FORGED IN STORMS AND SHADOWS

FORGED IN STORMS AND SHADOWS

BRITTANY OLDROYD

To my family—
Who taught me that, with love, all things are possible.

PART I

THE LIGHTNING DEMON

1

KALADRIA ASTRANA

The planet Earth sits below the window in my uncle's office, the lush world a clear reminder of why I do what I do. It's beautiful, even peaceful at this distance. I lean against the window, watching the planet I'm sworn to protect. Uncle Xalin is lucky. Many would kill for such a view.

A high-pitched ringing sounds at my side. I pull out the small communicator to find a single message, bearing the official seal of the Protectorate.

An unidentified ship has been spotted just outside the Border. No communication has been successful. If no contact can be made, destroy on sight. Coordinates are attached.

I swipe to a new message, forwarding the information to my team. *Time to go, boys.*

I push away from the wall but hesitate in the middle of the room. Disappointment sinks in. I'd hoped to see him before they shipped me off again. But it seems that, yet again, I don't have time to see him before I go. I wonder how much trouble I'll get in if I delay my departure long enough to…

The door swings open and Xalin Astrana himself steps inside. My uncle closes the door with an exhausted huff, slumping back.

Chuckling, I look my uncle up and down. True to the heritage we share as both members of the Astrana family and members of the race that calls Saturn home, Xalin's face carries the distinctive features that set our people apart. Short-cropped white hair, bright blue eyes, electricity sparking under his pale skin.

He heaves a sigh, frazzled.

I smile as I take a step closer. "Uncle? Are you alright?"

He looks up and his gaze instantly softens. "Kala?"

I grin and he runs a hand through his hair, slumping into the nearest seat. "When did you get back to the Satellite?"

"This morning." I sigh. "And, as it turns out, I'll be leaving again shortly. The Protectorate wants me back at the Border."

Xalin raises both eyebrows. "Again?"

I shrug, though I understand his concern. It's not uncommon for the Protectorate to send a squad to the Border. What is unusual is how often they've been sending me. My squad has been sent to the Border a lot lately, while much more experienced Protectors remain on the Satellite. I wonder if that's due to my squad's skill or the other captains' desire to keep me out of sight. Not that I care one way or another.

"An unidentified ship was spotted, near Mercury," I say. "I've been asked to handle it."

Xalin frowns, clearly troubled. I try very hard not to roll my eyes. "Don't worry, Uncle. This isn't anything I haven't done a thousand times before. I'll be fine." I push extra confidence into my smile. "Besides, you know my squad will never let anything happen to me."

He knows it's the truth as well as I do. My squad is fiercely loyal, if a little crazy at times. If I were to die, I'm fairly certain the four of them would find some way to yank me back into the world of the living.

Still, that reminder doesn't seem to be as comforting for Xalin as I hoped it would be. He just nods, almost absentmindedly.

I sigh, placing a hand on his shoulder. "Uncle, you're the one that encouraged me to join the Protectorate." I frown at him quizzically. "Why would you do such a thing if you were going to worry about me this much?"

He puts his hand over mine. "I didn't do it for me, Kala," he says quietly. "It was for you."

His words spark less pleasant memories and, suddenly, his hand over mine becomes an anchor. I clutch his hand, the rough calloused touch my only comfort. The months after the funeral were awful. We both know that. I fell apart in every way imaginable. I would have been lost if Xalin hadn't pushed me to become a Protector.

I clear my throat, pushing past those memories. "I love you, Uncle. Try not to worry. It's just another day at the office." I kiss his cheek. "I'll be back as soon as I can."

I slip my hand off his shoulder, turning toward the door with a small wave. Just as I step into the hall, I can hear his soft voice wishing me good luck. I don't bother turning. I know I don't have to tell him that, with my squad, I won't need it.

I ABSOLUTELY DESPISE THE SATELLITE. If I didn't have to hand in my reports to the Council and if Xalin wasn't here, I would never step foot on this station. As it stands, I walk through long silver hallways with tightly clenched fists and a rigid spine.

I know what everyone else calls me when they think I can't hear. *The Lightning Demon.* A captain whose very name has become akin with death and destruction.

My gaze flashes to the left. Several young Protectors stare at me, whispering amongst themselves. I can't hear their words but the intent is clear. The monster is on the Satellite and they'd better pray a bloodbath doesn't follow. It's stupid, really. I've never caused the Satellite to become a war zone. But the missions I'm sent on almost always end with my enemies being completely obliterated so everyone assumes I must enjoy the destruction I tend to leave in my wake.

I clench my hands into tight fists, forcing myself to keep walking so I don't throw myself at them. *Keep it together, Kaladria,* I remind myself. *Don't start a fight that will confirm what they already believe you are.*

5

I step onto the docks. My ship comes into view and my relief is almost palpable. The *Resistance* gleams silver, contrasting heavily against the darkness of space. With long wings and a sleek body, the *Resistance* appears as sharp and lethal as I know everyone sees me. Fitting, that I would be its captain.

Exhaling, I slip past the people around me, resisting the urge to growl as they shuffle away from me in an attempt to give me space. I focus on the *Resistance*, letting its presence quiet the frustration building inside of me. I can feel its electricity buzzing through my veins, my own power tuning in to the ship's energy.

I force myself to keep an even pace as I stride across the docks and into the safe embrace of my ship. I exhale as I step through the airlock, every tensed muscle relaxing as I listen to the familiar thrum of the *Resistance.* Leaning against the wall, I close my eyes, calmed by the familiarity of the electricity powering my ship.

"You okay, Kala?"

I look up, startled by the sound of my lieutenant's voice. Zeru Neshani, my oldest and most loyal friend, leans against the wall of the airlock, eyebrows slightly raised.

"Zeru." I straighten. "I'm fine. Just feeling a little shaken up." I let out my breath and, with it, all the emotions raging inside of me. "I really hate coming to the Satellite."

"The stares?" he guesses.

Instantly, I think of that group of Protectors on the Satellite, staring at me with wide eyes, whispering to each other behind their hands.

"It's like they don't think I can see." I wrinkle my nose. "Everyone looks at me like I'm some sort of monster."

"No, they look at you like you're some sort of god."

I scowl. "Very helpful."

Zeru grins. "Come on, Kala. You had to know it was going to be like this." He nudges me. "Not only are you captain of the most renowned ship in the Protectorate but you're also the youngest captain in our history. People are just curious."

I sigh. People *are* curious. But they've been curious about me long before I became captain of the *Resistance.* They've been curious about me since my parents' funerals, since Xalin proved he could raise me on his own, since I joined the Protectorate. Even before then, people were always staring at my parents. I suppose there's never been a time when people weren't curious about my family. The Astranas are simply not known for blending into the background.

Zeru nods to the door. "The rest of the team is already on the bridge."

I nod, leading the way out of the airlock. We make our way to the bridge, moving in silence. Zeru whistles softly, as calm and carefree as ever. I resist the urge to roll my eyes.

I slow my step, our progress quickly halted by the sight of two engineers checking the engines. When they notice me approach, they both stop. "Captain," one salutes.

"At ease." I glance between the two of them. They stand stiffly, clearly uneasy. I try not to be annoyed. "I suggest you make your way to the docks. The *Resistance* leaves for the Border."

They share a nervous look. "Now?"

"Now."

Both nodding fervently, they rush to the elevator at the end of the hall. No one, not even my own engineers, wants to be on board the ship of the Lightning Demon when she goes to the Border.

I shake my head. It's unclear if their fear is caused by the possibility of being near me during a potential firefight or going to the Border itself. Probably both.

We continue on our way. Zeru wisely makes no comment on the engineers' overzealous departure. We step into an elevator and I look up at the ceiling, studying it for a moment. At least, until I can feel Zeru's eyes on me.

"What is it, Zeru?"

"You look tired."

He says it matter-of-factly but I can still hear the question burning behind his words. *Why?*

I sigh, studying his face. Those silver eyes have always been so blasted observant. And, having served as my lieutenant for years, Zeru knows me better than anyone. Many wouldn't see a couple of years as enough time to be so in tune with each other but Zeru and I have fought side by side through so many battles, I'm almost surprised he hasn't figured out how to read my mind yet.

"I haven't been sleeping much," I admit. I refrain from telling him why. I don't tell him how the nightmares that have plagued me for half my life are getting worse. Or how I wake in the middle of the night, terrified of losing Xalin or Zeru or anyone else the same way I lost my parents that fateful day.

Zeru's eyes soften with sympathy. He opens his mouth but snaps it shut as the elevator doors open. I shake away darker thoughts, shrugging back my shoulders as I step onto the bridge. Then, I stop at the sight before me.

"What took you guys so long? Decide to stop for a nap?"

Azar Losali sits in *my* chair, feet up on the monitor, looking far too comfortable for my liking. I raise an eyebrow but the tall Venutian only grins.

"You know how it is, Azar," Zeru says with an easy smile. "Everyone wants Kala to tell them they're doing a good job."

I scowl and Azar's smile widens. I cross my arms, striding over to him. Azar doesn't move, white teeth flashing against his crimson skin.

"Up. *Now.*"

The tall Protector's grin turns mischievous. "Make me, Kala."

Eyes narrowed, I flick my fingers in his direction, releasing a small spark of lightning. There's a sharp buzz and Azar jumps to his feet. He yelps in surprise, the sound hardly masculine for the burly soldier. Standing, he crosses his arms, clearing his throat in an attempt to cover the yelp.

In the corner, Hassuun bursts into laughter. "Come on, man. That was dumb." He shakes his head, still chuckling. "She could totally fry you."

Azar scowls at his friend but wisely stays silent. He can't deny it. As a soldier of Venus, he may have fire at his fingertips but fire is no match for my lightning and he knows it.

Smirking, I brush past Azar. I take my seat, settling back and crossing my legs in ladylike fashion, like a queen taking the throne. I'm sure to make a show of it, pointedly reminding him that this is *my* ship. He gets the message, huffing with annoyance. Still smirking,

I shake out my fingertips, dispersing the lightning still sparking there.

As the laughter dies down, I glance between my squadmates. Hassuun shakes his head and Azar scowls at him. Zeru rolls his eyes, chuckling. And then there's Vale. He watches the whole scene in silence, carefully studying each of his squadmates, our new pilot the quiet calm amongst the chaos that so often plagues my ship.

Azar and Hassuun, full of wild energy as usual, begin taunting each other, calling each other names like they're a couple of children instead of two of the most dangerous Protectors in the system. Azar puts Hassuun in a headlock. Hassuun jabs him in the stomach. I silence their antics with a sharp look. "Vale," I say as they quiet down, "Get us out of here."

Wordlessly, Vale punches coordinates in on the dash. His fingers move silently, steady eyes focused entirely on his task. Hassuun settles back in his seat with a carefree smile and Azar sinks into his own chair, rubbing his arm when he thinks I'm not paying attention. Zeru's lips twitch with amusement as he takes the seat next to mine.

We retreat from the dock, leaving the Satellite behind and slipping into the blackness of space. I watch as the Satellite and Earth's moon disappear and we catch just a small glimpse of Earth. The blue planet is marbled with clouds that swirl above its surface, wreathing the entire planet in white.

"There's something beautiful about it, isn't there?" Zeru asks thoughtfully.

"It certainly has its own charm," I agree, watching as Earth disappears behind us.

"We wouldn't be here if it didn't," Hassuun comments.

I nod. I know the stories better than most. I was raised on stories of our ancestors. My parents were obsessed with them.

"What's the plan?" Azar asks, rolling back his shoulders, ready for a fight, as usual.

I glance at each of my squadmates in turn. "A ship has been spotted near Mercury," I say. "They have not responded to the Protectorate's attempts at contact. Our orders are to keep them from coming any closer, at all costs."

"What do we know?" Zeru asks.

I shake my head. "Very little." I glance at Hassuun. "Establish a comm link. Let's see if we can figure out what that ship is doing here."

Hassuun gets to work on the comms. Next to me, Zeru continues to whistle quietly. I shake my head at his contentment. No matter what we're doing, Zeru's spirits are never dampened.

I close my eyes, drumming my fingers across the arm rest of my chair while I wait for Hassuun to make contact. There have been an alarming number of ships pressing on our Borders as of late. Sometimes I wonder if they're looking for something. Sometimes I wonder if they know what we're protecting.

"No response, Kala."

I open my eyes. Unsurprising. If the Protectorate can't make contact, we usually can't either. "Prepare our guns, Azar. Zeru, turn on stealth systems." I look to Vale. "Take us in. Let's see what we're dealing with."

As my team gets to work, I stand. I step up to the window, arms crossed. We pass by Mercury, slipping around the planet quickly. And then the ship in question comes into view. Its shape is easily recognizable. Dark plating blends its form into the blackness of space, a rudimentary attempt at camouflage. There's a crude set of guns at the base of the ship. As I focus, I can feel the too familiar buzz of their shields.

I exhale, shaking my head at the dark form of the slaveship. Unsurprising, that it would be slavers refusing to answer our attempts at contact but disturbing nonetheless. Behind me, Hassuun curses and Azar spits.

"Keep it together, boys," I say quietly. "We knew there was a good chance it'd be slavers."

Still, my eyes are narrowed as I look at the ship. I can understand their disgust. Of everything we face on the Border, slavers are the most common. And this ship's lack of communication all but confirmed it. Slaveships are notorious for refusing all attempts at communication and then kidnapping the Protectors that investigate. They steal our soldiers, selling them to the highest bidder.

Of course, these slavers don't realize who they're dealing with.

Xalin had many run-ins with slavers in his soldiering days, some of which cost him squadmates. His training has ensured nothing similar will ever happen to me.

"How close can you get us, Vale?"

He looks up at me, gray eyes steady. "Not much closer than this. Unless you want them to spot us through a window."

I nod. "Let me see what I can learn."

I close my eyes, reaching a hand toward the window. Latching onto the electricity living inside of me, I search the space around me. I can feel the thrum of my ship the strongest, the *Resistance*'s power buzzing through me. But I can feel the slaveship too, the buzz almost deafening in a ship so large.

I open my eyes. "They have their shields up, full strength."

"Any weak spots?"

I point to the belly of the ship. "Hit them there, right above the guns."

Azar nods. "Ready when you are, Kala."

"Fire."

The sounds of the guns are thunderous. Azar shoots the base of the ship as directed and the deafening buzz goes out. Soon after, the ship explodes.

Everyone relaxes as the slaveship's broken form floats through space, each squadmate relieved to be rid of another slaver. "Zeru, inform the Protectorate that we've dealt with the threat," I say. "Let's do a quick scan for survivors and get out of here."

2

MALCOLM FARAWAY

"What about Emma Blake?"

I let out a weary sigh, dropping the pile of papers in my lap. They scatter in front of me, a mess of scribbled blueprints. I look up at my roommate reluctantly. "What about her?"

Tyler, sprawled across the couch, tosses a baseball between his hands. "You should ask her out."

Not this again.

"I told you, Tyler. I don't have time for dating right now." I wave the pile of papers at him for emphasis. "I've got too much work to do."

"Come on, dude. The lab isn't going anywhere."

I heave another sigh. "Help me out, Dean."

Dean grins from where he sits at the kitchen table. "It's no use, Ty. In all the time we've roomed together, I've only convinced Malcolm to go on one date."

"And it was horrible," I add.

Tyler's eyes flit between us, curious. "Why?"

"It was fine until she asked me what I do for work," I grumble.

That's when it always goes wrong. It's always fine until a girl realizes I'm a little *too* interesting for them. Either they don't realize what I'm telling them or they think I'm absolutely insane.

I shake my head. That date was particularly bad. The moment I explained what it is I do, what I'm building, she completely shut down. She was ready to get out of there. Honestly, I'm surprised she didn't make a run for it, based on the way she was looking at me.

"To be honest, dude," Tyler says, "I still don't really get what it is you do for work."

I glance at him, sighing as I shuffle through my notes. I've lost track of how many times I've explained it at this point. "The science department is paying me to research the possibility of using wormholes for space travel. I'm building a wormhole generator that will allow us to open portals to travel through space."

"See, you could totally be speaking a different language and I wouldn't even know the difference."

I roll my eyes as I stand. "I've got to go. I'll talk to you guys later."

I sling my bag over one shoulder, hefting the papers in my arms as I push open the door. Dean waves from his seat at the table. "See ya later."

Tyler throws in a casual salute. "Bye, dude."

I slip out of the apartment, walking down the street in the direction of campus and my lab.

<hr />

THE LAB IS dark and quiet when I get there. Adjusting the stack of papers still in my arms, I flip on the light switch. The room is mostly empty except for the two stainless steel desks in the room and the bookshelves lining the back wall. The desk on the far end of the room is clean and organized, its surface mostly cleared of all clutter. My desk is a completely different story. The entire thing is covered in paperwork, old blueprints and plans spread across the desk and mixed in with several dozen stacks of research.

I take the paperwork I brought with me from home, adding it to the pile. I pull out my laptop and set it on the desk as well.

Unlocking the top drawer in the desk, I pull out a small metal orb. I inspect it, turning it in my hands. It's just small enough that it fits easily in my hand but just large enough that my fingers can't quite curl around it completely. I brush my thumb across its cool surface, feeling the thin lines engraved into it, crisscrossing in every direction. It's simple in design but, hopefully, still effective.

I turn on my computer's camera and face the laptop toward my body, focusing it on the orb in my hand. My fingers move quickly across its surface, turning it in my hands as I rotate its pieces, spinning the interlocking parts until its lines form a new pattern. Then, I set it down with a deep breath.

Here goes nothing.

The orb thrums to life, lifting off the ground. It hovers several inches in the air. For a moment, I think it's actually going to work. But then the orb starts to spin erratically, dropping back to the ground with a loud thump.

I groan, dropping my head into my hands.

Behind me, the door swings open and closed. I lift my head from my hands as Emma Blake steps into the room. And, thanks to Tyler's insistence that I ask her on a date, I'm paying too much attention.

Emma Blake is not the kind of girl you would expect to find working in a lab. She's tall and thin, with dark hair and deep brown eyes that glitter when she speaks. She pauses in the room, taking in the scene with a small smile that curves up her lips.

"Problems?" she asks, taking in the orb on the floor.

I sigh, crouching down to snatch up the orb. "Darn thing isn't cooperating."

"What's wrong?"

I take a moment to scrutinize the orb. "Not sure. It started off well. It even hovered for a moment." I sigh. "I think it might be a problem with the power. Maybe a short in the wiring."

Emma smiles sympathetically. "I'd offer to help but I don't know a thing about mechanics." She blushes, as if this is something she should be embarrassed about. "Sorry."

I shrug. "I'll figure it out. Eventually."

I examine the surface of the orb. Deciding there's no more information to be had from the outside, I pry the device open and set its two halves on the desk. My mind spins with possible power solutions as I study the inner workings of the device.

Emma hesitates, standing in the middle of the room, surprisingly awkward. She takes a step closer to my desk. "So, Malcolm," she says slowly, tucking a loose strand of hair behind her ear, "I was wondering if you would want to get dinner with me on Friday?"

"I can't. I'm supposed to get this thing working this week." I barely look up, mind still focused in my work. *I wonder if I...*

Emma rubs her arm as she nods. "Oh, okay." She clears her throat, walking over to her own workspace. She sits down, starting to shuffle through some paperwork.

I fiddle with the orb for a moment. *Come on, you coward.* I sigh. "What about lunch?"

Emma turns, surprised. "What?"

"Do you..." I take a deep breath. "Do you want to get lunch on Friday?" I clear my throat. "With me?"

Emma's smile is dazzling. "I'd like that."

I exhale, smiling despite myself as I get back to work. Tyler will be proud. Mom will be beyond thrilled. I just hope they don't blow this out of proportion.

I turn the orb in my hands. Now, if I can just get this thing to work, I'll consider today a pretty good day. Hesitating, I glance at Emma. She slips on a lab coat, flipping back her hair. She turns to her computer but glances back once to smile at me.

I wave awkwardly. I suppose today might be a pretty good day anyway.

3

KALADRIA ASTRANA

"You going to join us, Kala?"

I glance at Azar, frowning up at him as I step out of the airlock. "For?"

Azar flashes a broad smile, dark eyes twinkling with mischief. "We're going to celebrate our success."

My frown deepens. "It was just another job. It seems hardly enough reason to celebrate."

Hassuun's eyes share Azar's sparkling mischief. "You're no fun, Kala. Any reason to celebrate is reason enough."

I roll my eyes at Hassuun's crazy logic. "You guys are nuts." I look at each of them, scrutinizing them each in turn. "You're all going?"

Vale shrugs, certainly not understanding what it is he's getting himself into. Next to him, Zeru winks. "Sure," he says. "Why not?"

I can think of a million reasons for why not, starting with how wild celebrating with Azar and Hassuun can be. It's a mistake I've made only once. I certainly don't intend to make it again.

"So?" Azar asks again. "Want to join us?"

I shake my head. "No thanks, guys. I've got plans already." I step away from them with a small wave. "I'll see you guys later."

"Your loss!" Hassuun calls.

I laugh, watching them go. They walk off the docks, completely ignoring the gazes that follow them. They may not be the Lightning Demon but, as my squad, people still find them a little intimidating. After all, who would willingly follow a demon into battle?

With a heavy sigh, I begin to make my way through the Satellite. As I walk, I can feel the gawking stares that follow me through the long corridors. It seems word of the *Resistance*'s latest exploits has already spread across the Satellite. I force my gaze forward, fighting the urge to grind my teeth.

I wonder if my parents felt differently about the way people watch our family. I wonder if they relished the attention. I certainly don't. I just want the whole system to stop treating my family like some sort of spectacle.

Holding my head high, I stride past a group of Protectors. One of the soldiers stares at me, whispering to another. "The Lightning Demon..."

I clench my fists, swallowing a growl. I force myself to keep walking. Even if I would prefer to grab him by the collar and demand he stop whispering about me like I'm not here.

As I reach my uncle's office, I let out a deep sigh. *Finally.* I push open the door and step inside, relieved to be free of the gossiping whispers.

Xalin sits at his desk, brow deeply furrowed as he stares at the monitor. His hands are laced in front of him and his shoulders slump forward in what I imagine to be boredom. He doesn't look up as I step inside the room, his mind obviously elsewhere.

"You look tired, Uncle."

He jolts in surprise, looking up. "Kala. That was fast. You were gone, what? A day?"

"I told you it was nothing major." I slip into the chair opposite his. "It was just a slaveship."

Xalin's face drops into a tight grimace. "I wouldn't say slavers are *just*."

I bite my lip, regretting my casual response. If anyone has the right to hate slavers, it's my uncle. Back in his own soldiering days, Xalin's ship was attacked by slavers. The rest of his squad was taken.

They never found them. I know it haunts him. I can see it in his face when he thinks I'm not looking.

"Uncle, don't worry. No slaver is going to catch me."

He relaxes, if only a little. "I suppose I did teach you better, didn't I?"

I grin. "You did."

"I assume everything went smoothly then?"

"Yes." My smile grows and I chuckle. "In fact, the boys are celebrating as we speak."

Xalin pauses to scrutinize my face. He looks suddenly troubled. "You didn't go with them?"

"Celebrations with Azar and Hassuun usually end with someone getting sick." I stand, smiling. "Besides, I had other plans today."

His eyebrows knit together. "Oh?"

I step around the desk and hold out my hand. "Lunch with my favorite uncle."

Xalin chuckles, not bothering to remind me that he is in fact my only uncle. He takes my hand and I haul him to his feet. We make our way through the Satellite but the stares begin almost immediately. I do my best to ignore them, lifting my chin.

"How's your squad, Kala?" Xalin asks, clearly trying to distract me.

I force out a breath, relaxing my clenched fists. "Just as crazy as ever," I answer. "Zeru is a tease. And Azar and Hassuun naturally keep things lively with their constant antics."

He smiles. "I heard you got a new squadmate. A pilot from Neptune?"

I nod. "My last pilot quit a month ago," I admit, feeling my cheeks redden. "He wasn't a fan of taking orders from a twenty-something old *child*."

Xalin scowls. "His loss. He gave up a prestigious position, serving under the most renowned captain in the Protectorate."

I smile softly. "Thank you, Uncle."

"So, tell me about this new pilot."

"Vale Taladauss. He's a skilled pilot and soldier from the heart of Neptune. He's closer to my age so it's not like I'm giving orders to someone twice my senior." I chuckle. "He certainly brings a change of pace to my ship."

"What do you mean?" Xalin asks.

"He's quiet. And serious. Honestly, it's a little refreshing."

Xalin chuckles.

"Anyway, Hassuun and Azar dragged him off to celebrate our latest success so I guess he's about to find out just how insane his squadmates are."

"Hopefully, you don't lose your new pilot."

I laugh.

I sit at the edge of the docks, legs hanging over the edge of the platform, a tray of food to my right. Reaching over, I scoop up a handful of nuts, popping them into my mouth. "Are you going home anytime soon?"

Xalin, sitting next to me on the platform, sets his cup down on the floor next to him. "I'm hoping to go later this week."

"Maybe I can join you."

Xalin raises his eyebrows. "Do you have time for that?"

"I'll make time," I promise. "The *Resistance* isn't the only ship in the Protectorate. Surely they can spare me for a day or so." I sigh. "Besides, I've got a lot of leave time built up. I'll get in trouble if I don't start using it."

Xalin opens his mouth. He pauses, glancing down as an intermittent buzz dances across the space between us. We both look down. Xalin sighs, picking up the communicator.

"The Council wants to speak with me," he says with a frown.

I frown, too. That's odd. Xalin does serve as an Advisor to the Council but he's one of hundreds. It's strange that they'd single him out.

I flick through my own messages, clicking on one with the Protectorate's seal. I scan through it quickly. *Unidentified ship spotted near Pluto.*

"I'm sorry, Kala. I should probably go."

I wave him off. "It's not a problem, Uncle. I need to go, too. Apparently, something has shown up on the scanners. I'm off to Pluto." I sigh. One meal hardly seems like a break but I guess I shouldn't be surprised at this point. "I guess I'll just let you know when I get back. Maybe we can go home together."

He smiles warmly. "I'll be sure to wait for you."

"We can watch the storm." I smile at the thought. While I often see him here at the Satellite, if even for such short intervals, it's been a long time since I was able to just sit and watch the lightning storms with him in our home.

Xalin nods. "Be careful, Kala."

"I will be." I stand. "I need to gather my squad. I'll see you later."

4

KALADRIA ASTRANA

ELECTRICITY SPARKS between my fingers as I slip a hand into the generator, looking up into the mess of wires with a tight frown. I finger them gently, feeling the electricity as I search for anything that might explain the shortage this room's power keeps experiencing.

"Kala?"

My head strikes the generator with a loud *thud*. I wince, extinguishing the lightning on my fingertips as I wiggle out from under the generator. I put a hand on my throbbing head, looking up at Zeru.

"Yes?"

His eyes dance with amusement. "What were you doing down there?"

"One of the engineers mentioned one of the generators has been acting up." I shrug. "I wanted to see if I could fix it."

Zeru offers a hand. "You know the engineers could have handled it once we got back to the Satellite."

I let him pull me to my feet. "And you know I prefer to take care of my own ship. I don't want to rely on some Satellite engineer that barely knows me or the *Resistance*."

"That's fair."

I scrutinize him. "So, did you need something? Or did you just come down to see why your captain was hiding under a generator?"

"We're approaching Pluto," Zeru explains. "And preparing to make contact."

I nod. "We should head up to the bridge then."

Zeru doesn't move. "Also, Councilor Verkire is on the comms," he says hesitantly. "He wishes to speak with you."

I frown. That's unusual. Most of our orders come from the Protectorate's generals. Very rarely does the Council get involved. For the Council to request a presence with Xalin and then a Councilor to call me personally is concerning. I can only hope it doesn't have to do with—

No.

The walls around that particular memory slam down and I push away that line of thought before it can form. I don't have time to worry about that right now.

Nodding slowly, I take a deep breath. "Let's go."

I follow Zeru into the elevator, rolling my eyes as he pushes off the balls of his feet, lifting off the ground. He hovers a few inches above the floor, a clear show of his Jovian gifts. "Do you always have to do that?"

Zeru grins. "Does it bother you, Kala?"

I shoot him a pointed look. "It makes you look like a show-off."

"Says the girl who blasts lightning out of her hands."

I scowl. "At least I don't go around parading my abilities."

"Like zapping people when they annoy you?" Zeru asks, eyes twinkling. "Because you *never* do that."

I give him a dirty look as I step out of the elevator, resisting the urge to release the electricity at my fingertips. It would only prove his point.

Clasping my hands behind my back, I face the comm link. "Hassuun, patch Councilor Verkire through."

Hassuun says nothing but only a moment passes before the holographic version of the Saturnian Councilor appears before me.

"Councilor," I say with a slight nod, "How may I be of service?"

"Captain Astrana," Verkire greets. "The Council wishes to meet with you on the Satellite. We have a bit of unorthodox mission for you. The matter is quite delicate so we would prefer to brief you in person." He hesitates. "Alone."

I nod, forcing the neutrality expected of me into my expression. Even if, inside, my heart thunders with sudden nervous energy. A private meeting with the Council can't mean anything good. What if it's about…

Stop it. There's no way this is connected to that.

"Of course," I say slowly. "I am currently away on a mission but I will do my best to wrap this up quickly. I'll return to the Satellite as soon as possible."

Verkire nods curtly. "Come quickly, Captain Astrana. Time is of the essence."

The comm call ends, the holographic Councilor Verkire disappearing. I close my eyes for a moment, taking a few breaths to refocus on the task at hand.

"We've got an unidentified ship trying to make contact, Kala," Hassuun says.

I turn away from the comm link with a tense frown. "Probably not slavers then." I face the comm link again, straightening my spine. "Put them through."

As the comm link comes to life, a figure appears before me in holographic form. The man before me is lithe, with long limbs and sinewy muscles. His skin is pale, his eyes a cloudy white.

"We had heard rumors of ships disappearing in this system," the figure says, "But we weren't sure what to make of them."

My eyes are narrowed. "I suggest you turn back unless you wish to become a part of those rumors," I say coolly.

The figure smiles, clearly unperturbed. "There are also rumors of a young race living in isolation on their home planet. The rumors claim this race believes themselves to be alone in the universe."

The tension on the bridge is almost palpable. No one should know about humanity. We've made sure no one could. Any ship that gets too close gets blown up so they can't spread word of the young race living in isolation on Earth. So, how does this man know about them? And who else knows?

My clasped hands must be white with tension. "The planet of

which you speak is under the protection of a Council of five very powerful races," I warn. "I suggest you leave while you still can."

"And abandon the harvest of ripe resources and billions of slaves?" he scoffs. "No, I don't think we will."

I scrutinize him. Perhaps he's not a slaver but he clearly has slaver connections. "I am under orders to keep all alien life from crossing our Borders. Move any closer and we will be forced to retaliate. This is your last chance to withdraw."

He sneers, baring his teeth. "Do you think me so much a fool to be afraid of a child?"

I bite my tongue to keep from snarling. Against any enemy, I can hold my own just as well as the older captains. But very few enemies consider me a threat. I'm too young, too small. A twenty-two year old *child*, too young to be intimidating.

"I urge you to reconsider," I say tightly. "You—"

He waves a hand aside, turning his back on me. Then, the comm link goes dead.

"He cut the connection, Kala."

I sigh, shaking my head. "It's always got to be the hard way."

Hassuun chuckles. "That's kind of typical with us, isn't it?"

I don't answer him, even if he is right. After all, there is a reason the other Protectors call me the Lightning Demon. Unclasping my hands, I stride across the bridge, stopping before the window. I study the enormous ship before us. I've never seen anything like it. It's much larger than the slaveships we normally deal with. And this ship's weaponry appears to be far more advanced.

"Azar, prepare our weapon systems," I order. "Vale, move us in as close as you can."

As my squad gets to work, a powerful thrum buzzes through the *Resistance*. It lights up the electricity in my blood, awakening the lightning inside of me.

"We're closing in," Vale says. "What are your orders?"

I lean forward, focusing my energy on our enemy. The whole ship is bright blue with electricity only I can see. It pulsates with power, growing hotter and hotter as the ship's electricity builds. I focus my attention on that heat. In it, I sense the ship's weapons, which are very suddenly thrumming with power.

"Evasive maneuvers," I bark.

Vale asks no questions, swerving the *Resistance* around, just as a beam fires from the enemy ship. The whole bridge jerks with his piloting and I hold out a hand to steady myself. As the ship rights itself, I exhale.

Eyes narrowed, I watch our enemy for a moment. There are no weaknesses in their barriers. This ship is simply too advanced for our usual tactics.

I grab my helmet. "I'll have to disable their shields from the inside."

Zeru stands. "Want a hand?"

Feeling a little on edge after being called a child *again*, I frown up at him. "Why? You think I can't handle it?"

Zeru rolls his eyes, grinning despite himself. "I'm more worried about unnecessary damage to the enemy. It's not their fault they don't realize who they're dealing with."

I shrug. "Fair enough." I glance across the bridge. "Keep them busy."

Azar flashes a smile. "With pleasure."

As Vale frowns at Azar, I purse my lips to hide my smile. Then, I turn, heading for the elevator. "Come on, Zeru. We've got a ship to board."

Zeru and I walk back to the elevator, heading down to the airlock. I lean back against the railing, looking over at him. "You look worried, Zeru."

"Is it that obvious?"

"You weren't assigned to the *Resistance* for your espionage skills."

He smiles wryly. "And yet, here I am, about to sneak on board an enemy ship."

"Hey, you offered." We step out of the airlock and I study his face. "What's bothering you?"

He exhales, blowing the air from his cheeks. "He'd heard rumors of ships disappearing within our Borders. But he didn't look worried about what those claims would mean for him and his ship. Doesn't that seem odd to you?"

"Maybe he's just arrogant?"

"I don't know, Kala. It seems awfully convenient."

I study his face, the tension in his brow, the troubled frown that turns down his mouth. I know better than to brush off his concerns. As carefree as he normally is, if Zeru is worried, it's usually with good reason.

"Do you think it's a trap?" I ask.

"I don't know." He thinks for a moment. "But I think we should use extreme caution on that ship."

I nod. Trap or not, a little caution couldn't be a bad thing.

Zeru and I slip on our helmets. I glance at him. "Ready?"

Zeru nods. His body turns transparent as he fades into his Ghost Form. "After you."

I take a deep breath, closing my eyes. I reach out to the explosive power coursing through my body. It lights up my blood, thrumming through my bones. Electricity spreads inside of me until I can feel it in every limb, every nerve. As I open my eyes, electricity sparking across my skin, I vault forward. There's a brief moment of nothingness before everything explodes in a torrent of lightning.

Within seconds, I stand in a dark hallway, no longer on the *Resistance*, but on the enemy's ship. I glance back as Zeru's pale form phases through the wall.

I reach behind my back to yank out my spear. Electricity sparks across its surface, blue light filling the space in front of me. "Let's go."

Zeru and I walk through the ship slowly, watching for signs of trouble. He carries a long dagger in one hand, eyes focused ahead. "How far to the shield generators?"

I pause, closing my eyes as I search for the energy. "Not far."

Zeru nods and we continue walking through the long darkness. I study our surroundings. Very little about this ship is distinguishable. The corridor is long and dark, only lit by dim red lighting strung across the floor, ensuring that I can only see a few feet in front of me. Along the ceiling hangs thick wire, running through the hallways and into various rooms. With each step, I can feel the electricity thrumming through the ship. Somewhere in the darkness, this enemy has very advanced technology, unlike anything I've ever sensed before.

I stop as Zeru puts his arm out in front of me, blocking our progress. His eyes are narrowed into the darkness.

"Did you see something?" I ask quietly, scanning the hallway.

I curse my own stupidity. I should have been paying more attention to where we were going and less attention to the ship. Xalin would scold me for such carelessness and rightfully so. My distraction would have cost us if Zeru hadn't remained so vigilant.

Zeru doesn't look at me. He watches the hallway in front of us warily. "Not sure," he says slowly.

"We should—"

Something slams into my shoulder hard, knocking my body sideways. I stumble, grimacing at the pale shape that blurs as it disappears again.

Zeru grabs my arm to steady me. "What…"

"I'm guessing it's some sort of speed manipulation." I scan the hallway for the pale form but I can't see it. At least for the moment, it's retreated. "It seems you were right, Zeru. They're ready for a fight."

"So are we."

I grip my spear, listening to the quiet thrum of electricity lighting up across the staff. Next to me, Zeru's eyes flash left and right. As we continue to make our way toward the generators, we are both on edge now that we have an idea of what we're dealing with.

Stopping, I place my hand against the wall, feeling the thrumming power on the other side of it. "We're almost—"

Shutting my mouth, I grab Zeru's hand and yank him out of the way as a white shape zips past us again with chiming laughter. I growl in annoyance. This game ends now. They might be fast but I have yet to meet an enemy faster than my lightning.

I lunge forward. Snapping through electricity, I teleport across the hall. As I reappear, I drive my spear up and through the white shape. She falls against the spear head, mouth tumbling open in surprise. Her pale eyes are wide, suddenly empty in death.

I yank out my spear and her body falls to the floor. "Come on. We're almost there."

We race into the next room, which is thrumming with deafening power. The kind of power that could only come from a power generator, and a very large one at that.

"You must be incredibly foolish."

I cross my arms, watching the pale figure that steps out from behind the generator. Though he looks a great deal like the woman I just killed, his voice gives him away as the man we'd spoken to on the comms before boarding their ship.

"I warned you that I would not allow you to cross our Borders," I remind him. "This system is protected."

"But you are only two," he replies.

I glare at him, head raised high. "Two is more than enough."

"Tell me," he says casually, "Are your people so desperate that they're sending children to war?"

I glance at Zeru. *Ready?*

He nods almost imperceptibly. If there's one thing I can count on, it's that Zeru will always be able to know my plan without me ever needing to voice it.

I turn my attention back to our enemy. "This isn't war," I answer coolly. "You aren't worthy of waging war with soldiers of the Protectorate of Five."

Electricity dances across my skin, bright blue lightning sparking around me. He takes a step back, with equal parts surprise and fear. I launch my body forward, teleporting through the electricity ripe in the air. I appear behind him, reaching for the generator. Despite its size, it takes little more than a small blast of lightning to send the ship into complete silence, the deafening hum of power falling silent.

I glance back. Zeru lifts his hand, urging his dagger forward without a touch. His telekinesis propels it forward and the knife launches through the air at his command. It plants itself in the chest of our enemy, who crumples without a sound.

Zeru opens his mouth, snapping it shut quickly at the chaos filling the previous silence. The sounds of gunshots and screaming fill the air, headed for our direction. *Time to go,* I think. I yank out Zeru's knife and take off running back the way we came.

We race through long corridors, moving much faster than we did on the way in. But then I catch sight of something in the corner of my eye. I skid to a stop, frozen for just a moment. I stare at the hallway to our left. *That can't be what it looked like, right?*

Zeru stops next to me. "Kala?"

I look over at him. "I need to check something," I say. "Go on without me."

"Kaladria—"

"That's an order, Zeru."

He sighs. "If you get captured by slavers, Xalin is going to kill me."

I turn away. "I'll catch up to you soon."

Muttering under his breath about my reckless behavior and how Xalin is going to murder him for tolerating my stupid heroics, Zeru turns away and starts running.

I take off in the opposite direction, running down a darkened corridor. As I run, I can't stop seeing it in my head. A black hand, with long fingers extending into sword-like talons. A nightmare given form.

I shake my head, continuing to run. *Just stay focused,* I remind myself.

Pausing in a new room, I take in my surroundings. There is no sign of the owner of the taloned hand. However, what I find is no less troubling.

I walk through the room, stopping at the conference table in its center. Images have been scattered across it. I pick one up, cursing at the image. The holographic photo depicts an Earthen city, with tall skyscrapers and streets packed with humans. I don't know how but, somehow, this ship has inside information on Earth.

Something is very wrong here. No one should know about Earth. And yet this ship has irrefutable proof that someone is spying on humanity. I need to get back to the *Resistance* so we can destroy this ship. Hopefully, that will be enough to protect humanity.

Turning away, I head back for the door. Clearly, the owner of that monstrous hand isn't here.

I pause, mid-step, at the sound of quiet sniffling. Turning back around, I crouch down and look under the table. A girl, no older than thirteen, sits beneath the table, hugging her legs. She has dark skin, almost purple in color, and has small horns peeking through her hair. She wears very little, nothing but a thin dress that's barely holding together. Clearly, a slave. On seeing me, she shrinks back.

I hold up my hands. "I'm not going to hurt you," I say gently. "I want to help you."

"W-who are you?"

"My name is Kaladria. What's yours?"

"Hedda," she whispers.

I smile, holding out my hand. "Why don't we get you out of here, Hedda? This ship isn't safe anymore."

Hedda stares at me for a moment. Then, nodding, she takes my hand. As I pull her to her feet, I glance at the door. I won't be able to take her with me, not onto the *Resistance*. Even if I wouldn't be breaking a thousand rules by doing so, she won't be able to teleport with me.

Holding her hand, I lead Hedda down the hall, toward the escape pods. As we reach them, I lead her inside, sitting her down and buckling her in. Then, I crouch in front of her.

"Why are you helping me?"

I grasp both of her hands in mine. "I'm the captain of a ship dedicated to protecting people," I say. "I wouldn't be doing a very good job if I left you here." I stand. "Stay buckled, okay? I'll come for you once I'm done here."

Hedda nods.

I squeeze her hands once before stepping out of the escape pod. I shut the doors, sending the pod off into space. Once Zeru and I return to the *Resistance*, I'll have to find her and take her to the Satellite. My superiors won't like it but they won't turn down a helpless girl. After all, the Protectorate exists to protect the helpless.

Turning away, I take off running, racing to catch up to Zeru.

When I find him, he hasn't made much progress. Likely disregarding my orders and waiting to make sure I caught up with him.

But I suppose I can't fault him for it, when I'm constantly disregarding the rules.

"Well?" he prompts.

I shake my head. "Later. Let's get out of here."

We start running. With him close behind me, I press a finger to the side of my helmet. "Vale, I need you guys back here. Now."

"Already on it," the quiet Neptunian replies. "Be ready to board in one, two, three…"

I glance at Zeru as he transforms back into his Ghost Form. Then, launching my body through lightning, I find myself standing back in the airlock of the *Resistance*. I turn, watching as Zeru floats back into the ship before turning solid once more.

"Shields are down," I say through my helmet. "Fire at them now."

"Firing," Azar replies.

As the sounds of our weaponry fill the air, I straighten. I yank off my helmet and glance at Zeru. "Let's get back up to the bridge. We'll search for possible survivors." I think of Hedda. I'll have to tell him about her once we get back to the bridge. I shrug back my shoulders. "Then, we need to hurry back to the Satellite."

Whether I'm ready or not, the Council is waiting for me.

5

MALCOLM FARAWAY

"I don't know what happened, Mom," I say, holding the phone against my ear with my shoulder as I fish out my keys. "I did everything right. I've been over the math a dozen times already. It should've worked."

"I don't know what to tell you, Mal. You know math and I don't exactly get along."

I chuckle. While my mom is super driven and can totally handle math, she's always hated it. It was a struggle for her in med school.

"I'm sure you'll figure it out, Mal. You're the smartest person I know."

I adjust the phone as I unlock the door, stepping into the lab. "Thanks, Mom."

"So," she says as nonchalantly as she can manage, "Are you excited for your date?"

I roll my eyes, regretting telling her about Emma Blake. I really did know better than to expect her to play it cool. Mom's been wanting me to bring home a girlfriend for years. It shouldn't surprise me that she's blown a simple meal way out of proportion.

I reach for the light switch. "It's not that big of a deal. Just lunch."

She lets out a heavy sigh. "Don't mess this up, Malcolm."

I laugh. "Mom, don't you think you're overreact…"

My laughter freezes somewhere in my throat as I look up into the lab, a gust of cold air sweeping through the room. The chaos sends papers flying across the room in a wild torrent. And, in the center of it all, I can see why. An empty void, forming a wide doorway into the blackness of space, a small silver orb spinning above it.

"Mal?"

"I have to go, Mom."

I slip my phone into my pocket, moving through the room slowly. I shield my face from the paperwork flying around. But, despite my caution, my foot still catches on something, sending me flailing into the desk. I catch myself, turning to see what I tripped on.

The floor looks like it's been split in two. A deep slash slices through the floor, as if someone took a knife and cut straight through it. When I crouch down, slipping a hand in, sudden cruel laughter echoes across the room.

I jump to my feet, stumbling away from the tear on the floor. What was *that*?

Silence fills the room. I whirl around in a circle, searching for the source of that cold laughter. But there's nothing. Whatever I heard—whatever I thought I heard—is gone.

I kneel down again, inspecting the scratch in the floor. I can sink my entire hand in and still not touch the bottom. Whatever happened to it is beyond me. The only thing I can think of that could have possibly caused it is some kind of freak accident connected to the orb. It's too much of a coincidence to be anything else.

The door swings open and Emma Blake steps into the lab with a sharp gasp, staring with wide eyes at the chaos across the room. "Malcolm, what—"

I shake my head. "I don't know."

I look back at the blackness surrounding the wormhole generator. The orb screeches loudly before dropping to the floor with a heavy thud. The darkness previously surrounding the orb disappears, the papers previously swirling around the room floating to the floor.

Slowly, I walk across the room. I finger the orb carefully, tapping it in case its trip through space has altered its temperature. When nothing appears to have changed, I pick it up. I frown, turning the cool metal in my hands.

Emma steps closer. "Did it…did it work?"

"I think so?" I frown, shaking my head. "It shouldn't have. I didn't turn it on. The wormhole generator was on when I got here."

Emma kneels down to look at the long scratch in the floor. I watch as she touches it. But she doesn't seem to hear the laughter like I did. "Did it make this?"

"I don't know. I don't see how." I sigh. "But I don't know how else it would be here." I shake away the sound of that laughter. "None of this makes sense."

Emma looks down at the orb. "You might want to keep that thing close for now. You probably don't want it turning itself on again."

I nod. Regardless of what happened and how it occurred, I don't want the orb making any wormholes unsupervised. Pocketing the device, I kneel down to pick up the papers strewn across the floor. Emma kneels down to help and, as we work to clean up the mess, I can't help but look back at the deep scratch in the floor, that cold laughter echoing through my head.

I don't know what could have caused the scratch or what sort of chain reaction could have caused such destruction. But something about it fills me with foreboding I can't shake off. Something deep inside of me is certain that this is not the last time I'll witness this level of destruction.

6

KALADRIA ASTRANA

THERE'S a large purple bruise forming on my shoulder. Pulling off my body armor, I can see it blossoming across my shoulder and arm. I touch it gingerly, wincing.

Xalin is not going to be happy.

Sighing, I grab the dress on the counter, slipping into the black fabric. I tug at the sleeves as I inspect my reflection. The dress is really too formal. Black satin hugs my body, imagining curves where I know there are none. There's a slit in one side, cutting through the dress's skirt and showing off one long leg. Even that much is showing too much skin for my taste. But at least its collar is high and its sleeves cuff at my wrists. I think I would die of embarrassment if it was any more revealing.

Smoothing down the black dress, I brush my fingers across my skirt. The Council always insists on a certain level of elegance when meeting with their Protectors. For any of the men on my squad, all that would entail would be black slacks and a blazer. But, for me, that means a slim black dress I feel utterly ridiculous in.

I adjust my sleeves, frowning at my reflection. The girl in the mirror mimics my frown, a stranger wearing my face. I've always felt out of place in this dress. I'm a soldier. I don't belong in dresses. I belong in armor.

Still, there's no denying that the girl in the mirror is me. Even with the elegance of the dress, I can see the lightning dancing under her skin. And despite her graceful appearance, I can see the roughness in her features, the light scar on her jaw, the sharpness of her cheekbones, even the fire in her eyes.

I heave a sigh. *Time to go.* Shoulders slumping in defeat, I leave my room and step into the elevator.

The silent ride up to the bridge is uneasy. It seems wrong that I'm the only one meeting the Council. They never single out members of the Protectorate like this. If they want to meet with me—specifically, *only* me—it can mean nothing good. I just hope this isn't wrong enough to somehow be connected to the last time I met with them in private like this.

I shake my head. That was a long time ago and I wasn't a Protector back then. This can't be the same.

I take a deep breath to steady myself before stepping out of the elevator. "Where are we at, boys?" I ask, crossing my arms as I step onto the bridge.

Azar grins, whistling jokingly. "You clean up good, Captain."

Warmth spreads across my cheeks. I flick out my fingers, zapping him. "Shut up."

"We're approaching the Satellite now, Kaladria," Vale interjects.

"Thank you, *Vale.*" I shoot Azar a pointed look. In the corner, Hassuun snickers and Azar rubs his arm, scowling.

I cross my arms with a huff of annoyance. "Where's Zeru?"

"Right here," Zeru says, stepping onto the bridge behind me. He takes in the scene before him, raising an eyebrow. "Do I even want to know why Azar looks wounded—"

"I do *not* look wounded."

Hassuun's snicker turns into bellowing laughter. Even Vale cracks a smile. Despite my anxiety about this meeting, I grin at Zeru. "You probably don't want to know." I pause. "Where's Hedda?" I ask over Hassuun's booming laughter.

"Waiting at the airlock."

I nod, glancing over at my other companions. Hedda is frightened enough without having to deal with Hassuun or Azar's chaotic behavior. "Vale," I decide, "Would you take Hedda to Protectorate Headquarters so they can sort out what to do with her?"

Vale nods.

I watch as the Satellite comes into view, my prior apprehension returning. I finger the sleeve of my dress, tugging it over my wrist. *Just another meeting,* I remind myself. *This is not a big deal.*

Zeru, noticing my fidgeting, leans closer. "You alright, Kala?"

"I'm fine," I exhale, pushing my nervousness away.

No one knows what happened that day. No one on my squad knows about the time I met the Council. Only Xalin and the Council are aware of the horrors I witnessed that day. I'd prefer to keep it that way.

After *it* happened, I'd met with the Council to explain what I'd seen. I remember standing in that huge room, a small child standing before the towering leaders of our people. I remember repeating what I'd seen with a kind of monotony no one would expect of a ten-year-old girl. I'm afraid of meeting with them again. I'm afraid of the memories I have pushed away for so long, afraid of what might come to light now. Afraid of that old monotony giving way to the emotions I have kept pent up for fourteen years.

I shake my head, heaving a sigh. I need to relax. This anxiety is going to get me nowhere. I take a few deep breaths, closing my eyes for a moment.

"Luna, this is *Resistance*, requesting permission to land," Vale says into the comms.

There's barely a moment of silence. "Permission granted, *Resistance*."

When I make no move to leave, Zeru touches my arm. "Kala?"

I nod, shaking my fears out at my fingertips. I turn to the elevator. "You have the ship, Zeru."

7

KALADRIA ASTRANA

MY ANXIETY DISSIPATES as I step off the *Resistance* to find my uncle waiting for me. Xalin stands on the docks, arms crossed as he leans against the wall. The skin around his eyes crinkles with a smile when he sees me.

I step forward to meet him. He wraps me up in a tight hug and I can feel my fears melt away. Still, I'm unable to hide a wince as a tight soreness spreads out from my shoulder.

Xalin frowns. He leans back, holding me at arm's length. "You're hurt."

I wave him off. "Zeru and I ran into some minor trouble aboard an enemy ship. It's nothing to worry about. Just a little bruise." When he sighs, I smile. "I promise I didn't do anything overly reckless." I clear my throat. "This time."

Xalin shakes his head but his eyes are sparkling and his lips are pursed together in amusement. No one knows my tendency for impulsive and reckless behavior better than him.

I look across the docks. "I need to see the Council."

He nods. "I know."

Xalin gestures across the docks and we start to make our way through the Satellite, which isn't as crowded as it normally is. Mercifully. I don't think my nerves could take the stares today. "Did they tell you what this is all about?" I ask.

He hesitates. "I should let them explain."

Anxiety creeps back into every nerve. "Uncle," I say slowly, "Is this…Does this have something to do with what I saw when my parents…"

I can't even finish the thought.

Xalin stops, taking in the tension in my face. Then, he puts an arm around my shoulders, guiding me forward. "No, of course not," he soothes. "This is something else entirely."

I exhale. "Good."

He rubs my arm comfortingly. "They didn't tell me much to begin with but it sounds like there's something they need you to investigate."

I nod absentmindedly. Though it's comforting to know that this has nothing to do with my parents, the whole situation is still rather troubling. The Council must be very concerned if they've already spoken to Xalin. They probably spoke with him to gauge my readiness. Which means they must be worried I won't be able to handle this new mission. That doesn't bode well.

I stop as we reach the door. I study the silver engraved in its panels, focusing on each individual swirl and coil in the metal. A final attempt to calm my nerves. "Well, I guess this is it."

"It sounded like they intended on sending you off as soon as you've been briefed. So this will likely be the last we talk until you get back."

I hug him, ignoring my shoulder's painful protest. "I love you, Uncle."

He hugs me back. "Be careful. I know where it is they intend to send you. This will be a lot more risky than most of your missions. Please don't do anything reckless."

"I'll be careful. I promise." I sigh. "I guess we'll have to hold off on that trip home."

Xalin squeezes me once before releasing me. "We can go home when you return." He steps away. His stature is calm but his eyes give away his own anxieties. Clearly, he's as nervous as I am. "Good luck, Kala."

I watch as Xalin walks back the way we've come, hands clasped behind his back. Then, I turn to the solid silver doors in front of me. *Show time.* I push them open with a deep breath. I step into the next room, waiting to be addressed. The Council is speaking to an Advisor, all of their expressions deeply troubled by whatever the Advisor says. It sets my nerves further on edge.

"Captain Astrana, please come in."

As the Councilors return to their seats on the other side of the room, I step all the way inside, clasping my hands behind my back tightly. "Councilors, how may I be of service?"

Councilor Verkire is the first to speak. "We have picked up an unusual signal on Earth. It's caused massive power fluctuations. We don't know what could have caused something like this. We've never seen anything like it."

I pause, studying their faces. "Are you worried humanity is progressing too quickly?"

It would be a valid concern. Anonymity plays a large role in how we protect Earth. If humanity developed technology too advanced too quickly, it would bring trouble to our Borders. Trouble much less manageable than slavers.

Councilor Corvar clears his throat. "We're worried that this energy spike was caused by something that could prove too dangerous for humanity. It's ludicrous to consider the possibility that humanity could have progressed that far. We are much more concerned that something has slipped past our Borders."

I think of what I saw on that ship, of the photographs of a city on Earth. If they had pictures of Earth, could they also be the ones responsible for this power fluctuation?

"We're sending you to Earth to investigate," Councilor Handrals says. "And, due to the sensitivity of this mission and our past experiences with humanity, we are sending you alone. Your squad is to remain on standby, in stealth mode just outside Earth's orbit."

I fight to contain a wince. *Oh, they are going to just love it.*

"Due to the delicate situation," Councilor J'sepp says, "We expect

FORGED IN STORMS AND SHADOWS

you to use the utmost caution. This is a mission of stealth, Captain Astrana. Humanity is not ready to know of our existence."

I nod. I understand. Humanity can't know about life past their own planet. They're too prone to violence when faced with something they don't understand. The last thing anyone wants is another massacre.

"Find the source of the power fluctuations and return to this Council immediately," Verkire orders. "Speak to no one of what you learn until you have briefed this Council."

"Understood. Am I to leave immediately?"

"That would be for the best," Corvar says. "Move quickly. We don't know the severity of the situation."

I slip into a stiff bow before turning on my heel. Walking back through the Satellite, I shake my head. No wonder Xalin was worried. It's been decades since the Council considered sending a Protector to Earth. The stories stemming from that massacre still serve as reminders why Protectors should always be ready for anything.

Still, it seems fitting. The Council is going to send me somewhere no one has dared to tread for years. Just like my parents, traveling across the universe to a system no one had occupied for centuries. I suppose I have more in common with them than I thought.

I just hope this ends better for me than it did for them.

THE ENTIRE BRIDGE is silent as I step out of the elevator. Zeru leans against the wall and Azar and Hassuun are seated at the window. Vale has returned from dropping off Hedda, sitting in his usual seat. All of them watch me, impatiently waiting for an explanation.

"The Council has a new mission for us," I say slowly, rubbing the back of my neck. "One that takes precedence over everything else."

"What is it?" Zeru asks.

"The Council has intercepted some sort of power fluctuation on Earth. They want it investigated immediately." I heave a sigh. "And they want me to go in alone."

Azar jumps to his feet, as does Hassuun. Both Zeru and Vale are quiet, their expressions troubled.

Hassuun shakes his head. "You can't be serious."

"That's insane!" Azar exclaims at the same time.

I roll my eyes, hoping to exude the confidence I'm not entirely certain of. "Please, guys, I'll be fine."

"This isn't a game, Kaladria," Zeru says, eyes worried. "You could be killed."

"Or worse," Vale adds under his breath.

I sigh. There's no fooling them. "I know that," I say. "Believe me, I don't like this much more than you do. But this is for the best. It's too dangerous for all of us to go."

"Then, send me," Zeru interjects. "Even if I was spotted, no one would be able to touch me."

In any other case, I would let him do it. It's not as if we haven't defied orders before. But this is different. I break the rules when it's the best option. But I can't agree that ignoring explicit orders is the best option in this case. Not with so little information regarding this mission. There could be *anything* down there.

"Not this time," I say quietly. "No one knows what's going on down there. I won't risk your life."

"But you'll risk your own? Kala, just—"

I shake my head. "No," I say firmly. "This is a direct order from the Council and I will not defy it. I am going to Earth and I am going alone."

"Kaladria," Zeru says. "It's too dangerous, even for you."

Vale clears his throat. "No one has been there in decades. We don't know what the humans would do if they found you or realized what you can do."

"I know that."

I look at each of them. Zeru has his arms crossed stubbornly. Hassuun and Azar, still on their feet, clench their hands into tight fists. Vale shakes his head disapprovingly.

"I appreciate the loyalty, guys," I say, "But this is one mission I'm going to have to do on my own."

"Kala—"

I step toward Zeru. Despite the height he has over me, I stand my ground, authoritatively looking up at him. Not as his friend, but as his captain. "Need I remind you that I am your superior?" I ask. "You know I hate pulling the captain card on you but I will if I have to."

Zeru says nothing, staring back at me. For a moment, I think he'll challenge me and force me to make an order I really don't want to make. But then he sighs, slumping back in his seat in defeat. "What are we supposed to do?"

I exhale. "Orbit Earth in stealth mode. As soon as I have the information the Council needs, you can come and pick me up."

Everyone is silent. Azar sinks back into his seat with a frown and Hassuun turns to glare out the window. Vale's jaw is set in a tense line, the Neptunian pilot far more upset than I would expect him to be for him having been a member of my squad for such a short amount of time. Zeru refuses to look at me, his frustration practically radiating off of him in waves.

"I'll let you know as soon as I figure out what's going on down there," I say softly, knowing there's little point in apologizing. "Until then, keep a low profile."

Zeru nods but he still won't look at me. "Don't worry, Captain. We'll take care of it."

I wince at his frigid tone. "Bring us down, Vale."

They work silently, the tense atmosphere putting me on edge. I sigh, turning to leave. If I'm going to Earth, I need to change into something more appropriate. Stepping into the elevator, I slump back against the wall as the doors close. I lean my head back, glaring at the ceiling.

"I hope you know what you're doing, Kaladria," I mutter. "For all of their sakes."

8

MALCOLM FARAWAY

"Thanks for this, Malcolm." Emma loops her arm through mine as we walk down the street. "It's been fun."

I clear my throat, trying to ignore the flip my stomach does at that small touch. "Hey, no problem. I could use the break. I'm pretty sure my mom thinks I'm turning into a hermit."

Emma smiles but says nothing. She looks down, watching her feet. We walk in silence and I look across the street, struggling to come up with something to say. But I was never any good at this.

"So," Emma finally says, "Has your wormhole generator turned on again?"

I shake my head, brows knitting together with a tight frown. "No. It's been dead since the other day."

"That's good, right? I mean, I don't know a lot about it but I'm guessing you wouldn't want to make a wormhole in the middle of the city or something."

I nod, a little mechanically. "Yeah, it is." But I'm still frowning. I can't get that lifeless laughter out of my head. And I can't wrap my head around how or why the wormhole generator would turn itself on and then fall silent. I want answers. But they don't seem to be forthcoming.

Emma touches my arm. "Malcolm?"

The *zing* that accompanies her touch jolts me out of my thoughts. "None of this makes sense." I shake my head. "Before yesterday, I couldn't get it to stay on for more than a few seconds. And, suddenly, it's opening wormholes on its own? It doesn't add up."

We both stop as we reach the lab. I unlock the door, flicking on the lights.

Emma approaches the long scratch in the floor. She crouches down, fingering the deep cut. As was the case before, she doesn't seem overly troubled by it. I wonder again if she can't hear the laughter I heard before.

"What about this?" she asks. "Any ideas?"

I shake my head. "I can't see how the wormhole generator could have made it."

Emma stands. "Do you think...?" She stops, thinking for a moment. "Do you think it's possible that something came through the wormhole?"

Instantly, the memory of that laughter echoes through my head. I shake it off. "What? Like an alien?" I raise both eyebrows. "You believe in that kind of stuff?"

"I—"

"Interesting. It seems like someone who could create a portal through space would be intelligent enough to know that something might be able to pass through it."

I spin around at the mocking voice. A pale form steps into the room, casually leaning against the wall. Incredibly thin and long-limbed, he looks almost as if his body was stretched out, like a rubber band that no longer snaps back into place. His eyes are cloudy, completely white, but his lips are turned up in a smirk.

"Who are you?" I ask, surprising myself with my own courage.

The stranger sighs melodramatically. "Perhaps you aren't as intelligent as I was led to believe."

He snaps his fingers sharply. A sudden *whoosh* blows through the room. A pale shape darts past me, too quick to see. The shape appears behind Emma, revealing itself as a second pale man, with limbs just as

45

long as the first man's, his eyes just as pale. He lifts Emma off the ground and she screams, kicking her legs out. He slaps a hand over her mouth, silencing her.

"Emma!"

As I move forward, the first man puts out a hand. "Stop right there, human. I have some questions for you. Cooperate and your friend will not be harmed."

My heart is pounding. *What is happening?* I look at Emma. She squirms but can't work herself free. I look back at the first man. "What do you want to know?"

He smiles approvingly. "Where is the Protector?"

"Who?"

"Wrong answer." He glances at his companion. He simply nods but it's the most damaging thing he could have done. Before I can blink, the man gripping Emma races out of the room with barely enough time for her to scream again.

I lunge forward, not entirely sure what I intend to do. "Emma!"

The first man points a strange-looking pistol, red light emanating from the barrel. "Stay right where you are, human."

I freeze, clenching my hands tightly. Everything is spinning. The only thing I can focus on is getting him to bring Emma back.

"Now, I'm going to ask again. Where is she? The one they call the Lightning Demon. Kaladria Astrana. I was told she'd been sent here. Where is she?"

I take a step back. There's something very dangerous in his tone. And I don't like the way his expression contorts with disgust when he says that name. This *Lightning Demon*, this Kaladria Astrana. He hates her. And if he's willing to kidnap strangers, I'm not sure I want to witness what he would do to someone he hates.

"I don't know what you're talking about."

"No? Perhaps, I should call for my man to kill your friend, then."

"No, please." I take a deep breath. "I really don't know who you're talking about. I've never heard of her."

The man purses his lips, clearly displeased. "How unfortunate. I had hoped she would show herself. I have a score to settle with her on behalf of my people."

I frown. What kind of girl is this? He said she's known as the Lightning Demon. What kind of girl gets a name like that? And what did she do to earn the hatred of an entire group of people?

He sighs, moving on. "Fine, then. Where is the portal maker? The wormhole generator?"

I stiffen, very suddenly hyper aware of the orb in the desk drawer across the room. Why does he want it? How does he even know about it to begin with?

"I have no patience for this." His eyes are narrowed. "Tell me where it is or I will kill you and your pretty friend."

I swallow past the sudden lump in my throat. He's placed an impossible choice before me. If I don't give it to him, Emma and I are done for. But if I give the wormhole generator to him, something tells me things will only get worse. I don't know what he wants it for but he's willing to kill two strangers to get it. Nothing good can come of giving him that kind of technology.

He shakes his head. "Have it your way, then."

He adjusts his aim, pointing the gun at my head. My heart is practically ramming out of my chest as I search for a way out of this mess. But there doesn't seem to be one.

Something whizzes past my ear, sending the gunman stumbling back. He drops his weapon, pressing a hand against his shoulder, blood gushing past the pale knife stuck there.

"You know, I'm getting really tired of you guys."

I whirl around, frozen by the sight of her. The woman stepping into my lab looks no more human than the man intending to kill me. Her white hair is long and straight, flowing around her. Beneath the black body armor, her skin is a pale bluish-white and bright light dances under her skin. Her eyes, bright blue, are set with a hard glint.

The gunman yanks the knife out of his shoulder. He smirks at her. "I was hoping you might show yourself. Shall I call you Kaladria? Or would you prefer the Lightning Demon?"

I look back at the woman. This is her? The woman his people want revenge on? At first glance, she doesn't seem like much of a threat. She's small, barely tall enough to be considered an adult. And yet…There's something about her that puts me on edge. A dangerous sharpness in her eyes.

Kaladria glares at the pale man. When he smirks, her expression turns terrifying. Her eyes are brighter than before, practically glowing, as she leans forward. Sudden electricity, like blue lightning, sparks around her. She vanishes from sight, only to reappear between me and my attacker. I stiffen as she grabs him by the collar, yanking him closer.

I blink. How did she do that? She crossed the room in half a second. It wasn't like the way Emma's kidnapper moved either. I could see a blurred form when he moved. The way she moved was something else entirely. One minute she was there, the next she was gone.

"You are not the first of your kind I have dealt with," she says with narrowed eyes. "How did you get here?"

He's still smirking. "You'd be surprised how large the hole is in your precious Protectorate."

"What is your interest in humanity?" she demands.

His expression darkens. "I have no interest in humanity."

"No?" She shoves him against the nearest wall, grabbing his arms. Bright blue lightning sparks around them both. He screams in pain. As the lightning disappears, he snarls angrily. She merely watches him, unperturbed. "Want to try again?"

He looks at me briefly. "I was paid to retrieve something from that human," he growls.

Kaladria doesn't turn. "And who is this employer?"

"I have nothing more to say to you," he spits. Without another word, he swings a knife, slicing through her stomach. She stumbles back in surprise. He shoves past her, turning to barely more than a speeding blur. It races in my direction with a glint of silver in its hand.

Kaladria spins back around, pale hair whipping around her, eyes ablaze with a fury I've never seen before. Gaze fixed on the blur, she reaches out a hand. As she extends her fingertips, lightning springs from her fingertips, sparking across the air before striking the blur.

My attacker stops, going suddenly rigid with pain. Then, he slumps to the ground in a smoking heap.

I stare at Kaladria as she steps across the room. *Lightning Demon.* Now, I understand the name. Because she's not a girl. She's a storm with skin.

What is she? I wonder. *What have I gotten myself into?*

9

MALCOLM FARAWAY

KALADRIA CROUCHES DOWN, fingers quickly searching the gunman. When she doesn't find what she's looking for, she stands with a heavy sigh, turning that sharp gaze on me.

I try to remember my manners. "You just saved my life. Thank—"

She lunges forward. Spear in both hands, she shoves me back against the wall. Her face is suddenly inches from mine as she stands on her toes, placing the long staff of her spear against my throat. She narrows her eyes.

"What have you done?" she growls.

I stare at her, blinking stupidly. "W-what?"

Her eyes are like ice. She doesn't remove her spear, scrutinizing my face. "He wanted something from you. What was it?"

"I-I don't know."

I can't stop stammering. I haven't had a problem with it since I was a kid but her gaze has brought the old habit back out.

She watches me silently, narrowed eyes studying my face. Like she's trying to decide if she believes me.

"Look." I swallow. "I don't know what's going on but they just kidnapped my friend." Fear sets back in at the thought of what they'll do to Emma. "You have to help her. Please."

She hesitates. "A human?"

"Yes, a human. What else would she be?"

I don't know where this sudden irritation is coming from. This can't be a wise course of action. I just saw her fry a man for making her angry. To make the same mistake would be lethal.

Kaladria sighs, lowering her spear a couple of inches. "I will do what I can to help your friend," she promises. "But first I need to know what they were after."

"They wanted to know where you were. They said they had a score to settle with you?"

She doesn't look bothered in the slightest. I wonder if she's used to people swearing vengeance against her. She certainly doesn't seem to mind that an entire group of people hate her. "I am quite familiar with this score," she says impatiently. "What else?"

I blink. "Well, he...he wanted my device."

She studies my face, her expression softening slightly with curiosity. "What device?"

I hesitate. While she did technically save my life, she seems more dangerous than the man she saved me from. Do I really want her to know about the wormhole generator?

The fire returns to her eyes, growing with her impatience. "Don't test me, human. I'm really not in the mood to play games. What is this device?"

I try to push her spear away. "Why do you want to know?"

Her eyes are electric with anger. She shoves her spear back against my throat. "What part of *don't test my patience* didn't you understand?"

"Okay, okay." I cough as she relaxes her stance. "I made a wormhole generator."

I expect her to stare, maybe even laugh at me, like everyone else does. But she doesn't. Her eyes spark with fury. "Of all the idiotic…" She slams her spear against the ground, sending electricity sparking across the floor. "Show me. *Now*."

KALADRIA ASTRANA

I LET the human slide past me, watching him carefully as he walks over to a desk, fumbling with a set of keys. As he unlocks a drawer, I lean back against the wall, crossing my arms.

A wormhole generator. I shake my head. It certainly explains how enemies crossed our Borders undetected. Hopefully, the damage he's done is reversible.

I glance at the still smoking form on the floor, thinking of the ship Zeru and I infiltrated. I remember all of those photos in that conference room. Were they performing reconnaissance for whomever hired them?

I shake my head. It would seem I have a lot to report on to the Council.

The human faces me, holding a small ball in his hand. When he holds it out to me, I take the small orb from him. As my fingers close around its cool surface, I raise both eyebrows. Its power thrums through my hands. Even in a dormant state, it gives off more electricity than I'd expect in something so small.

I look up. This must be the source of the power fluctuations the Council was concerned about, though it is certainly not what they were expecting.

"Have you used it?"

He hesitates. "Not intentionally. It sort of turned itself on," he says slowly. "There was this huge wormhole in the middle of the room yesterday." He points across the room. "And then I found this."

I follow his gaze, frowning at the enormous tear in the floor. I kneel down and place my hand inside of it. But I draw it out immediately at the sound of cold, lifeless laughter. I look around the room, lightning sparking on a closed fist.

The human stares at me and I shake my head. *Easy, girl.*

I look back down at the floor. Whatever did this must be immensely more powerful than—

I stop, jerking my head toward the open door. Something outside is giving off a massive amount of power. But it doesn't feel like the sort of power I'm used to. It must be some sort of electricity or I wouldn't be able to sense it but the energy is weird, off somehow.

Clenching my fists, I jump to my feet. I toss the orb back to the human, who catches it clumsily. "What's—"

"Stay where you are." I push urgency into my voice, hoping he has the sense to hear it this time. When he stiffens, I lift my fingers, letting electricity spread from my hands. Walls of pure energy rise up, surrounding the human in barriers made of lightning.

He looks slightly panicked as he clutches the orb, staring back at me. I raise a hand. "Stay calm. You'll be safe in there. This isn't over quite yet."

He swallows, then nods.

I turn away, facing the open door. Lightning sparks across my skin and I clench my hands around my spear, ready for the eminent fight. But the very moment the intruder steps through the room, I can't move. Terror wraps itself around my chest, lungs crushed by the panic snaking its way through my body.

Two tall monsters step into the room. They are incredibly tall, likely several heads higher than even Hassuun or Azar. Their fingers are too long to truly be considered fingers and are sharp like long talons, built like curved swords. Their skin is black and tight over bony bodies, lightly scarred beneath the obsidian armor they wear. Their faces are horrible, skeletal things, their tar-like skin stretched over their skulls. At the sight of their lipless mouths and soulless eyes, my fingers are trembling.

I stare at those hauntingly familiar talons, unable to push away the memory of the first time I saw them.

"Dad!"

My father waves at me through the comm, the skin around his eyes crinkling with a smile. "Hello, Baby Girl!"

Behind me, Xalin winks. "I leave you to it, kiddo."

He leaves the room, shutting the door behind him, and I plop down on the couch in front of the comm link, smiling brightly. "Where's Mom?"

Dad turns away. "Dalla!" he calls. "Come say hello to your daughter!"

My mother steps into view, kissing my father's cheek as she sits down. She smiles brightly. "Hello, my little Kala!"

I'm beaming as I lean forward. "Where are you?"

My father stretches out his arms, assuredly stiff from the long journey through dark space. "We're not sure. It will probably take some time to figure out exactly where we are."

"We hope we're close to the Zeta Arae system and the Home Worlds," Mom adds. She shrugs. "But only time will tell."

I frown. I don't particularly like the sound of that. It's already been weeks. As much as I love Uncle Xalin, I miss them. I miss Mom's singing and Dad's stories. I miss the days when we're all together at the house.

"When are you coming h—"

A loud crash resounds through the air and they both turn to look. Dad stands slowly, frowning. "Sorry, Baby Girl," he apologizes. "I better check that out." He blows me a kiss before disappearing.

"What's going on, Mom?"

She shakes her head with another shrug. "No idea. Probably just a faulty generator." She smiles encouragingly. "Don't worry, sweetie. I'm sure it's nothing major."

I open my mouth but snap it shut at the sound of a scream.

"Run, Dalla!"

My eyes widen. That was Dad's voice. Mom jumps to her feet, staring at something I can't see.

"Mom?"

Her face turns white as she staggers back a step. Lightning sparks in her hands, held up far too defensively for any of this to be nothing to worry about.

"Mom!"

She doesn't respond, tripping as she stumbles back. A loud gasp tears through her chest as black talons rip through her body.

I scream.

Gasping, I stagger back, ripped free of the memory. My spear slips from my fingers, clattering to the floor uselessly. I stare up at the monsters. *No. It* can't *be.* But the monsters that haunted my nightmares since that day are as real as they were the day they killed my parents.

They slink into the room, assessing the situation with empty eyes. As they draw closer, I know I have to fight but all I can do is stand there and blink stupidly. My chest feels so tight as heavy gasps rack my lungs, sending spasms of pain through my body.

These monsters—these *things*—shouldn't be here. They should be halfway across the universe.

My gaze flits over to the human, to the orb in his hands. The wormhole generator. It must have brought them here when it turned itself on.

"You look afraid," mocks one of the monsters.

In an instant, terror turns to fury. I roar, vaulting through the electricity in the air. As I reappear, I lunge at the monster. But it merely swings its talons, lazily slashing through my armor like it's made of butter.

I fall, gritting my teeth as I place an arm over my stomach. Blood drips past my attempts to staunch the bleeding, and I stagger to the side.

The monster steps forward, talons curling around my throat as it lifts me off the floor. "You are not human." It inspects my face, the monster's skull-like face mere inches from mine. It smiles, baring teeth. "No. You're one of those *Protectors.*"

I dig my fingers into the talons, legs dangling uselessly.

The monster smirks. "Ah, yes. We have heard of you. Kaladria Astrana, the Lightning Demon. You are the Protector the Council of Five sent."

It drops me. I slip to the floor, my breath sharp as knives as I gasp. The monster turns its attention to the human and the barriers I created around him. The human stiffens, staring up at the monster with wide eyes.

I grit my teeth. *Get up, Kaladria. You have to get up.* Somehow, I manage to force myself to my feet, stumbling to the side.

The monster reaches its talons toward the barrier but stops short of touching the electricity. Shaking its head, it looks back at me. "You've certainly complicated things, haven't you, Lightning Demon?"

I lunge for my staff. Clutching it in both hands, I dive at the monster. It turns slowly, grabbing my spear and yanking it out of my hands. Like I'm merely a child instead of the soldier so many have come to think of as a demon for the destruction my power can cause.

It tosses me to the ground, snatching up my jaw as it yanks me back up. The monster studies my face, black eyes narrowed. "Very well. If we cannot have the human, we will have to settle for you."

11

MALCOLM FARAWAY

I CAN'T CATCH my breath. I stand in the middle of her barriers, watching as the tall monsters snatch up Kaladria Astrana's limp form. Her head falls forward as they drag her out of the lab, talons curling around her arms.

Trapped between walls of bright blue energy, I sink to the floor, sitting down with the silver orb in my lap. I shiver, staring at the door the monsters disappeared through. They were nightmares. With grotesquely long limbs and sword-like fingers, they were the kind of beasts I'd expect to find under the bed of a child or hiding in the closet.

And the look on Kaladria's face...

From the moment she appeared in my lab, there was a ferocity about her, equal parts frightening and awe-inspiring. At least until those black-taloned monsters showed up. At the sight of them, something inside her snapped.

I don't want to think about what they'll do to her. The way they spoke, it's clear they only took her to punish her for protecting me.

Looking down, I clench a fist around the small orb in my lap. A large part of me is tempted to throw it through the electric walls surrounding me.

I never should have made the wormhole generator.

Some would argue that the chance to travel across the universe is worth the damage. And maybe, at one point, I might have agreed. But not now. Not having witnessed a friend's kidnapping because of it. Not after watching a stranger be dragged off, bruised and bleeding, because of it. Nothing—no achievement, no adventure—is worth this.

I lift my head at the sound of voices outside the lab. I stare at the door as a tall shadow falls across it. But it's not long-limbed monsters that step through the open door. Four men walk into the room. But, as unusual as their appearances are, they resemble Kaladria more than the monsters that took her.

The first to step into the room is tall and lean, his skin paper-white and his eyes pale. He holds a long dagger in one hand, eyes scanning the room carefully. My gaze falls on the ground below him. His feet aren't touching the floor. He hovers just above it, the balls of his feet a few inches above the floor.

Behind him, another man steps into the room, perhaps the most ordinary in appearance out of the four of them. His skin is pale but his eyes are a fairly typical gray and his hair is dark. He steps into the room slowly, scanning the scene as carefully as the man before him.

The final two are perhaps the strangest in appearance. Both big and burly, they stand out amongst the other two. One has pale green skin, red web-like veins just barely visible beneath his skin. His long hair is dark, braided away from his face. Next to him stands a man with huge muscled arms and gruff features. His skin is a dark crimson, his wild black hair swept away from his face.

The first man, still hovering above the floor, stops in the middle of the room. He looks at the tear in the floor and at the pale gunman dead nearby, still smoking from Kaladria's lightning blast. Finally, he looks at me and the sparking electric barriers still around me.

He flicks a hand, almost dismissively. A powerful blast sweeps across the room. I fall back, catching myself with my hands as the forceful gust rages through the room. The barriers around me flicker and then vanish.

"What happened here, Human?"

I hesitate, uncertain of my next move. I want this over. I want to push my troubles onto someone else, let these men take care of the immense issues plaguing my mind. But I don't know who they are or if they can be trusted. After all, the men that kidnapped Emma were more like these men than the monsters that took Kaladria. They could as easily be here to kill me as they could be here to help me.

"I doubt he knows anything, Zeru," the green-skinned man says impatiently.

Zeru exhales. He closes his eyes, brow tense with worry. Looking at the rest of them, I realize they're all worried. The pale, dark-haired man frowns, face deeply troubled as he looks down at the dead man on the floor. Their companions—the man with red skin and the man with green skin—both cross their arms, continuously looking outside as if they expect trouble.

Either this is a well-planned ruse or they truly are worried. The latter seems more likely. And, if that's true, they can't be looking for me. They're looking for her.

"Are you..." I hesitate. "Are you looking for someone called Kaladria?"

Zeru's eyes snap open. "Yes," he says, urgency filling his words. "She's our friend and we think she might be hurt."

I wince at the reminder of the injuries Kaladria sustained from those monsters. Then, studying the four of them, I hesitate. I have to be absolutely sure I can trust them. "How do I know you don't mean her any harm?"

Behind Zeru, the red-skinned man raises his eyebrows.

I raise my hands, defensive. "She was dragged off for protecting me. I just have to be sure I'm not making a mistake by trusting you."

Zeru's eyes soften only slightly. "If I were going to hurt you, I already would have."

I study his face, surprised by his bluntness. His face is still contorted with intense worry. If he's lying and Kaladria isn't his friend, he's very good at pretending she is.

I sigh. "Something took your friend."

"Can you be a little more specific?"

"I don't know what it was." I shake my head. "I don't think it was human."

"None of us are." Zeru crosses his arms. "What was it that you saw?"

None of you are? I blink. "Um, your friend saved me from the guy you see on the floor. He'd told her that he'd been employed to find something I made." I hold up the wormhole generator for his inspection. "Long story short, this device can create wormholes through space. The things that took Kaladria wanted it, too."

"What were these things that took Kala?" the green-skinned man asks.

"They were very tall, with really long arms and legs. And they had these long talons instead of fingers." I hesitate. "They knew who she was."

Zeru's brow furrows and he glances at his companions. "I don't recognize any race by that description. It doesn't sound like anything we've ever faced before."

"She seemed to recognize them," I say slowly, remembering the horror on her face as the monsters stepped into the lab. "I think she was afraid of them."

The red-skinned man snorts. "Don't be stupid. She's not afraid of anything."

Zeru shoots him a look before meeting my gaze again. "What makes you think she was afraid?"

"Before they showed up," I say slowly, "She was more frustrated than anything else. She acted quickly and without remorse. But, when she saw those *things*, she froze up."

Zeru rubs the back of his neck. "May I see the wormhole generator?"

I hesitate, thinking again of how many people are after this thing. Then, I sigh, handing it over. If he really wanted it, he could probably just take it by force.

Zeru studies the orb for a moment. His expression remains deeply troubled as he turns it in his hands.

"Zeru, we need to find her," the green-skinned man says. "We have to go."

"We should report to the Council," the dark-haired man adds. "If whatever took her really is dangerous enough to scare her, we're going to need some back up."

Zeru pinches the bridge of his nose. "I—"

Something loud sounds just outside the door, a high grating sound filling the air like nails on a chalkboard.

I can feel the color drain from my face.

"We've got company." Zeru passes the orb back to me. He twirls his knife, turning toward the door. "Azar, Hassuun, Vale, I want you to go to the *Resistance*. Take the human with you. I'll be there shortly."

"Zeru—"

"I'm not asking. Now *go*."

The warning tone in his voice sets all three of them on edge. "Come with us, Human," the green-skinned man sighs, clearly displeased with the arrangement. "Quickly."

I follow him out of the room, glancing back at Zeru. Hovering just above the floor, he twirls his knife between his fingers. His body fades away, becoming almost ghost-like in appearance, his body suddenly transparent.

Turning away, I allow his companions to rush me outside. We start running, racing out of town and through the forest.

"Who are you guys?" I ask, panting as I run beside the three of them, struggling to keep up with their fast pace. "And where are we going?"

"We'll explain everything on the *Resistance*. I suspect you'll have a hard time swallowing it all. And, right now, we have to hurry."

I say nothing, refraining from asking what the *Resistance* is. I keep running, my mind spinning with the implications of everything that's happened today. Emma was kidnapped. And a girl with *lightning powers* was taken for protecting me. And now I'm running through the forest with three men who are no more human than Kaladria Astrana.

I push away desperate thoughts, trying to not imagine what Emma must be going through, what Kaladria must be facing. It's hard to imagine those monsters having rules about how they treat hostages.

Gripping the wormhole generator tightly, I keep running. Nothing makes sense anymore. First, there was the accidental wormhole that never should have happened. And then the huge scratch in the floor, followed by that bodiless laughter. Not to mention all the people I've met with bizarre abilities. It can't be real. It's all too impossible.

"There it is," the green-skinned man pants.

I stop, staring at the space between several trees. It shimmers before revealing a huge silver shape. It appears to be some sort of advanced plane, with long wings and a sleek body, far too advanced in appearance to belong anywhere but between the pages of a book.

"The *Resistance* is a plane?"

The red-skinned man claps me on the back, hurrying up the ramp. "Oh, she's much more than that. Come on."

I hesitate, unsure what I'm walking into. But then Zeru appears behind me. He trudges up the ramp, carrying a dagger in one hand, Kaladria's spear in the other. He looks mostly unharmed but his shoulders are set tensely and black blood is splattered across his armor.

"Come on, Human," he says quietly as he steps up the ramp.

I follow him onto the ship, looking back only once, hoping this isn't the last time I see home.

12

KALADRIA ASTRANA

THE ONLY THING I'm truly aware of is that my fingers are trembling.

I curl my knees up to my chest, staring into the blank wall in front of me. I can feel the manacle around my neck, its chain clinking somewhere behind me. My breath comes out in tight gasps as it forces its way out of my lungs.

I thought I was stronger than this. I really thought I could be braver than that little girl screaming in front of the comm link. But perhaps fear is inescapable. Perhaps my entire life has always been leading me right here.

Shivering, I wrap my arms around my sides. I wonder what happens now. Zeru probably went to Earth when I didn't contact them. The tracker in my arm should still be giving feedback. Which means the ship will have sent Zeru errors regarding my injuries. He'll have retraced my steps, leading him straight to that human. Hopefully, before these monsters return for him and the wormhole generator.

Exhaling shakily, I look down at my hands. The lightning flickers weakly in response. Not a good sign for my powers.

The Lightning Demon with no lightning. If only the rest of the Protectorate could see me now.

I stiffen as a black shape steps into the room. But this one is different from the rest. He's taller, his stance more authoritative. Clearly, a leader amongst the rest of them. His body is covered in more scars than the others, a warrior with experience. He watches me with black eyes, his smile curling up in mockery.

"Your parents would be so disappointed," he sneers. "I almost wish we'd kept them alive, just so they could see how pathetic their daughter is."

Sudden fury swells within me. I lunge forward, fingers clenched into tight fists. But the manacle pulls tight, leaving me inches from the monster. He laughs.

I glare. "What do you want from me?"

"From you? Nothing." He smirks as he steps closer. "You are nothing but a tool, a means to lure the human here."

My laughter is wild and humorless. "He doesn't even know what I am. He will have all but forgotten me by now." I lean forward. "If you're going to kill me, you might as well get it over with."

"So ready to die, are we?" The monster grabs my jaw between taloned fingers, inspecting my face. "Do you know what I am, Saturnian?"

"I know you killed my parents," I spit. "That's enough."

He releases my jaw, pushing me back. "My people call me the General," he says, almost conversationally. "My people and your people have quite the...history." His smile darkens. "I am sure you are quite familiar with us. We're called the Aklev'Zol."

I stiffen, suddenly lost to the memories. Of the stories my father used to tell. About the Aklev'Zol and our ancestors' escape from their clutches. How our people fled our system hundreds of years ago to escape the Aklev'Zol, how it brought us here. It was due to the Aklev'Zol's brutality that our ancestors created the Protectorate in the first place, vowing that Earth would remain under our protection, that humanity would never lose all that we had lost.

I can't breathe. "That's not possible."

The General smirks. "Your people should have kept better records of what we look like."

My voice is trembling. "You can't be—"

"Your parents were searching for us, were they not?" He bares his teeth in a feral smile. "Well, they were successful in their search."

I grind my teeth. My parents never expected to actually find the Aklev'Zol. Not alive, not hunting us. Not after all this time.

"I'll admit, I was rather surprised anyone would actually want to find us. Your parents must have been rather stupid."

I snarl wordlessly, lunging forward. But, once again, the chain and manacle yank me back.

"And now that foolish human has led us straight to your system," the General continues. "Now, we can finish what we started."

I grit my teeth. "You're a fool if you think you can just waltz in without a fight."

"Why? Even centuries ago, your people were cowards. They *ran*." Still smirking, he grabs a fistful of my hair, yanking my head back to inspect my face. "Besides, your presence here proves how wrong you are. You are supposed to be the best, are you not? Do your people not view you as a hero?" He chuckles. "If we can stop you—the dreaded *Lightning Demon*—so easily, how do you expect your people to fare?"

I clench my fists.

"Don't fret, Captain Astrana. You will not live long enough to witness their destruction. Once we have the human, we will have no use for you."

13

MALCOLM FARAWAY

"Does anyone want to explain what's going on?" I ask, stumbling as I spin around to look at my surroundings.

I stand on a platform on the *Resistance*'s top level. The floor is silver, as are the walls. Huge windows look out the front of the *Resistance*. Monitors are strewn across the room, their thin screens set in front of the chairs spread throughout the room.

"Hassuun, put us in stealth mode. Vale, get us out of here," Zeru orders. "We make for the Satellite." He sinks into a chair before looking at me. "This isn't a plane. It's a ship, designed for space travel." He waves a hand around the ship as he speaks. "We're not from your planet."

Silently, I try to process what he's implying, what I've been piecing together since Emma's kidnapping and Kaladria's arrival. *Aliens.* So many theories have been made, claiming why life outside of Earth was or wasn't possible. And, here I am, standing amidst the irrefutable proof that they do indeed exist.

Zeru looks at each of his companions in turn. "Each of us comes from a different planet. We're all sworn to protect Earth from those who wish to harm humanity."

My head is still spinning. "Which planets?"

"Azar is from Venus." Zeru nods to the red-skinned man slumped back in his seat with arms crossed. "Hassuun is from Mars." The green-skinned man salutes casually. "Vale is from Neptune." The gray-eyed man barely glances my way before turning his attention back to the panel in front of him. "And I'm from Jupiter."

I frown. "How can you be from Jupiter? Isn't it just gas?"

"We have technology that allowed us to build our cities right on top of the atmosphere," he explains. "It's due to the planet's less than solid state that I can do this."

He turns into a ghostly version of himself, slipping his hand through the nearest wall.

"Do you all have abilities like that?" I pause, thinking of that bright blue electricity. "Kaladria shot lightning out of her hands."

Zeru turns solid once more. "Kaladria is from Saturn, which is ravaged by constant lightning storms. Her people are practically made of lightning."

"Not that this isn't all fascinating," Azar says dryly, "But aren't we in a hurry? The longer we waste time, the more danger Kala is in."

Zeru nods. "Inform the Council we have critical information to share regarding Kaladria's mission to Earth."

Azar turns back to a panel in the wall, fingers moving across it quickly. I glance at Zeru. He rubs the back of his neck, grimacing.

"You alright?"

He exhales. "I'm worried about Kala. If you're right and these things really scared her, I'm afraid we are in more trouble than anyone bargained for. Kaladria doesn't scare easy."

I think of her eyes, of the bright fire in them as she wielded her lightning. She was wild and fierce and completely unafraid.

I swallow. "I got that impression."

Zeru sighs. "I hope she's alright. The last time we spoke..." He shakes his head. "We didn't leave on good terms. I need to make that right."

"You all seem pretty close," I note.

Zeru nods but says no more on the subject.

"We're approaching the Satellite," Vale announces. He swipes his fingers across the panel in front of him. "Luna, this is *Resistance*, requesting permission to land."

"Permission granted, *Resistance*."

I step closer to the window, my jaw falling slack. An enormous satellite comes into view. The space station is huge in size, with colossal turrets and dozens of ships flying to and from the satellite. The whole thing shines brightly against the darkness of space, glittering in contrast to the pale moon.

"How did we miss this?"

Zeru glances over. "We're careful to ensure that you did."

I frown. "Why all the secrecy? If you're here to protect humanity, why not reveal yourselves?"

Hassuun snorts. "How about because of the mass chaos it would cause?"

"Hassuun is right," Zeru agrees. "Humanity isn't ready. The last time we sent anyone here was decades ago. It didn't end well. I suspect it will be a very long time before we try again."

I frown, watching as Vale docks the ship. I wonder what could have been so bad to cause them to keep their distance. Bad enough they would keep their existence a secret. And, yet, not bad enough that they would forsake their vows to protect Earth.

Vale stands, clearing his throat. "We should go."

"I alerted the Council," Azar adds. "They want to meet with us as soon as possible. And they want us to bring the human."

Zeru glances at me. "We never asked for your name."

"Malcolm."

He stands. "Well, Malcolm, I'm sorry to drag you into this but, as you were the last person to see Kaladria, we could use your help."

I nod.

Zeru glances across the bridge. "Come on. We should speak to Xalin before meeting with the Council. He should be the first to know what's happened."

"Who's Xalin?"

"Kala's uncle," Azar explains. "I told him to meet us on the dock. I'm betting he's outside waiting for us."

Zeru steps toward the elevator. "Then let's go."

14

MALCOLM FARAWAY

As we step off the Satellite and onto a silver platform, there's a man waiting for us. Based on the white hair and bluish skin, he must be Kaladria's uncle. And, based on his expression and fidgeting fingers, he must not have been told exactly what happened to his niece.

He looks at Zeru as we draw near. "Kala?"

Zeru looks down, shaking his head. "I'm sorry, Xalin. Things went awry." He lets out his breath. "It seems she's been taken hostage. Some sort of Outsider force."

Xalin rubs his face, the tight lines in his forehead becoming suddenly pronounced. "Are they related to what the Council sent her to find?" The lines deepen. "How did they get to Earth? How did they make it past our Borders?"

Zeru hesitates, glancing briefly at me before focusing on Xalin again. "It's—"

I clear my throat, stepping forward. "It's my fault."

Xalin looks at me, raising both eyebrows. He looks back at Zeru, incredulous. "A human?"

"Kala was protecting him when she was captured."

Xalin's face is suddenly unreadable as he glances back at me. "Why?"

I rub the back of my neck. "I'm still trying to wrap my head around all of this," I admit, "But I think it's my fault. I created this….device that makes wormholes. I think I let them through by accident. They wanted the wormhole generator. Your niece prevented them from taking it or me so they took her instead."

Xalin's eyes are suddenly cold. Instantly, I can see the resemblance between him and Kaladria. His eyes are as intense and piercing as hers.

I force myself to meet his gaze, even as my shame and guilt beg me to look away. "I'm sorry," I say quietly. "I had no intention of causing trouble." I straighten. "I promise to do whatever I can to get her back."

Xalin sighs, looking at Zeru. "Do you have a plan?"

"Convince the Council to send the Protectorate after her." Zeru grimaces, as if this will be the most difficult thing he's ever had to do. "I've seen the Outsiders that took her, Xalin. We will need all the help we can get if we're going to get her back."

Xalin exhales. "It will require a substantial amount of convincing. The Council is spooked by this whole business. They'll be reluctant to risk their armies, even for their best soldier."

"And for a human?"

Zeru frowns at me. "What?"

I look at him, head spinning as the wheels begin to turn. "Before Kaladria showed up, my friend was kidnapped too. If your people are protecting Earth, wouldn't this council care if a human was captured as well as Kaladria?"

Xalin is thoughtful. "Was this friend of yours taken by the same Outsiders that took my niece?"

I shake my head. "No. But I got the impression that the men that took my friend had been employed by the aliens…I mean, the Outsiders that took Kaladria."

"I might be able to work with that." Zeru looks at Xalin. "Even if the Council refuses to act, I won't abandon her. We're going to find her, even if it's without Council support."

Xalin nods mechanically. "I assume the Council is waiting for you?"

Zeru nods.

"Let me know what the verdict is. And let me know how I can help."

Without another word, Xalin Astrana walks away. His hands are clasped tightly behind his back, his shoulders slumping as he walks. This news is hard for him, to know that someone he cares about is in so much danger, that he's helpless to stop it.

And it's my fault. All of it is my fault. Without the wormhole generator, Emma would be safe, Kaladria would never have come to Earth in the first place. If anything happens to either of them, I will be wholly responsible.

"Come on."

Zeru leads the way off the dock and through the Satellite. As we walk, I stumble along, unable to keep from staring. The Satellite is huge, its long silver hallways extending on forever. The corridors of silver open up to room after room on either side of us as Zeru continues to lead the way forward.

I slow my pace, noticing the shocked faces of those around us. Men and women stare, gasping and muttering amongst themselves as they watch with wide eyes. *At me*, I realize.

Hassuun notices. He leans in. "No one here has ever actually seen a human before."

I glance to my left. A woman with red skin and dark hair freezes, clearly horrified. I swallow. "They look...afraid."

Hassuun sighs. "Like Zeru said before, the last time anyone went to Earth ended in disaster."

"Disaster?" I prod.

"Our Protectors were murdered and studied in a rather...brutal fashion. They became the humans' science experiments, dissected and torn apart to be studied organ by organ."

I wince. "So when they look at me..."

Glancing over, I can see a young mother watching me. She holds her child close as she stares at me with frightened eyes.

They see a monster. The kind of monster that would slaughter them for the sake of knowledge. It's a wonder they kept protecting Earth after that.

"They just don't know what to make of you," Hassuun says. "Or why you would be here. Kaladria being sent to Earth...It was all very hush-hush. If everyone knew that the Council was sending a renowned Captain to Earth, there would have been mass chaos. The Council wanted to avoid a panic."

I glance at a pale-skinned man, who watches me with narrowed eyes. Suspicious.

"It looks like there might be one anyway."

Azar grins. "I wouldn't worry about it too much. No one will bother you while you're with us."

I tear my eyes away from the stares to look at him. "Oh?"

"The *Resistance* is sort of the most famous ship in the Protectorate," Azar brags, still grinning. "We're basically heroes."

Zeru stops in front of us to turn and roll his eyes at Azar. "You mean *Kala* is a hero. She's the one people look at like she's some sort of god."

Azar shrugs.

"Why?" I ask. "What has she done?"

"Well, for starters," Hassuun says as Zeru keeps walking. "She's the youngest captain in the history of the Protectorate."

"Most captains have decades of experience before the Council gives them their own ships and squads," Azar adds. "But not Kala. Our captain served as a Protector for just one year before she was made captain of the *Resistance*."

"That seems like it would make other people jealous," I say.

Hassuun smiles. "To be honest, I think most of the other captains were just relieved."

Azar nods his agreement. "Making Kala a captain was the best solution."

"Solution?"

"Kaladria is a great soldier. She's aggressively efficient on any mission thrown her way and has always been very much in control of her lightning," Hassuun says, "But she's not great at taking orders."

"Only giving them," Azar adds with a chuckle.

"Making her captain allowed Kaladria to call the shots. So, instead of defying direct orders, she was giving them. It allowed the Council to keep her in the Protectorate without having to dismiss all the insubordination."

"It was the right call," Azar says, nodding. "Kaladria has gained a lot of renown as a captain. She's proven to be a capable adversary for anyone who dares to cross our Borders."

Blue lightning flashes through my mind as I think of the way she fought. Capable is an understatement. "Some of the Outsiders called her the *Lightning Demon.*"

"A nickname she earned due to her power," Azar explains. "Kala tends to leave destruction in her wake."

"That's why people treat her like she's different? Because she's powerful?"

"That and all the rumors swirling around her family," Hassuun says in a hushed tone.

I glance at him, brow furrowed.

"The Astranas have some strange history. Kala's parents disappeared in deep space about a decade ago. Xalin took her in after that. From what we've heard, he used to be a pretty skilled Protector himself. But he took an office job when he took Kaladria in."

I swallow. *Lost in deep space.* That's a little too close to home.

Exhaling, I shake away those thoughts. Now is not the time for them.

"They sort of disappeared off the map for years," Hassuun continues. "Until Kala joined the Protectorate, the family had sort of become an enigma."

I shake my head and force myself to focus on Zeru. He stops in front of a set of huge doors, glancing back. "Let me do the talking," he says, attention on Hassuun and Azar in particular. Then, setting his shoulders back, he pushes open the doors.

Five figures wait against the far wall. At the end of the line of chairs sits a woman with pale skin and dark hair, clearly from Neptune. Next to her, there's a man with pale electrified skin and surprisingly bored eyes for a Saturnian, considering the fire I've seen in both of the Astranas' eyes. Seated in the middle of the five chairs is a man with skin as white as Zeru's. Next to him is a green-skinned man and next to him is a red-skinned woman with intense black eyes. All are wearing black suits and dresses. They all sit poised, wearing stoic faces.

"Protector Neshani," the man in the middle greets, "Come in."

Zeru bows slightly. "Councilor Corvar."

"Where is Captain Astrana?" asks the Saturnian Councilor. "Is she not with you?"

"No, Councilor Verkire," Zeru says. "Captain Astrana was captured by an unknown race of Outsiders. She was, however, able to confirm what caused the power fluctuations before her capture."

I listen as Zeru explains the situation, quickly telling the Council what happened to their captain and my involvement in her capture. I keep my head down, the intense weight on my shoulders burying fleeting courage beneath shame.

"Where is this human?" asks the green-skinned Councilor.

I lift my head, looking at Zeru. When he nods, I take a deep breath. Azar and Hassuun—previously flanking me—step aside so I can stand next to Zeru. I force myself to hold my head up as the five Councilors look me over.

"Is this true? You have a device capable of creating wormholes?"

"Yes, it's true." I swallow hard. "And I will take responsibility for everything that has happened because of it."

I can feel Zeru's eyes on me, curious, perhaps even surprised. I keep my eyes on the Council, forcing myself to keep my head up. *You created this mess*, I tell myself. *You'll have to accept whatever punishment they deem appropriate.*

"Though we agree that this device has created quite the disaster, that is not the purpose of this meeting," Councilor Verkire says indifferently. "Right now, our focus must be on ascertaining what to do about Captain Astrana."

"Councilors," Zeru interjects, "Kaladria wasn't the only one taken by the invaders. A human has been kidnapped as well."

Several of the Councilors lean forward, trading apathy for sudden concern.

I clear my throat. "A friend of mine was taken, before Kaladria arrived."

The Venutian Councilor drums her fingers against her armrest. "Well," she sighs, "That certainly complicates things."

The Saturnian Councilor studies my face. "What can you tell us of the Outsiders that took them?"

"There were two sets of them," I admit. "The first came and took my friend when I didn't give them the wormhole generator. They were extremely fast."

Zeru speaks up. "Councilors, Outsiders such as these were trying to cross the Border near Pluto a couple of days ago. We destroyed their ship when they refused to turn back."

"It would seem then that their people are seeking retribution. What of the second set of Outsiders, Human? The ones that took our missing Protector, I assume?"

I nod slowly. "I think they'd employed those first Outsiders to take the wormhole generator. Soon after they failed, this second set came in search of the device."

"What did they look like?"

"They were tall and lanky," I remember. "They had black skin and really bony bodies. Their fingers were more like super long talons." I hesitate. "They knew who Kaladria was. They called her by name."

"And did she know who they were?"

I remember the sudden switch in her countenance when those monsters appeared, the way she went from a ready soldier to a terrified girl. "I believe so."

The Councilors share a look, clearly having come to some sort of conclusion.

"Councilors?"

"Protector Neshani, did Captain Astrana ever tell you about her—"

The doors slam open and a young man rushes into the room. The Martian bows quickly, almost as an afterthought. "Councilors, I apologize for the intrusion. But there's an unidentified Outsider on the Comms, requesting an audience with you directly."

Councilor Corvar nods. "Patch them through."

A hologram appears in the middle of the room. The hair on the back of my neck stands up. The hologram clearly depicts a tall, long-limbed monster with sword-like fingers. Next to me, Zeru steps forward with narrowed eyes.

"Ah, the Council of Five," the monster sneers in a guttural voice.

The Neptunian Councilor waves her hand dismissively. "Do not waste our time with your mockery, Outsider. I believe it is safe to presume you are responsible for the kidnapping of a human girl and our missing Protector. What is it you're after?"

The monster's eyes slide over to me, a cruel smile twisting up its lipless mouth. I force myself to hold its gaze, despite my desire to shrink back. Zeru steps in front of me and once again his other squadmates flank me.

The monster points a talon at me. "Give us the human and the wormhole generator."

Councilor Verkire shakes his head. "You know why we are here and what we protect. You can't honestly expect us to hand over a human."

Verkire's words only fuel the monster's dark smile. "Really? Not even for one of your own?"

Councilor Corvar crosses his arms. "And do you expect us to take it on faith that you have kept her alive?"

As smug as ever, the monster nods to someone out of sight and none other than Kaladria Astrana stumbles into view. Gagged, with chains encircling her wrists, the Captain of the *Resistance* is held firm by taloned hands on her shoulders.

Gone is the fear I saw in her eyes as she first laid eyes on these monsters. It's been replaced by a bright fury only contained by the inability to act. She glares at her captors with a hatred that chills my spine. Despite her current predicament, despite the injuries I know she received in my lab, she stands tall, head held high, chin jutted out defiantly.

I glance around me. Zeru is stiff with tension. Both Azar and Hassuun clench tight fists, ready to jump through the hologram. Vale sets his jaw, expression suddenly cold. All ready to wage war for their captain.

I look back at Kaladria, finally noticing what I had missed before. The tightness in her stance, the stiffness in her shoulders. And now I understand. She's not keeping her eyes on her captor purely out of defiance. She's keeping her eyes on the monster so she doesn't meet her squad's eyes. So they don't see her fear.

The Outsider grabs her jaw. "Do you intend to leave your best Protector behind to rot?"

Silence greets him. Seeing his words have elicited no response from the Council, the monster shrugs, pushing Kaladria back. She disappears, no doubt dragged off by one of her unseen captors.

"I see that you are willing to sacrifice Captain Astrana," the Outsider says, focusing on the five Councilors. "Very well. But what of the girl? After all, she is one of the humans your people have supposedly vowed to protect."

I freeze as the Outsider drags Emma Blake into view. Dark hair swirls around her face and her dark eyes are wild with terror. She's been gagged and tied up like Kaladria but, unlike the captain of the *Resistance*, she is completely hysterical. She sobs past her gag, squirming against her captor's grip.

The monster pays little attention to her struggling, his focus on the Council. "Now, correct me if I am wrong, but I do believe you are willing to leave Captain Astrana in our hands, despite everything she's done for your Protectorate?" When the Councilors say nothing, he continues. "And what of the human girl? What do you say? One human traded for another?"

I swallow. *Do it. Emma doesn't deserve this. Not for me.*

"You know that is not a trade we can afford to make," the Venutian Councilor says stiffly.

The Outsider shrugs. "The offer will stand for the next twenty-four hours. After that, both the human and the Protector will be executed. If you do not give us what we want, it will be them that pay the price."

15

MALCOLM FARAWAY

As the hologram disappears, I stare numbly at the empty wall. The Outsider's last words echo through my head. *They're going to kill them. They're going to kill both of them.* I pinch my eyes shut. Everything that happens next will be my fault.

Zeru clears his throat, the first to recover from his shock. Even still, his voice trembles slightly. "Councilors, we don't have to trade Malcolm or the wormhole generator. We have Kaladria's coordinates from the tracker in her arm. We could send a team through a wormhole with Malcolm's device. We'd be there and back before anyone knew what was happening."

The Councilors share a look. Verkire shakes his head and several others merely look down.

"We are sorry, Protector Neshani," Corvar says, "But we will not risk the wormhole generator falling into their hands. Kaladria Astrana—"

"But—"

"Kaladria Astrana was well aware of the risks of being a Protector when she joined our ranks," Corvar finishes, as if Zeru hadn't even spoken.

"And the human girl?" Vale asks, crossing his arms.

"An unfortunate situation," Verkire says slowly. "However, if these

78

Outsiders had the wormhole generator, they would be capable of destroying the entire human race. No one is worth risking that."

I can't breathe all of the sudden.

"You can't just leave them to die," Zeru protests.

Verkire sighs. "Their sacrifices will be remembered."

"That's it?" Azar snaps. "You'll let them both die?"

The Venutian Councilor shakes her head. "This matter is not up for discussion. And, if you insist on pushing it by going after them yourselves, this Council will consider it treason."

"Until this matter can be resolved," Verkire adds, "We will be grounding the *Resistance*."

Corvar holds out a hand. "The wormhole generator, if you will."

I stiffen but don't move, watching Zeru. I wait for him to argue. He looks ready to. His eyes are hard and he works his jaw. But he doesn't speak, likely knowing the Council isn't going to budge on the matter.

"Malcolm," he says quietly.

I grip the wormhole generator tightly. Then, with a heavy exhale that curves my shoulders inward, I hand him the silver orb.

Zeru places the wormhole generator on the floor in the middle of the room. Then, bowing stiffly, he spins around and walks out of the room. Flanked by the rest of his team, I follow him out into the hall.

As we step into an elevator, Zeru slumps back against a wall.

"What are we doing, Zeru? This is *wrong!*"

Zeru looks at Azar. "We will not abandon either of them. We're just going to have to work behind the Council's back. Figure out a way of getting the ship off the Satellite."

My mind is spinning with the choice placed before us. "The Council said you'd be committing treason," I say quietly. "Are you prepared to face that?"

"How can you say that?" Hassuun growls. "Kaladria saved your life. If she dies, it will be because of *you*."

I cringe against his words, wishing I could deny them. "I know that." I swallow the lump in my throat. "I meant what I said before. I will do everything I can to help. I just want to make sure you're all willing to face any consequences that may come of this. Because, if you aren't, you could always do the trade and give me to them in exchange for the two of them."

The thought of being anywhere near those monsters terrifies me. But not as much as the possibility of letting both of them die for me.

"No, we couldn't," Zeru sighs. "First of all, it would go against everything we stand for, everything we've vowed to protect. And it wouldn't solve anything. If these Outsiders had the technology to make wormholes, they could just come here and kill us all."

"Not to mention that Kaladria would skin us alive," Vale mutters.

Zeru nods his agreement. "We'll face whatever comes of our treason. Kaladria would do the same for any one of us."

I lean back against the elevator. "You said you know where they are? The exact coordinates? At this very moment?"

"We keep track of all our Protectors through a tracker in the arm. I can get the coordinates of her tracker off the *Resistance*."

"Then, we need to get the wormhole generator back." I pause, lowering my voice. "We'll need to steal it. But, if we can get it, I think I can open a wormhole from inside the ship. We could make one to wherever they are, grab Emma and Kaladria, and be back without ever technically leaving the ship."

Zeru considers for a moment, rubbing the back of his neck thoughtfully. Finally, he nods. "Alright. But I'm going through the wormhole alone."

Azar frowns. "Zeru—"

"I'm the only one they can't touch. If anyone gets too close, I'll just use my Ghost Form."

Azar lets out his breath in defeat.

"Let's get back to the *Resistance* and get those coordinates," Zeru says in a low voice as the elevator doors open. "Then, we need to steal back the wormhole generator."

16

MALCOLM FARAWAY

"Protector Neshani!"

Both Zeru and I stop on the docks, mere feet from the *Resistance.*

Councilor Corvar glances between Zeru and I as he approaches. Drawing closer, he slows, clasping gloved hands together behind his back.

"Councilor Corvar," Zeru says coldly, "Is there something else? As you have decided to sentence my captain to death."

"That was a Council-wide decision. But I'm willing to reconsider, perhaps even try to convince the rest of the Council to change their minds on the matter. Just let me speak with the human in private first."

I look at him in surprise but he's not looking at me. He's still looking at Zeru.

Zeru crosses his arms. "Why?"

Corvar shrugs. "Curiosity. We did not anticipate that humanity had progressed far enough to make such great bounds in space travel. Let me speak to him privately and I will return the favor by speaking to the other Councilors."

"I don't think—"

"I'll talk to him."

Zeru's frown is troubled. "Malcolm…"

"Neither Emma or Kaladria have much time," I whisper quietly. "Let me see what I can do."

Zeru sighs, nodding.

Corvar clasps his hands together. "Excellent."

"Meet us back on the ship," Zeru mutters. He walks down the dock toward the *Resistance*, his squadmates following behind him with backward glances. I look at Corvar, who waves a hand for me to follow him.

As we walk back through the winding hallways of the Satellite, I study Corvar. Maybe I can learn something about him and how he thinks. Maybe even something that might help me convince him to save Emma and Kaladria.

It's obvious, looking at his pale skin and white hair, that he's from Jupiter, just like Zeru. But that's where the similarities between the two of them end. While Zeru always seems prepared for a fight, Corvar is almost too relaxed for being charged with leading a Protectorate of soldiers. He walks with his hands behind his back, clasping gloved fingers loosely. His expression is too at ease for a man considering sending an army through space for a rescue mission.

Corvar leads me into a small office. As he slips a hand in his pocket, he places the wormhole generator on the desk. Heart hammering, I watch Corvar. If I can't convince him to help them, I'll have to find a way to steal it.

Corvar sits down slowly before studying my face. "Now, tell me, Mr. Faraway, what is your interest in all of this?"

"What do you mean?" I frown. "My friend—"

"Yes, yes, I understand your desire to help a friend," Corvar interrupts. "However, I believe you are a man of logic. Do you really think it wise to choose two people over an entire galaxy?"

I hesitate, choosing my words carefully. So much is at stake. Two lives could be the cost of failure here. I need to show him why saving them is the right thing to do, despite the risks.

"If I were to let them die, does that really make me better than the monsters that took them?" I ask slowly.

"I do not follow your line of thought, Human."

"My friend, Emma Blake. She's innocent in all of this. She had no part in the creation of the wormhole generator. She just happened to be with me at exactly the wrong time. And Kaladria Astrana saved my life. I'd be dead if it wasn't for her."

Corvar purses his lips. "As was stated before, Captain Astrana has always known the risks of her chosen occupation."

"That's not the point." I shake my head. "This isn't about her. It's about me. Everything that's happened, anything that might happen, is because of me. If I let them kill Emma and Kaladria, I might as well have pulled the trigger. People aren't just numbers. Yes, it might risk far more lives if we rescue them. But, if we don't, we will give in to the same brutality that our enemies claim gives them the right to execute both of them in the first place. If we don't save them, our hands will be just as dirty as the Outsiders that kill them."

"Oh? Does our neutrality not keep us in the right?"

"You can't claim to be doing the right thing by avoiding the situation. People who do the right thing stand up for the helpless. Neutrality prevents you from doing the right thing. So, turning a blind eye makes you just as bad as the murderers."

Corvar studies my face for a long time. I meet his gaze, even if my heart is pounding. I don't know what else I could say to convince him.

Finally, Corvar sighs. He leans back in his seat. "Alright, I see your point." He pauses to collect his thoughts. "I have a proposition for you."

I wait, clinging onto the hope that I may have just found a way to rescue Kaladria and Emma, maybe even without getting Zeru and his squad in a lot of trouble.

"I am not keen on losing our best captain," Corvar says. "Nor do I like the thought of being responsible for the death of an innocent girl. However, I like the idea of risking some of our best soldiers a lot less."

My heart sinks.

"Which is why I am going to propose a third option."

"A third option?"

"I have acquired Captain Astrana's coordinates. What I am

suggesting is you open a wormhole right here and I will personally go get her and Miss Blake myself."

I hesitate. Something feels very wrong about this proposition. I feel suddenly uneasy about being alone with this stranger. His curiosity seemed innocent enough before but now...

I don't understand his thinking. It doesn't make sense for him to refuse to risk anyone for one soldier and now all of the sudden he's willing to risk his own neck. Besides that, he told Zeru he wanted to speak to me because he was surprised humanity had progressed enough to create a wormhole generator. Yet, he hasn't spoken a word about it since I got here.

"Wouldn't the odds be more in our favor with more than just you going through the wormhole? Wouldn't it make more sense to get the whole Council on board?"

Corvar stands. "It would, if we had more time. However, I do not think I will be able to convince my fellow Councilors to change their stance before it's too late for Miss Blake and Captain Astrana."

"But isn't it dangerous for you?"

"No more dangerous than it would be for Zeru Neshani." His look is pointed. He knows what we were planning to do. "I was a soldier long before I was a Councilor. Besides, if anyone gets too close, I can slip into my Ghost Form. As brave as Protector Neshani may be, I am much more experienced. My chances of success are much higher than his would be."

I hesitate. Everything inside of me protests this plan. Something is wrong. He's been far too calm about all of this. And it was far too easy to convince him to help. It's strange he'd offer to do this in secret, rather than in front of the rest of Kaladria's squad.

"I assure you, Mr. Faraway, this is your best option," he says. "If you do not take it, you will likely get the squad of the *Resistance* killed, or at least arrested for treason."

The offer is tempting. I already feel responsible for what happened to Kaladria and Emma. I don't want to be responsible for what happens to Zeru, too. But I can't take this decision lightly. I can't afford to make the wrong choice. Too much is at stake.

I let out my breath. "I'll need to speak to Zeru first."

Corvar's expression falls with disappointment. "I can't allow you to do that."

My expression freezes in place at his words. I try to work through them, trying to make sense of them.

Corvar straightens, wordlessly slipping off his gloves. And now I understand why he's been wearing them. One hand is the pale, colorless skin of a Jovian, but the other hand is black, his fingers stretched out into talons.

I can feel the color drain from my face. "What are you?"

Corvar reaches into the desk, picking up a gun. "I am a Jovian," he says in a low growl, pointing the gun at my chest. "Now, pick up the wormhole generator."

Even though my heart is almost ramming out of my chest, I glare at him. I pick up the wormhole generator, clenching my fingers around the orb.

Corvar smiles. "It's nothing personal, Mr. Faraway, but they've promised to undo the damage to my hand if I turn you over."

"You can't seriously believe they'll keep their word."

Corvar cocks the gun. "Open a wormhole."

I don't know where my courage comes from. But, even with a gun pointed at me, all I feel is anger. My fear is replaced with it, fueled by his betrayal of his people, his willingness to sacrifice lives for his *hand*.

Still glaring, I shake my head. "No."

Corvar's eyes are narrowed. "Do you really value your life so little that you would rather die?"

"You won't kill me. You need me to open the wormhole."

His expression darkens and my smile is hard. I'm no use to him dead and neither is the wormhole generator. I'm the only one who knows how to use it. He can't turn it on without me.

"I may not be able to kill you," Corvar says slowly, "But what about your new friends? The squad of the *Resistance* would never expect an attack from a Councilor." When I grit my teeth, he continues. "And what of Miss Blake? I could certainly speed up her demise. All it would take is a call."

I clench my hands into tight fists. He's right. Zeru is smart and seemed fairly guarded around the Council but he would never expect Corvar to outright attack him. I release my clenched fists. It might not save Emma or Kaladria. But it will certainly save Zeru and the others on the *Resistance*.

"What are the coordinates?"

17

KALADRIA ASTRANA

MY BODY IS COMPLETELY numb as I sit on the floor, hands still tied in front of me, the gag still shoved in my mouth. I stare at the empty room, oddly grateful for my isolation. They've returned the human girl to her cell, having served her purpose on the comm call.

I lean my head back against the wall with a heavy sigh. Zeru will likely try to convince the Council to come for me. Maybe even try to use the human girl as reason to come for both of us. Not that it matters. The Council would never risk it. One Protector and one human is simply not enough to risk our captors getting their hands on the wormhole generator.

As I sit on the cold floor, I remember black talons ripping through my mother's chest. *Is that what awaits me?* I shiver. I've never feared death, not in all my time as a soldier. But those black talons have haunted me for as long as I can remember and I would rather face anything else before I faced death at their hands.

I open my eyes, suddenly motionless. A single point of light splits apart the room, extending out, creating a hole in my cell. As the hole widens, it opens up into a new room, one with silver walls and a familiar hum I've felt a thousand times before.

That's an office on the Satellite.

My heart feels like it's going to pound out my chest and my head is spinning. Regardless of who has opened that wormhole, it means trouble. If my squad was that foolish, they are now in as much danger as I am. And if it was anyone else, it will mean trouble for the human and his device.

My worst fears are confirmed as two figures appear on the other side of the wormhole. The human who invented the wormhole generator stands in the Satellite office, glaring at the figure across from him. His hands are slightly raised. But it's the sight of the figure standing across from him that truly shocks me. Councilor Corvar stands across from him, pointing a gun. My gaze falls on Corvar's free hand, clearly black and taloned, just like the Aklev'Zol.

I stare, frozen at the realization of exactly what he's done hits me. He's giving up the human and the wormhole generator. At gunpoint.

Traitor.

I jump to my feet, fury boiling inside of me. Launching as far forward as the chain encircling my neck will let me, I jerk against the bindings around my wrists. If I had my lightning right now, I would fry him.

Corvar doesn't even look at me, focused elsewhere. I turn my head, grimacing as the General steps into the room. He looks at the open wormhole. "Ah. Well done, Councilor."

Corvar nods to the human, saying something I can't hear. Jaw set, the human steps through the wormhole slowly. His eyes brush past mine before he glares back at Corvar.

"I'm surprised, Councilor," the General says. "I wasn't sure you'd be able to follow through."

I grit my teeth. Everything has unraveled in mere minutes. Was the General right? Are we doomed?

"My hand," Corvar says hoarsely as he holds out the taloned hand. "Fix it."

The General flicks long talons dismissively. "Enough, Councilor. You will get what you desire soon enough. Now, give me the wormhole generator."

Shoulders slumping, Corvar grabs the small orb hovering above the wormhole and tosses it to the General. Immediately, the wormhole evaporates, closing into itself. The General inspects the small orb for a moment before smirking at my fallen expression. "I'll let the two of you get reacquainted."

I glare into his back as he turns, shutting the door behind him with the finality of a tomb. I exhale, slumping back against the wall as I look back at the human.

He hesitates only a moment before stepping closer and pulling out my gag.

"What happened?"

He exhales. "You've got a traitor on your Council."

"I gathered that." I shake my head. "How did you end up here?"

He leans back against the wall next to me. "Your squad found me and brought me to the Satellite. Corvar wanted to speak with me privately. He was offering to convince the Council to plan a rescue in exchange for a conversation with him."

"And you agreed?"

"It seemed like the best thing to do at the time." He sighs. "When he took me to his office, he threatened to kill Zeru and the rest of your squad if I didn't open a wormhole for him."

I sigh. As good as they are, none of my squadmates would expect to be attacked by Corvar. None of us would have. He's a renowned ex-Protector, as well-known as I am. He's completely above suspicion.

"You protected my squad?"

He nods slowly.

"Thank you."

He opens his mouth but snaps it shut quickly. We both turn as the door swings open. I grimace at the sight of the General with the human girl in tow. He tosses her forward. The human boy catches her as she stumbles. When she sobs, he pulls her close to his side, glaring at the General.

I have to hand it to him. He's braver than I'd expected.

"Cute." The General smirks. "Do you really think you can protect her, Mr. Faraway?" His eyes slide over to me and he laughs cruelly. "*She's* the soldier and she can't protect anyone. What makes you think you can do better?"

I grit my teeth, looking at the humans and then back at the

General. I want to prove him wrong but I know there's little I can do. He's too strong. Even if I wasn't chained up, I wouldn't be able to do any damage. Not without my lightning.

"Now," the General continues, "I think it's time I kept my promise to the Council of Five. A little early but we know they won't be sending any help. Wouldn't you agree, Captain Astrana?"

Hands clenched into tight fists, I watch as several more Aklev'Zol step into the room. I want to shrink back into the wall. All I can think about is those black talons tearing through my mother's chest.

The General notices, his smile as smug as it is disturbing.

I glare, forcing myself to stand a little taller, to be the soldier Xalin trained me to be. *You are bigger than your fear,* I tell myself. Clenching my hands tighter, sure my knuckles are white with tension, I lift my chin stubbornly.

"You do know what happens next, don't you, Captain Astrana?"

I swallow my fear, blinking it away. But I know the stories of the Aklev'Zol better than anyone, thanks to my father's fascination with our history. I know exactly what it is the Aklev'Zol are capable of.

The General is still smiling. "The humans may not yet know what it is we do to prisoners but I believe you—"

"Let them go. You've got what you wanted."

The General watches me and I force myself to hold the gaze of the monster I have feared half of my life.

"And what about you, Captain Astrana?" he mocks. "Am I to release you as well?"

With a deep exhale, I force the tension from my fingertips. *You are bigger than your fear.* "No. I suspect I am too much of a threat for that."

"How noble. However, I will not be releasing either of them." He glances at the two humans. "I still need the boy. And the girl provides an excellent opportunity to show you exactly why your ancestors feared us so much."

He waves two Aklev'Zol forward. Their long talons snatch the girl back. She screams, sobbing.

"Emma!" The human boy lunges forward, only to be dragged back by another Aklev'Zol.

I clench my hands into fists, only able to take a single step forward before the manacle around my neck tugs me back. Two Aklev'Zol hold the girl in place as the General steps forward.

"Stop." I lean forward, metal biting into my neck. *"Stop."*

The General, ignoring both the girl's sobbing and my weak protests, jabs one long talon into her arm. She cries out, squirming as the talon sinks beneath her skin, quickly drawing blood. The bleeding stops as the General removes the talon. In place of a puncture wound is a black spot the size of a fingertip. But the blackness is growing, spreading through her arm. It moves down her wrist and up her sleeve, presumably spreading up into her shoulder.

The Aklev'Zol release her. She falls to her knees, still sobbing. Her fingers dig into the skin at her wrist, as if she could somehow claw away the heavy blackness spreading across her body.

The General smirks at the human boy, whose face mirrors my own horror. "You've seen and met many powerful aliens, haven't you? The Saturnians with their lightning, the Jovians with their Ghost Forms. But their ancestors came to your system centuries ago to flee from *our* power."

The human girl sobs again.

"You can see the black mark spreading across Miss Blake's skin," the General continues. "When it has spread to every inch of her skin, she will no longer be human. She will be Aklev'Zol, just like me or any of my soldiers."

I pinch my eyes shut. All the stories my father used to tell were true. Stories of the Aklev'Zol turning our people into enemies. Stories of our own soldiers turned against us, becoming dark and twisted monsters, completely committed to the Aklev'Zol.

The human girl sobs again and I force my eyes open. The black mark has spread all the way down her hand, turning once delicate fingers into long talons, sharp and pointed like daggers.

"Please," she begs, still sobbing, and I realize she's speaking to me. "Please, help me."

I swallow. *I am so sorry.*

The General laughs. "She can't help you. She can't even help herself."

I glare but say nothing.

The General smiles. "Fascinating, isn't it? The process is rather nasty. You see, the more fear Miss Blake feels, the faster the infection spreads. I suspect it won't be long now."

I lunge forward, just inches from the General's smug face when the chain yanks against my neck.

The General's grin is wicked. "Infuriating, isn't it? When was the last time you felt this helpless, Captain Astrana? Was it when your mother died?"

I grit my teeth.

The General turns his attention back to the human girl. The blackness continues to spread more and more quickly as she frantically claws at her skin.

The human boy jerks an arm free. *"Emma!"*

I turn my head away as the girl lets out one final terrified scream, wordless and raw, before the sound is cut off. Swallowing the lump in my throat, I force myself to look at the new Aklev'Zol. She stands slowly, talons scraping against the floor.

"E-Emma?"

I look at the human boy. He stares up at the newest Aklev'Zol with horror and confusion. His eyes are wide, his face pale, his entire body tensed with fear.

"I'm not Emma," the Aklev'Zol-Emma purrs as she slinks closer. "The girl you led into this...interesting situation is *dead*."

The human boy slumps forward, bowing his head in defeat. The Aklev'Zol release him and he collapses to the floor, broken.

I clench my fists, digging nails into the palms of my hands. The pain is a welcome distraction.

So many people are at fault. My parents for trying to discover a past better left buried. The human for creating the wormhole generator. Corvar for betraying us all. And me, for letting my fear blind me. I should have been faster, I should have been stronger. I'm supposed to be the Lightning Demon but, when it counted, I was useless. If I hadn't let fear overtake me on Earth, I could have prevented all of this. I could have protected the human, I could have rescued the girl.

The General, noticing my distress, smirks. "I'll be back for you later," he promises before leading his soldiers and the Aklev'Zol-Emma out of the room.

As they walk out, leaving only me and the human boy, I sink to the floor, hands still clenched tightly. The door slams shut and I look over at the human. He stares at the door, a familiar sort of pain in his eyes as he tears his fingers through his hair.

I pinch my eyes shut, trying to force normalcy into my breathing. I don't fear death. Zeru has teased me more than once for running headfirst toward danger. But, even if I'm not afraid to lose my life, I am terrified of the kind of death the Aklev'Zol can provide. If I'm going to die, I want to be buried in the ground, not turned into a twisted monster dedicated to serving the worst kind of enemy.

I only wish I could choose the kind of death they're going to serve. I wish I could be so lucky.

1 8

MALCOLM FARAWAY

SHE DIDN'T DESERVE THIS.

Emma was completely innocent in this mess. She didn't deserve to be afraid like that until it twisted her into a monster. She shouldn't have died. She—

"It's not your fault."

I look up at Kaladria but she isn't looking at me. She sits on the floor, leaning against the wall. She glares at the ceiling, bound hands resting in her lap.

"You sure?"

Kaladria exhales, looking at me wearily. "Yes. This is on the General and the Aklev'Zol. There is nothing you could have done to prevent this from happening."

"If I hadn't made the wormhole generator—"

"The Aklev'Zol would have found another way eventually. This was inevitable."

But it didn't have to be Emma. It didn't have to be now.

I close my eyes but immediately decide that's a bad idea. The memories flow too freely behind closed eyes.

"What's your name?"

I look up. "What?"

Kaladria's eyes are on me. "Your name," she repeats. "I never caught it before."

"Oh." I frown. "It's Malcolm."

She leans forward, grimacing in pain. I look down at her stomach. There's a deep cut in her armor. The dried blood covering her side is dark blue. "Well, Malcolm," she says, "Do you think you can help me up?"

Silently, I nod, dragging myself to my feet. I grab her arm and help her to her feet as gently as I can. She staggers once, exhaling through grit teeth. I keep a hold of her arm as she flexes her fingers against her bindings.

"You may want to take a step back," she mutters.

I release her arm, taking a few steps away from her. Kaladria closes her eyes tightly, as if in intense concentration. After a moment, she opens them, her expression falling with unsurprised disappointment. "They've dampened my abilities."

I frown. "Is that possible?"

"Evidently. I haven't been able to use my lightning since I got here." She sighs. "The Aklev'Zol have been hunting us for centuries. I suppose they've been looking for our weaknesses. It must have led them to find a way to block our powers."

She sinks to the floor. I sit down next to her hesitantly. As she closes her eyes, I stare ahead at the blank wall, trying to ignore the pounding memories in my head.

Whatever comes next, I hope it comes quickly.

1 9

KALADRIA ASTRANA

MALCOLM and I sit in silence for a long time. He leans his head back against the wall, staring up at the ceiling. I finger the manacle around my neck, skin burning from the chafing caused by the metal.

I wonder how long before Zeru realizes something is wrong and Malcolm is no longer with Councilor Corvar. I'm guessing not long. Zeru has never had any love for the Jovian Councilor or his political mind. He must have been pretty desperate to even let Malcolm go with him in the first place. It won't be long before he goes looking for Corvar. And that will put him in danger. I suspect Corvar will do anything to keep his secret. Even kill a fellow Jovian.

I clench my fists "We need to find a way out of here."

Malcolm glances at me. "*Is* there a way out of here?"

"I just need to get out of these chains." I gesture to my manacled neck with my bound hands. Then, I frown. "Somehow."

Malcolm lets out his breath with a weary sigh, getting to his feet. He looks around, eyes slightly narrowed as he assesses the room. He walks over to the wall behind me, fingers skimming its surface.

"What are you…?"

I trail off as the wall makes an awful grating sound. Malcolm pushes a panel aside, revealing a mess of brightly colored wires. As he leans in, examining wires, I stare at him. I would never have thought to check for something like that. But, then again, I suppose someone smart enough to invent a wormhole generator would be smart enough to find a secret panel.

I close my eyes, breathing deeply against the pain in my side, wondering how long we have until the General returns. I doubt no amount of time would ever be enough.

I open my eyes, jolting upright with a surprised gasp that yanks itself free of my chest as electricity surges through my body. Its heat dances across my skin and suddenly I am alive with power. When I look down, a wave of lightning shoots down my arms before disappearing.

I look at Malcolm, straightening as I scrutinize him. "What did you do?"

"Did it work?"

"It worked. I can..." I trail off, sensing a force outside the door, tainted with that strange energy. "Return the panel," I order. "Quickly. They're coming."

Malcolm returns the panel, stepping away from the wall. "What are you going to do?"

I set back my shoulders, glaring at the door. All my thoughts are on the General's cruelty, Emma Blake's screamed pleas, my own mother's shock as those horrible talons ripped through her chest. These monsters have much to answer for.

"I'm going to show them why no Outsider has ever crossed the Protectorate's Borders and lived to tell the tale." I exhale, still glaring at the door. "It's time the Aklev'Zol remembered that they're not the only ones with power."

Malcolm opens his mouth, perhaps to warn me to be careful, but doesn't get the chance. The door opens and two Aklev'Zol soldiers step into the room, their tall forms towering over both of us.

I watch them carefully, unmoving. Neither the Aklev'Zol-Emma or the General are here. *Lucky.* Even still, I'm going to have to do something risky if I hope to pull this off. My electricity wasn't enough to stop them before. I have to make sure it is this time.

One of the Aklev'Zol soldiers looks down on Malcolm. "How do we use the wormhole generator?"

Some tension leaves my shoulders. They haven't figured it out yet. Good. We still have some time to stop this before the damage is irreparable.

I watch Malcolm. There's a familiar sort of anger in his eyes. A fierce iciness that I know all too well. I have to hand it to him. I never would have expected to see it in him. For a human, he handles his fear well. He doesn't even look afraid, just furious.

"You don't really expect me to tell you that right off the bat, do you?" he asks coldly.

One of the Aklev'Zol soldiers grabs him, lifting him up by the shirt. "This isn't a game, boy."

To his credit, Malcolm doesn't even flinch. He stares back at the Aklev'Zol, his expression cool and collected. "I never said it was," he says. "But I'm not afraid of you."

"You will be," the Aklev'Zol snarls, reaching talons for his face.

It's now or never.

I take a single step forward, letting out my breath. The electricity in my blood buzzes to life, sending heat coursing through my body. Then, everything explodes into lightning.

20

MALCOLM FARAWAY

My eyes widen, my jaw falling slack, as Kaladria takes a step forward, eyes tightly closed. Her skin glows with the energy carried beneath her skin. When she opens her eyes, they are the brightest blue I've ever seen, sparking like lightning.

Everything explodes, the static energy from her power making the hair on the back of my neck stand up. I look away, blinking away the sudden light. When I look back, Kaladria no longer resembles anything close to human. She's become lightning. Her body has transformed into electricity. Her forms sparks wildly, barely discernible in the chaos her power has created. She floats above the floor, her entire form bright blue with electricity.

In her new form, she slips free of her bindings effortlessly, the manacle previously encircling her neck dropping to the floor. She glides forward, extending long strings of lightning-like fingers. Electricity springs from her fingertips and hits the Aklev'Zol holding me. The monster drops me with a shriek of pain and Kaladria points another hand at the other Aklev'Zol. They both crumple to the floor.

I watch as she turns toward the door, touching it with a burst of power. That single touch is enough to send a chain reaction through it. The metal door flies off its hinges, clattering to the floor in the hallway.

Electricity sparks around her once more before going out. The room is suddenly darker as her lightning form is replaced with flesh and blood. Kaladria drops to the floor, landing on her hands and knees. She gasps, limbs shaking with exertion.

I rush to her side. "Are you okay?"

She stares at the floor, breathing hard. She looks almost sick, her normally pale blue skin even more colorless than normal. "I've never done that before," she pants. "We're not supposed to use that form."

"Why not?"

"It's volatile." She shivers. "And extremely unpredictable. Unlike some of my squadmates' second forms, the Lightning Form of a Saturnian is too hard to control. One wrong move and I could split apart and lose myself to the lightning. It wouldn't be the first time we'd lost someone that way."

"I guess they didn't give you much of a choice."

Kaladria tries to stand but her arms give out and she collapses back to the floor. I lean down, grabbing her arm and draping it over my shoulders as I pull her to her feet.

"We need to find that wormhole generator." She nods to the hallway, where the door still lies on the floor. "And then we need to get out of here."

I hesitate in the doorway. Guilt assaults every nerve. After what happened to Emma, after what came of my decision to invent the wormhole generator, I wonder if I even deserve to leave. Surely Kaladria deserves to live. But do I? After everything I've caused, isn't a cruel death exactly what I've earned?

"She would want you to live, Malcolm," Kaladria says quietly.

I look over at her. Kaladria leans against me, sweat beading her forehead. She'll never make it out on her own.

Sighing, I nod. Holding her arm more tightly, I help her through the hallway. But we stop very suddenly as several Aklev'Zol come down the hall. They freeze at the sight of us in the hallway before launching forward.

Kaladria curses, grinding her teeth. Then, she reaches out a hand and blasts them with lightning.

"Are you sure you should be—"

"Just go!"

I snap my mouth shut, continuing to guide her down the hall. As more and more Aklev'Zol come to stop us, Kaladria keeps blasting electricity. But, with every burst of lightning, her steps become more and more sluggish.

I grip her arm more tightly as she stumbles into me. "Any idea where they'd have the wormhole generator?" I ask.

Kaladria grimaces, forcing her head up. "I can feel its electricity." She nods to a room at the end of the hall. "It's that way."

I nod, leading her into the next room. As I stop inside the room, I glance over at Kaladria. Her face is drained of all color and her eyes are unfocused.

"Kaladria, are you okay?"

She blinks, looking up at me weakly. "What?" she asks dizzily.

I open my mouth to repeat myself but then she staggers to the side. She collapses, head falling forward, legs crumpling uselessly beneath her. She leans into me, her weight dropping against my side.

"Kaladria!"

She doesn't respond, exhaling as she slips into unconsciousness.

I put an arm around her waist as I look across the room. At least for the moment, we're alone in here. But I doubt that will last for very long.

I glance down at Kaladria. The lightning beneath her skin flickers weakly. I wonder if she drained too much energy by going into her other form. I set her down on the floor. She barely stirs and I walk through the room, searching for the device that got us in this mess in the first place.

The room is mostly empty, except for a long metal table. On it, there are a couple of long knives, glowing brightly with some sort of energy, hot electricity arcing through the blades. I pick one up, fingering it as I glance back at Kaladria. It has to be hers. The electricity glows as brightly as she does.

I stop, noticing the silver orb sitting on the edge of the table. I grab it, turning it in my hands. I slide the orb's interlocking pieces, fingers moving quickly to input the coordinates of the first place that comes to mind. The wormhole generator begins to spin, creating a portal in the middle of the room.

I spin around rather abruptly as the door slides open. An Aklev'Zol steps into the room. Luckily, it's not the Aklev'Zol-Emma or the Aklev'Zol that had changed her. Still, my heart is pounding as I look across the room, at Kaladria still unconscious on the floor.

The Aklev'Zol pauses in the room, assessing the situation. The monster looks down at Kaladria's unconscious form. Then, he looks up and a horrifying smile contorts his features. "Well, you are certainly more resourceful than we were led to believe." The Aklev'Zol steps toward Kaladria. "Not that it makes any difference."

The Aklev'Zol leans down, talons curling around Kaladria's jaw. As he lifts her up, inspecting her face, I grit my teeth. Emma's hysterical screams echo through my head.

"Stay away from her," I snap, finding courage I didn't know I had, "Unless you really want to find out how resourceful I can be."

The Aklev'Zol drops her. Kaladria falls back to the floor, still unconscious. The Aklev'Zol faces me, smirking. "Do you really think," he asks slowly, "That I would seriously consider any threat given by a human child?"

I take a step back, heart pounding. "You should."

"You humans are such terrible liars. It's laughable." He shakes his head, taking another step closer.

As the Aklev'Zol reaches for me, I snatch up one of the daggers on the table. The monster grabs my arm, talons closing around my wrist. I swing up the knife with my free hand and stab the knife directly into the center of the monster's skull. The Aklev'Zol falls to the ground soundlessly.

Exhaling shakily, I look over at the wormhole. It's fully formed now. Fingers trembling, I slip the rest of the knives in my jacket's pocket before leaning down to pick up Kaladria. She barely stirs, exhaling softly as her head falls against my chest. I take a shaky breath before stepping through the wormhole.

I set Kaladria down and face the wormhole. Another Aklev'Zol, possibly the Aklev'Zol-Emma based on the way she has a hand on her hip, appears on the other side. Her eyes widen and she steps forward.

Don't do something foolish, I tell myself.

I snatch the silver orb out of the middle of the wormhole. The Aklev'Zol-Emma lunges but not before the wormhole vanishes.

I lift Kaladria's form back into my arms. Glancing left and right, I make my way across the street. As I walk through the city, I feel suddenly out of place. So much has happened since I was last here. After everything I've witnessed, it's insane that the world could just keep on turning, oblivious to the war raging around it. And yet it has. The world lives on, oblivious to the rest of the universe.

I walk up a set of steps, pausing as I reach the door. I take a deep breath. *Here goes nothing.*

Opening the door, I try very hard to ignore my roommates. They're both on their feet, gaping. I wonder if they're staring because of my disappearance, my disheveled appearance, or the bizarre girl in my arms.

I shoot them a look that I hope demands silence before slipping into my room. I set Kaladria down on the bed and face the window. I lock it and shut the blinds, though I'm not sure that would do much to deter the Aklev'Zol if they found us here.

I let out my breath. I'm going to have to face them sooner or later. I slip out of the room, facing the door as I close it. I take a deep, steadying breath before facing my roommates. Tyler has both eyebrows raised, the question in his eyes clear. I told him I didn't have time for girls. And now, here I am, bringing a girl to the apartment. I don't bother answering the unspoken comment by explaining that Kaladria isn't here because she likes me.

"What the heck happened to you, Mal?" Dean asks in disbelief. "No one has seen you or Emma Blake and the police found a dead guy in your lab. We didn't know what to think."

I exhale, rubbing the back of my neck. "It's all a mess." I drop into the seat next to Tyler on the couch. "I know about the dead guy. I was there."

"What happened, dude?" Tyler asks, eyebrows knitting together. "Why is there a dead guy in your lab? And what happened to Emma?"

I hesitate. It's going to sound crazy. And it might not be wise to get them involved in my messes like Emma was. But the Aklev'Zol are targeting me. They killed Emma, just to make a show of their power. I don't want Dean and Tyler blindly stumbling into that kind of trouble. Despite the dangers, despite the absurdity of it all, it's still safer for them to know what we're up against.

I hold up the silver orb. "It's because of this."

"The wormhole generator?" Dean frowns. "Why?"

I exhale, blowing the air from my cheeks. Then, I tell them everything. About the Outsiders that kidnapped Emma and about the Aklev'Zol. When I explain how Kaladria showed up and used her powers to save me, Tyler stops me.

"She can shoot lightning?" His eyes are wide with awe. "Dude, I think I'm in love."

I roll my eyes. "*Anyway,* Kaladria wanted to know about the wormhole generator and about it turning on before. After I showed it to her, two of the monsters I mentioned before showed up. She made these electric barriers around me so they couldn't get me or the wormhole generator." I sigh. "So, they took her instead."

"She saved your life?"

"It's sort of her job." I shrug. "Amongst her people, she's a pretty famous soldier."

"So, basically, she's your knight in shining armor."

I don't bother responding to that. I continue my story, explaining about meeting Zeru and the rest of the squad of the *Resistance.* I tell them about going to the Satellite, about Corvar's betrayal and getting captured by the Aklev'Zol. As I explain about what the Aklev'Zol did to Emma, both Tyler and Dean are silent.

I lean my head back to glare at the ceiling. A part of me still thinks I should have stayed behind, that I deserved to suffer as she had. But, even if I'm not sure I deserve to be here, I know Kaladria never would have made it out without me. And she definitely deserves to survive this mess.

"So," Tyler says, too quiet for his normally lively nature, "What are you going to do now? Do you have a plan?"

"There's not much I can do until Kaladria wakes up. I don't know the coordinates of her ship so I can't use the wormhole generator to get us to her squad. Until she wakes, we'll just have to lay low."

I slip the wormhole generator back into my jacket pocket. There's no way I'm letting it out of my sight now.

"So, this girl," Tyler says casually, "She's pretty hot. For an alien, I mean."

I shake my head in exasperation. "I'm not going to have this conversation with you right now."

"No, seriously, dude. You created the wormhole generator for the good of science or whatever and instead it unknowingly led you to a hot babe. How can I get in on this action?"

I sigh. "I'm going to check on Kaladria. Don't answer the door for anyone."

Standing, I stride back into my room. I shut the door quietly and turn to face the bed. Kaladria is still unconscious, pale hair fanned out around her. Her body is curled around itself as if she's protecting herself, even in sleep.

Exhaling, I pull out the chair at my desk and slump into the seat. Within minutes, my head drops to my chest.

21

MALCOLM FARAWAY

"Dude, she's still asleep?"

Shutting the door behind me, I scowl at Tyler in annoyance. "She's kind of been through a lot."

Tyler shrugs. "So, what did she say when you told her about the wormhole generator?"

I roll my eyes, knowing exactly what he's alluding to. Too bad for him it's not going to be what he wants to hear. "She was absolutely furious."

"Bummer."

I shake my head, glancing at Dean. "How—"

The door crashes to the floor, knocked off its hinges. I stiffen as black talons curl around the door frame. My heart rams in my chest. I didn't know where they'd been keeping us but now it's obvious. It must have been on Earth. It's the only way they could have gotten here without the wormhole generator.

The tall form of an Aklev'Zol steps into the room. Those soulless eyes bare into me, sending chills down my spine.

"Mr. Faraway," the Aklev'Zol sneers. "That was very clever, using the wormhole generator to escape."

I glance across the room, toward the kitchen table. Kaladria's knives glint under the bright kitchen lights. I curse silently, kicking myself for not keeping one closer.

"Where is—"

Tyler rams into the Aklev'Zol's black form, causing the alien to stagger back in surprise. For the first time, I'm grateful for my wild roommate's rash behavior and especially grateful for his obsession with football.

I look across the room. This might be the only chance I'll get. "Dean!"

He's staring at the Aklev'Zol.

"Dean!"

He rips his eyes away from the monster. Lunging for one of the knives, he tosses it in my direction. Miraculously, I manage to catch it, fingers closing around the hilt. As the Aklev'Zol shoves Tyler aside in annoyance, I swing the knife.

The Aklev'Zol dodges my attack easily, shifting to one side before grabbing my wrist. "What now?" the monster mocks, yanking me forward.

My heart thunders in my chest. *A lot of good that did.* But then I stop, listening to the one sound that could save me. It's the most dangerous sound in the world. Crackling energy sparks in the room and I can see blue light in the corner of my eye.

Unable to help myself, I grin. "Now, *that.*"

The Aklev'Zol barely turns as Kaladria appears behind him. Body wreathed in lightning, she kicks him in the chest. As the Aklev'Zol stumbles back, releasing my wrist, she looks at me, hand outstretched.

I toss her the knife. She turns it expertly between her fingers, driving it through the Aklev'Zol's chest. Coughing and sputtering, the monster falls to the floor.

I look at Kaladria. "Hey, good…"

Her face is dangerously pale as she stumbles, tripping over her own feet as she pitches forward. I lunge forward to catch her before she hits the ground.

"Thanks," she mutters, eyes falling on the dead Aklev'Zol. "We need to get onto the *Resistance.*"

"It's grounded on the Satellite."

She sighs wearily, repeating a set of coordinates.

I frown. "How do you know?"

"The *Resistance* comes and goes often enough that it has a designated spot on the docks," she says. "Use the wormhole generator to get us there."

"What about us?" Tyler asks, rubbing his shoulder.

Kaladria, not bothering to ask who Dean and Tyler are, closes her eyes. "You will be far safer with us gone."

I look at Dean and then at Tyler, making a split second decision. "Go to my mom's house. You shouldn't have any trouble without me and Kaladria around but I'd rather play it safe. Tell my mom everything and tell her I'll come home as soon as I can."

Dean is staring at the dead Aklev'Zol. "I can't believe…"

"We'll keep her safe, Malcolm," Tyler interjects.

"I'm sorry you guys got thrown into this mess." I look down as Kaladria lets out her breath, falling unconscious once more. I look back up. "Don't let anyone know where you're going. And be careful."

Quickly, I input the coordinates Kaladria gave me into the wormhole generator, twisting and spinning its parts until its ready. Then, I set it down, waiting for the portal to open. I take a deep breath, preparing to carry her through the wormhole.

"Malcolm." I glance at Dean as he straightens. "Good luck."

I nod. "Get going."

As they head across the apartment, making preparations to leave, I step through the wormhole, letting out a heavy sigh. I feel strangely relieved to find myself in the sleek ship again.

"Malcolm?"

Zeru sits upright in his seat, completely bewildered by my sudden appearance. As his eyes fall on Kaladria, he jumps to his feet. "What happened?"

"Grab the wormhole generator." When he snatches it out of the air, effectively closing the portal, I heave a sigh. "It's a long story, probably for another time. Kaladria has fainted twice now."

Zeru frowns, clearly troubled.

"We have to get off the Satellite." I hesitate. "And as far away from Councilor Corvar as possible."

His frown deepens.

"I'll explain more later but he's a traitor to your Council. Trust me, Zeru. He can't know we're here."

At this point, I doubt he'd risk discovery by openly attacking us here but Kaladria isn't in a state for us to take any chances.

Zeru nods slowly. "Come on, then."

I follow him down a long corridor, struggling to keep up with his quick pace. He only stops once, poking his head in an open door. When I peer inside, I can see the rest of the squad, all slumped back in their chairs.

Azar launches to his feet at the sight of Kaladria. "How—"

"Vale, get up to the bridge and tell Xalin to head to Saturn. Make sure the message is encrypted," Zeru orders. "Azar, Hassuun, watch the airlock. No one gets on this ship, regardless of their rank. Make sure Councilor Corvar in particular stays away from here."

Hassuun looks bewildered. "Corvar?"

"Later. Right now, you have somewhere to be."

Hassuun nods. He and Azar rush out of the room, running for the elevator with Vale right behind them. Zeru leads me down the hall, opening a single door. I step inside and set Kaladria down on the bed.

"Go get some rest, Malcolm. Two doors down, you'll find an empty bed. I'll wake you when I figure out how to get this ship off the Satellite."

I nod, suddenly hyper aware of the exhaustion in my limbs. I feel almost numb as I turn and walk down the hall. I slip into the room he mentioned and flop down on the bed with a heavy sigh. Within seconds, sleep overcomes me.

22

KALADRIA ASTRANA

I WAKE with a sharp gasp that arcs my back. My neck burns from the manacle and my body aches with a dull sort of pain. I can still feel the sting of the deep cuts running across my front side from the Aklev'Zol in Malcolm's lab.

"Kala."

Still breathing heavily, I almost throw off the arms pushing me back into the bed. But then I realize who it is leaning over me. My lieutenant watches me, pale eyes intense with worry.

"Zeru."

He leans back. "How do you feel?"

"Probably about the same as I look." My head falls back on the pillow. "I used my Lightning Form."

Zeru shakes his head. "Sometimes, I really do wonder if you want to die the most horrible kind of death."

I'm not sure if I want to burst into laughter or burst into tears. I keep seeing it. The Aklev'Zol and their soulless eyes, their skull-like faces. I keep remembering Emma Blake and the infection. I can think of no death more horrible than that.

Zeru misinterprets the pain in my eyes. "Kala, about before, when you went to Earth. I'm sorry. We were wrong to react like that. You were just—"

"It's alright, Zeru." I shake my head. "You guys were just worried about me. With good reason. Evidently, I shouldn't have gone alone."

It's a cruel irony. The one time I determined I shouldn't ignore orders was probably the time I should have. If Zeru had gone with me, it wouldn't have mattered if the Aklev'Zol had caught me off guard. They wouldn't have done so to him. Even if they had surprised him, his Ghost Form would ensure he wouldn't have been captured.

Corvar is undoubtedly responsible. He must have convinced the Council to send me alone so the Aklev'Zol could capture me.

I shake my head again. Corvar will have much to answer for before this is over.

"What happened, Kala?"

I sigh. "I think it would be best to explain it to everyone at once. I'd rather not repeat myself. Does my uncle know I'm alright?"

"We're hoping to meet him on Saturn but the Council has grounded the *Resistance*."

Surprising even myself with the sly smile that touches my face, I flick my fingers. Electricity surges through me and the ship thrums to life. "What was that?"

Zeru grins. "I missed you, Kala."

I FIND Malcolm in the cargo hold. He's got the wormhole generator with him. He keeps tossing the small orb from one hand to the other, glaring at the wall in front of him with his brow furrowed.

"You know," I say, sinking to the floor next to him, "If you miss catching that thing, you might break it."

He doesn't look at me. He just keeps tossing the orb between his hands, his expression sullen. "Don't tempt me."

I sigh, snatching the ball from him. "Are you alright?"

Malcolm drops his head, running his fingers through his hair. "I just…" He sighs. "I can't stop thinking about everything the wormhole generator has resulted in. And everything that could have been prevented if I'd just never invented it."

"You couldn't have known. You didn't know what was waiting on the other side of that wormhole."

He doesn't look at me, silent.

"I'm sorry about Emma."

Malcolm exhales. "Yeah, me too."

"I'm sorry I couldn't save her. I…" I stop, not sure what to say. I can't think of anything that would make him feel better. Nothing ever made me feel better. "Well, I'm just…sorry."

Malcolm looks down at his hands. "It's not your fault," he says softly. "It's not like you opened a wormhole and let those *things* through."

"It wasn't your fault either." I lean my head back against the wall. "I've seen a lot of death, Malcolm. More than my share. I've witnessed a lot of pain. But it's taught me something very important."

He waits.

"You can't save everyone. Sometimes, people die and there's nothing you can do to stop it." I close my eyes as the memory of my mother gasping in pain flashes through my mind. "What you can do is honor the memory of those left behind."

Malcolm is silent.

I look up at the ceiling, quiet too. I wonder what my parents would think about the path I've chosen. I wonder what they'd think about the daughter becoming the Lightning Demon.

Malcolm sighs, lifting his head. His eyes slide over to meet mine. "I never got the chance to thank you. You saved my life."

I smile slightly. "I was just doing my job. You've more than repaid me. I'd probably be dead if not for you."

Or worse.

Malcolm opens his mouth but snaps it shut as Vale's voice sounds above us through the intercom. "Kaladria, we're approaching Saturn now."

I stand, holding out a hand for him to take. "Come on. You're going to want to see this."

23

MALCOLM FARAWAY

KALADRIA LEANS BACK against the railing in the elevator, arms crossed. She's exhausted but she's hiding it well behind a straight spine and a stubborn chin. She rubs her neck absentmindedly, fingers trailing across the skin rubbed raw from her time as the Aklev'Zol's prisoner. Her expression is composed but there's a haunted look hiding in those intense blue eyes.

I follow her out of the elevator and onto the bridge. As we step out of the elevator, all eyes are on her. Vale nods. Azar winks and Hassuun grins. Zeru salutes casually.

Kaladria clasps her hands behind her back. "How are we doing?"

"Stealth systems are on," Hassuun says.

"And we're entering orbit now," Vale adds.

Kaladria exhales, releasing the tension in her shoulders. Her expression instantly softens as she steps toward the window. She stands on her toes as she looks out the front of the ship.

"Come here, Malcolm."

I jump, surprised by the summons, but she doesn't turn. Hesitating, I follow her to the window. Kaladria doesn't turn, nodding outside. As I look, I can see why she called me over.

We pass one of Saturn's rings before a city comes into view, surrounded by a thick fog. The city shimmers gold, everything glittering with bright light that glows amongst the dark storms surrounding the city. The buildings, connected by long bridges encased in glass, float in the middle of the atmosphere. Around the city, lightning flashes in a torrent of electricity, as bright a blue as Kaladria's own power.

My jaw goes slack at the sight of it. A city suspended in the air, surrounded by a breathtaking storm.

"What do you think?"

I can't tear my eyes off the city. "It's beautiful."

"It's also one of the more dangerous of our planets," Zeru comments. "The storms are treacherous for those of us who aren't from Saturn."

Next to me, Kaladria smiles. "That's kind of what makes it beautiful, Zeru."

"Leave it to you to find something beautiful about life-threatening danger."

Kaladria sticks out her tongue as the ship comes to a stop next to a golden building with huge glass windows. I watch the windows as lightning flashes again. "What happens if lightning strikes a building?"

"Everything is built to last the storm." Something that I don't recognize crosses her face, like a longing sadness. But it disappears as she turns away from the window. "Come on."

"Kala," Hassuun says, "You cool if we show Malcolm around the city?"

Kaladria glances at me, a question in her eyes. "If he wants to." When I shrug, she looks back at Hassuun. She scrutinizes the tall Martian, her gaze flicking over to Azar. "And if you promise to be on your best behavior."

Azar scowls. "Who are you, my mother?"

Kaladria jabs an accusatory finger at the two of them. "You two are like the twin brothers I never asked for. Don't get Malcolm into any kind of trouble."

"I'll go with them," Vale offers.

"That would make me feel a great deal better."

I purse my lips against a smile. Hassuun and Azar wave me toward the elevator. As I step into the elevator, I glance back at Kaladria. She turns to face the window once more. Just before the elevator doors close, I think I might see her shoulders slump.

24

KALADRIA ASTRANA

"You going to be okay, Kala?"

I glance at Zeru, nodding. "I'm getting there." I don't bother trying to hide the fact that I'm not quite okay yet. He's always been able to read me so easily. Lying would get me nowhere.

"I'm going to check on a few things," Zeru says. He steps off the bridge and into the elevator, likely to ensure we haven't been tracked down by Corvar or the Aklev'Zol.

I stay on the bridge for a few more minutes, watching the storm. With every lightning strike, my body responds, sparking energy exploding beneath my skin. There's something soothing about being so connected to the storm, something that calms my fears, if only for a moment. Still, I know it can't last. There are people I need to see, things I need to do.

Sighing, I turn away from the window and head for the airlock.

The moment I step off the *Resistance*, I collapse into my uncle's arms. Xalin barely stumbles as he catches me, hugging me tightly. The composure I've been forcing myself to keep for too long drains out of me. I exhale shakily, holding onto him.

Xalin says nothing. He just scoops me up and carries me into the house like I'm ten years old again. My head is spinning too quickly with memories for me to even consider being embarrassed by my lack of composure as he sets me down on the sofa.

This house has so much history. Xalin and I waiting by the window for my parents to come home from one of their travels. Sparring with him in preparation for my induction into the Protectorate. All those nights curled up at the window, watching the storm and trying to ignore that one horrible memory.

Xalin tucks my hair behind my ear, watching me silently. He's clearly exhausted. Dark circles ring his eyes and his face is gaunt. What this must have been like for him...He always worries about me on Protectorate missions. To hear that I'd been captured by something far worse than slavers must have been terrifying.

I inhale deeply, trying to shake off the numbness in my fingertips. "I wasn't sure I was ever going to see you again."

Xalin loses a bit of his own composure. He yanks me forward, holding onto me. "What happened, Kaladria?" he asks huskily.

I rest my chin on his shoulder, blinking quickly. "It's them, Uncle," I whisper. "The Outsiders that killed Mom and Dad."

He doesn't move but his sharp inhale gives him away. "You're sure?"

"I'd recognize them anywhere. That's how they caught me. I didn't..." I sigh. "I froze up, Uncle." As he rubs my arms for comfort, I swallow. "They're claiming to be the Aklev'Zol."

Now, he jerks back. "What?"

"All those stories Dad used to tell were true," I say softly. "I saw them do it. The Aklev'Zol turned a human girl into an Aklev'Zol."

"Have you told anyone else this?"

"Not yet. I wasn't...I'm not sure how to tell them. The Aklev'Zol are the cruelest sort of monsters, far worse than anything we've ever faced."

"I know." His eyes are solemn. Despite everything he witnessed as a Protector, all the cruelty he's seen, he knows as well as I that none of it compares to the Aklev'Zol's darkness. "Still," he says quietly, "They should know what we're up against."

I look out the window. "Do *we* know what we're up against?"

Xalin sighs. "We should go through your father's notes. Perhaps there's something in the stories he gathered that can help."

I swallow the lump in my throat. He's right. I know he's right. But I haven't given much thought to my father's journals in a long time. I'm not sure I'm ready to relive those late nights with him lying next to me on my bed, weaving stories until I fell asleep. Still, his notes may be the only thing that can save us now.

"You scared me, Kala. There were rumors that someone was holding you hostage with the intent to execute you."

I lean my head back. "I wish I could say those rumors were false. The Aklev'Zol seem to have some sort of vendetta against the Astrana family."

Xalin is silent. I look back out the window. Lightning flashes, sparking across the city. The storm forks across the sky, splintering before disappearing again. I almost smile. Despite what Zeru believes of the dangers Saturn presents to most, the storm's presence is peace-giving.

"You should get some rest, Kala."

I don't look at him. "I want to watch the storm for a while. I'll rest after I've told the others what's going on."

Xalin stands, leaning forward to kiss my forehead. "Don't push yourself. You're not invincible."

"Believe me, I know."

25

MALCOLM FARAWAY

THE SATURNIAN CITY IS A PARADISE. As lightning strikes the sky, the golden buildings spread through the city shine even brighter with each flash of the storm. Glass encased walkways are suspended in the air between buildings, stretching across the air like stairways to heaven.

I stumble behind Vale, Hassuun, and Azar in complete awe. Staggering, I watch as a group of Saturnian children run through the walkway with playful squeals. I stare up at the huge structures around me, certain I look like a fool. But I can't help it. It's magical, a fantastic world weaved out of the pages of a book.

Hassuun chuckles. "Very subtle, Malcolm."

I tear my eyes away from the golden buildings. "Sorry. I've just... I've never seen anything like this."

"I don't blame you," Vale says as he looks up at the sky. "Saturn is certainly one of the most beautiful planets in the Protectorate."

"What about Venus?" Azar scoffs.

Hassuun rolls his eyes. "You live in the most inhospitable place in the galaxy, Azar. Malcolm wouldn't even be able to step foot there."

"What's it like on the rest of your planets, anyway?" I ask.

"Well, Venus is the hottest of our worlds, due to its proximity to the Sun," Vale says. "It's not a very pleasant place to visit unless you're Venutian."

"Neptune isn't much better," Azar points out.

Vale shrugs. "True. Neptunians are the only ones that could survive the cold."

"Mars isn't so bad," Hassuun offers.

I glance at him. "Yeah, I was going to ask about that. How do you avoid detection? Humans have sent stuff to Mars before."

"The cities are underground. Martians are rarely on the planet's surface."

I pause. "Zeru mentioned Jupiter's cities are built in the air?"

Vale nods. "One of the safest of our planets, along with Mars. The Jovians have technology capable of creating flooring right on the lower atmosphere."

I jam my hands in my pockets as we continue through the city. Outside the walkway, lightning flashes, illuminating the pathway. Mom would love this. She's always sitting on the porch during thunderstorms. As a kid, I used to find her out there with a book, just listening to the storm. She always said she felt most at home in a storm.

"We should head back," Vale says. "Figure out what's going on."

He glances at me briefly but I say nothing, simply nodding. I am far from ready to talk about what I witnessed. And, as much of a coward I am for making Kaladria explain things that clearly haunt us both, I know she understands what all of this means better than I do.

We walk back to the Astrana home quickly. As I step inside, I take a moment to look around. The house is huge, the walls engraved with gold. The front door leads into an open room with huge windows that line one wall. There's a sofa pushed against another wall but the room is otherwise empty except for the few pictures adorning the walls.

Kaladria stands next to the window, leaning her head against the cool glass as she watches the storm. She turns away from the window with a slight smile. But it doesn't quite reach her eyes. "I trust no one was hurt in the festivities?" she asks, glancing at Vale.

The Neptunian pilot smiles. "They behaved."

Azar scowls but Xalin chooses that moment to return to the room, interrupting Azar's retort. "We all need to talk."

Kaladria nods reluctantly as she pushes away from the window. As she sits down on the sofa, I remind myself that it's better they hear about this from her. Still, I can't push away my guilt as she clenches her hands in her lap. "There's something I've never told any of you," she says quietly, looking at her squadmates. "Something I didn't want anyone to know about."

The silence is practically palpable in the air. I glance at the four of them. Azar and Hassuun look surprised and Vale looks simply curious. Zeru doesn't seem particularly surprised but he seems to know her better than the others. Even if he didn't know what she was hiding, he must have known she was keeping something secret.

"I assume you know my parents died when I was ten?" she asks.

As everyone nods solemnly, Kaladria looks down at her hands, fidgeting with her fingers. "The Council kept the details of their deaths private, as a favor to the Astrana family, but I saw them die."

Xalin puts a hand on her shoulder and she sighs. "They were off on a mission, exploring a region of space in search of the system our ancestors came from. I was on the comms with them when it happened." She shivers. "The same Outsiders that murdered my parents are the ones that came through the wormhole."

I stiffen. *Is that why...*

I shake my head. It all makes sense now. Her sudden fear when the Aklev'Zol stepped into the lab, how they could stop her so easily. It seemed so out of character for her to be caught off guard so abruptly. I understand now. She was ten when she first saw the Aklev'Zol. I look at her face, at the haunted look in her eyes, the exhaustion set in her features. How many years has she feared that memory? For how long have nightmares of black, taloned monsters terrorized her?

"I know who they are now," she continues, glancing at me briefly. "The Aklev'Zol."

Zeru clears his throat. "Kala—"

She turns on him, eyes hardening at his disbelieving tone. "Malcolm and I saw them do it." She looks at me, expression softening in a wordless apology. "The human girl, Emma Blake, was infected with their dark matter. And she's not the only one. Corvar's hand also bears the infection. He's a sleeper agent. That's why he betrayed the Council. I suspect he urged the rest of the Council to send me to Earth alone so I wouldn't be able to stop them."

Zeru stiffens at the implications. Corvar would have been very much responsible for Kaladria's death if we hadn't escaped.

"What I don't understand is what would drive them to cross the universe just to find your people," I say slowly.

Kaladria grimaces. "Their leader calls himself the General. He seemed rather content to watch this entire system burn."

"I've been looking into the stories we have of the Aklev'Zol," Xalin says. "As the story goes, they weren't always obsessed with destruction. But they became so when they sought power from an entity only ever referred to as the Queen of Tethra. According to the stories, the Queen of Tethra granted them their ability to infect and transform other beings."

Kaladria frowns. "The General didn't mention a queen."

"It's possible the queen is just a story. Centuries have passed since we last saw the Aklev'Zol. The truth could have easily been stretched in that time." Xalin shrugs. "Regardless, we should be wary. Queen or not, the Aklev'Zol have proven desperate to continue to infect all of our people."

I pull the wormhole generator out of my pocket. "Is that why they want this thing so badly? So they can invade?"

"Without it," Kaladria says, "They will have to cross an entire universe to reach us. Only a handful of them are in the system at the moment. But, with the wormhole generator, they could have every Aklev'Zol in the system within hours."

A deep silence follows her words. I look down at the wormhole generator. "Maybe we would be better off if this thing was destroyed."

Kaladria shakes her head. "The General knows you invented it. If we destroy it, he will just hunt us down until you make him another."

"So, we make sure no one gets their hands on that device," Vale says.

"I'll keep it," Kaladria offers.

"No." Xalin shakes his head. "If they find us, they'll expect it to be with you or Malcolm. I'm the least involved person here. I'll keep it."

"Uncle—"

Xalin's expression hardens, his eyes as fiercely stubborn as hers. "Don't worry about me, Kala. Even if Corvar or the Aklev'Zol could make it into this house, I doubt they'd make it as far as my room, with five Protectors staying here."

I watch their exchange silently but I know he's right. Kaladria alone has proven to be a worthy adversary for the Aklev'Zol. Not to mention the other four Protectors. It's unlikely that anyone could get past all of them.

Kaladria crosses her arms. "And if they do?"

"I was a soldier long before I was your uncle," he reminds her. "I can handle them."

As Kaladria sighs, Xalin holds out his hand. I barely hesitate before passing over the orb. It's far safer in his hands.

"I suggest you all get some sleep," he says. "I think we're in for a rough couple of days."

As the others begin to leave the room, Kaladria pulls me aside. "Hold on, Malcolm." She jerks her head toward the door. "Come with me."

As we start walking, leaving the others behind, I look over at Kaladria. "What's up?"

"You've sort of been thrown into this mess without any knowledge of what's at stake. Everyone else knows the stories of the Aklev'-Zol. I figured the least I could do was make sure you knew as much as everyone else."

I pause. "Do you know much?"

Kaladria sighs. "Not as much as I'd like. However, my parents were rather interested in the stories so I know more than most. I was practically raised on the stories my father gathered regarding the Aklev'Zol."

"That sounds...terrifying."

She smiles slightly. Then, as she leads me into a new room, she stops.

The room is small and cramped, littered with books, the floor covered with documents. When I glance at Kaladria, I frown. She watches the room with sad eyes, brushing a finger across an old book on the table, almost as if greeting an old friend.

"Kaladria?"

She looks up, then sighs. "This is my father's office. Xalin and I have mostly been ignoring it since my parents died. But my father collected all the stories here. It seemed like it was time to take a look in here."

I swallow, wondering what I should say, wondering if there's anything *to* say.

Kaladria takes a breath, picking up a book. She blows dust from it, fingering the worn leather. Then, she passes it over to me. "My father was compiling stories of the Aklev'Zol in one place. He didn't finish but what's there should tell you what you need to know."

I take book from her, opening it to the first page. Then, I begin to read.

It's said that the Nadarani were once a thriving people with a bountiful empire. Their peace and prosperity was well-known across the universe, their advanced technology and high society setting the standard for the rest of the galaxy. But every empire must come to an end. And so their society began to slip, falling into a deep decline. Their numbers dwindling. Though no one can be sure what caused their fall, there is no doubt that there resulting desperation set things in motion that forever altered the course of history.

The Nadarani were desperate to save their crumbling empire. They searched for a way to survive, a way to prolong their lives and boost their numbers. This search led them to a being so powerful and so ancient, the only name she is ever known by is the Queen of Tethra. This being, in her immense power, offered the Nadarani a solution.

But the Queen of Tethra deceived the Nadarani. She granted them the power to extend their lives while stripping away all that they once were. They became her slaves, husks of her terrible power, incapable of doing anything but her will. And so, the fall of the Nadarani's empire was complete. Those who had once been members of that once-thriving race became known as the Aklev'Zol, the Dark Ones...

I glance at Kaladria. "You said the General never mentioned a queen?"

Kaladria shakes her head.

"Your father talks about her."

Frowning slightly, Kaladria leans in to examine the journal. I blink, breath hitching at her sudden closeness. But she doesn't seem to notice, focused on her father's writing.

Finally, she sighs. "I've been trying so hard to forget about what happened..." She shakes her head. "It was foolish to suppress the memories of these stories."

"I don't think anyone would fault you for it." I pause, glancing down at the unfinished journal. "How did the Aklev'Zol come into contact with your people?"

Kaladria rubs her forehead, clearly still troubled. "According to legend, the Aklev'Zol swept across the universe, conquering planet after planet, changing all they found into Aklev'Zol. It wasn't until the Aklev'Zol came to the Zeta Arae system that they found any resistance."

"That's where the Protectorate came from?" I guess.

She nods. "The ancestors of the races that serve in the Protectorate all come from the Zeta Arae. Our ancestors fought back against the Aklev'Zol, killing many of them. But, in the end, the Aklev'Zol's numbers overwhelmed them. Those that survived the onslaught left the system and fled across the universe. That's how our ancestors ended up here. We formed the Protectorate and split up across five planets surrounding Earth, vowing that humanity would not lose as we had once lost. But that was hundreds of years ago."

I look down at the book in my hands. "I guess the Aklev'Zol fell into legend?"

Kaladria leans her head back against the wall, studying the ceiling. "We focused on smaller threats, such as slavers or curious Outsiders. But, with time, we forgot what we'd created the Protectorate for." She exhales slowly. "Most of the Protectorate sees the Aklev'Zol as myth. Stories to frighten children into behaving."

I'm silent. Even if the Protectorate forgot about the Aklev'Zol, it would seem that the Aklev'Zol didn't forget about them. Whether the

Queen of Tethra exists or not, the Aklev'Zol have been hunting for them for hundreds of years.

I look up at Kaladria. She's still studying the ceiling but her eyes are half-closed, as if she's trying very hard to not fall asleep.

I clear my throat. "I'm sorry. You must be exhausted."

Those half-closed eyes slide over to meet mine. "Truth be told, I wasn't quite ready to sleep yet." She stands, shrugging back her shoulders. "But I suppose we both ought to get some rest." She waves me toward the door. "Come on. I'll show you to your bed."

26

MALCOLM FARAWAY

LATE INTO THE NIGHT, I lay in bed, listening to the storm with my eyes closed. Thunder crashes outside, the sound muffled by the walls of the Astrana home. Despite the soothing sound of it, I can't fall asleep.

My mind is still reeling. I'm sitting in a floating house in Saturn's atmosphere. All the while, evil aliens are plotting to steal my invention and use it to turn every living being in the galaxy into one of their soldiers.

I keep thinking about everything Kaladria told me, about the Aklev'Zol and how her ancestors came into contact with them. The Aklev'Zol were monsters. If the Queen of Tethra did exist and was controlling them, I'm not sure I want to know.

Stiffening, I open my eyes, surprised to find a hand pressed over my mouth.

Zeru puts a finger to his lips, nodding to the open door. A black shape slinks past the room, long taloned fingers hanging at its sides. Its shadow practically blends into the hallway.

I hold my breath, watching as the monster passes by us, creeping further into the house. As the shadow disappears, Zeru removes his hand from my mouth. "Warn Kaladria," he whispers. He pulls out a long dagger. "I'm going to make sure they don't reach Xalin." He flips the dagger around, pressing it into my hand. "Be careful."

I grip the knife tightly. It's almost impossible to ignore how comfortable a weapon has begun to feel in my hands. I slip out of the room after Zeru. As he turns left, he nods. *Good luck.* I turn the other way, hurrying toward Kaladria's room. As I round a corner, I stagger back as a black shape slips into her room.

Frozen, I grit my teeth. *What do I do?* I'm not a soldier. Every encounter I've had with these monsters has proven that. The one time I actually managed to best one of them feels like an accident, nothing but dumb luck. But I can't just stand here and hope she can handle it.

Stepping into the room, I stop breathing. The Aklev'Zol's long talons curl around her neck, shoving her back into the nearest wall. Dark blue blood runs down her forehead, assuredly from the Aklev'-Zol's talons, and the lightning sparking beneath her skin seems less vibrant than usual. Gasping for breath, she swings out her legs.

The Aklev'Zol sidesteps her attack, stroking her cheek with a long talon. "The Lightning Demon," the monster croons, "You will make such a good soldier."

I don't know what overcomes me but, at the thought of these monsters turning her into one of their cruel soldiers, something inside of me snaps. With the Aklev'Zol solely focused on her, I rush forward and slam the dagger into the middle of his back. The Aklev'Zol releases Kaladria with a gasp, falling to the floor.

Kaladria drops into a crouch, coughing. Breathing heavily, she looks up at me. I stare back at her, panting hard. Then, my eyes fall on the dead Aklev'Zol. I feel suddenly sick at the sight of the dead monster.

Looking down, Kaladria yanks the knife out of the Aklev'Zol. She stands, pressing the dagger back into my hand. "I don't think we're done yet."

I nod mechanically. "Zeru went to find Xalin."

Kaladria nods. She snatches up her spear before grabbing my hand and leading the way out of the room. "Come on."

27

KALADRIA ASTRANA

I STEP into the hallway first, peering down the hallway. When I can't see any Aklev'Zol, I slip out of the room. I hurry toward Xalin's room, tugging Malcolm along behind me. As we make our way down the hallway, my heart is pounding. How did I let him convince me that he should keep the wormhole generator? As brave as my uncle may be, it's been years since he fought anyone. And he's never faced anything like the Aklev'Zol before.

I slow my step, breath freezing in my throat. *That energy...*

I start to turn, fingers tight around my spear, but I'm too slow. Malcolm's hand is ripped from mine as an Aklev'Zol yanks him back. He cries out in surprise, stumbling.

The Aklev'Zol sneers. "Ah, if it isn't—"

I bring up my spear, swinging the electric staff up and sending his jaw skyward. The Aklev'Zol staggers, releasing Malcolm.

"I've had just enough of your stupid monologues," I growl.

Face twisted with anger, the Aklev'Zol lunges for me. I step to the side. The Aklev'Zol spins around, claws outstretched. I slide past its talons, grabbing the monster's skull with lightning on my fingertips. The Aklev'Zol goes rigid, body convulsing against the lightning as it collapses to the floor.

Malcolm pushes himself to his feet. I grab his hand, yanking him forward as I race for Xalin's room. *Come on, come on.* He has to still be there. I have to be fast enough. *I can't lose you, too.*

As we reach the door, I push it open with my shoulder. I refuse to slow my pace as we rush into the room. But the instant we enter the room, I drop my spear. Zeru is laying on the floor in a pool of blood. Just out the window, an Aklev'Zol strides toward a ship, my uncle slung over its shoulder.

"No!"

I rush forward, slipping in and out of lightning. But by the time I'm staggering outside, the ship is already taking off. It's too far for me to consider attempting to teleport inside. *I'm too late.*

I fall to my knees.

28

MALCOLM FARAWAY

As Kaladria releases my hand to teleport outside, I run across the room, where Zeru lies. His face is even paler than normal, almost corpse-like. His body is surrounded by colorless Jovian blood. I press two fingers to his neck, relieved to find a pulse. Then, I push both hands against his side to staunch the bleeding.

I keep my hands pressed to his stomach as I look around. *What do I do?* There's nothing I can do to stop the bleeding, not without help. But Kaladria isn't in a position to offer it. I look back down at Zeru. He's going to die if I can't find a way to save him.

I look up as Vale rushes into the room, arms covered in ice. Relief floods through me. Pausing, Vale looks first at Kaladria kneeling outside in the storm and then down at Zeru. He kneels down next to me.

"We have to stop the bleeding." Silently, I thank my mother for the little medical training she passed on to me growing up. "He's losing too much blood."

Vale nods. "Move your hands, Malcolm." When I do so, he places his hand over Zeru's stomach. Eyes still closed, the Jovian grimaces as ice spreads from Vale's hand, spreading across Zeru's torso as he freezes the wound.

"The ice will only work as a temporary solution," Vale says quietly. "There's an infirmary on the *Resistance*. Let's get him patched up."

I nod and Vale stands, lifting Zeru's limp form. I glance back at the window. *Later,* I think. Zeru is in more immediate need of help than Kaladria is. Still, walking away from the Saturnian captain kneeling in the rain feels like a great betrayal.

I clench my hands at my sides, continuing to follow Vale out of the room. *I'll be back,* I think. *You don't have to face this alone. Not this time.*

HOURS AFTER VALE and I took care of Zeru's injuries, Kaladria is still outside in the storm. She sits in the rain, seemingly oblivious to the lightning raging around her.

At first, I thought Azar or Hassuun, maybe even Vale would go out and bring her inside. But, so far, no one has dared to approach her. I know that's partially due to the raging storm but I no longer think that's the only thing holding them back. As close as they are as a squad, none of them has ever really seen Kaladria as anything but a soldier. She's brave and reckless, completely unafraid. But it's not the Lightning Demon kneeling outside. It's a broken girl grieving for yet another loved one stolen from her. And none of them know what to do.

"Malcolm."

I turn. Zeru stands in the doorway. His face is gaunt and drawn and he leans heavily against the door frame. Still, he looks more alive than he did earlier.

"You're awake."

"I understand I have you to thank for that."

I wave him off. "I really didn't do much. You should be thanking Vale for his quick thinking."

Zeru nods outside, where Kaladria still kneels. "How long has she been out there?"

I sigh, looking outside. Kaladria is slumped forward in the rain.

Her hair is soaked but she doesn't seem to care. She shivers slightly but doesn't move.

"A couple of hours. Since they took Xalin."

Zeru sighs, too. He steps forward, slipping into his Ghost Form. He phases through the window, stepping out into the storm. He kneels before Kaladria, still in his Ghost Form. Kaladria lifts her head, ripping her hands through her hair as she says something to him. Zeru releases his Ghost Form, ignoring the dangers of the storm and tugging her into a fierce hug.

I glance over as Hassuun steps over to the window, standing next to me. He watches Kaladria and Zeru with a troubled frown.

"Are they...?"

"Together?" Hassuun guesses. "No. Azar and I sort of wondered if they were when we were assigned to the *Resistance* but they're just really close."

Zeru pulls back, hands on her shoulders as he says something. Kaladria nods, again ripping a hand through her drenched hair.

"From what I've heard," Hassuun continues, "Kaladria's never been interested in anyone like that. For a long time, we thought she was just keeping her romantic life a secret. She's always been so private. But I think she didn't feel she had time for dating. She must have been trying to deal with what happened to her parents."

I look back at Kaladria's grief-stricken face. "I'd believe that."

29

KALADRIA ASTRANA

I sit on the floor of Xalin's room, back against the wall. I stare out at the lightning striking outside, lips pressed together to hold in the scream threatening to rip me apart. I twirl a knife between my fingers as I glare out into the storm.

I feel hollow. I stare at the window, trying very hard to not think about what will happen to him. They didn't have to take him. They could have taken the wormhole generator and left him behind like Zeru.

"Kaladria?"

This is a personal attack on me. The General is reminding me that I am powerless to stop them from finishing what they started centuries ago.

A heavy exhale fills the air and someone sits down next to me. "Kaladria," Malcolm says slowly, "I'm sorry. I know—"

Grief splits through my composure. I whirl on him, pressing the knife to his throat. *"Don't,"* I snarl. "Don't you *dare* tell me you know what I'm going through. This is your fault."

He swallows hard, eyes wide.

I drop my arm, standing and tossing the knife across the room. It sticks in the wall with a dull thud. Hands clenched into fists, I storm out of the room, slamming the door behind me.

"That was a little cruel, Kala."

I don't look up. I focus on the panel, stripping back a wire. "I don't know what you're talking about, Zeru."

He sinks to the floor with a grimace of pain. "You're not being fair. Malcolm isn't a soldier. In fact, before a few days ago, I doubt he'd ever held a weapon."

I sigh. "So?"

"So, he's been through a lot the last couple of days. He just got thrown into a war he didn't even know was possible. He's handling it pretty well. As I recall, he's already saved your life several times."

I close my eyes. He's right. I told Malcolm this was inevitable, that the Aklev'Zol would have come for us eventually, even without the wormhole generator. I don't get to take those words back now, just because things are getting hard.

"You can't blame him for this, Kala. It's not fair. He didn't know what would happen when he designed the wormhole generator. He never intended to let the Aklev'Zol through. It was a mistake, one that has already cost him dearly."

I swallow hard. I know better than anyone what the wormhole generator cost him. I know exactly how heavy all of this weighs on him. After Emma Blake was changed, he nearly convinced himself he deserved to die there.

I sigh. "I know. I lost my temper."

Zeru's smile is slight. "You have a habit of doing that."

I scowl. "Shut up."

Zeru stands. "Talk to him, Kala. He deserves to know that sometimes you say things you don't really mean."

As Zeru leaves the room, I sigh. Then, standing, I walk out of the room. I stride through the ship in search of Malcolm.

I stop as I reach the cargo hold. Malcolm sits on the floor, his back against a crate. He stares ahead at the blank metal wall in front of him, expression worn. He holds his glasses in one hand, his other hand on the back of his neck.

I exhale. Wrapping my arms around my waist, I sink to the floor next to him. I pull my knees up to my chest. Resting my chin on my knees, I turn my head to look at him.

His skin is fair, almost ashen in the dimly lit room. His light brown hair is all wild curls, almost as if he just tore his fingers through it. His eyes are soft, colored a startling mixture of green, blue, and brown that reminds me of the nebulas my father used to send me pictures of when he and Mom were away. I find myself searching his face, this strange human who has taken the brunt of my temper too often. I study the strong set of his brow, the straightness of his nose. As my eyes trail down to his lips…

Embarrassment burns on my cheeks. I turn my attention to the wall instead. I clear my throat. "I'm sorry. I shouldn't have reacted like that."

"You were right though," he says huskily. "It is my fault."

"No, it's not. I was angry and looking for someone to blame. But I shouldn't have blamed you. I told you before that the Aklev'Zol would have come even without the use of the wormhole generator." I look at him. "You made something incredible. It's not your fault the Aklev'Zol turned it into a weapon."

"But—"

"Just take the apology, Malcolm."

He stops, studying my face. I look back stubbornly and he sighs, smiling slightly. "Alright. Thanks."

I settle back, looking at the ceiling. The silence between us is easy, peaceful even. It's a welcome change from the chaos of the last couple of days.

"So, you really think the wormhole generator is incredible?"

"Are you kidding? The first time I held it I couldn't believe how powerful it was. I've never sensed so much energy in anything before."

"Says the girl who is basically a bolt of lightning," he jokes.

I chuckle. Leaning my head back, I close my eyes. But it's a bad idea. Behind closed eyes, it's too easy to think of Xalin and what might have happened to him. Did they infect him? Kill him?

I grit my teeth. No. I have to believe he's alive. *You are bigger than your fear*, I remind myself.

"Kaladria?"

I sigh, grateful for the distraction. "Yes?"

He hesitates. "Can I be honest with you?"

Turning, I watch him carefully. "I'd like it if you were."

"I can't stop thinking about the things I've had to do lately. I've killed a couple of them." He shakes his head. "Logically, I know it was self-defense and the Aklev'Zol are monsters who certainly deserve it. But I still feel a little guilty."

He has such a good heart, I think. His kindness is something to be treasured. Still, it surprises me. I'm the Lightning Demon, known for destruction. It's been a long time since I've met anyone with so much compassion. I almost envy him.

"I'd be worried about your sanity if you didn't," I say softly.

"It doesn't seem to bother anyone else around here."

"That's because everyone else is a soldier who has killed too many to name." I nudge him gently with my shoulder. "I don't think there's anything wrong with feeling a little guilty. Life is precious and you're a good person for trying to protect that as much as possible."

Malcolm falls silent. He leans his head back against the wall. He looks out the small window, at the lightning storm raging across the black sky. "You know," he says after a long time, "I always wanted to go to space."

"Is that why you built the wormhole generator?"

"Not exactly."

He exhales heavily. His shoulders slump as a dark grief falls across his face. It's the same sort of heartbreak that has dragged me down a thousand times before. Instantly, I regret my question.

"You don't have to tell me," I say softly.

"No, it's okay." He sighs. "My father was an astronaut. But, when I was little, he left for a mission he never came back from."

I swallow hard, thinking of my own parents.

"Something went wrong," Malcolm says quietly. "His shuttle just vanished." He shakes his head. "At the time, no one knew what happened. But I figured it out. It was a wormhole. His shuttle passed right through it."

I nod, thinking of the few times our own ships have vanished. It's extremely rare but it does happen. "He was lost to space?"

Malcolm looks down. "The coordinates that had been imputed when the wormhole generator turned itself on that first time…"

"That's where the wormhole took your father?"

He nods.

I sigh, finally understanding. "You were trying to find him."

Malcolm looks away, his throat bobbing with emotion. "I'm not sure I want to now. The Aklev'Zol probably got to him."

I never would have expected to share so much with a human. But Malcolm and I share more than I could ever claim to share with anyone else. If anyone could understand what it's like to lose a parent like that, to know the Aklev'Zol likely gave someone you love the worst death imaginable, it's me.

I reach over, grabbing his hand and squeezing it. "I am so sorry, Malcolm."

He clears his throat, cheeks slightly flushed as he pulls his hand free of mine. "So," he says, clearly ready for a change of subject, "Why did you end up becoming a soldier anyway?"

"What?"

Malcolm shrugs, almost sheepishly. "You just seem like the kind of girl that could do whatever she wanted. Why a soldier?"

"It was Xalin's idea actually." I lean back against the wall. "He thought I could use the distraction. The years after my parents' deaths were difficult, to say the least." I shake my head. "As it turned out, joining the Protectorate was the best decision I've ever made."

"Because of the distraction?"

"At first." I tilt my head, thinking. "But, with time, it became much more than a distraction." I glance at him. "You have to understand. I've never had many friends. Growing up, particularly after what happened to my parents, I was so serious. It was hard to get to know people. The first time I felt like I had friends was on this ship.

"Zeru was the first assigned to my squad. He took my solemnity in stride. He was always teasing me, saying stupid stuff just to make me smile. Eventually, it wasn't so hard anymore."

"Is that why you made him your lieutenant?"

I lean back. "I made him my lieutenant because I trust him. And I knew he would always be honest with me. Those early days were difficult enough without worrying about politics. I wanted a lieutenant that would tell me what needed to be done, rather than what I wanted to hear." I let out a breath. "There was a lot of pressure to do well in those early days. I had a lot to prove. The Council had put so much trust in me when they made me captain of the *Resistance*."

"Azar said you were made a captain because you never follow orders."

I laugh. "Azar isn't any better." I shake my head. "Still, you're right. I've never been good at silently doing what I'm told. I can't blindly follow orders if it means someone might get hurt. Sometimes, doing the right thing means breaking the rules society sets for us."

Both Malcolm and I fall silent. He slips his glasses back on, looking down at his hands. I smile to myself, thinking of those early days. My captains all hated me. I questioned every order. I never did as I was told if it jeopardized a squadmate's life. It drove them all crazy. I'm certain they were all relieved to learn the Council was making me Captain of the *Resistance*.

"We should go." Exhaling, I stand. "It's time to find Xalin."

MALCOLM FARAWAY

I CAN'T FIGURE her out. This girl who goes from ice queen to kind-hearted friend and back again in an instant. There are moments I'm certain she's going to electrocute me. And then there are moments when I think she might hug me. Every time I think I've got her figured out, she does something that goes against what I think she is.

As we step out of the elevator, she sheds her previous friendliness, going back to the serious soldier she seems to be most comfortable with. Kaladria strides onto the bridge, arms crossed, eyes hard. "We need a game plan. Do we have any idea where they could have taken Xalin?"

No one speaks, all eyes suddenly cast downward.

They don't want to hurt her. They don't have the slightest idea what to do but none of them want to see her grief again.

Zeru sighs. "We know so little about the Aklev'Zol—"

"Kaladria," Vale interrupts, "Councilor Corvar is on the comms."

Her expression changes in an instant. She turns from a cool-headed soldier to a vengeful niece. Her lips turn down in a very unladylike expression, almost like a snarl. She clenches and unclenches her fists. Then, Kaladria exhales. She relaxes, her expression turning cold, almost empty.

"No one else speaks," she says firmly. "Let me do the talking." She glances at me. A strange expression crosses her face and she waves me over. "Come stand with me, Malcolm."

I frown, hesitantly joining her. "What are we doing?"

"Trust me," she says quietly. I take a deep breath, nodding. Kaladria faces the comms. She glances at Vale. "Patch him through."

Lorkan Corvar appears on the comms, the holographic copy of the Jovian Councilor sending chills up my back. His hands are gloved and his face is neutral but I can still see disdain in his eyes. "Captain Astrana," he says with a nod that is far too polite, "We were pleased to know you had escaped the clutches of your captors."

Kaladria glances at me, bringing attention to the fact that I'm standing next to her. "Yes, we were very lucky," she says smoothly.

Corvar's expression freezes. It's just for a moment but it's enough.

He's afraid of what she'll do, I realize. *He's afraid she'll tell the Council about him.*

I glance at Kaladria, wondering for a moment why she doesn't do just that. But then I see her eyes. While filled with that cool fire, there is something like fear there. And suddenly I understand. The Aklev'Zol have Xalin. There's no telling what they would do if she revealed Corvar as their sleeper agent. Until we have Xalin back, her hands are tied.

Corvar clears his throat. "We've been informed that Xalin Astrana was taken prisoner by the same Outsiders that took you hostage before."

Kaladria doesn't even flinch. "That is correct, Councilor. You'll have to excuse us from any upcoming missions. My first priority is finding my uncle."

Corvar's expression remains neutral. "I would try to convince you otherwise but I know there is little I could do to stop the *Lightning Demon.*" His tone borders on degrading but his face remains emotionless. "So, I will give you information instead. We've picked up another energy spike on Earth. It's quite possible it has come from the wormhole generator. Following its signature could lead you to your uncle, since he was the last to have it. It should at least lead to some information that might help you find him."

I keep expecting her to lose her calm façade but she doesn't. She just nods. "Then, that is where we will go."

"I will send you the coordinates," Corvar replies.

I glance between Corvar on the comms and Kaladria standing next to me. They're both playing a dangerous game, dancing around a precarious situation. And yet they both look so calm, as if this is just another day on the job, despite Corvar's obvious disdain and Kaladria's barely contained anger.

Kaladria's façade cracks, a hard glint sparking in her eyes. "Oh, and Councilor, we will be sure to inform the Council of all involved parties after we find Xalin. Be sure to inform the other Councilors of that."

Corvar's expression freezes in place. Kaladria waves a hand, signaling for Vale to end the call. For a moment, everyone just stands in silence.

Azar chuckles. "Kala, I think you're my hero."

KALADRIA ASTRANA

"Why are we going where Corvar told us to?" Zeru crosses his arms, watching me carefully, almost like he thinks I've lost my mind. "It's undoubtedly a trap."

"Oh, I'm absolutely positive it is." My smile is wry. "That's exactly why I wanted Malcolm to stand next to me during the call."

Malcolm frowns. "I don't follow."

"Corvar has undoubtedly been informed that the Aklev'Zol have the wormhole generator. But I doubt they know how to use it yet. They still need Malcolm for that. I knew, if Corvar saw that we were both on the *Resistance*, he'd send us to some sort of trap to get Malcolm."

Malcolm's brows furrow together with concern.

Zeru frowns. "And we want this because?"

"Whatever this trap is, it will involve the Aklev'Zol. And where we find them, we'll find some leads to Xalin and the wormhole generator."

"Are we sure we're ready to face them?" Vale asks, concern knitting his eyebrows together as he glances at Zeru. "They beat us pretty easily last time."

"We'll just have to be smart." I grin. "Worst case scenario, Zeru can use his Ghost Form to rescue the rest of us later."

"Very comforting," Zeru says sourly.

I chuckle. "Take us down in stealth mode, Vale."

The coordinates Corvar gave us leads to an old house on the edge of a human city. It's clearly been abandoned. The shingles are falling off the roof and the whole outside of the house almost looks like it could be blown over by little more than a light breeze. Wooden boards cover the windows and the door looks like a good kick would knock it off its hinges.

Next to me, Malcolm exhales, a little shakily. As he looks up at the ominous house, he swallows.

I frown. "Hey, you okay?"

"Fine." He clears his throat. "We humans just aren't fond of abandoned houses. A lot of scary stories start in houses that look like this."

I look back at the house. I watch it for a moment, as if I expect to see something move behind the messily shuttered windows. "Well, we know there's going to be *something* in there. Probably nothing paranormal though." I step closer to him, studying his troubled expression. Then, leaning in, I lower my voice. "You don't have to come."

Malcolm shakes his head. He sets back his shoulders, looking back at the house with determination. "I'm not going to wait around the ship while the rest of you risk your lives."

I nod, not really surprised. Malcolm has already proven more than once that he'd rather be useful than be safe. He'd rather face a creepy old house than risk something happening to the rest of us while he sits on the ship.

I step onto the porch, which creaks loudly. Reaching behind my back for my spear, I glance behind me. "Be ready."

Azar shifts to his flaming form and Hassuun shrugs back his shoulders, his entire body suddenly made of stone. Vale coats his arms in ice. Zeru pulls out a knife, slipping into his Ghost Form. Malcolm nods, straightening.

I turn back to the door, taking a deep breath. Then, I kick it hard with my heel.

The door flies open. I grip my spear in one hand as I scan the darkness. "Azar," I say softly. A rush of heat fills the room as he flicks fiery fingers, an orb of bright flames flickering ahead, floating in the middle of the room.

The inside of the house doesn't look any better than the outside did. Floorboards are missing and shattered glass covers the remaining floor. A layer of dust has settled over most of the house, which is almost completely devoid of furniture, except for a couch in the corner. The couch is flipped on its side, the worn leather shredded.

I glance up. Above us, the floor creaks loudly. I look at each of my companions in turn, finger pressed to my lips, as I move toward the dilapidated staircase. I move up the stairs slowly, a spark of lightning in my clenched fist.

As I reach the last step, I pause. I scan the room but, without Azar's flames, it's too dark to see much. I step further into the room, allowing my companions to join me. But, Azar's fire lights up the room, a low snarl fills the air.

Something shimmers across the attic. A dark shape appears, suddenly visible in the dim lighting. It looks like some sort of mechanical beast, with a wolfish body and silvery eyes. Its body is long and lean, shimmering silver in the darkness, metal parts grating as it lunges forward.

I dart forward to meet it, slipping in and out of electricity. I ram my body against the monster and we both fall to the ground. I roll away from the beast as it snaps its jaws. As I stand, the beast lowers its head, baring silver teeth.

Grimacing, I watch the beast. Thanks to my father's collected notes, I know what it is. A Zol Beast, one of the Aklev'Zol's machine beasts. Stories claim it's practically invincible, relentless in whatever task its masters give it.

I guess it's time to see how close to invincible it really is.

Slipping into a crouch, electricity sparking in my hands, I wait for it to lunge. The Zol Beast rushes forward but not for me. For Malcolm.

Hassuun steps in front of him, swatting the beast aside with a rock-armored arm. The beast skitters, sliding across the floor. It lets out a small whine before scrambling to its feet. Then, it launches forward again. Azar blasts the creature with fire but the flames barely lick the creature's silver body before disappearing. The Zol Beast leaps forward and Vale places a hand on the floor, layer of ice seeping into the floorboards. The mechanical wolf slides across the floor again before crashing against Hassuun's fist. And this time, when it hits the ground, the beast doesn't get back up.

"That was kind of awesome," Malcolm says as he steps forward to look more closely at the downed creature. He crouches down several paces away from it, pushing up his glasses as he studies the beast.

I roll my eyes. "It's…"

I trail off, looking at the beast. It thrums back to life, so quiet I know only my attunement to electricity will notice.

I spring into action. Launching forward, I teleport across the room, putting my body between the Zol Beast and Malcolm. It barrels into me and suddenly we're tumbling. My head strikes the floor as it pounces on top of me. I barely have time to suck in a breath before the creature's jaws snap around my shoulder.

My breath stops, frozen somewhere in my chest. The Zol Beast's long teeth dig into my skin. It jerks its head, ripping through my shoulder. I grit my teeth against a scream, trying to push it away.

Hassuun and Zeru yank the Beast off me. It snaps its jaws at Zeru, who promptly returns to his Ghost Form. The Zol Beast turns on Hassuun, latching onto his rock-covered arm, but he swats it aside.

I watch the creature carefully, staggering to my feet. I grit my teeth against the sharp pain in my now shredded shoulder.

Malcolm meets my gaze. Something flickers across his face. Fear? Or is it guilt? He barely glances at the beast before darting past the fighting. As I stumble again, he catches my arm. "Thank you," he whispers.

I nod, watching as the creature swipes at Vale. The Neptunian dances to the side. "Any ideas?" I ask Malcolm.

"What?"

I grimace. "I'm sort of fresh out."

Malcolm pauses, studying the creature for a moment, eyes slightly narrowed as he watches the way it moves. "It's probably got some kind of protective plating. Based on how little damage you guys have been able to do to it, I'd guess the only way to stop it would be to open up the plating and—"

"Overload the systems," I realize. I look up. "Guys, keep it busy!" I call.

"What do you think we've been doing?" Azar shouts back as he dodges the creature's claws.

I look at Zeru. "I have a plan. Can you tear a hole in its armor?"

Zeru nods and I glance at Malcolm. "Step back. You shouldn't be too close to me when I do this."

Malcolm opens his mouth, perhaps to ask what I'm planning, but then thinks better of it. He steps away.

I watch as Zeru launches forward in his ghostly form. The creature ignores him, focused on the others. But, just as he's passing the creature, Zeru flicks back into his solid form, sliding his dagger across the creature's side.

As the beast roars in fury, I launch forward. Focused on the lightning sparking inside of me, I exhale. A sudden heat takes hold of my body. I can feel the change as I release my power, letting the energy take over as I shift into my Lightning Form. Zipping forward, straight through the creature's side, I tear through the hole in its armor with my power.

As I drop back to the ground, shifting to my normal body, I glance back at the creature. It stiffens. Then, it falls to the ground, the low thrum finally falling silent.

"Geez, Kala." Azar shakes his head. "Way to show everyone up in the cool department."

I sink to the floor. "Get the rest of its armor opened up. There might be some sort of memory chip. Maybe something we can pull information from."

As my squad gets to work peeling back the silver armor, Malcolm sits next to me on the floor. "Are you okay?"

I keep my fingers pressed tightly over my shoulder. "I don't think I'm going to answer that." I lean my head back. "Let's just hope using my Lightning Form doesn't knock me out cold again."

Malcolm nods his agreement. "Now doesn't seem like the best time for sleeping beauty."

I frown. "Sleeping what?"

His cheeks redden slightly. "It's a human story." Still seeing my confusion, he waves a hand dismissively. "Never mind. It's not important."

"Kala, I think we've got it," Zeru calls. He holds up a small silver chip, laced with circuitry.

I exhale. *Some good luck at last.* "Let's—"

Stiffening, Zeru inhales sharply. He slaps his neck in surprise. Then, he drops to the ground, the small chip slipping from his fingers.

"Zeru!"

Jumping to my feet, I spin around the room, looking at the cracks in the boarded windows. We're too exposed here. Clearly, the machine beast was not Corvar's only play.

"We need to—"

There's a sharp prick at my neck. I slap my hand up, feeling the blood. I yank out a small needled dart. "Oh…"

I stumble, my bones suddenly melting into the floorboards. I barely have time to look at Malcolm. His eyes are wide with shock and I think he says my name. Then, I collapse, eyes drooping until there is nothing but blackness.

32

MALCOLM FARAWAY

A GASP WORKS its way out of my body so quickly it wrenches my head back.

"Mr. Faraway."

I blink several times, until the dark spots disappear. Someone slides something across the table in front of me. I look down, picking up my glasses and sliding them on.

The room I'm sitting in is small, with only a single table. There are two men in the room with me. One stands at the door. He stares ahead, holding a rifle in both hands. Across the table from me sits a second man, with graying hair and hard eyes. Both wear military uniforms.

I rub the back of my neck, fingers trailing over the small prick. And it all comes flooding back. The old house with the Aklev'Zol's machine beast, Kaladria using her Lightning Form. Zeru finding its memory chip. And then everyone slowly crumpling to the ground. The sharp pain followed by an insane sort of drowsiness. And then nothing.

I force myself to sit up straight. "What's going on?" I look at the gray-haired man. "Why am I here?"

"You are at a top secret military base," he replies. "We need to ask you some questions."

My heart is practically ramming out of my chest. I think of all the people that had been with me in that house. And I remember what Hassuun had said before, about the last time humanity interacted with Protectors. They turned the Protectors into science experiments and dissected them like lab rats.

"Where are my friends?" I ask, nauseated.

The gray-haired man shifts in his seat. "Your friends are fine. I suggest you cooperate and answer my questions. The sooner you do, the sooner you and your friends can be on your way."

I relax but only slightly. Has he not figured out what they are yet? It seems unlikely, considering their unusual appearances. Vale or even Zeru might be able to pass as human if they didn't look too closely. But I know the rest of them can't. Even if they could, I can't see Azar and Hassuun being idle. And Kaladria? Even without the lightning clearly displayed beneath her skin, I've seen her temper. If she believes, even for a second, that her squad is in jeopardy, she will attack.

"What do you want to know?" I ask slowly.

"You have…unusual friends. How did you come to meet such extraordinary people?"

I don't like the look in his eyes. It's hungry. He definitely knows about them, at least enough to think he can use them. I clench my jaw, trying very hard to not imagine them being cut open or tortured in some brutal fashion.

"Mr. Faraway, I do not have a long fuse," he warns.

I look down at the table, determined to keep my silence. Telling him anything will just put them in more danger. Anything I tell him would only fuel any desire he already has to use them as experiments. I refuse to play any part in that.

He sighs. "Let's talk specifics then. What about the girl?"

I'm surprised by the anger that curls my fingers into tight fists. I stare down at the table, grinding my teeth. "What about her?"

"I had her examined. She is unbelievably powerful."

I stiffen. *He had her examined …*

I push away the possibility of Kaladria strapped down to a table. "If you've hurt her…" I say through my teeth, though I don't know what I would do if they had. He's holding all of the cards and I don't think there's a single thing I can do to gain the upper hand.

"She's fine," he says indifferently. "She will remain so as long as we get the cooperation we need."

Meaning they will hurt her if I don't tell them what they want to know.

"Our scientists are under the impression that her body houses some sort of energy. They say it carries more electricity than a bolt of lightning. And it's constantly running through her like a current. Do you want to explain that?"

Now, I understand the hunger in his eyes. He doesn't care about the rest of them. He only cares about her. As powerful as her squad is, Kaladria is the most powerful out of all of them. She's the one with enough electricity living in her body to become a living storm.

Keep your mouth shut, I tell myself. Even if he threatens to hurt her, I can't give him any ammunition against her. If he knew what she really is, if he knew exactly how powerful her lightning can be, he would never let her go.

I glare. "No, I don't."

He stands, pursing his lips. "I suggest you reconsider. I'll be back shortly. For the sake of your friends, I recommend you seriously consider answering my questions." He turns toward the door. The soldier there steps aside, letting him out before placing himself before the door again.

I drop my head into my hands.

33

KALADRIA ASTRANA

I HAVE TO ESCAPE, I think as I glare at the wall in front of me.

They have me completely immobilized. My body is stiff against cool metal, wrists manacled to the surface behind me. My ankles have been similarly bound. They've also removed my body armor, leaving me exposed in a thin shirt and pants, my feet bare. And, while they did wrap up my injured shoulder, their bandaging has done little to ease the pain.

None of those things are what troubles me though. What does worry me is that there are wires everywhere, connected to my arms, my legs, my temples, like I'm some sort of machine. Though I suppose, to them, I must be.

I exhale, very slowly. Indignant anger floods my senses. When I first woke in this room, it was in a rage. My captors had me strapped down, poking and prodding me like I'm some sort of lab rat. They ran tests on me before chaining me up like I am now. That fury, knowing they don't even truly see me as a person, has barely diminished. But I know I can't strike. Not until I know it won't mean trouble for my friends.

Closing my eyes, I wonder about the rest of my squad. Azar and Hassuun will be in the most jeopardy, due to their complexions and their inability to lay low. Vale and Zeru should be relatively safe. They just look like very pale humans. If they bide their time, it's unlikely the humans will think much of them. Malcolm is probably the safest out of all of us and I know he's smart enough to keep out of trouble.

I look up as a man steps into the room. He's followed by two armed soldiers. I watch warily as he steps closer. He studies me in silence, eyes scrutinizing my electrified skin like it's on display in a museum. I glare back at him, hands clenching into fists.

"Do you have a name?" he asks.

I say nothing. Jaw set in a hard line, I wait. Perhaps my silence will be enough to deter him from asking questions I refuse to ever answer.

"My people say that you have a very unique nervous system," he continues, "But that you have neglected to share how it's possible."

I still say nothing. He wants to know how my body functions, how the lightning works. But, if he thinks I'd ever tell him, he's about to be disappointed.

"This will go much faster if you cooperate, Miss. We don't want to hurt you—"

My laughter is wild, humorless. "Don't *lie*."

He stops, obviously surprised by the outburst.

"If you didn't want to hurt me, you wouldn't have me strapped down like this." I lift my head, eyes cold. "In my experience, these exchanges run much more smoothly if both parties are just honest with each other."

He pauses, straightening his suit. He understands now that he's not dealing with just a strange girl, but with someone who has been trained for these kinds of situations, accustomed to being a prisoner and even being tortured. "Very well. My name is General Hugh Callaghan. I am in charge of this facility. And you are?"

I press my lips together in a thin line.

"Miss, I thought we were going to be honest with each other?"

"No, I said being honest would help things run smoothly." Quiet rage twists my expression. "However, you have kidnapped me and my friends, treated me like an *animal*, and I have strong doubts that my friends are being treated much better." I spit. "I have no interest in helping you."

Callaghan shakes his head, eyes narrowed. "Have it your way."

He signals for his soldiers to follow him out of the room. I exhale heavily as I'm left alone. But my relief quickly vanishes as the cool surface behind me thrums to life with a powerful kind of energy. I turn rigid.

The whole room is alive with the quiet buzz of electricity. It moves through the surface behind me before hitting the wires connected to my body. My breath stops somewhere in my chest, an unfamiliar sort of power pulsing through those wires. It's like my skin is cracking apart from the pressure, like lightning is trying to force its way out through every inch of skin.

My entire body sparks with electricity. *That's exactly what they're trying to do,* I realize. *Force it out without my permission.* The air fills with me electricity, lightning striking through the air, the crackling sparks deafening out every other sound.

Agony explodes through me and my breath rushes out in the form of a blood-curdling scream.

34

MALCOLM FARAWAY

I JUMP TO MY FEET, knocking my chair back. I feel suddenly sick at the sound that fills the room. A high-pitched scream erupts through the air, barely muted by the closed door.

"Kaladria," I whisper.

It's her. It has to be. She's the one they're so interested in.

She will remain so as long as we get the cooperation we need...

This is my fault. I wouldn't tell them anything about her and now they've taken matters into their own hands. She's being tortured because I wouldn't tell them what she is or what she can do.

I'm sorry, Kaladria. I'm so sorry.

The soldier at the door moves a step to the left at the sound of a knock. The gray-haired man steps back into the room. I glare at him, clenching my fists tightly, as he closes the door behind him, muting her screams.

"What are you doing to her?" I demand.

"Sit down, Mr. Faraway," he says, dismissing the question.

Anger outweighs any kind of logic. "I'll stand, thanks." Glaring, I tense as another scream pierces the air. "What have you done to her?"

"As you neglected to give us any information, we had to take matters into our own hands." He glances back at the door, listening to another barely muffled cry. "Taking knowledge by force is never pleasant."

I can't breathe. She sounds like she's in agony.

"I warned you she would only be harmed if you didn't cooperate," he reminds me. "Are you ready to talk now?"

I pinch my eyes shut. "What do you want to know?"

"Tell me about her lightning."

I watch him silently. His eyes are once again filled with that greedy hunger. *It's not going to end,* I realize. If I tell him what Kaladria is, how she can do what she can do, he will never stop. The memory of her Lightning Form flashes through my mind. She'll be tortured and experimented on, just like the last Protectors to come to Earth were. They'll kill her, cut her open and use her body to fuel their experiments.

I think of her holding my hand as I told her what happened to my father and I clench a fist. *I won't play any role in her pain.*

My knuckles are white with tension. "I can't."

"Then, I'm afraid this continues."

He turns on his heel, striding out of the room. I slump back against the wall, desperately trying to think a way out of here.

35

KALADRIA ASTRANA

I SLUMP FORWARD with a heavy gasp as the pain stops. Electricity dissipates from the air and a sudden silence fills the room. In the absence of the lightning trying to break through my skin, I'm freezing. I tremble, body shaking with violent tremors.

I stiffen, clenching every muscle in a failed attempt to stop my shivering as General Callaghan returns to the room. "Are you ready to talk now?"

Clenching my hands into tight fists, I force my body to be still. "It will take more than a little torture to make me tell you anything."

Callaghan watches me for a long time. A shadow falls across his face as he decides his next move. "And if I torture your friends?"

My eyes are narrowed. "They'll never tell you a thing."

"Even Mr. Faraway?" Callaghan asks smoothly.

I freeze at the thought of Malcolm, of that human boy who was always too kind to be following the destruction the Lightning Demon leaves in her wake.

"Touch him and I will show you exactly what I'm capable of," I snarl.

"I don't think you're in a position to be making threats."

My fingernails dig into the palms of my hands. "What do you want from me?" I ask through my teeth.

"You have an extraordinary gift. If we could harness it, humanity would be capable of so much more than we currently are. With your help, we could push humanity into the future by leaps and bounds."

My eyes are narrowed. Power, then. He hopes to use me to make himself stronger, to earn the respect of his people, to gain fame amongst the humans.

"I'm not some kind of glorified battery," I growl. "I won't be a tool for you to use to gain popularity."

"I was rather hoping you would see reason," Callaghan sighs. "Very well. This will have to continue then."

As he turns on his heel, I steel myself for what's coming. But nothing can prepare me for that pain.

The moment the door shuts, my body is rigid with it. Electricity is amplified through the room. But this time it's worse, like they're stealing the lightning more aggressively than before in retaliation for my continued obstinance. It's impossible to stop my body from quivering and my screams feel as if they're going to tear my throat apart. If I continue to refuse his demands, this room will certainly be the death of me.

36

MALCOLM FARAWAY

"You neglected to mention how *skilled* the rest of your companions were."

I look up as the gray-haired man returns, wearing a sour expression. His mouth is twisted into a tight grimace and he narrows his eyes as he looks down at me.

Zeru and the others must be giving him trouble. I wonder if they heard Kaladria's screams. Nothing would put the four of them in more of a rage. They would tear the whole world apart to save her. Likely, they escaped and are causing mass chaos now.

I press my lips together. He has no idea who he's dealing with. Vale and Zeru alone are formidable. But Azar and Hassuun? If those two are free, he's going to have a hard time staying in control of the situation.

"You didn't seem all that interested in them." I fail to hide a smirk. "You wanted to know about the girl. You never said you wanted to know what the rest of them could do."

He puts on the table, huffing in frustration. "Perhaps it's time we discussed them instead."

Crossing my arms stubbornly, I glare back at him. "I think I'll let you figure them out on your own."

I don't quite understand what's come over me. I've always been logical, inclined to think before I speak. But this man has released a rage within me I didn't even know existed.

He scrutinizes me for a long time. Then, he lets out a long sigh, shaking his head in disappointment. "Clearly, this line of questioning is getting us nowhere." He signals to the soldier at the door. "Let's go for a walk."

The soldier wears a detached expression as he grabs my arm and leads me out of the room behind the gray-haired man. They lead me down long hallways, past more and more soldiers, but I feel too numb to even consider an escape plan.

It's getting louder. With every step, Kaladria's screams fill more and more space in the air around us.

We stop before a huge glass wall. As I look through it, my breath stops.

Chained up, her body has been manacled against a silver wall with wires connected to her skin. She's rigid, convulsing with pain. Her eyes are pinched shut and tears stream down her cheeks. Her mouth hangs open in a wordless scream, her entire body arcing with every cry. Her skin practically glows with electricity. Lightning sparks around her, striking across the room in a wild torrent of bright blue light.

They're drawing it out of her. Like she's some kind of generator.

I clench my jaw. She's nothing more than an energy source to them, barely worth considering alive.

"Your male companions seem capable of handling themselves," the gray-haired man says slyly, "But *she* doesn't appear to be quite so fortunate."

I jerk my arm but the soldier tightens his grip. "You're making a mistake."

"Am I? I'm not the one letting a friend suffer for your silence."

I look back through the glass. Kaladria's skin glows brighter with every scream, which are more and more hysterical by the moment. How long can she do this? How long before their efforts become too much for her to handle? As strong as she is, a body can only handle so much pain before it gives out.

I stare at her, swallowing the lump in my throat. Everything is so twisted. She's the soldier. She's the one trained to be both a weapon and a shield. And yet, here I am, desperately searching for a way to save her.

Screaming hysterically, Kaladria arcs against her bindings in an effort to free herself, and I lose it. "Fine," I snap, glaring at the gray-haired man. "You want to know what she is? You want to know why she's so powerful?"

He raises an eyebrow, not at all troubled by the sharpness in my voice.

"Because she has to be. Because she's spent *years* risking her life to protect Earth from enemies we can't even imagine. And, if you keep this up, you're going to kill the world's best chance for survival." I lean forward. "I hope you're okay with being responsible for the destruction of the human race."

He studies me for a long time. I stare back at him, waiting to see if my words mean anything. Then, without a word, he signals to another soldier. The lightning around Kaladria vanishes as she falls forward. I exhale, hoping my words were enough to save her.

37

KALADRIA ASTRANA

THE PAIN VANISHES SO QUICKLY that my body becomes suddenly and impossibly heavy. I slump forward, panting hard, trembling violently against my chains.

The door swings open and I can hear the sound of shuffling foot-steps. *Look up,* I tell myself. *You can't let them beat you yet.* With a groan, I force my head up. But it isn't Callaghan that steps into the room. It's Malcolm.

He rushes to my side. "Kaladria!"

I don't think I've ever been so tired before. Even using my Light-ning Form doesn't make me this weak. This machine has stolen every ounce of energy from inside of me. My body is shaking, convulsing with exhaustion. My face is covered in a sheen of sweat and my throat is on fire. I can barely breathe.

Hesitantly, Malcolm reaches out a hand. He presses it to my cheek. "Breathe, Kaladria," he murmurs softly.

If had the energy, I might be surprised by his tenderness.

I try to take a deep breath. I focus on the hand still pressed to my cheek. His hand is warm and his long fingers extend all the way up the side of my face and into my hair. As my breathing starts to normalize and he drops his hand, I exhale. "Malcolm, you shouldn't…"

I stop, snapping my mouth shut. My body stiffens with pain, that familiar tightness wrapping itself around my body, starting at the wires. Agony wraps around my body like a cocoon. Suddenly, I'm hyper aware of Malcolm standing next to me.

As the electricity begins to leave me, I arch my back, screaming as I pull the lightning back into my body. But I can only hold onto it for a moment. The exertion it takes to keep the lightning in my body is too much to hold onto.

The pain yanks and the lightning is freed, snapping out of my body more aggressively than before. It blasts Malcolm back and his head strikes the floor.

I scream. *"No!"*

38

KALADRIA ASTRANA

A NEW KIND of pain now racks my body. It's far worse than anything I've felt since waking in this place. I thought I could handle anything Callaghan threw at me. Physical torture is nothing. I would gladly die for any of my friends. Even if the pain their machine supplies is enough to make me convulse, to beg for mercy in ways I never have before, I would rather feel that a hundred times over than feel what I'm feeling right now.

This is the kind of pain that has always been my destruction. Being helpless. I watched the Aklev'Zol kill my mother, watched the light fade from her eyes as I stood there, unable to stop it. I listened to Emma Blake beg for help as the General turned her into a monster. I couldn't do anything when the Aklev'Zol dragged my uncle to who-knows-where, knowing it should have been me they took in his place.

And this is exactly the same. Callaghan used my body, my power, against me. He used it to hit Malcolm with far more lightning than I know he can survive. I won't stand for it. Not this time.

I've watched too many people die. I've lost too much due to my own weakness. I refuse to be helpless again. I won't let them do this. Not to me, certainly not to him.

I scream again. But this is different than before. It's so unlike the agonized cries that have filled this room in the last hours. This is a battle cry of unbridled fury, a wild roar full of the wrath of the Lightning Demon.

Limbs shaking from the effort, I pinch my eyes shut in concentration. A scream rips through my lungs as I draw the lightning sparking in the room back into my body. The wires around me are fried in the process.

Keep going, I tell myself, pressing forward.

I force my body to teleport in and out of lightning, despite the fatigue threatening to overtake me.

I move through electricity, stumbling before Malcolm. I fall to my knees. My fingers tremble as I grab his wrist, searching for a pulse. But there's nothing. I lean down, pressing an ear to his chest, only to be greeted by silence.

"No," I breathe.

I start compressions, pushing down on his chest, counting the beats. After a few minutes, I pinch his nose, leaning down for a rescue breath. Still, nothing.

"Dang it, Malcolm!" Trails of hot tears streak down my cheeks. I slam a hand against the floor. *"Breathe!"*

I can almost feel the ghost of his hand on my cheek and I bow my head. He can't die.

Drawing in every ounce of what little lightning is left inside of me, I fill my hands with electricity. I take a deep breath, placing my hands on his chest, pushing the lightning through my fingers. His chest lifts and falls and then is silent.

I've failed.

Crying out in defeat, I drop my head to his chest. I pinch my eyes shut, the tears flowing freely now. My shoulders shake with grief. "I'm sorry," I whisper. "I'm so sorry."

My heart hurts. It's been shredded by my failure, by the knowledge that the Lightning Demon has led yet another into death.

Why does this always happen? I cry out in my mind. *Why must everyone I care for die?*

Malcolm gasps, inhaling sharply.

I lift my head. "Malcolm?"

His eyes remain closed but his breath continues, chest shuddering with slow and shaky breaths. I drop my head, relief flooding through me with a heavy exhale. But I barely have time for more than that long sigh before the door swings open again. Soldiers step into the room, followed by Callaghan.

"That was an incredible display," he comments. "I must admit, I wasn't quite sure what you planned to do."

I wish I had enough strength left to blast him. "You're insane."

Callaghan ignores my snarled outburst. "You'll be happy to know that Mr. Faraway didn't give you away." He smirks, as if there's something funny about Malcolm's loyalty. "He only claimed you're protecting Earth from certain destruction."

I narrow my eyes at his tone.

Callaghan, still clearly amused, shakes his head. "I find it interesting that the two of you would protect each other so adamantly."

I look down at Malcolm. His chest lifts and falls with ragged breaths, as if each one is excruciating. I place a hand on his cheek, absolutely certain of my next words. "You're going to let him go," I say without looking up.

"What was that?"

I lift my head to look at Callaghan, hoping my gaze is cold enough to slice through his amusement. "Let him go. If you release him, I'll do whatever you wish of me."

Callaghan recovers from his initial surprise quickly. "As I said before, you're in no position to be making demands."

"That's where I'm going to have to disagree with you." I stand shakily. "You want my power? You're going to have to give me something in return."

For a moment, Callaghan says nothing. He watches me, testing my resolve. I hold my head high, eyes bearing into him. I will not submit, not this time.

Finally, Callaghan chuckles, shaking his head in disbelief. "I was beginning to think you were incapable of such sensibility," he says slyly. "Your uncle would be so proud."

At first, I am so still, frozen by his words. But, as they sink in, fury overtakes me. I launch forward with a roar, moving in and out of electricity. I disappear from my position standing over Malcolm, reappearing in front of Callaghan. Before his soldiers can react, I knock him back into the nearest wall. "What game are you playing?"

Callaghan looks behind me, holding up a hand to signal his soldiers to stay where they are. Then, he focuses on me again. "It's no game. Just business." He shrugs. "A strange man came to me with quite the offer the other day. I was to capture your team and keep you out of his way by any means necessary."

I grit my teeth. *Corvar.*

"In exchange for my…services, he handed over a very interesting prisoner, with abilities very similar to your own. He would be the perfect weapon, if he wasn't as stubborn as you are."

Anger burns inside of me at the thought of Xalin being tortured the way I have been. The Aklev'Zol must have had Corvar hand Xalin over to the humans. Likely to punish me. And likely to keep me on a wild goose chase.

"You have no idea who you're dealing with," I warn. "You think you've found an ally that can provide you with soldiers and technology far beyond your own. But you couldn't be more wrong. He will turn on you the very moment it suits him."

"I think you have other concerns right now." He signals to the soldiers behind me. Hands wrap around my arms, pulling me off him.

"Don't make this mistake, Callaghan. It will not end well for you or your soldiers."

Callaghan waves a hand dismissively. "I suggest you cooperate. For your uncle's sake, as well as for the sake of Mr. Faraway."

I look down at Malcolm. His breathing is still so shallow. I can't let them hurt him again. He's too weak to survive it a second time. My surrender may not free him from this place but it might prevent them from killing him.

My shoulders slump with my defeat. "So be it."

3 9

MALCOLM FARAWAY

THERE'S a tight pain in my chest when I wake, as if there's some invisible weight sitting on top of me. Every breath feels like it's going to tear my lungs apart. But then I remember why. *Kaladria.* I was standing right next to her. I remember touching her cheek, trying to still her shaking. And then the lightning started to spark around the room. The last thing I can remember is that she was screaming.

I open my eyes, staring up at a blank ceiling. The implications of it all makes my head spin. They'd thrown me in that room with her, knowing what would happen when they used her lightning against her, against me.

Grimacing, I sit up slowly. I'm still in the room where Kaladria was being tortured. But she's not here anymore. The chains remain locked against the silver wall and there's a mess of half-melted wires strewn across the floor but Kaladria is nowhere in sight.

I look at the door. The soldier previously guarding my interrogation room stands there. But, unlike before, his eyes aren't fixed on the wall in front of him. He's watching me with an unreadable expression. "How do you feel?"

I lean my head back against the wall. "Not good." I groan. It feels like my chest is in a vice. "What happened?"

"You were struck by lightning."

"After that," I clarify.

The soldier hesitates. "I'm not sure I really have answers for you. I don't know what happened. The girl...Kaladria? She got out of her bonds somehow." He shakes his head, as if he still doesn't believe what he saw. "It was like she sucked all the lightning back into her body." He studies my face. "She restarted your heart."

I stiffen. "It stopped?"

My mind is spinning and I have a million more questions to ask but the soldier is no longer looking at me. His gaze has snapped forward once more. The door swings open and the gray-haired man steps inside. "Ah, Mr. Faraway, you're awake."

I glare. "You almost killed me."

"No," he disagrees. "That was *her* doing."

I swallow. Does she know I'm okay? Or did they drag her off, letting her believe that her lightning had killed me?

"Where is she?" I ask.

The gray-haired man clasps his hands behind his back. "She and I have come to an agreement. I'll be taking her to a different facility shortly."

In the corner of my eye, I can see the soldier standing at the door. A muscle in his jaw tics, his expression darkening.

I look back at the gray-haired man. "I don't believe you. She'd never surrender. Not for anything."

"Not even for the boy she almost killed? She was rather distraught, you know." He smirks. "And whether you believe it or not is completely irrelevant. Miss Astrana will be moved to a new facility and you will remain here."

I grit my teeth. *To keep her in line, no doubt.*

He says no more, turning on his heel. As he leaves the room, I lean my head back, closing my eyes. It feels surreal. I was sort of dead. Even if only for a moment, it still happened.

"She was protecting you."

I look over at the soldier. "So, she did make a deal with him?"

"General Callaghan is holding all the cards," he says. "I don't think she felt she had much of a choice. Callaghan wasn't lying when he said she was distraught. Until that moment, nothing has affected her.

In every interrogation and through all the torture, she's been cold, almost detached. But she lost it when your heart stopped."

I sigh, leaning my head back. "What will they do to her?"

"They will either use her as a weapon or as a generator. They'll drain her electricity and harvest it to power new weaponry, maybe even a whole facility. They'll likely do so until she has nothing left to give."

I grit my teeth at the thought. I don't like the idea of an obedient Kaladria. From the moment we met, I knew she was uncontrollable. She is a storm with skin and the possibility of her letting anyone order her around makes my heart hurt. Especially when I consider why she's submitting. She's doing what they want to protect me. And, even if I think I'd rather get hit by that lightning a thousand times over, I know she'll keep protecting me for as long as she thinks she has to.

The soldier pushes away from the wall. "I've cut the power to this room."

"What? Why?"

"Because I'm not one of Callaghan's dogs." He reaches a hand down and pulls me to my feet. I stagger a step and he steadies me before letting go. "My name is Noah Hilliard. I'm from Criminal Investigation Command. I was sent here to look into some claims about General Callaghan."

I blink. "You're a cop?"

"Undercover, yes. Callaghan doesn't know why I'm here. Otherwise, I doubt he would have let me see what he was doing here, regarding Miss Astrana."

"I'm guessing your investigation is classified."

"Good guess." He smiles shrewdly. "I will say I was not anticipating finding him torturing a young woman with supernatural abilities. I don't know how I'm ever going to explain my report to my superiors." He shakes his head. "Regardless, my top priority is getting you out of here. I can't let Callaghan keep using you and Miss Astrana against one another."

"You're going to help me?" When he nods, I hesitate. "What about my other friends? What about Kaladria?"

"Your friends have turned the prison level of this facility into a warzone. I don't think there's much we can do for any of them."

"I'm not leaving without them."

He sighs, clearly exasperated.

"Look, Callaghan was willing to kill me, just to get a rise out of Kaladria. I don't want to know what he'd do if he decided he wanted to use the rest of them." I take a deep breath, straightening. "They've all risked their lives for me. I won't abandon them."

Noah sighs again, still reluctant. "You do realize if we're caught, Callaghan will win."

I stand a little taller. "He's not going to win," I vow. "I'm not going to let him keep hurting her. She's too important."

He rubs the back of his neck, studying my face silently.

"Either you help me save my friends or you leave me here. Either way, I am not going without them."

Noah shakes his head, then sighs. "Very well. Let's go for your friends in the prison level first. If you intend to free Miss Astrana, you'll need all the help you can get."

I nod. "Let's go."

He leads the way out of the room, gripping my arm tightly. I stumble along, grinding my teeth. It strikes me just how weak my body is. I feel like I was hit by a train. Every movement is laced with pain, every inch of me aches. I don't envy anyone who has ever been struck by Kaladria's lightning.

"Stay close," Noah says in a low voice, "And follow my lead."

We make our way down the hall. I do my best to keep up with him, staggering as I ignore the pain in my chest.

"So, what's the story with my friends in the prison level? What's it like down there?"

"Not really sure." Noah leads me down a new corridor. "Apparently, the four of them have destroyed some of the walls and convened in one cell. I guess they've made some sort of barricade. Callaghan's men are having a hard time breaching it." He shakes his head. "It's been mass chaos down there."

I grin. These soldiers have no idea who they're dealing with.

We make our way down a staircase. I can hear the chaos Noah

mentioned. Men are yelling, their voices followed by the sound of gunshots. I hear something like an explosion, followed by the hiss of ice.

As we reach the bottom step, Noah holds out a hand. "Stay back," he mutters.

He lets go of my arm and I lean against the wall with a frustrated huff. I feel utterly useless. *Just like always,* a voice in the back of my head reminds me. I push it away.

Noah rounds the next corner and I peek around, watching as he strides down the hallway. There are a dozen soldiers there, hiding behind crates and backed up against another wall. Across the corridor, there's a wall made of stone. Fire and ice flash across the air.

As Noah steps into the hallway, several of the soldiers stop. "What are you doing down here?" one asks.

Noah pauses, straightening. "Stand down, soldiers. This—"

One of the soldiers scoffs. "Who are you to order us around, recruit?"

Noah pulls something from his pocket, holding up a small badge. "Special Agent Noah Hilliard, of the CID. I suggest you all stand down before things get ugly."

"Not likely. We answer to Callaghan. And only Callaghan."

"Callaghan has committed crimes against his country, including the murders of several fellow soldiers."

Murder? Is that what Noah was investigating?

He shrugs back his shoulders. "He's got you all being paid under the table, correct?"

"You—"

"Stand down. This is the last time I'll ask."

Several of the soldiers lift their weapons. "Not happening."

As one of the soldiers fires a weapon, Noah dodges to the side. As he straightens, he swings around the rifle previously slung across his shoulder. Then, he leaps into action.

Noah fires again and again, hitting several of the soldiers in various limbs. As they begin to return fire, Noah rolls to the side, crouching behind a crate. He glances at me, probably ensuring I haven't been spotted. Then, he begins to fire again. Before long, all the soldiers are down.

Noah stands, approaching the staircase. I push against the wall, cursing when I trip, nearly face planting on the floor. Noah grabs my arm and guides me forward.

"Remind me not to get on your bad side."

He half-smiles. "Update your friends quickly. If you still intend to rescue her, we will have to be fast."

I nod, using the wall as a crutch as I approach the barricade. "Guys?" I call.

The rock wall crumples apart, revealing Azar, Hassuun, Vale, and Zeru. Only Zeru looks worse for wear. The Jovian lieutenant grimaces, leaning against the nearest wall.

"Zeru? Are you alright?"

He exhales. "The walls here are a little thicker than I'm used to. The humans appear to have figured out how to dampen my abilities."

"You can't use your Ghost Form?"

Zeru grimaces. "I'm afraid not."

I glance at Noah. "Could Callaghan do that?"

"Callaghan has committed many crimes." Noah shrugs. "He did have a machine capable of forcing Miss Astrana's lightning out of her body. Nothing would surprise me."

Zeru's expression darkens. "Is that why she was..." He shakes his head, glancing between me and Noah. "Malcolm, who's your friend?"

I shake my head. "We can go into it later. Right now, we have to hurry. They're taking Kaladria somewhere. If we don't hurry, we'll lose her."

Zeru's face falls with sudden frustration. "I'm afraid I won't be much help," he says, rubbing his temples.

"Me, neither," I admit. "Apparently, my heart stopped not too long ago. I'm having a hard time getting around, let around doing anything useful."

Zeru studies my face, like he wants to ask for details but then thinks better of it. He looks at Azar and Hassuun. "Find her. The two of you have the best chance of getting to her without being stopped."

Noah steps forward. "I'll show you the way."

Azar nods curtly. The three of them take off down the hall, Hassuun taking on his Rock Form and Azar lighting his arms and hands on fire. Vale glances between me and Zeru. "We need to get the two of you out of here."

I grimace. If we ever get out of here, I swear to myself that I'm going to learn to be useful, to be able to fight alongside these Protectors instead of just getting dragged along all the time.

Zeru shakes his head. "I need you to do something first," he says to Vale. "Find our stuff. I had that memory chip when we were captured. If we make it out of here, we're going to need it."

Vale hesitates.

Zeru's expression is obstinate. "Consider it an order from your acting captain. We'll meet you outside."

Vale sighs. He takes off running in the opposite direction as the way Azar, Hassuun, and Noah went, leaving Zeru and I alone in the hallway.

Zeru studies my face for a moment, taking note of the way I slump back against the wall. "Now, what's this about your heart stopping?"

40

KALADRIA ASTRANA

A NEWFOUND SORT of determination lives inside my chest as they lead me down the hallway. Ever since the Aklev'Zol revealed themselves on that fateful trip to Malcolm's lab, my uncertainty has been growing. At first, it was almost imperceptible. But, the longer I ignored it, the stronger it became. My doubt that I didn't know how to stop the Aklev'Zol turned to fear that I might no longer be capable of protecting anyone from the monsters that have already stolen so many.

Callaghan changed that. He turned me into a weapon against someone I didn't realize I cared so much about. It snapped something inside of me. And learning about Xalin? That was the final straw.

I will play the role Callaghan wants me to play. But the moment he slips up, the moment he gives me an opportunity to turn on him, I'll show him that allying with Corvar was the wrong move. I'll prove to him that making an enemy of the Lightning Demon was a grave mistake.

As I follow him through dimly lit hallways, I allow his soldiers to drag me forward, keeping hold of my arms. After all the lightning I lost, I'm not sure I'd be standing without them anyway. Still, I keep my head high. I force myself to ignore the weakness in my limbs and

the dull ache in my shoulder from my previous encounter with the Aklev'Zol's machine beast.

I stop. Chaos erupts somewhere behind me. And it isn't long before I hear Hassuun and Azar amongst the gunshots and screams. I look behind me.

Azar stands there, with ember eyes burning as brightly as the flames in his hands. Hassuun, in his rock-like form, clenches tight fists.

I stiffen. I could break free of these soldier's grips. If I could just teleport to my squadmates, I'd be safe. Even as weak as I am, they'd never let them touch me again. But I know I will never get this close to finding Xalin again. If I escape now, I may never see him again.

I look at Azar. He will undoubtedly be the first to attack. As he steps toward me, I shake my head. He freezes where he stands, surprised and confused. But he still clenches his jaw in stubbornness.

I hope my eyes portray just how serious this is. *Please,* I mouth.

Azar grimaces.

Track me.

He exhales. For once, he doesn't ignore the order. Perhaps seeing my desperation, Azar puts out a hand to stop Hassuun. The rock-covered Martian frowns, looking at me and then at Azar. Eyes still watching me, hating every moment of this but respecting me too much to ignore my plea, Azar nods.

As the two of my most reckless squadmates disappear back the way they've come, I let out a heavy sigh and allow the soldiers to drag me away.

176

MALCOLM FARAWAY

"Zeru?"

Stopping outside a hallway, Zeru frowns, his eyes suddenly unreadable. He holds up a hand, flexing his fingers. "I think it might be wearing off." Wordlessly, he pushes a transparent hand through the nearest wall. Still, the motion is slow and his expression is strained. He removes his hand, turning solid once more.

"It's not all the way there but I think whatever they did is wearing off. I should be able to phase normally soon."

I nod absentmindedly. My thoughts are focused on Kaladria. What if they can't find her in time? What if Callaghan spirits her away before anyone can stop him? Noah's words echo in my head. They'll steal her lightning until she has no more electricity left to give. Can she survive without it? Or will their efforts kill her?

Zeru glances at me. "You doing okay?"

I sigh as we continue to make our way through the base. "I'm just trying to wrap my head around all of this. Callaghan is just as cruel as any of the Aklev'Zol. He would have killed me in an effort to elicit some kind of reaction from Kaladria." I shake my head. "It's hard to believe anyone would want to protect humanity, would want to protect men like him. Maybe humanity isn't worth protecting."

Zeru slows his pace. "Callaghan may not deserve the protection the Council and the Protectorate provides but there are plenty of others that do. We cannot condemn an entire race based on the actions of a few evil men."

I'm quiet as we step out of the building and into the dark night. I follow Zeru as he slinks past a truck and a couple of soldiers, stopping at a fence.

"Let's go," Zeru says. "We need to figure out where we are. I suspect we've got a long way to go to find the *Resistance*."

AS WE REACH THE SHIP, walking up to the bridge, I slump into the nearest seat. Vale, having caught up to us outside, glances at me before going to his seat. Zeru leans against the wall with his arms crossed, watching me carefully.

I close my eyes, leaning my head back. We were lucky the ship was so close to the military base. It didn't take us long to get here. Hopefully, it won't be long until the others arrive as well.

Despite my exhaustion, sitting down makes me feel suddenly anxious. I think of Kaladria, slumped forward in that room, sweating and shaking and impossibly frail. I don't ever want to see her like that again. But if they couldn't save her, I might not have a choice.

I exhale. *No.* I have to believe that they found her in time. Hassuun and Azar are an impossible force. And I saw Noah fight. Even without any of the special abilities the others have, he's powerful, too. With the three of them, Kaladria will be fine.

As the elevator doors slide open, I look over. Hassuun and Azar step onto the bridge, both looking uncharacteristically worried.

My heart sinks.

On seeing them, Zeru frowns. "Where's Kala?"

Hassuun grimaces, glancing at Azar. "She doesn't want to escape. At least, not yet. She wants us to track her."

I think again of those horrible screams, of the pure agony in her face. I can feel my brow furrow. "Why?"

Azar shakes his head. "We didn't have time to ask. But I didn't dare cross her. She's never looked at me like that. This time, we need to trust her judgment."

My mind is going a hundred miles an hour. I can't imagine why she would want to remain Callaghan's prisoner. I think again of what Noah said, about Callaghan holding all the cards. Clearly, he still has something over her.

"Where's Noah?" I ask.

"We told him everything," Hassuun explains. "He wanted some time to process it all. He's in the cargo hold."

I glance at Zeru as he stands, walking over to a monitor. He touches it a few times, swiping his fingers across the screen. But then he stops, stiffening slightly, in either surprise or shock.

"Zeru? What is it?"

He doesn't turn but his body remains rigid. "Her tracker is gone."

"What?"

"Her tracker. It's not giving any sort of feedback anymore. It's just gone."

Azar curses. "They must have removed it."

"How would they even know to do that?" Hassuun asks with a frown. "How would they even know she had one?"

Zeru turns, shaking his head. "The same way they knew how to keep me from using my Ghost Form. The same way they had a machine meant to draw out Kaladria's power. The same way they found us in the first place. They have inside information about all of us."

The implications are dangerous. I doubt many would willingly tell Callaghan how to defeat all of them. And I suspect there are even fewer with the technology to turn Kaladria's lightning against her. Honestly, I can think of only one force capable of both of those things. A force that has been hunting for me, that is responsible for sending us into that house. It's the only thing that makes sense but I sincerely hope I'm wrong.

I look up, biting my tongue. Everyone else is too on edge for theories right now.

Zeru lets out his breath. "I can at least get us the coordinates of the last place the tracker was giving feedback."

"Noah might be able to get us to the facility from there," I say. He was investigating Callaghan, after all. If anyone would know where to find Kaladria now, it would be him.

Zeru repeats a set of coordinates to Vale. "Get us there as quickly as you can." He pauses, glancing across the bridge. "And give Malcolm the memory chip."

I frown as I accept the chip. "What do you want me to do with it?"

"See if you can find anything on it. We lost a lot of time in that base. As soon as we find Kala, we'll need to figure out where the Aklev'Zol are hiding Xalin."

I look down at the chip. "I'm not sure I'll be able to find anything, Zeru." I shake my head. "This tech has got to be way beyond humanity's."

Hassuun smirks. "And a wormhole generator isn't?"

Zeru smiles. "Do your best, Malcolm." He straightens, glancing at Vale. "How long?"

"We'll hit your coordinates in a few hours. The hard part will be figuring out where this mysterious facility is from there."

"Good. Gear up, everyone."

42

KALADRIA ASTRANA

YOU CAN DO THIS, I tell myself as we arrive at the new facility. I take deep, calming breaths.

As I'm escorted inside, I try very hard not to think about what is about to happen. I'm at peace with my decision but that doesn't make the thought of getting my lightning ripped out of me any more alluring.

Reaching a hand down as we walk, I finger the bandage around my arm. The inside of my forearm stings where they used a scalpel to remove the tracker.

I wonder what my squad must be thinking right now. They were counting on using my tracker to find me and now it's gone. I can't say I feel great about it either. There are no longer any assurances of rescue for either me or Xalin now.

As we stop, Callaghan draws closer, studying my face. "I'm impressed with you, Miss Astrana. I didn't expect you to be so cooperative."

My jaw is set in a hard line. "Where's my uncle?"

Callaghan signals to one of the soldiers. "This way."

The soldiers drag me forward and Callaghan leads the way down the hall. I let them guide me but my anxiety grows with every step. Having the lightning sucked out of my body was absolute agony. I can't imagine what they might have done to Xalin since Corvar handed him over.

My fears become reality as Callaghan stops in front of a large glass window. The soldier gripping me tightens his hold, keeping me still. As I look through the window, bile rises to my mouth.

Xalin is tied up exactly as I had been, wires attached in a similar fashion. His skin glows bright blue and lightning sparks across the room. Unlike I had been, Xalin is still. His jaw is rigid and his back is stiff but he keeps his eyes closed and his mouth shut.

I jerk against the soldier's grasp. "Stop," I plead. "I'll do whatever you ask, just stop hurting him."

Callaghan's smile is cruel. "How much do you think he can take? Does your kind survive on the electricity? What would happen if we drew all of it—"

I scream, lunging forward, but the soldier yanks me back.

Callaghan smirks. "You have no control over what happens now, Miss Astrana. You gave away that right the moment you agreed to come here." He looks at the soldier still gripping my arm. "Take her to her cell."

MALCOLM FARAWAY

"Noah?"

He barely glances at me. "Malcolm."

I sink to the floor, trying to not think too much about being in the cargo hold. This is where she held my hand, where I told her things I've never told anyone else. I think of those sharp eyes and my chest aches. Will she ever…

I stop that thought. *We'll get her back,* I tell myself. *You haven't said goodbye yet.*

I look over at Noah. "You look a little sick. You going to be okay?"

He rubs the back of his neck. "This is a lot to take in. I went to that base to investigate several soldiers' deaths. Finding out Callaghan had captured a girl capable of wielding lightning was crazy. But aliens? An impending intergalactic war? This is a whole new level of unbelievable."

I nod, understanding completely. I never had time to consider how crazy all of this is, how insane it is to be traveling across the universe with a group of alien soldiers in an attempt to save Earth and the rest of the galaxy from nightmarish monsters. If I had, I probably would have felt the same way he does.

"What are you going to do now?" I ask. "Do you need to make a report on your investigation?"

"Not yet. I've got some time still before I need to report to my superiors." He scrutinizes me for a moment. "You said before that Kaladria Astrana was Earth's best chance for survival. Did you mean that?"

I nod.

Noah shrugs back his shoulders. "I'd say my first priority is helping you rescue her. Then, I want to do what I can to help with the Aklev'Zol threat. I think that's a little more of a pressing issue than reporting Callaghan's crimes."

I exhale. "At this point, I think we could use all the help we can get."

Noah leans his head back against the wall. "So, I hear this all began with a wormhole generator?"

I grimace. "Yeah. I…"

I trail off as Zeru appears in the doorway. "We're landing." He glances at Noah. "We could use your help. We stopped receiving data from Kaladria's tracker but we've gone as far as we can. Do you think you could help us figure out where to go from here?"

Noah nods slowly. "I know of a couple of other facilities Callaghan has access to. He likely took her to one of those sites."

The two of them leave the cargo hold. I stay where I am on the floor, leaning my head back against the wall. The pain in my chest has lessened since returning to the *Resistance* but I still feel infuriatingly frail. It takes too much energy to even walk around the ship. I hope I can be more useful when they find her.

You don't have to protect me anymore, I think. *This time, I'm going to protect you.*

I let out a heavy sigh. I hope that's a promise I can keep.

———

It takes two days to find her. By the time Noah has managed to track down which facility she's at from what little information we have, my body has more or less healed from my dance with death.

Everyone aboard the *Resistance* is on edge. Azar and Hassuun are fighting nonstop, their normally rambunctious teasing transformed by fear for their captain. Vale is even quieter than usual and Zeru can't hold still for longer than thirty seconds at a time.

Of course, when we do find where Callaghan took Kaladria, no one seems any less agitated. But at least now everyone has something to focus on.

As everyone prepares to leave the ship, Zeru glances at Noah. "We could use your help again."

Noah nods. "I was planning on going in."

"I'm coming, too."

Zeru looks at me uncertainly. "Malcolm—"

I shake my head furiously. "No. There's no way I'm going to sit here on the ship, twiddling my thumbs, while some madman is torturing her." He sighs and I continue. "Besides, what am I supposed to do if you fail? Wait for the Aklev'Zol to come and force me to show them how to use the wormhole generator?"

He concedes. "Alright. Come on, then."

Zeru leads the way off the ship, where Vale, Hassuun, and Azar wait. He glances at everyone in turn, setting back his shoulders.

"I'm going to stay in my Ghost Form. I don't want them hitting me with one of those darts again. Azar, Hassuun, go cause some sort of commotion. Vale, you and I are going in after them as quietly as possible to scout ahead." He glances at Noah and I. "You guys follow after us. Hopefully, we can find Kala without too much trouble."

I nod and Zeru pulls out a dagger, flipping it around as he passes it over to me. "If memory serves, this worked well for you last time."

I take the knife, holding it tightly.

Zeru glances at Azar and Hassuun again. "Do whatever you can. Cause as much destruction as possible. Just make sure they stay focused on you guys until we get Kala out of there."

Azar grins. "Got it."

I watch them go. Azar lights fire across his arms and Hassuun shifts to his rocky form. I don't envy the soldiers that find them.

Zeru looks at Vale. "Come on. Let's see what we can learn."

44

KALADRIA ASTRANA

HAVING BEEN ORDERED to continue harvesting my electricity, Callaghan's men have strapped me down as before. I can feel the power thrumming through the wires connected to my skin. Even in its dormant state, the power of their infernal machine makes my head spin.

I have no idea how long I've been here. Hours? Days? It all blurs together as they turn their machine on and off, sending lightning sparking through the room and then letting it disperse, again and again and again. It's been long enough that I'm confident my body will give out even if they release me from my bindings.

Waiting for the machine to start up again, I close my eyes. I don't understand how Xalin could have been so still, how he could endure it in silence. Every time they turn it on again, it requires all my willpower to not beg for release. But I suppose it was Xalin that taught me how to be still in the midst of pain. If anyone could withstand this kind of torture, it would be him.

"What do you know? The Lightning Demon has been reduced to a living battery."

I stiffen, opening eyes to find Corvar in the room, watching me with disdain.

He's changed. It's not just his hand that is tainted with the Aklev'-

186

Zol's dark matter now. The blackness has begun to creep up his neck. He'll be hard pressed to hide it from the other Councilors soon.

"I'm surprised you were foolish enough to go where I instructed."

I clench my fists. "Did you really expect anything less? I've never been one to run from a fight."

"I suppose so." He smirks. "Do you know what happens next, Captain Astrana? Callaghan gets to experiment on you, drawing your lightning out until you are nothing but a husk. Then, his scientists will dissect your body and harvest your organs for the sake of their science."

I set my jaw, clenching my body against the chill that runs down my spine. *You are bigger than your fear. You are bigger than your fear...*

"You should have—"

A sound like thunder, accompanied by some sort of explosion, fills the air. It's followed by an earthquake that rattles the entire room. I've witnessed those two events together too often to not recognize what caused them. *Azar and Hassuun.* They've found me. Despite all the odds, despite not being able to track me, they still found me.

I grin. "It seems you've forgotten about the greatest squad in the Protectorate."

His expression turns almost feral. He grabs my jaw, black talons clawing into my cheeks. "And you've forgotten who they face."

He calls down the hall. In an instant, two Aklev'Zol soldiers drag Callaghan into the room. Callaghan glares at Corvar. "What is this?" the human general growls.

"I have no further use for you," Corvar says dismissively.

Callaghan looks at me. And now he knows. My warning held true. Corvar has discarded him, just as I said he would.

Corvar looks at the two Aklev'Zol gripping Callaghan. "Change him."

Callaghan yells, struggling against his captors as they throw him to the floor, holding him down as one drives a talon through his body, infecting him with their darkness.

I turn my head, pinching my eyes shut. I've already witnessed one infection. I'd rather not see another.

Long minutes pass before his screams fall silent. I open my eyes, teeth grit at the sight of the Aklev'Zol soldier that has replaced Callaghan.

Corvar looks at the three Aklev'Zol. "Change them all. Infect every human on this base," he orders. "Kill anyone that tries to stop you."

I squirm against my bindings. "No!"

Corvar barely looks at me. "And someone turn on this blasted contraption."

4 5

MALCOLM FARAWAY

Noah and I make our way across the street, sneaking across the shadows made by the facility. Fire explodes across the building's wall, followed by a quake that shakes the ground around us. Soldiers take off running, rushing to see what's caused the commotion.

"Are we sure they can handle this?" Noah asks in a low voice.

"Yeah, I've seen them fight. When they use their other forms, Azar and Hassuun are practically untouchable."

Noah nods. He grips his gun tightly as we round a corner, running through the long hallways. As we hit a dead end, he sighs. "Let's—"

Black talons curl around my arm. "Mr. Malcolm Faraway."

Time speeds up. Adrenaline lets me take in everything so much faster than I'd think possible. The tightening of the talons around my wrist. Noah lunging forward, only to be thrown back by the Aklev'-Zol's other hand. My fingers tightening around Zeru's knife.

While the Aklev'Zol is distracted by Noah, I whirl the dagger around, driving it straight through the monster's chest. As I yank the knife back out and the Aklev'Zol falls, I look at Noah. He stands, grimacing.

"You good?"

He nods slowly. "Was that...?"

"Aklev'Zol. If they're here, then things have gotten a lot more complicated. We need to find Kaladria. *Now.*"

After so long, after how much lightning has been drained from her body, Kaladria is in no position to fight the Aklev'Zol. We need to get her out of here before they get to her.

Noah and I make our way further into the building, more slowly now. Every once in a while, we stop at the sound of talons sliding across the wall or the heavy footsteps of soldiers. But, eventually, we find ourselves before a wide window. I freeze at the sight of lightning sparking inside.

I race over to the window, expecting to find Kaladria inside. But I stop at the sight of the figure manacled to the wall. *Xalin.*

Stumbling forward, I reach for the monitor outside the window. Fumbling with Zeru's knife, I slice through the wires that connect the monitor to the wall. Instantly, Xalin relaxes and the lightning dissipates from the air.

Without waiting for Noah, I run into the next room. I yank Xalin free of his bindings. He stumbles forward and I catch his arm to steady him.

"Malcolm? What are you doing here?"

"I could ask you the same thing," I say. "What are you doing on Earth?"

Xalin grimaces. "Part of a deal between Corvar and Callaghan. I was offered up as an experiment if Callaghan did everything in his power to distract Kaladria."

I grimace. *I hate it when I'm right,* I think, remembering my own theory on how Callaghan was so well-prepared to capture us, how he could have blocked Zeru's abilities and remove Kaladria's tracker.

Noah steps into the room, rifle in hand. "We need to keep moving."

Xalin, forcing himself to stand on his own, assesses the human soldier.

"Xalin, this is Noah. He's helping us." I let out my breath, shaking my head. "We don't have time to explain everything that's happened. Kaladria is here somewhere."

Xalin rubs a hand across the side of his face, worry darkening his features. "Then, we need to find her quickly." He hesitates, closing his eyes in concentration. When he opens his eyes, he points down the hall. "There's a huge spike of electricity in that direction. It has to be her."

I nod. "Let's go."

We take off running down the hall, with me and Noah following Xalin as he races through the building. For someone who had been tortured similarly to Kaladria, he isn't doing too badly. Xalin moves quickly, not stumbling or shaking or doing any of the things I saw Kaladria do after they tortured her.

But, as a glass window appears several paces ahead, Xalin stops, hands trembling at the sight of the blue lightning sparking in the room and his niece tied up, screaming hysterically. Kaladria tilts her head up toward the ceiling, tears streaking down her cheeks.

Face grim, I look outside that room, where Lorkan Corvar stands. He watches from outside the room, his hands clasped behind his back, two Aklev'Zol soldiers at his side.

My fingers tighten around the dagger. He's just *watching* her, like this is some sort of sick game, a spectacle for his enjoyment.

Next to me, Xalin clenches his hands into fists. Lightning sparks across his knuckles. "Get Kala," he says in a low voice. "I'll handle them."

He doesn't wait for me to respond. He strides into the hallway, barely pausing as Corvar faces him.

"Xalin," Corvar drawls, "What a surprise."

Xalin doesn't stop. "This madness ends now."

Corvar's smile is slight as he pulls out a gun. "Agreed. The Aklev'Zol made a mistake keeping you alive. You're more trouble than you're worth." He points the gun. "A problem I will quickly remedy."

I tense but Xalin merely shakes his head. "You're forgetting something, Corvar."

"What would that be?"

Xalin teleports forward. Hastily, Corvar pulls the trigger. But he's too late. Xalin reappears in front of him, swinging a fist. Lightning sparks across Corvar's cheek as his gunshot ricochets against the wall behind Xalin.

Xalin's hands are still sparking. "Kaladria Astrana learned everything she knows from *me*."

I blink, staring at Xalin. Suddenly, it makes sense how Kaladria could have become so powerful so quickly. Because she was being taught by someone equally as dangerous.

Corvar launches forward, talons outstretched. As Xalin dances to the side, the Aklev'Zol soldiers launch forward. Next to me, Noah lifts his gun and fires at one of the Aklev'Zol. As the monster stumbles, Noah rushes forward to attack the Aklev'Zol once more.

As Xalin and Noah keep Corvar and the Aklev'Zol distracted, I peer around the corner. Noah hits an Aklev'Zol with the butt of his rifle and Xalin sends Corvar stumbling back with a roar of fury. Past them, I can see Kaladria through the window, obliviously screaming at the ceiling.

I remember the promise I made myself. She's risked herself protecting me too many times. Now, it's my turn.

Darting past the fight, I duck under the window, cutting the wires to the monitor. As I peek up into the window, I exhale as the lightning disappears from the air. Kaladria falls forward, barely held up by her bindings.

I run into the room, yanking her free. She falls forward and I catch her, both of us slipping to the floor.

"Malcolm?" she whispers hoarsely.

"Hi." I brush the wires from her skin. "You okay?"

"No." Kaladria shivers. "I'm not."

As she continues to shake, I pull her closer. She feels like ice. I rub her arms, trying to warm her, but it doesn't do anything to stop her shivering.

She closes her eyes. "How did you find me?"

"I had help. Zeru and the others are here somewhere."

She opens her eyes, sharp anger sparking in her expression. "They left you *alone*?"

I smile. "No." I pull her to her feet, careful to keep an arm around her waist so she doesn't fall. "Let me show you who's with me."

She stumbles, peering out of the room as we near the door. One of the Aklev'Zol soldiers is slumped over on the floor. Noah fights the other one. Kaladria frowns. But, as her gaze falls on Xalin, who lets out a cry of fury as he blasts lightning in Corvar's direction, tears fill her eyes.

"I have to…"

She tries to push away from me. I grab her arm, pulling her back to my side. "Don't even think about it. You can barely walk."

Kaladria grimaces. She looks back at Xalin with a sigh. As if to prove my point, she sags into my side, allowing me to hold her up. Still shaking and shivering, she leans her head against my chest, her entire body racked with pain from what Callaghan did to her.

I swallow, holding her tightly.

46

KALADRIA ASTRANA

I FORGOT how capable my uncle is. It's been years since I saw him fight, over a decade since he quit the Protectorate in order to take care of me. In that time, I've forgotten it was he that taught me how to hold my own in a fight, it was he that taught me to use the lightning as a weapon.

Still, I never expected to see such fury in him. His expression twists with a roar as he pummels Corvar again and again, eyes full of a wrath that's completely foreign to me.

Corvar staggers back, ducking under a blast of bright blue energy. His face is ashen. He understands now the mistake he's made in making an enemy of my uncle. It's something he won't soon forget. Xalin strikes again and again, relentlessly blasting lightning through the hallway. Corvar stumbles back, shifting to his Ghost Form as he runs down the corridor, leaving the dead Aklev'Zol behind.

I try to stand on my own but end up slumped back against Malcolm. I curse my inability to move on my own. "Help me," I tell him as Xalin rushes over, extinguishing the lightning still sparking on his skin.

Malcolm guides me across the hallway, only releasing me as I collapse into Xalin's arms. "Kala." He exhales, hugging me tightly. "Are you alright?"

I look up at him, thinking of his calm face as they tortured him the same way they were torturing me. "Are you?" I challenge.

Xalin's smile is slight. "It takes a lot more than that to drain me."

"Clearly." I shake my head. "I can't believe you could hold so still. It felt like they were ripping me apart from the inside."

Xalin rubs my arms. "I've had a little more time practicing how to handle pain than you have."

I open my mouth, not completely satisfied with that answer, but I snap it shut as the human stranger previously fighting the Aklev'Zol soldiers steps forward. "We need to keep moving," he says. "There's bound to be more."

I raise an eyebrow, looking back at Malcolm. "You want to tell me what's going on?"

"Later. Right now, we need to get out of here."

47

MALCOLM FARAWAY

"WELL, NOW WHAT?" Hassuun asks.

I glance at Kaladria. She leans against the wall, shivering with her eyes pinched shut. Her face is pale and dark circles ring her eyes, as if she hasn't slept in days.

"I seriously doubt that many Aklev'Zol will give up looking for us," I say slowly.

"The memory chip is on the *Resistance*," Zeru says. "We should take it to the Council and tell them what's going on."

"Take the *Resistance* to the Satellite," Kaladria says, eyes still closed. "Inform the Council that Corvar is a traitor. Tell them everything that's happened since they sent me to Earth."

"What about you?"

She doesn't open her eyes. "I should remain here. You'll reach the ship faster without me."

"I'll stay with you," Xalin offers.

Kaladria opens her eyes, shaking her head. "No, you need to go with them. Having you there will solidify anything Zeru tells the Council. Corvar can't dismiss anything about your capture if you're standing right there."

"Kala, if you think—"

"I am in no condition to be traveling to the Satellite. Besides, the

196

Aklev'Zol will be watching for the *Resistance*, not a single Protector on Earth. If anyone gets attacked, it's going to be you guys. I'm not in shape to be fighting anyone. I need to lay low. I'll be safer away from Corvar and the Satellite."

"Kala—"

"I'll take her somewhere safe," I interject.

I glance at Kaladria, waiting for her to argue, perhaps tell me she doesn't need my protection. But she doesn't. She simply closes her eyes again, weariness clearly seeping into every feature.

"I'll stay, too," Noah adds.

Xalin sighs and Zeru frowns, troubled. "I don't like this. The three of you will be very vulnerable."

"Don't make me order you, Zeru," Kaladria sighs, forcing her eyes open. "I am your captain and I will make this an order if necessary. Go to the Satellite. We'll be fine."

Zeru sighs, too. "Where will we find you when we're done on the Satellite?"

"I'll take her to my mom's house," I decide. "It should be safe enough."

Nodding, Zeru reaches into a pocket, tossing me a small disc. "That's a comm link. Send me the coordinates and we'll come and get you once we're done on the Satellite."

I nod, pocketing the device.

Xalin looks at Kaladria sternly. "Be careful, all of you. We'll be back soon."

Kaladria nods slowly. "I know. Good luck."

JUST AS WE near the front door of my mother's house, Kaladria stumbles, tripping over her own feet as her knees buckle. I catch her arm. "Kaladria?"

"I'm…I'm fine…"

She doesn't look fine. She looks like she's going to collapse again. She's shivering and her face is an alarming shade of white. Even her eyes are unfocused, almost distant.

I scoop her up, a little surprised by her lack of protests. She huffs a soft sigh, sinking into my arms. Eyebrows knitting together with worry, I glance at Noah. "Give the door a knock for me."

Noah raps his knuckles against the door. Then, he glances back at the street, as if he expects trouble to come barreling in behind us at any given moment.

The door opens a crack before swinging wide to reveal a surprised Tyler. "Dude, you're back." He glances at Kaladria. "And she's unconscious again."

I sigh in exasperation. "Let me in. And go get my mom. I need her help."

As Tyler hurries down the hall, I step inside the house. I glance at Noah, who continues to watch the street. "I'll hang out here," he says without looking at me. "Keep an eye on things, just to be safe. You get her taken care of."

I nod gratefully. The last thing we need is the Aklev'Zol sneaking up on us.

Hurrying back inside the house, I carry Kaladria into the next room. I set her down on the couch, kneeling next to her. Her shoulder is drenched in blood, the skin still shredded from the Aklev'Zol Beast's claws. How long has it been this bad? I wonder if the shivering was due to this injury as much as the torture she's endured.

I shake my head. Self-sacrificing, as per usual, I guess.

Carefully, I examine her other arm. I unwrap the bandage to find a nasty cut in her forearm. Likely where they cut out and removed her tracker. Luckily, it looks like it's healing okay.

"Malcolm?"

I turn as she steps into the room. She's wearing her scrubs, as if she just finished a shift at work. Her gray hair is piled on top of her head, eyes full of concern.

I exhale. "Hi, Mom."

She looks at Kaladria, not asking any of the questions I'm sure she wants to. She kneels down, gently pulling Kaladria's sleeve away to examine her shoulder, going into doctor mode. "What happened?"

"Some sort of...beast bit her. It ripped her shoulder open." I sigh.

"She's also suffered a fair amount of trauma since then that may have reopened the wound."

My mother nods, focusing on the gash in Kaladria's arm. "And here?"

"She had a tracking chip in her arm but someone removed it. I'm guessing that's where it was."

Mom pauses, then nods again. "Get the first aid box. Quickly now."

I hurry across the room, opening the box up. "What do you need?"

"Needle, thread, antiseptic, bandages, the bottle of anesthesia."

I dig through the box, grabbing the things she's asked for in silence. As I hurry back to her side, my mother takes the antiseptic from me. She pours it over a cloth, pressing it to Kaladria's open shoulder.

Kaladria's eyes fly open and she cries out in surprise. Instinctively, I grab her hand, squeezing her fingers.

Mom glances at me briefly before looking back at Kaladria. "Try to hold still, sweetie. You need stitches."

Kaladria nods curtly. She closes her eyes, letting out her breath. Keeping a hold of my hand, she squeezes it back.

Mom takes the syringe and fills it with the antiseptic, pushing the needle into Kaladria's shoulder. Eyes closed more peacefully, Kaladria squeezes my hand again before relaxing.

Mom stitches her shoulder up quickly. I keep a hold of Kaladria's hand while she works, frowning as Kaladria shivers again. As Mom finishes, she gathers up the first aid things, placing them back in their proper place and shoving the box back under the table.

I look down at Kaladria as she sighs, fingers suddenly slack against mine. Releasing her hand, I stand. "Thanks, Mom."

"It's the least I could do." Mom's smile is kind. "Dean tells me you owe her your life."

I look back down at Kaladria. She turns on her side, a mess of white hair falling around her. "Yeah, I do," I say softly. "Several times over."

Mom studies my face. "You seem very close to her. Much closer than I was expecting, considering how long it's been since you met her."

I nod slowly. I'm not sure what to tell her, how to explain what it is Kaladria and I have come to share in the short time we've known each other. It feels insane that I could have met her a few days ago. But I know I would trust her with my life. And, it seems—since we're here—she trusts me with hers.

"She's very pretty," Mom comments.

I groan. "You're as bad as Tyler."

Mom winks, shrugging. "I'm just saying. You can't honestly tell me that you haven't noticed." As my face reddens, Mom gives me a suddenly pointed look, almost accusatory. "I saw you holding her hand."

I roll my eyes. "She was in pain. That's why I was holding her hand."

"And that's the only reason?"

"I don't know, Mom."

My feelings regarding Kaladria Astrana are so jumbled. She's intimidating and powerful and often seems more like a storm than an actual person. But I've seen so many other sides to her. I've seen her fear and her grief and sometimes even laughter. Her friendship has come to mean more to me than much else. I just don't know if there's anything else between us that might complicate an already very complicated situation.

Sensing my unease, Mom drops the subject. "So," she says slowly, "Do you want to explain to me where you've been? All Dean could tell me is you had to get her to her ship."

"I went to Saturn."

She watches me, listening intently.

"You would have loved it, Mom. It was beautiful. Saturn has these crazy storms so there was blue lightning everywhere. And the city is suspended in the lower atmosphere. It just sort of floats there. It was amazing."

"It sounds like you wish you could have stayed there."

"And leave you here all alone? No way."

Mom smiles. "What brought you home?"

"The Aklev'Zol." I glare into the floor. "They kidnapped Kaladria's uncle and stole the wormhole generator."

"Is that how she got hurt?"

I shake my head. "No, that happened here on Earth. We ran into some trouble, a trap set by the Aklev'Zol. They had this wolf...thing, some kind of machine beast." I swallow, thinking of how Kaladria teleported between me and the beast. "She got hurt protecting me from it."

Mom looks over at Kaladria, her face unreadable. I look too, watching as Kaladria shifts in her sleep.

"So, did you come straight here after Kaladria was injured?" Mom asks.

I shake my head. "Not exactly." I tell her about being captured by Callaghan, how he had tortured Kaladria. But I gloss over the details, not wanting to tell her about getting struck by lightning. The last thing she needs to hear about is my heart stopping, even if Kaladria got it started again. I finish by telling her about Noah helping me escape and about saving Xalin and Kaladria.

"So, the Aklev'Zol were behind all of it?" Mom pauses. "What about the wormhole generator?"

I grimace. "The Aklev'Zol still have it."

"Do they know how to use it?" Mom asks. "The way you described it...Well, it sounded complicated."

"It is. As far as I know, they haven't figured it out yet. Hopefully, they don't. If they open a wormhole..." I trail off, not wanting to finish that sentence.

"Dean told me about Emma Blake."

I pinch my eyes shut. Once again, guilt spreads through me at the memory of Emma Blake screaming as that horrible blackness spread across her skin.

"There's so much at stake," I say softly. "So many people will get infected like Emma was if we don't stop them."

Mom is silent for a long time, her face troubled. Then, she sighs. "You're going to leave again, aren't you?"

I let out my breath in a heavy *whoosh*. "I have to. The Aklev'Zol are here because of my wormhole generator. I have to make that right.

Besides, whatever is going on between Kaladria and I..." I sigh. "I can't just sit around and wait to hear if she gets infected or killed. I..."

"I know." Mom sighs, too. "I am proud of you. Just promise me that you'll be careful. Please."

"I promise."

48

KALADRIA ASTRANA

WHEN I WAKE, my shoulder aches and my limbs feel impossibly heavy but at least I can feel my lightning again. It courses through my body, sparking across my skin. A reminder that no one can take my power away from me, not forever.

I push my hair out of my face, raking it back. I look over at Malcolm, surprised to find him leaning against the couch, asleep on the floor next to me. His head rests against the couch and his jaw is slack, glasses askew on his face.

I press my lips together to suppress laughter. Sitting up slowly so I don't wake him, I slide off the couch silently. I lean down to take his glasses off, setting them on the table. Then, I stand, walking through the house.

In the next room, a woman sits at the table. Her gray hair is messily piled on top of her head and she wears glasses low on her nose. She doesn't look much like Malcolm but her eyes are that same strange nebula-like color.

She looks up when she sees me, surprise coloring her features. "Oh, you're awake."

"I'm sorry," I say, strangely embarrassed to have been noticed. "I didn't mean to bother you."

"Nonsense." She smiles warmly. "I'd intended to check on you soon anyway."

She waves me forward, patting the seat next to hers. I sit down, slipping my shirt down to show her my shoulder. "Mrs. Faraway—"

"Call me Lori, sweetie."

I smile. *Oh, I like her.* She's so warm. Even just talking to her for a moment has put me at ease, as if I belong here, as if this is as much my home as it is hers.

"Lori," I start again, "I just wanted to thank you. My shoulder has been in pretty bad shape for a few days now. I appreciate the help."

"It's not a problem." She stands, putting her glasses on top of her head as she examines my shoulder. "It looks good. You should heal nicely as long as you don't tear the stitches open."

I adjust my shirt. "I'll do my best. However, I do need to stop a galactic invasion and that means I'll be fighting quite a few battles. I can't promise I won't open up any injuries in a fight."

She gives me a sharp look. "You will, if you don't want that shoulder of yours to get infected," she says sternly. "I strongly recommend you avoid reckless heroics, if you don't want to end up with permanent damage in your arm."

I concede. "Yes, ma'am."

She sits down once more, her expression softening. "Malcolm tells me you received this injury protecting him."

I say nothing, biting the inside of my cheek. While she's right that my shoulder was hurt when I stepped in between Malcolm and the Zol Beast, I can't help but feel like it was rightly deserved. If I hadn't let him come into the house, he wouldn't have been captured by Callaghan along with the rest of us. He would never have been struck by my lightning.

"Kaladria, I want to thank you for looking out for him."

I grimace. "I wouldn't thank me yet. As best as I've tried to keep him safe, your son keeps having to be the one to protect *me*." It feels so absurd. I'm the Lightning Demon. I shouldn't need protection from anyone. And yet Malcolm has stood with me in more deadly situations than almost anyone. I shake my head. "I'm sorry for putting him in that kind of position."

Lori's eyes soften and she leans back in her chair. "Sweetie, you have nothing to apologize for. From the sound of things, you two have been protecting each other. There's nothing wrong with that."

I study her face. "Don't you worry about him?"

"Of course I do. The last thing I ever want is to see him get hurt. The idea of him facing off against those monsters is terrifying. But expressing those fears might make him question his chosen path and that's the last thing I want."

I can feel my eyebrows knit together.

"Malcolm has been certain of very little in his life. The design and invention of that wormhole generator was the only thing that drove him for a long time. But, meeting you, working to stop the Aklev'Zol, I've seen a side to my son that wasn't there before. He's driven, determined. Malcolm knows the path he needs to take now and I can't take that from him, not even to soothe my fears."

Now, I understand. Because I can see the worry, the concern in her eyes. Hidden behind a smile but there all the same. She's afraid but she won't ever let Malcolm see that. She doesn't want to stand in the way of his growth.

"Lori, I promise I will protect him. Regardless of where this path leads, I vow here and now that your son will be safe."

Sudden tears brim in her eyes. "Thank you, Kaladria."

I nod. "I…"

I trail off as Malcolm's two friends walk into the kitchen. In an instant, Lori's tears fade away and she smiles at the two of them. "Good morning, Dean, Tyler."

"Morning, Lori," Dean says. Then, he looks at me. "Hi, Kaladria."

I smile. He looks much calmer now than he had the last we'd met. The last time I'd seen the two of them, Dean had looked about ready to pass out. Not that I would have blamed him. At the time, he'd just witnessed me kill an Aklev'Zol in the middle of his apartment.

"I don't think we've actually met." Tyler winks. "I'm Tyler."

I merely raise an eyebrow.

"You can ignore him," Dean assures me. "I do."

As Tyler scowls, I chuckle. "Nice to meet you guys. You know when I'm not stabbing monsters in the chest." I frown. "Or fainting."

Lori shakes her head.

I stand smoothly, touching Lori's shoulder as I pass her. "I'll talk to all of you later. I need to check on a few things."

———

As I walk out onto the porch, Noah Hilliard glances back at me. "Miss Astrana."

I sit down on the floor next to him. "You can call me Kaladria." I prop my chin in my hand. "Has there been any trouble?"

Noah shakes his head, continuing to watch the street. "Nothing. It's quiet."

"Hopefully, it stays that way."

He nods, glancing at me. "How are you feeling?"

I sigh, looking down at my hands. The lightning beneath my skin sparks intermittently. "It may be some time before my lightning functions properly again."

"I'm sorry for what they did to you."

I look over, scrutinizing him. "I never got the chance to ask. Why did you help us?"

Noah continues to watch the street. "I already knew there was something wrong with that base. Callaghan was paying his men under the table, developing technology he intended to sell to the highest bidder. I was gathering information for my superiors."

"And then he captured a bunch of aliens?" I guess.

"I didn't know you were an alien at the time. But it was evident you did not deserve to be tortured like that."

"So, you saved Malcolm, rescued my squad, and even helped to free me." I exhale. "Thank you."

He nods curtly.

"You should go get some rest. I can watch for a while."

Noah glances over. He thinks about it for a moment, then nods. "Need a weapon?" he asks, offering his rifle.

I smile, shaking my head. "I'll be fine without it."

Noah leaves, stepping back into the house. As the door swings shut, I look down at my hands. I clench my fists, electricity sparking

FORGED IN STORMS AND SHADOWS

across my skin before fizzling out. I frown. Clearly, Callaghan's machine has left quite the impression on my body.

The door swings open again. "Kaladria?"

I glance back at Malcolm. He stands on the porch, his expression surprisingly pale, his eyes filled with...fear.

I stand. "Hey, what's wrong?"

Malcolm shakes his head. "It's nothing. I'm fine. Just a bad dream." He lets out his breath. "I want to ask you for a favor."

Stepping closer, I look up at him. "Of course. What do you need?"

"Can you..." He hesitates. "Can you teach me how to fight?"

I pause. Of all the things he could have asked of me, that was not what I was expecting. "You want to learn how to fight? Why?"

"You said it yourself. The Aklev'Zol still need me to use the wormhole generator. I'd like to be able to defend myself next time they attack."

"I can protect—"

"You shouldn't have to." As I stand there, stunned and silent, Malcolm sighs. "Will you please teach me?"

I study his face. He in turn watches me, stubborn and determined. Finally, I sigh. "I won't go easy on you," I warn him. "But, if you're serious about this, I'll teach you."

He nods. "Please."

"Very well. I'll teach you what I can."

4 9

MALCOLM FARAWAY

As KALADRIA SWINGS A PRACTICE STAFF, sweeping my legs out from under me, I fall on my back. I blink up at the sky, dazed.

Kaladria chuckles, holding out a hand. "Need a break?"

With a grunt, I force myself to stand. I pick up my staff. "Let's go again."

She nods, spinning her staff between her fingers. "Come on, then."

For a moment, I just stand there, thinking and studying. Since we're still waiting for Zeru and the others to complete their business on the Satellite, Kaladria has offered to go ahead and start teaching me. Which means a lot of sparring.

At first, I worried about her shoulder and the new stitches holding it together. But, in each of our sparring sessions, Kaladria hasn't used that arm at all, likely ensuring the stitches remain intact. I thought that might give me an edge, with her only using one arm to fight. But it hasn't. As it turns out, Kaladria is just as lethal fighting one-handed as she is with both hands.

She raises an eyebrow. "Well?"

Taking a breath, I launch forward. I swing the staff toward her but Kaladria blocks it easily, pushing me back. She swings her staff again, going for my legs. But I'm prepared this time. I dance away to avoid being knocked onto my back again.

"Good!"

She swings again, faster this time. It's as if, by avoiding her attack, I've passed some test and she's ready to provide the next one.

Swinging again and again, Kaladria pushes me further and further back. As my back hits a wall, I huff in frustration. *This is never going to get me anywhere,* I think. *She's too good.*

"Come on, Malcolm," Kaladria says quietly. "An enemy has you backed up against the wall. What do you do?"

I take a breath. *Think.* She's not invincible. And, while her movements are fast and powerful, there has to be a way to beat her.

As Kaladria swings her staff again, I duck and jump to the side. Then, I reach out to grab her staff. As I yank, the motion pulling her toward me, she staggers.

I swing my staff hard. It strikes her in the side, making her stumble again. As I strike again, she raises her staff. Her eyes sparking, she grins. "Let's see how long you can last."

With that, she pushes me back and swings again. I block her and, as she strikes again, a sort of dance begins as we exchange blows. Again and again, we move. Her blows are fast and sharp, leaving only just enough time to avoid getting smacked. I swing in return, doing my best to keep up with her speed. Until finally—

Kaladria drives her staff forward, hitting me in the stomach. With a grunt, I stumble back. By the time I've recovered, she's got the tip of her staff to my chest.

She smiles, lowering the staff. "That was pretty good. You're improving."

"We can keep going," I offer.

Kaladria shakes her head. "As admirable as your dedication is, rest is important for this kind of training…"

She trails off, turning to look at the house with narrowed eyes.

"Kaladria?"

She keeps watching the house. "Stay here."

Without another word, her lightning lights up across her skin and she teleports away, leaving me standing alone in the yard.

50

KALADRIA ASTRANA

I TELEPORT STRAIGHT into the kitchen, causing Lori to gasp in surprise, nearly dropping the plate in her hand. "Kaladria, what..."

Shaking my head, I face the opposite wall, turning toward the strange power I can still sense outside. I clench my fists, electricity sparking across my skin before going out again. *Come on. Not now.* Gritting my teeth, I force the lightning back on my fists.

"Stay behind me," I tell Lori. Then, I glance out of the room, hoping Malcolm has the sense to stay outside until I've dealt with this.

With Lori standing behind me, I watch as Lorkan Corvar phases through the kitchen wall. His hands aren't gloved for once, leaving his taloned hand completely visible. "You really are predictable," he tells me.

"If I'm so predictable, then why are you here, instead of stopping my squad from telling the Council everything?" I force a smirk. "I suspect they've already arrived. By now, the Council knows everything."

Corvar stiffens. "No one will believe them. The Aklev'Zol are little more than legend to the Council."

"Oh? And what if my uncle went with them? What if they also had the memory chip stolen from a certain robotic wolf?"

Corvar glares.

"I suggest you leave," I say in a low voice, straining to keep the electricity sparking on my fists from going out. "It's over."

"Not yet, it's not," he disagrees.

Corvar launches forward, talons outstretched. A snarl twists his expression with tight anger as he tries to grab me. I go low, ramming into him. He falls back. I swing a fist but my electricity disappears in my exhaustion. Corvar smirks as he launches his own attack.

"You're weak." He grabs me by the hair, slamming my head against a wall. As Lori screams my name, I try to wriggle free. Corvar holds me still, shoving my cheek against the wall. He grabs my arm, twisting it behind my back. I jerk but I can't break his grip.

"What's wrong?" Corvar taunts, voice menacingly low. "Are you truly useless without your lightning?"

I grit my teeth. "Why are you doing this, Corvar? You can't seriously want the Aklev'Zol to succeed."

"They will succeed, with or without me. But the longer I cooperate, the longer I extend my own life. This is a matter of survival."

"You're a coward. You *swore* an oath to protect humanity. You're giving that up for what? To live an extra day?"

His talons dig into my skull. "I don't answer to you." He waves a hand, using his telekinesis, to open the door behind him. A single Aklev'Zol slinks into the room. I struggle against Corvar's grip, cursing my inability to use lightning right now.

Lori pales, staggering back, as she stares up at the tall monster.

"Change her."

"No!" I writhe, trying to squirm my way free. Corvar holds my head firmly against the wall, talons drawing blood as he keeps me still.

Just before reaching Lori, the Aklev'Zol stops, suddenly frozen in the middle of the room. As it falls, I see the long dagger in the middle of its back.

Malcolm stands in the hallway, hand still outstretched, glaring at Corvar.

I blink. *Did he throw that knife?*

"You," Corvar snarls.

Malcolm's eyes meet mine before falling on Corvar once more. "Let her go."

"No one is going to be rescuing Kaladria Astrana this time."

I snarl. "Who said she needs to be?"

Elbowing Corvar in the stomach with my free arm, I break his grip. As he releases me, I whirl around. I lunge for him but he's suddenly translucent and I pass right through his Ghost Form. I turn around but he's already stepping back toward the door.

"See you on the Satellite," I say flatly.

He glares with hatred but says nothing more. He disappears out of the house, leaving the dead Aklev'Zol on Lori's kitchen floor.

MALCOLM FARAWAY

I HURRY to my mother's side, stepping over the dead Aklev'Zol. "You okay, Mom?" I ask in a quiet voice.

She nods but she's trembling. Mom stares at the monster on the floor, her face ghostly white. Not that I blame her in the slightest. I hug her, rubbing her arm. I look over at Kaladria as she steps toward the open door with a worried frown.

"Kaladria?"

She glances back. "I'm going to find Noah."

As she steps outside, lightning sparking against her skin once more, I glance at the stairs as Tyler and Dean come running down. Dean stops at the sight of the Aklev'Zol. "You guys good?"

I nod, silent.

"Dude, is it always like this?" Tyler asks wryly, looking at the Aklev'Zol.

"A lot of the time, yeah," I say slowly. "Kind of comes with the territory."

Mom looks up at me, studying my face with worry. "That's not the first time you've had to kill, is it?" she asks quietly.

I sigh, knowing she's not going to like my answer. "No, it's not."

Mom swallows, closing her eyes for a moment. "Oh, Malcolm..."

I say nothing. I'm not even sure what else I could tell her. That it's fine? Perhaps that would make her feel worse, knowing her son had begun to not fear the endless battles. Shaking my head, I look out the door, where Kaladria disappeared. She told me to stay outside, knowing Corvar was nearby.

You're still helpless, a little voice in the back of my head tells me. Clenching my fists, I push away that voice. No, not anymore.

"Malcolm…"

Mom snaps her mouth closed and we both look up as Kaladria returns with Noah. She has an arm around him and Noah stumbles next to her, his face gaunt.

"What happened?"

"Zol Beast," Kaladria explains. "Clearly, I underestimated the Aklev'Zol's desire to remove me from the equation. We should get a hold of Zeru. I think it's time for me to go."

I open my mouth but Kaladria is already hurrying into the next room to help Noah sit down. Sighing, Mom follows, leaving me standing in the kitchen with Dean and Tyler. I watch Kaladria. She keeps her arm around Noah as she walks. But, after attempting to use lightning after escaping Corvar, she looks exhausted. Her shoulders are slumped forward and her fingers tremble ever so slightly.

Tyler notices me watching her. "Dude, you totally like her."

I roll my eyes. "This really isn't the time to be trying to set me up, Tyler."

"Oh, come on, man. She's *hot.*"

I sigh wearily and Dean shakes his head. "Let it go, Ty." He frowns, scrutinizing me. "You okay, Mal?"

I nod, mechanically, looking down at the dead Aklev'Zol.

"Malcolm?"

I clear my throat. "Yeah, I'm fine." But, even as the words leave my mouth, I wonder when lying became so easy.

5 2

KALADRIA ASTRANA

ONCE NOAH HAS BEEN BANDAGED up, I slip out of the room in search of Malcolm. I find him sitting on the porch, hands folded in his lap, shoulders slumped forward slightly.

"Are you sure you should be out here alone?"

He doesn't look at me. "Probably not."

I sigh, sinking down next to him. "Something is bothering you."

His eyes slide over to meet mine. "What makes you say that?"

"I'd like to think that, after everything you and I have been through, I know you at least well enough to know when you're upset."

Malcolm takes off his glasses with a weary sigh. "Everyone around me keeps getting hurt. First, there was Emma. And then you were captured and tortured, treated like some kind of living battery." He shakes his head. "And now the Aklev'Zol almost kill my mother."

I swallow. I've taken for granted how well he's handling all of this. I forgot that he's not a soldier. Fighting monsters, protecting innocents, that's part of *my* normal life. But not his. I can see it on his face now, the uncertainty, the weariness. And I remember how he looked when he asked me to teach him how to fight. He's tired of watching people get hurt, tired of not doing anything about it.

"Your mother is safe. Largely thanks to you. And I'm okay, too. Thanks to you and the others, I'm free of Callaghan's machine."

"And your shoulder?"

"Malcolm, do you really think I wouldn't jump between an enemy and any of my squadmates? If someone was about to hurt Zeru or Azar or any of the others, I would jump in their path without a second thought. You're not helpless. You've already proven that. I stepped between you and the Zol Beast, just as I would have if it attacked anyone I care about. That's not a reflection on you but one on me."

He doesn't look at me but his face softens a little at least.

I reach over, touching his arm gently. "Nothing that's happened is on you."

He takes a deep breath. Then, as the haunted look leaves his face, he looks at me. "Thank you, Kaladria."

I smile faintly.

As we both fall silent, I look down at my hands. Lightning flickers weakly and I sigh, wondering how long it will take for my powers to get back to normal. *If they get back to normal,* I add with a touch of fear.

"So," I say finally, knowing we both need a change of subject and there are other things we need to discuss, "We never really talked about what happened before, in that military base."

"What do you mean?"

"Have you forgotten? Your heart stopped."

He glances at me. "I think that's actually bothering you a lot more than it's bothering me."

I say nothing, studying his face. He studies my face in turn, strangely calm now. I suppose he's right. What happened in that facility isn't bothering him at all. But it's all I can see when I close my eyes. I suspect my despair in that moment is a memory that will live with me for the rest of my life.

"You weren't breathing, Malcolm. I thought you'd died."

"Is that why you told me to stay outside when Corvar showed up?" he asks quietly.

I sigh, looking down. "I told you to stay outside because I didn't want to see you get hurt again," I say quietly. "Because when my lightning hit you, I have never felt so desperate. I never want to feel that way again."

"Kaladria, I'm fine," he says softly.

I look up, exhaling sharply as I meet his gaze. He's just a breath away now. When did he get so close? When did I?

"Malcolm—"

"Kaladria, someone is here to see you. Zeru, I think?"

Heat rises to my cheeks. I stand, slipping passed Lori as she sits with her son on the porch. He smiles wearily at her. Whatever just happened between us has passed. Still, I can't help but wonder if he felt it, too.

I shake my head. I have far too much to focus on to worry about that right now.

As I face Zeru, he gives me a pointed look, raising an eyebrow. "You'll be fine, huh?"

Not particularly feeling like a lecture, I meet his pointed look with one of my own. "I'm not hurt, am I?"

Zeru sighs.

"How did it go?"

"Slowly. The Council wants the data from the memory chip analyzed. And they want someone...uninvolved to investigate our claims about Corvar."

I shake my head. How the Council can brush off so many witnesses is beyond me. I really hate politics. "Figures."

"What now?"

I think carefully. "We go to the Satellite. I'll convince the Council to move more quickly. The more time the Aklev'Zol have, the worse I feel." I pause. "Corvar is becoming more and more Aklev'Zol. The Council will not be able to ignore our claims if we can force him to show himself."

"And if he won't?"

I shrug. "We'll worry about that when it happens."

Malcolm stands, stepping away from his mother. He sets back his shoulders, his expression like steel. "I'm coming with you."

I study his face. I've never seen this kind of determination in him before. His eyes are hard and his jaw is set stubbornly. I have no doubt that he would go to the end of the universe to see this fight through. Even if I wish he wouldn't.

"Malcolm..." I hesitate, lowering his voice. "I can't ask you to do that. You should take care of your family. You should be here."

He shakes his head. "I'm coming with you, Kaladria."

Looking at his face, I remember what Lori told me. *Malcolm knows the path he needs to take now.* As much as I hate it, I know I can't force him away from this path.

I sigh. "Alright. Get ready to go, then."

53

KALADRIA ASTRANA

I smooth down my dress as I step out of the elevator, trying to ignore how out of sorts I feel without my body armor. Going to the Satellite now feels like going to war and I'm stuck wearing this stupid dress.

Stepping out of the elevator, I take a moment to assess my squadmates. The four of them wear the black blazers required of the men who serve the Protectorate. I scowl at Zeru, who smiles knowingly at the annoyance written all over my face.

I really hate this dress.

Malcolm looks at me in surprise, appraising me with both eyebrows raised.

I can feel the heat rise to my cheeks. "The Council requires a certain level of formality when meeting with their Protectors."

"Old traditions," Xalin explains.

"Tradition or not," I say, fidgeting with my collar, "I feel silly."

"You don't look silly," Malcolm assures me, also looking a little fidgety. He looks away quickly, clearing his throat.

My blush deepens as Xalin glances between the two of us, clearly amused. I scowl, daring him to say anything. But he merely smiles, turning to look out the window.

I shake my head, taking a deep breath. *Focus, Kaladria.* Turning my attention to the task at hand, I look at Vale. "How are we doing?"

"I told the Council you wished to speak with them. They're expecting us as soon as we arrive." He pauses. "We're almost there now."

"Good." I exhale, trying to shake off the sick feeling in the pit of my stomach. But I can't seem to rid myself of the sense of foreboding warning me that war has arrived on our doorstep. "Let's get this over with."

I LEAD the way out of the airlock, taking a breath before striding through the Satellite. Holding my head high, I clasp my hands together in front of me so I don't end up striking one of the people staring at me.

As we walk through the Satellite, I keep my gaze fixed forward. *You have bigger things to worry about today,* I remind myself. *The Aklev'-Zol, Corvar, the missing wormhole generator...*

Still, my fists are clenched so tightly and I bite the inside of my cheek to distract myself. Not that it's working.

Suddenly, Malcolm is at my side, his clear human features drawing the attention of two Saturnian women. Now, instead of them watching me, they're staring at him, whispering behind their hands.

Malcolm brushes the back of his hand against mine before putting his hand in his pocket. The intent is clear. *I'm here.*

Swallowing, I blink back sudden tears for what he's given me. It's a chance to walk freely without every person here staring at me like I'm a monster. I doubt I'll ever be able to repay him for it.

I set back my shoulders, taking a breath. "Thank you," I whisper.

We step into the room where the Council waits, all five Councilors there. Corvar stands with them, gloved hands clasped behind his back, eyes barely narrowed.

I watch him carefully. If he was smart, he would have stayed far away. He knows I intend to reveal his true nature. If I succeed, he'll have nowhere to run. But I suppose Corvar is rather arrogant. He probably doesn't think I'm capable of revealing his secret.

I turn my attention away from Corvar, looking at the other Councilors as Councilor Verkire clears his throat. "Protectors, we understand there is more you would like to discuss?"

Here we go.

"Yes, Councilor Verkire." I step forward, my tightly clasped hands the only sign of the anxiety wrapping around my body. "First, I would like to ask if you were able to pull any information from the memory chip my squad brought you."

"We were not," Verkire replies. "It self-destructed before we could examine it."

I glance at Corvar but his face remains neutral. There is definitely something else at work here. Corvar is too at ease. He's clearly annoyed by my presence but still relaxed in his stance. Either he is foolishly proud or he's got something else up his sleeve.

"No matter," I say, as if the destruction of the Zol Beast's chip changes nothing. "And what of the claims regarding Councilor Verkire?"

"This Council sees no reason to distrust Councilor Corvar. He has served this Council faithfully for years."

I bite my tongue to keep from speaking out of turn. It wouldn't help my case and would likely lead to us being dismissed and the *Resistance* grounded. Still, it's insane to think they can ignore all the testimonies building up against Corvar.

"I urge you to reconsider your stance," I say slowly, choosing my words carefully. "What if I were to prove, right now, that Councilor Corvar has committed treason and allied himself with the ancient race known as the Aklev'Zol?"

"That would be quite a feat, especially since the Aklev'Zol are a story."

Behind me, someone snarls, indignant. Azar, most likely.

I hold up a hand to signal for his silence, even as anger heats the lightning in my veins. I resist asking them how *a story* killed my parents.

With a slow exhale, I release my suddenly clenched fists and face Corvar. "If you would be so kind to remove your gloves, Councilor?" I ask smoothly.

Corvar stiffens. But he quickly regains his composure, raising an eyebrow. "My gloves?" His smile is polite but his eyes are cold. "What would that prove, Captain Astrana?"

I hold out a hand. "If you have nothing to hide, why not remove them?"

As Corvar works his jaw, I smile. *Your move.* He has nothing to hide behind now. The other Councilors are watching him too carefully, their expressions troubled by his sudden refusal to prove his innocence.

As he looks at me, I can see it in his eyes. He knows he's been beaten. "Very well, Captain." He yanks on the fingers of his glove. "You win."

Corvar pulls the gloves off, tossing them to the ground. At the sight of the black taloned fingers that clearly don't belong to the Jovian Councilor, a deep silence fills the room. The rest of the Councilors stare at him.

"Lorkan..."

He ignores them, hatred-filled eyes focused entirely on me. His face twists into a livid snarl. "You think you've won, don't you?"

Hardly, I think. *One sleeper agent outed isn't much of a victory at this point.*

I meet his gaze. "You have betrayed everything you once stood for, Lorkan Corvar. The proof is in your hand. You are becoming one of them. With every day, you become less Jovian and more Aklev'Zol."

He steps forward. "You're going to regret this," he promises. Face still contorted in anger, his eyes harden into something dangerous.

I tense. Something is very wrong. I can feel it deep in my bones. Every fiber of my being is warning me that something bad is about to happen.

Corvar reaches a hand into his pocket. As he fingers something there, I stiffen. I know that electricity. I lunge forward but not before he pulls out the small, round object. As he spins its parts, I reach for my power.

Realizing the same thing I have, Malcolm launches into action. "Get back!"

But it's too late. Corvar tosses the device into the middle of the room. And then everything explodes.

54

KALADRIA ASTRANA

CORVAR HAS WEAPONIZED the wormhole generator.

As the orb hits the ground, I am fully prepared to fight whatever comes through that portal. What I am not prepared for is the explosion of dark matter that follows. Black energy explodes through the air as the wormhole forms, slamming through the open portal. The blast throws me back, knocking me into the wall.

I blink, rolling onto my side. I grimace as I push myself to my feet, looking across the room at the sudden chaos. Following the explosive dark matter I saw in the air moments ago are the black forms of the Aklev'Zol. They dart through the wormhole, snatching up anyone too close, tossing them back through the open portal like rag dolls. As the noise draws other Protectors into the room, they launch forward to fight the sudden onslaught.

My team is nowhere in sight, likely thrown back by that black energy. And with so many Protectors in here now, it's impossible to tell where anyone ended up.

I search the room in desperation, choking on my relief at the sight of Xalin. He's across the room, standing slowly as he leans against the wall.

I dart forward. But an Aklev'Zol yanks me back, talons curling around my arm. Without a moment's hesitation, I blast the monster with lightning. I grit my teeth against the all too familiar exhaustion that still threatens to overtake me every time I use my power.

Shaking my head, I rush to Xalin's side. "Uncle!"

He grabs my arms. "Are you alright?"

"I'm fine." I look across the chaos. If Xalin is fine, perhaps there's still hope for everyone else. "Get to the *Resistance*. If you see Zeru or anyone else, tell them to go there. We have to get off the Satellite."

"What about you?"

My eyes flit across the room in a panic. He was the closest to the explosion. Did he get pulled in when the Aklev'Zol came through?

"I have to find Malcolm," I say, still searching.

Xalin hesitates.

"Uncle, *please*." I push him toward the door. "Go."

Xalin grips my shoulders tightly, face intense. *Don't you dare do anything stupid.* Then, he exhales. "Hurry, Kaladria."

As he turns away, I start across the room, continuously scanning the chaos. A Protector darts in front of me, fiery fists slamming into the body of an Aklev'Zol, only to cry out as the Aklev'Zol shoves a talon into his side, the black taint already spreading across his skin.

I swallow, forcing myself to keep going. *You can't save everyone,* I remind myself as I race across the room, pushing past Protectors and Aklev'Zol alike.

An Aklev'Zol grabs my wrist, wrenching me forward. I use the momentum of his attack to launch forward, swinging a lightning-covered fist. The Aklev'Zol sneers as the lightning vanishes just before I hit him. The Aklev'Zol starts to drag me forward but I drop my weight, forcing him to release me. Then, I unsheathe the knife tucked at my ankle, shoving it into the monster's chest as I stand.

I start running again. *Come on, come on.* He's still here somewhere. He has to be.

As I near the wormhole, I stop, panting heavily. I can't find him. Not anywhere in this room. I clench my fists. This can't be...

I stop. An Aklev'Zol grips Malcolm by the shirt, just outside the wormhole. He glares back at the monster, as impossibly brave as ever.

Gritting my teeth, I launch forward. I force myself to teleport across the room. But I can't hold onto the lightning long enough. Just paces away from Malcolm and the Aklev'Zol, I stagger out of the electricity.

The Aklev'Zol prepares to throw Malcolm through the portal and I scream. "No!"

Malcolm grips the dagger Zeru gave him and stabs the Aklev'Zol in the chest. As it drops him, I race forward, helping Malcolm to his feet.

"We have to run."

Malcolm nods. Then, holding the dagger tightly, Malcolm grabs my hand. Together, we take off running in the direction of the docks.

We sprint through the Satellite, dodging various battles as we run. I hold onto Malcolm's hand tightly, head spinning. The whole situation just unraveled in mere minutes. We hadn't had time to stop it, even if we'd tried.

As we near the docking port where the *Resistance* waits, the ship thrums to life. It hovers just a few feet from the dock. Xalin must have made it. Hopefully, so did everyone else.

An Aklev'Zol lunges for us and I throw a bout of lightning, grimacing as the sparks dissipate. Malcolm throws his dagger. As it strikes the Aklev'Zol, he snatches it up, tugging me toward the *Resistance*. Exhaling, I run toward the ship as the airlock opens to reveal Zeru.

I let go of Malcolm's hand, pushing him toward the ship. I follow as he runs ahead. He jumps as he reaches the edge of the dock. Zeru reaches out and catches his hand, pulling him onto the ship.

Looking back at the docks, I stop. Sudden uncertainty grips me. What about the others? Hassuun and Vale and Azar? Did they make it? Or are they still somewhere on this mess of a battlefield?

I turn as a crash resounds across the Satellite. I look at one of the many turrets lining the exterior of the Satellite as it fires on one of the docked ships. The Aklev'Zol must have taken control of the Protectorate's weapon systems.

"Kala!"

I look back at the *Resistance*, praying I'm not about to leave anyone behind. Then, I take a deep breath, staring at the airlock. If my lightning fails me now, I'll be in more than a little trouble.

Leaping forward, I jump through electricity, fingers catching the side of the airlock. But, right then, one of the Satellite's turrets hits the side of the ship. The blast reverberates against the *Resistance*'s shields, sending tremors through the ship.

I lose my grip on the airlock. My fingers slide right off the edge of the ship. Malcolm lunges forward, catching hold of my wrist. I grit my teeth as my arm is nearly pulled out of its socket, my legs dangling uselessly beneath me.

Malcolm starts to pull me up, grabbing my arm with his other hand. Next to him, Zeru throws out a hand, likely throwing his power across the docks to keep the Aklev'Zol from getting too close.

Sudden, sharp pain tears into my ankle. I bite down a cry as talons dig into my ankle, yanking me back. Malcolm loses his grip on all but my fingers.

"Kaladria!"

I look down, silently cursing the black talons digging into my ankle, the snarled expression twisting Corvar's face. It would seem that, if he's not going to survive today, he'd rather I didn't either.

I'm not going to make it.

As that realization sinks in, I lift my head, looking back up at Malcolm. His expression is surprisingly aggressive as he grips my fingers more tightly. "Don't you dare let go."

I search his face, the intensity in his gaze, the grim determination there. I think of him stepping next to me earlier to avert the stares away from me, of his fingers brushing past mine. That kindness is something I will cherish for as long as I live.

My throat is suddenly raw. I look at Zeru, who continuously sends Aklev'Zol back with blasts of his power. He barely stops to look at me.

I swallow. "Save them."

Zeru's face contorts with pain but I know he understands.

I look back at Malcolm. "I'm sorry."

"Kala—"

I slip my fingers free of his.

55

MALCOLM FARAWAY

"KALADRIA!"

As she slips her fingers free of mine, I lunge forward. But it's too late. I nearly tumble out of the *Resistance* after her. Zeru grabs my arm, yanking me back into the airlock. We watch helplessly as she falls back onto the Satellite, immediately lost to the war raging across the space station.

I can't breathe. The walls are closing in around me as she vanishes from sight. I grip the edge of the airlock tightly. *You stupid, helpless human,* the voice in my head whispers. *You did nothing.* I shove it away, forcing myself to look away from the chaos ravaging the Satellite.

"Zeru, we can't leave her!"

He rips his fingers through his hair in indecision. Another bout of thunder attacks the side of the ship and his shoulders slump in defeat. "We have to." He grits his teeth. "She's gone."

I drop my knees. *Kaladria...*

Zeru slams a hand against the wall, shutting the airlock. He hits the button for the intercom. "Get us out of here, Vale," he says hoarsely.

I pinch my eyes shut, resisting the urge to open the airlock again. Zeru is right, even if we both wish he wasn't. She's gone, likely already struck down by the black matter the Aklev'Zol so readily provide to their victims. Jumping out there would only result in my own death. We can't go back. We have an army of monsters to destroy. No matter how much I want to, I can't jump off this ship, I can't die a meaningless death.

Zeru claps a hand on my shoulder wearily. Then, he walks off, no doubt headed up to the bridge to update the others.

I stay where I am, opening my eyes to glare at the closed airlock. I replay it in my head a thousand times, searching for something I could have done differently, some way I could have saved her.

I should have held on more tightly. I should have pulled her up faster. I'd promised myself I'd be strong enough to protect her the way she protected me. But I failed.

Exhaling shakily, I clench my fists tightly. "I'm sorry, Kaladria."

56

KALADRIA ASTRANA

My back strikes the ground hard. I roll across the docks before catching myself with my hands.

Corvar rolls past me, pulling himself up with those taloned hands. There's very little left of the Jovian Councilor. Just those pale eyes and a patch of skin on his face. Everything else has already been lost to the Aklev'Zol's darkness.

I drag myself up. I look back at the *Resistance* as it takes off, disappearing into the blackness of space. A few shots from the Satellite's turrets reverberates off its shielding but it does little to slow the *Resistance* down.

I watch the ship disappear. "Keep fighting, boys," I whisper.

Turning my attention back to Corvar, I reach behind my back and yank out my spear. I fall into a low crouch, watching him warily.

Corvar pushes off talons, launching at me with hatred in his eyes. I roll to the side, swinging my staff around and knocking him off his feet. Corvar merely lunges again. I bring up my spear, but not fast enough to completely block his attack. One hand makes it past my spear. Long talons slice through my body, from hip to shoulder, ripping through my stitches.

I cry out, kicking him with both feet. As he stumbles back, I force myself to stand. I press a hand over my shoulder. My body aches with dizzying pain and I know I don't have the strength to pull out the lightning right now. Skill is all I have left.

A sudden scream works its way out of Corvar's throat. I freeze, turning my head away as the sound is silenced, the remaining bit of him lost to the Aklev'Zol he has become. When I look back, there's nothing left of the Jovian Councilor.

I clench my fists around my spear. As the monster lunges, I raise my weapon. The motion causes a spasm of pain, particularly in my shoulder, and my breath hitches.

The Aklev'Zol-Corvar grips my spear, leaning in to yank me closer. "What will you do now that your friends have abandoned you?" the monster mocks.

I rip my spear from his grasp with a growl. He staggers and I shove the spear's end straight through his chest. The Aklev'Zol-Corvar freezes, mouth tumbling open in a surprised gape.

"That's for taking me away from my family," I whisper.

I yank out the spear, watching him fall. Then, turning my attention to the battle being waged across the Satellite, I grimace. The Aklev'Zol soldiers drag Protectors, Council Advisors, and regular citizens away. Some are unconscious but others are screaming, jerking their limbs as they struggle. All of them have been infected, the black mark spreading across their bodies.

I clench my fists. *Come on, Kaladria,* I think. *The Lightning Demon can't go out like that.*

Groaning with the effort, I leap forward. I teleport over and over again. I refuse to let them see me long enough to grab me. Constant motion is my only defense now.

I stop as I near the wormhole. Falling into a crouch, I peer into the room from around the corner. Aklev'Zol prowl through the room, digging their talons into their captives before pushing them through the wormhole.

I clench my teeth, letting out my breath in a tight hiss. If I stay on the Satellite, they'll infect me and turn me into one of their soldiers. And, while I'm not confident I can avoid that fate forever, I want to avoid it for as long as possible.

I look past the Aklev'Zol at the open wormhole. I must be insane.

Taking a breath, I vault through electricity. I stagger on the other side of the wormhole. As I stand, I find myself on a barren world of black obsidian. The ground is laced with deep crevices that open to reveal an intense blackness similar to the Aklev'Zol's own skin, the swirling dark matter beckoning with tendrils of power.

It must be one of the Aklev'Zol's worlds. Maybe even the first one.

At the sound of voices, I rush forward, diving behind a building's corner before I can be spotted. I peer around the corner, gritting my teeth.

An Aklev'Zol soldier grabs the wormhole generator and the wormhole closes itself back up.

Yanking my fingers through my hair, I lean back against the wall. *You can do this,* I think. *You have to.* I have no choice now. This is the path I've chosen and I'll have to stick to it. Whether I like it or not.

My hands are shaking as this new reality sinks in. I'm going to die here on this forsaken planet. But, until my end comes, I know there's one final mission for the captain of the *Resistance*. I'm going to spend every last moment bringing the Aklev'Zol down from inside.

5 7

MALCOLM FARAWAY

"Malcolm!"

I stop, shoulders slumping. I can't look at her as my mother wraps her arms around me. "Malcolm," she says softly, noticing my desolate expression. She touches my cheek. "What happened? Where's Kaladria?"

My knees wobble. I can barely suppress the image of Kaladria tumbling back onto the Satellite. "The Aklev'Zol opened a wormhole in the middle of the Satellite. Kaladria didn't…" I choke on the words. "She didn't make it."

Mom stops, silently putting her hand over her mouth. Tears prick her eyes. Then, she hugs me tightly. "I am so sorry, Malcolm."

I pinch my eyes shut. I can't stop seeing it. I can't stop trying to work my way around the truth. Even having seen her fall, my mind can't stop trying to find some way to reject what my heart knows. Even Kaladria Astrana couldn't have survived on the Satellite with so many enemies. She's gone and she's not coming back.

I shake my head. *Focus, Malcolm. Focus on what comes next.*

"The others have returned to their prospective planets," I say quietly. "The Aklev'Zol will be coming for everyone now. After today, most of the Protectors will have been changed into the Aklev'Zol. Those that escaped left to warn their people, to prepare for war."

33

Separating was Vale's idea. As the only one coherent enough to form a plan, he'd suggested we split up. It's our best chance to keep the Aklev'Zol from completely obliterating life in our system. Hassuun returned to Mars, Azar to Venus, Vale to Neptune, Xalin to Saturn. Zeru took the *Resistance* with him to Jupiter.

I swallow the lump in my throat, thinking of the lot of them. On hearing what happened, Hassuun was yelling, Azar had punched Zeru for telling them to go without her, Vale wouldn't look at anyone. Xalin would have run to the airlock if we hadn't stopped him.

"And Earth?"

I force myself to look at her. I take a deep breath, forcing away the memories still threatening to overtake me. I have to do something. I can't keep sitting around, thinking myself into endless circles. I need to focus on something else, on anything else.

"They'll be coming for us, too." I heave a sigh. "Where's Noah?"

Mom nods back to the house.

I squeeze her hand before stepping up the porch and into the house. I find Noah sitting on the couch, eyes closed.

"Noah."

He opens his eyes, grimacing as he stands. "You're back."

"The Aklev'Zol have control of the Satellite," I say grimly. "They'll be coming for Earth very soon. We need to get every army on Earth to work together and mobilize."

Noah exhales slowly, shaking his head. "Alright. I might have some contacts that can help with that. Let me see what I can do." He walks out of the room, pulling out a phone.

I slump down on the couch, head bowed. I hold Zeru's dagger in my hand, squeezing the hilt tightly. There's so much that needs to be done. Somehow, I have to convince Earth that an evil alien race is going to attack any time now and convince all of them to work together. Humanity has never been good at that but the last thing we can afford right now is to fight amongst ourselves.

"Dang it, Kaladria," I whisper. "How am I supposed to do this without you?"

PART II

THE SHADOW QUEEN

58

KALADRIA ASTRANA

I DART across the planet's cool surface, barely paying attention to the empty sky as I teleport in and out of lightning. I appear in front of a couple of Aklev'Zol soldiers, just long enough for them to notice me. As they lunge, I dart through the lightning again, teleporting away. I wait for them to give chase before teleporting a short distance away once more.

I let them chase me, moving across the dark planet at an aggressive speed. I don't stop until I've gathered a decent amount of Aklev'Zol soldiers. They move in to surround me.

I stop, forcing a smirk. "Well, well, are you all here to play?"

"Astrana, you're supposed to be dead," one of the Aklev'Zol growls with narrowed eyes.

"You're a fool for coming here," another adds.

I keep my smirk in place. Over the last year, I've learned the best way to catch them off guard is with a carefree attitude. My smirks might be false but they've served me well so far.

The Aklev'Zol press forward from all sides. I glance at the one who last spoke. "Perhaps," I concede. "But not as much of a fool as you for thinking you could stop me after so long."

"Grab her!"

The Aklev'Zol all charge and I let out a furious cry. I push the lightning out of my body, surrounding myself with it. Electricity sparks around me, spreading out in a wild storm. It hits the Aklev'Zol with a heavy enough blast to kill them all. Or, at least most of them.

I straighten, watching the one furthest from the blast stagger to the side, talons over his stomach. "You can't defeat us," the monster says weakly. "There are more every day."

"Maybe not." I lunge, driving my spear through his chest. "But I will never stop trying."

Wordlessly, I jerk my spear free as the Aklev'Zol falls dead. I stand, looking across the empty sky. There are only a few dim stars blinking back at me.

I shiver, strapping my spear to my back. I make my way across the planet in search of more soldiers. That Aklev'Zol soldier wasn't lying. There are more every day, limitless numbers for me to take down. I know I'm only seeing a very small portion of their army too, just those that remain on this planet, unlike the hundreds of thousands attacking Earth and the Protectorate worlds.

As I walk, my thoughts drift to all those worlds, to everything I left behind. I'm fairly certain none of our worlds have fallen yet but I know most of them are close. I can only hope my friends remain amongst the living.

My heart aches at the reminder of those I left behind. I miss all of them. I miss the way Xalin's eyebrows knit together when he's worried I'm going to do something stupid. Zeru's grin when he's teasing me about being the *Lightning Demon*. The comfortable silences with Vale and Hassuun's easy smile. I even miss Azar's relentless jokes, which is something I didn't think I'd ever miss. And Malcolm…

I swallow hard. Then, I stop, pressing my body against the nearest wall. I peer around, at the two Aklev'Zol soldiers guarding the door. Their eyes alert, they stand tall, talons at the ready.

Clenching my fists tightly, I let the electricity spark across my skin. Then, wordlessly, I rush them with the lightning ready in my hands.

5 9

MALCOLM FARAWAY

I HURRY DOWN THE STREET, a rifle slung over one shoulder. I slip past people in the street, doing my best to ignore their stares. They're looking at me the same way people used to look at *her* and I am definitely not comfortable with the comparison. I'm not as good as she was. I know I never will be.

Shaking my head, I shoulder past the soldiers running down the street. I look up at the barricade as I approach. The huge wall is made of various stones, sheets of metal, as well as smaller pieces of rubble. A bit rudimentary but it's served us well so far.

Noah, with his back against the huge wall, shouts orders to soldiers before turning to face the barricade, firing a few shots before turning to face me. "Malcolm."

I glance at the barricade as it quakes, shaking the air around us. Then, it explodes, a good portion of the barricade flying apart, a gaping hole breaking the wall. Ducking down, I swing my rifle around as an Aklev'Zol soldier slinks through the wall. I fire quickly. As the Aklev'Zol falls, I lower my weapon.

"Fix the barricade!"

As human soldiers rush forward to repair the damage, I lunge forward. Noah is right behind me as I dart for the opening. Noah and I fire at the incoming Aklev'Zol, giving the soldiers the time they need to repair the barricade. A wolfish Zol Beast dives through the hole in the wall. I swing the butt of my rifle at its head. The beast stumbles and I fire my weapon in between its armor plating, sending it sprawling back.

Once the soldiers finish putting the barrier back together, Noah and I step back, exchanging a look. I sling my rifle over my back. "They're awfully determined," I remark.

Noah nods. He glances back at the barricade as it shakes again. It holds in place this time but the wall still quivers.

"They're losing patience. This street has held for a long time. They find that maddening."

Good, I think. *Their desperation makes them foolish. That'll keep us alive.*

I pause at the sound of a high-pitched ringing. I pull out the comm device, answering the call. Immediately, I'm greeted by a small hologram of a Jovian soldier crouching down behind a broken wall.

"Zeru."

Face weary, armor stained with a smear of black blood, Zeru holds out a hand to steady himself. An explosion sounds through the air around him, striking the hologram. "Malcolm, how are you holding up?"

I can't decide if he's asking about me personally or about Earth in general. And, as is typical in these conversations, I treat it as the latter. "We're hanging in there." I glance back, listening to the deep boom against the barricade. "How's Jupiter?"

Zeru grimaces. "We've lost the city and have retreated to the outskirts. We've got a plan in place but we're still working out logistics."

"What about everyone else? Is anyone faring better?"

"They're all alive but the situation is…" Zeru stops, looking away at something I can't see. "I have to go." A sharp cry fills the air on his end of the comm link. "Get down!" Zeru yells suddenly.

"Zeru!"

The comm link breaks off and the hologram disappears. I take a breath, pocketing the device. All I can do is hope and pray that Zeru makes it out of whatever situation just drew him away.

I glance up at the sky, then back at the barricade, frowning as another blast hits it. "We sure could use a little lightning right now, Kaladria," I mutter.

More than anything, I wish she could give it. I wish she was here to help in this fight. She *should* be here.

I shake my head. I have to keep moving. If there's anything I've learned in the last year, it's that standing still always brings back the memories I am not ready to relive.

60

KALADRIA ASTRANA

I CAN HONESTLY SAY I never expected to last this long.

With the entire planet turned into the dark matter that makes up the Aklev'Zol and the infection they wield, the very ground flattened by darkness, there are very few places for me to hide. The only sort of sanctuary I've found is on rooftops.

Standing on one such rooftop, I cross my arms, studying the empty horizon. As usual, the sky is black. Even the days here are overshadowed by the darkness, as if even the sky knows this is a place of evil, a place not even sunlight dares cross.

That's depressing. I shake my head. Being here for so long is starting to really mess with my head. But, in all fairness, this isn't the kind of place I can thrive in. It's a miracle I'm even breathing.

When I arrived on their world, I promised myself I would wreak havoc on their forces until the day I died. I didn't think it would take this long. But the days turned into weeks and weeks into months and the Aklev'Zol have yet to catch me.

I turn around, crossing the roof. Then, using my spear to pry open a crate, I throw the lid off, revealing a score of food and supplies. I snatch up a piece of fruit, shaking my head. When I first came here, I never would have imagined the Aklev'Zol would eat something so ordinary. But I suppose even monsters need to eat sometimes.

After I'm done, I hit the supplies with a blast of lightning that destroys the crate. I consider hiding the evidence of my crime but then think better of it. Let the General see what I've done, let him know that the Lightning Demon is laying waste to his soldiers and his supplies. He'll never catch me. My actions are too erratic. A crate destroyed here, a few Aklev'Zol killed there. There's no scheme for him to discover, no grand master plan to stop.

I'm about to vault off the roof but stop when I sense the strange dark matter of the Aklev'Zol that has always felt so similar to the electricity I'm so accustomed to sensing.

Crouched down, I peer over the edge of the rooftop, listening to the Aklev'Zol soldiers below.

"Earth is certainly putting up more resistance than we'd expected."

"Faraway's doing, no doubt," the other soldier spits, contempt and disgust tainting his words. "Our forces report he's been rallying humanity together since the fall of the Satellite."

Pride swells within me. I knew he could do it. If anyone could bring together the entire human race, it would be the compassionate human who once followed the Lightning Demon into a war none of us were prepared for.

"The General isn't worried about him," the first Aklev'Zol says. "The other planets are already falling. It won't be long before Earth follows."

I close my fingers into tight fists. *Not if I have anything to say about it.* I launch myself through lightning, teleporting between the two Aklev'Zol. I swing up a leg, smashing my heel against one of their chins. As he staggers, I grab the other by the jaw, lightning sparking on my fingertips. Snarling, he shoves me back. As both stumble, I pull out my spear.

"Astrana."

"The General wants to see you."

I narrow my eyes. "He'll have to catch me first."

I stab my spear forward, impaling one of the Aklev'Zol. I blast the other with lightning. As they both fall dead, I step away. I ready myself to dart through the lightning and out of sight but then I stop, stiffening.

Whirling around, I freeze at the sight of a single figure darting across the barren land. A human woman rushes across the planet's surface, barely turning to fire a gun at the Aklev'Zol chasing her.

My knees nearly buckle. A *human*. She must have been thrown through the wormhole to be infected and escaped. And if she hasn't been infected yet, if she's still free of their taint...

I'm not alone.

Racing forward, I teleport through lightning and strike the Aklev'Zol closest to her. When it falls, I strike another. The human woman fires a rifle, shooting one of the remaining Aklev'Zol.

I barely pause to nod to her, shoving my spear through another enemy.

The Aklev'Zol fall, one by one, until only one Aklev'Zol soldier remains. I turn to launch through the lightning but this Aklev'Zol is faster than his companions. The human woman barely turns before the Aklev'Zol stabs a talon through her gut.

My breath stops and I freeze. Then, I launch forward with a roar. I throw a blast of lightning at the monster. It crumples in a smoking heap, releasing the human woman.

Racing forward, I slide as I fall to my knees next to her. I curse at the sight of the blackness spreading from her stomach.

"It's happening, isn't it?" She grimaces. "I'm going to turn."

Somehow, I manage to keep my voice even. "Stay with me. The calmer you remain, the slower the infection's progress."

"I don't know who you are or what you're doing here but I need to ask you for a favor." She sets her jaw. "You have to kill me."

"What?"

She exhales shakily against the fear spreading through her limbs. "Even if I thought I could control my fear and slow its progress, I'll never be able to stop it. Eventually, I'll turn into one of them, no matter how brave I try to be. Unless you kill me before I can turn into one of their monsters."

"I can't do that."

"If you don't, you'll be forced to kill me in the form of an Aklev'-Zol. How is that any better?"

I grit my teeth, pinching my eyes shut.

"Just promise me you'll find a way to stop this madness. Someone has to stop them."

I open my eyes. Her expression is so hopeful, like she truly believes someone can still turn the tide in this war. I can't steal that from her. I place a hand on her shoulder. "I promise."

"Good." She lets out her breath in a tight hiss. "You better do it now. Before it's too late."

My hands clench into tight fists.

"It's okay." She takes a deep breath. "Just make it count."

I yank out my spear, driving it through her stomach quickly. With a sharp gasp, she falls back, the blackness no longer spreading from her chest.

61

MALCOLM FARAWAY

I DART THROUGH FORGOTTEN STREETS, dagger in hand, a sniper rifle strapped to my back. I barely look behind me at the Aklev'Zol giving chase.

I slow my pace at another soldier, who fires at the Aklev'Zol chasing me. "Faraway," he greets. I nod and together we fire at the Aklev'Zol. I drop to a knee, firing at the Aklev'Zol as they charge. He fights at my side, firing a pistol. We keep firing until none are left. As the last one falls dead, I straighten. "Thanks."

The soldier lowers his weapon. He opens his mouth, perhaps to say something else, but not before the sound of a Zol Beast's snarling cuts him off. We both whirl. I grimace at the sight of several Aklev'Zol soldiers with the Zol Beast.

This isn't over yet.

I launch forward, firing at the Aklev'Zol. They lunge, a few of them moving past me to attack the other soldier. I swing up the butt of my gun, sending one staggering back. I drive my dagger through its chest before moving on to the next one.

Before long, they're all dead, leaving us standing in an empty street littered with corpses. Hopefully, that's all for the moment. I turn around to thank the soldier but pale at the sight of the black mark tainting his skin. It's moving quickly.

His breathing labored, panic fills his eyes. It occurs to me that he might have not been a soldier for long. Likely, he was a civilian before the war.

"Soldier, calm yourself. You—"

I realize what he intends to do as he pulls out a knife. I leap forward but it's too late. With one swift movement, he aims to cut off the infection, slicing through his arm. But the moment the knife cuts through his flesh, black matter explodes.

The blast throws me back. I land on my back, several feet away. When I look up, all that's left of him is a mangled black corpse.

I rip a hand through my hair, swearing under my breath. That's the danger of the Aklev'Zol's infection. Not only is there a high chance of joining their ranks but, if you try to remove it, the infection removes you from the picture.

I step toward the body but stop at the sight of more Aklev'Zol soldiers. *They're getting persistent.* Cursing myself for leaving the body, I turn and run. I have to get to back to the barricade. The open city is simply full of too many Aklev'Zol.

As I run, I clench my fists. *I'll make this right,* I think. *Somehow, I'll fix this.*

I TRUDGE up to my mother's house, clenching my fists. My footsteps feel heavy as I think of the man who, in his terror, tried to cut out the Aklev'Zol's infection.

It hasn't gotten any easier. I've become no stranger to death in the last year. I've killed more than I can count, witnessed more deaths than I can ever forget. But seeing it again, witnessing someone else being killed in this stupid war, it hits me as hard as it did the first time.

"Malcolm!"

As my mother slams into me, I wrap my arms around her. Panic swells through me and my fingers itch for my weapon. She sounds so scared.

I grip her arms. "Mom? Are you alright?"

She won't look at me. "I heard there was trouble in the city outskirts. I was terrified."

Of course.

I sigh. "I'm fine, Mom." I rub her arms comfortingly. "There was a little bit of trouble but nothing I couldn't handle."

"I know it's been a year and I should be used to all this but..." She exhales. "I can't lose you."

"You won't."

The words feel like a lie. I don't know that they're true. With the entire system falling to the Aklev'Zol, it seems impossible for us to pull through this. Earth has become a bomb and it's explosion is inevitable.

Mom takes a deep breath, taking a seat on the porch.

I rub the back of my neck, taking the seat next to her. After what just happened, she's not going to like what I have to say next. "I'm going to have to leave for a couple of days. I need to check on the other bases still standing. Unity is really our only defense at this point."

She tries to hide her fear with a weary smile. "Look at you, my little soldier."

"Not really." I blush. "Kaladria was the soldier."

We both fall silent. I look down. I can't believe I just said her name. I've barely spoken of her to anyone, not since the Satellite fell. I haven't wanted to. The words just slipped out before I could stop them.

"It's been a year," I say softly.

"She'd be so proud of you, of everything you've accomplished. Without your efforts, the Aklev'Zol would have conquered us in a day."

"That seems like an exaggeration." I shake my head, unable to ignore the memory of that bright blue lightning. "If she were here, the Aklev'Zol would be running away like dogs with their tails between their legs."

"Now, who's exaggerating?"

I shrug. "You should have seen her, Mom. The way she wielded her power..." I shake my head. "She was amazing. A little frightening sometimes but still amazing."

Again, that lightning flashes in my mind.

I sigh. She was the fiercest creature I'd ever laid eyes on, the bravest person I've ever had the pleasure of knowing. The universe will never be the same without her. Even if we manage to survive the Aklev'Zol, the system will always feel empty, almost broken.

As Mom leans her head against my shoulder, I tilt my head up to look at the sky. I watch the stormy sky, putting an arm around her.

I hope you're proud, I think. *I hope you're watching us fighting back and I hope you're rooting for us, wherever you are.*

As if in answer, lightning flashes across the sky.

6 2

KALADRIA ASTRANA

I stay with the human woman's body for as long as I dare.

Sitting on the cold ground next to her, surrounded by the bodies of slain Aklev'Zol, I wish I could bury her or at the very least burn the body. They might not be able to infect her anymore but I doubt that will keep the Aklev'Zol from finding some other way to desecrate her body.

I shake my head, leaning over her to brush her eyes closed. "I'll find a way," I say softly. "I'll save the system."

I don't know how I'll ever manage it. After a year trapped on this world, escape feels further off than it ever has before. And yet...

For this brave woman who was willing to die before being turned into one of their soldiers, I'll find a way. I have to.

I stand, readying myself to dart through the lightning, but then I stop. A familiar burst of energy sparks through the air somewhere behind me.

Whirling around, I face the building behind me. A spike of electricity fills the air again, stealing my breath. Shock rolls through me. I know of only one thing that thrums with that much raw power.

"The wormhole generator," I breathe.

I step toward the building. Since the beginning of their invasion, the Aklev'Zol have created much larger versions of Malcolm's device.

But each has been too heavily guarded on both ends for me to even consider jumping through. It's been months since there was any indication of the original device being used.

I exhale shakily. *This is it.* My one and only chance out of this world, back to my own system and everyone I love. My last chance to save the system I once protected.

Glancing down at the human woman's body, I take a deep breath. "Guess it's time for me to keep my promise."

I lunge through lightning, heading for that building. All the while my focus remains on the power the wormhole generator is giving off.

As I near the building, I blast the two Aklev'Zol soldiers standing guard outside. Without stopping, I teleport across the threshold, heading inside the building.

Time to go home.

I slink inside the building with my spear in one hand, lightning in the other. I move quickly and quietly through the winding hallway, feeling for the wormhole generator's electricity. All the while, my heart feels like it's about to beat right out of my chest. I'd accepted my fate a long time ago and now there's a chance that I don't have to. There's a chance to see my friends and family again, to fight by their sides.

Exhaling, I slow my pace. I step into a large room, which is mostly empty. Except for the wormhole generator hovering in the center of the room, spinning quickly.

I take a few steps toward it but stop when I see where it is the wormhole leads. Just on the other side of the portal is my old home on Saturn. It looks trashed but those huge windows are easily recognizable. Lightning sparks behind them, bright blue power striking across the sky. I can see the sofa flipped on its side, a dozen cracked pictures on the floor around it.

I take a step back. This is too easy. Too much like a message, a warning even. And then I can sense it, the dark matter that I have become all too familiar with.

"You're either incredibly stupid or incredibly reckless."

Fists clenched, I spin around to face the Aklev'Zol now blocking my exit. She's thin, standing with one taloned hand at her waist. Her skull-like features and soulless eyes are much like most of the soldiers I fight but there's something different about her. Something in the cruelty of her sharp smile, something about the familiarity of her voice.

I grip my spear. "How about a little bit of both?"

She bares her teeth in what I think is supposed to be a smile. "You don't remember me, do you?"

"Frankly, I just don't care. You're all monsters."

She smirks. "Oh? Even if I'm the *monster* that used to be that simpering little idiot? What was her name again? Emma Blake?"

I grit my teeth. *Of course.* That's why she seems so familiar. This was the girl who once begged for me to save her before she was turned into a taunting monster. She loves to mock now. She has since the moment they made her into an Aklev'Zol.

"I suppose it was too much to hope that you would have died in the last year," I growl.

"Oh, you are hateful, aren't you?"

I glare. *You have no idea,* I think, remembering how Emma's death had haunted Malcolm. It had torn at him the same way my parents' deaths tear at me. I will always hate the monster that stole from him what was stolen from me.

The Aklev'Zol-Emma steps closer. "The General wants to see you."

"If you think I'm going to just let you lead me to him, you are sorely mistaken," I say, lightning sparking across my fists.

She grins. Then, she launches forward, talons extended. I dance out of reach, watching as she stumbles past me, hitting the wall.

I smirk.

The Aklev'Zol-Emma whirls around. I lunge for her, swinging my spear. She raises a hand, yanking it out of my hands. As she tosses it aside, it clatters to the floor several feet away. "What now?" she purrs.

I glare, electricity sparking across my arms. Then, I swing a lightning covered fist. She stumbles back as I strike her jaw. She rubs it as the lightning dissipates. Then, she launches an attack of her own, eyes full of rage. The Aklev'Zol-Emma swings her talons. I stumble, ducking back to avoid her claws. She swings again, launching forward wrathfully. As she presses me back against the wall, I duck under her talons. Then, I ram into her stomach, pushing her back.

Lunging forward, I reach for her throat. She dodges my attack at the last second, taking a step back before launching forward again. I try to sidestep her but then she drives her talons straight through my side.

Gasping, I release my lightning. She hooks her claws under my skin, digging them into my side. I cry out, trying to jerk free of her grasp.

No. No, no, no. I can't be changed yet. I—

"Shh, shh. Stop struggling." She grabs my throat, using her other hand to twist the talons in my side. I try to get free but she digs even deeper. "Don't worry, Captain. I'm not going to change you. Not yet. The General has other plans for you."

As she jerks her talons out, sending blue blood splattering across the floor, I drop to my knees. Sharp pain shoots through my side. I press my fingers over the wound, gritting my teeth.

The Aklev'Zol-Emma lifts her bloodied hand, signaling to several Aklev'Zol soldiers. They step into the room, crowding around me. As they drag me to my feet, I look wistfully back at the wormhole generator. I should have taken my chance when I still had it.

"Come on, little demon," the Aklev'Zol-Emma mocks. "It's time to go."

As she leads the way further into the building, I glare into the Aklev'Zol-Emma's back. She strides ahead, long taloned fingers at her side. My blood still drops from the ends of her talons, leaving a trail of dark blue droplets on the floor. Her entire body sways as she moves, weirdly feminine. Almost as if she sees herself as a seductress instead of a hideous monster.

She stops as we enter a room. The General stands against the wall, watching me with a cruel smile. He looks the same as I remember him. His body is covered in thousands of scars and he looks at me as if I am still nothing but a child screaming for her parents.

"It's been a long time, Captain Astrana."

I force my expression into something icy. "General."

He studies my face. "I understand you've been disrupting my operations."

I smirk. "And yet it still took you a year to catch me."

His expression darkens but he masks it with a shrug. "I was curious. A single Protector living on our home world with little more than a single spear? How much damage could you really do?" He chuckles. "I thought you had some master plan to bring us down but you don't, do you? You're just poking the beast to buy your friends a little extra time."

"I don't need to buy them time. From what I hear, they're doing well enough without me."

"Oh, they're surviving. But just barely. Soon enough, there will be nothing left of your precious Protectorate."

My heart stutters with fear and I push it away. I force a smirk back into place. "Is that so?" I ask smoothly. "And what about Earth?" As his expression darkens, I continue, "It must be so frustrating to be thwarted by a human you once claimed couldn't protect anyone."

The General lunges forward, inhumanly fast. He grabs my throat, dragging me forward. "He is *nothing*." When I smirk, he shoves me back. He takes a breath, forcibly collecting himself. "Now, I believe there is someone here who will want to see you before we decide on your fate."

My heart hammers in my chest and I swallow the sudden lump in my throat. *Please don't let it be anyone I love. Please let them all be safe, away from this horrible purgatory of a world.*

63

KALADRIA ASTRANA

THE GENERAL and his soldiers lead me through a set of long, winding hallways. Their talons are tight around my arms, dragging me forward. Every step sends sharp pain through my stomach, blood still dripping down my side.

I try to work through where they're taking me, wondering who could possibly want to see me. Again, I pray it's not a friend. The General knows about everyone I love. I can only hope he's been too busy to worry about capturing them.

Then, as we stop, so does my heart.

There's a single pane of glass before me, opening up to an almost empty room. A cot has been pushed against one wall, where a man sits. He rakes his fingers through his hair anxiously. His skin is pale, covered in grime and gore, but I still see the tint of blue that marks him as Saturnian. But his pale eyes are so weary, devoid of the normally bright blue that sets apart our people.

But seeing a fellow Saturnian isn't what stops me. It's the obvious resemblance to the man who raised me, the sharp features that I know as well as I know my own face.

He looks like Xalin. I can see my uncle in the set of his jaw, the way he clenches and unclenches his hands as he stares at a blank wall. I can see the tight lines in his expression, tensed with worry. Of course, he doesn't have the hardness in his eyes Xalin does when he's upset. There's a kindness there that I have only witnessed in one person.

Tears streak down my cheeks and I jerk against my captors' grips. I stare through the glass, memorizing every feature. "Dad," I whisper.

"Ah, so you *do* recognize him." The General bares his teeth in a feral smile. "I'd wondered if you would."

I grind my teeth. The General lied. He let me believe both of my parents were dead, when in fact my father was here the whole time. I'd foolishly assumed they killed him when they killed Mom. But he's been here this whole time, their prisoner for the last fourteen years.

The General leads me into the room, his soldiers keeping a firm hold on my arms. I stumble along, my heart pounding its way out of my chest. I can barely feel the gash in my side, numbed by the realization that I'm not alone anymore.

My father looks up, eyebrows knitting together as his eyes meet mine. *He doesn't recognize me.* My heart sinks. My own father is looking at me like I'm a stranger.

"Astrana," the General greets.

As my father's eyes flit over to the General, his demeanor changes from confused to suspicious. "What are you playing at?"

"Don't tell me you don't recognize her," the General scoffs, mockingly.

I jerk against the talons holding me in place. "As if you expected anything different," I snarl.

Smirking, the General signals for his soldiers to drop me. But, rather than just letting me go, they toss me forward. I stagger. Instinctively, my father reaches out a hand to steady me. His fingers curl around my arm, catching me.

With that small touch, I'm trembling. *He's alive.* He's right here, with me. Fourteen years of nightmares, of shoved away fears and grief, and suddenly he's back.

He reaches another hand over, grasping my hand to steady its shaking.

My throat is suddenly raw. He doesn't know who I am. But he's

FORGED IN STORMS AND SHADOWS

still showing so much compassion to someone he believes to be a stranger. He hasn't changed at all.

His gaze remains on the General. "What have you done to her?" my father demands, still not understanding.

"You still haven't figured it out?" The General laughs. "Come now, Herren. You're supposed to be brilliant."

Dad's eyes are narrowed as he glances between me and the General.

"I've done very little to her, compared to you." The General smirks. "After all, you're the one who abandoned her."

My father looks at me again. He takes in my stricken face, my tear-stained cheeks. As our eyes meet, I know he sees it. The bold sharpness the Astrana bloodline is known for. Sudden recognition lights up in his eyes.

"Dad—"

He pulls me close, protectively holding me to his side. He glares at the General, an unfamiliar sort of rage flashing in his eyes.

"Yes, I see you've caught up now," the General sneers. "I'll give you two a few minutes."

"How kind," Dad says dryly as the Aklev'Zol file out of the room. When they're gone, he yanks me into a tight hug. "Kaladria."

I wrap my arms around him tightly, trying to still the shaking in my fingertips. "Hi, Dad," I whisper.

Dropping my head to his chest, I slide my hands around his waist, half expecting him to vanish. Head spinning, body shaking with tears, I pinch my eyes shut.

It's too much. After fourteen years of being certain I'd never see him again, after this last year of complete isolation, it feels too impossible to have him back.

He exhales, holding me tightly. "It's alright, Kaladria," he whispers. "I'm here. I'm here."

I close my eyes, taking a shaky breath. I have to calm down. The last thing I want is the General coming back in here to see me in so many broken pieces.

Looking down at my feet, I focus on my breathing, taking slow breaths until the tears stop. I wipe the back of my hand across my cheeks. Then, I look up.

Dad touches my cheek. "Look at you," he says softly. "You're so grown up."

That nearly sets me off again. I close my eyes, biting the inside of my cheek to keep from sobbing. "I'm sorry." My voice cracks. "I've just been alone for so long and to see you again…"

He hugs me again. "Oh, Baby Girl, I am so sorry."

"I thought you were dead."

He leans back, tucking my hair behind my ear. "The General decided to keep me alive for information, gathering intel for their impending invasion." He exhales, looking down. "Your mother was not so lucky."

"I know." I shiver at the memory. "I saw."

Pain flits across his face. "You never should have seen that."

I look down. "It's really not the worst thing I've witnessed."

He frowns, worry etched into his features as he thinks on my words and what they must mean. "How did you end up here?"

"That's sort of a long story."

"I think we have the time."

I sink down on the cot and he sits next to me. "Xalin took me in. He left the Protectorate so he could raise me. He took a job as an Advisor to the Council."

My father barks a laugh. "My big brother? A Council *Advisor*? What has the world come to?"

I smile. "I know he used to be pretty reckless but he's changed. He's been pretty solemn in the years since you and Mom disappeared. He got very serious when he took me in. Sometimes, I wonder if he worries too much." I swallow, wondering for the millionth time what he must have done when he learned what happened to me. "Raising me really aged him, I think."

"Well, you *were* a bit of a handful."

I roll my eyes.

"What brought you here? Were you on the Satellite when they invaded?" When I raise my eyebrows at him, he sighs. "The General ensures I remain informed on the progress of their invasion," he explains. "To taunt me, I imagine. I feared the worst for you."

"Well, it certainly hasn't been easy." I lean my head back. "And yes, I was on the Satellite when they invaded. I was meeting with the Council when the Aklev'Zol invaded."

His brow furrows.

"I'm a captain in the Protectorate." I frown. "Or, I was. I have strong suspicions that the Protectorate no longer exists."

"You're a soldier," he says, grimacing.

"Don't give me that look. I know you would have preferred I became a scientist or a teacher or—"

"I would have preferred you became anything but a soldier."

"Dad," I say very quietly, "I was very good at it. And, believe it or not, I was happy. There was something about wielding the lightning in the service of others, using it to fight for what's right...It made me feel *alive*."

He sighs, shooting me a sideways glance. "You sound like Xalin."

I can't help it. I grin.

He studies my face. "Tell me about your life as a Protector."

And so I do. I tell him about joining the Protectorate and the other captains' annoyance with my rule-breaking streak. I tell him about becoming the captain of the *Resistance* and my missions as its leader.

"What's your squad like?"

Even as my heart aches, I smile. "They're family."

As his eyes soften with a smile of his own, I tell him about them. I tell him about Vale and the easy quiet he brings to the *Resistance*. I tell him about Zeru and his incessant teasing. But I also tell him of his loyalty, that willingness to fight by my side when the odds were far from our favor. As I tell him about Azar and Hassuun, I can't help but laugh.

"Reckless, wild, troublemakers," I say. "Azar has always enjoyed antagonizing me. He has since the day he joined my squad. He's felt my lightning more than most. And Hassuun usually goes along with his wild plans, unless it includes antagonizing me. Hassuun knows better."

Dad chuckles. "It sounds like you're a tight knit group."

"We are, or we were. I could always count on them. And we only got closer as the Aklev'Zol prepared to invade."

Sighing, I lean my head back, wondering what they must have thought that day. Azar and Hassuun were probably furious. It's hard to say with Vale. He was always so reserved but I'd witnessed his loyalty more than once. And Zeru...

I hope he doesn't blame himself for the order I gave him, the order he chose to accept. Leave me behind to save everyone else. But, as much as I want to believe he'd understand that this choice was mine and mine alone, I know he'll blame himself.

Thinking of those last few moments, I find myself thinking of Malcolm. How he'd gripped my fingers as I dangled over the edge of the airlock. *Don't you dare let go...*

I shake my head. "There was one more," I say softly. "Before the invasion, we sort of ended up with another member of our team, even if he wasn't a Protector."

"Oh?"

"A human." I smile. "Despite being thrown into quite the disaster without much of an idea as to what was happening, I really consider him a member of my squad. He saved my life more than once."

"How did you come to meet a human?"

"When this was all starting, the Council sent me to Earth to investigate some kind of power fluctuation," I explain. "As it turned out, this human had invented the device giving off the energy the Council sensed. It was a wormhole generator."

"A *human* created the wormhole generator the Aklev'Zol used to invade?"

I nod. "He's very smart."

"I'll say." Dad leans back, eyes lighting up as the wheels of his mind begin to turn. "A machine of that scale would require some very advanced tech."

"It gives off some pretty powerful electricity," I agree.

We both fall silent, my father assuredly still considering the powerful tech required for Malcolm's wormhole generator. I lean my head back, staring up at the ceiling. Sitting in the silence, I'm reminded of my promise. *Just promise me you'll find a way to stop this madness.* The fulfillment of that promise keeps getting further and further away. And yet I know I have to find some way to do it.

"Well," Dad finally sighs, "I'm still not sure about my little girl being a soldier. But I am proud of you. You've found a worthy calling, Baby Girl." He smiles softly. "I'm sure your mother would be proud, too."

Swallowing the lump in my throat, I reach over and squeeze his hand. "Thanks, Dad."

64

KALADRIA ASTRANA

THE GENERAL DOESN'T GIVE us as much time as I would like. After giving us just long enough to explain myself to my father, he returns with two soldiers.

I narrow my eyes, watching them carefully with my head held high. The General has already seen my fear too often. I will not give him the satisfaction of seeing it again.

Wordlessly, the General nods to his soldiers. My father tenses as one of the Aklev'Zol steps closer to him. I glare at the General when his other soldier grabs my arm.

"What?" I scoff. "No mockery? No monologues?"

Ignoring my poor attempt at sarcasm, the General steps forward, holding a small syringe. It's immediately clear my father knows what it is. Eyes widening in horror, he lunges forward. But he's quickly dragged back by the Aklev'Zol soldier standing next to him.

"Kaladria!" my father cries, struggling once more.

As my eyes falls on the General's cruel, mocking gaze, I lift my head, chin jut out stubbornly. But that pride very quickly vanishes as the General administers whatever is in the syringe.

Pain shoots through my skull, the pressure of it squeezing every thought from my head. I stagger back as the Aklev'Zol previously gripping my arm releases me. I grit my teeth, fingers over my face. I slip to the floor, closing my eyes against my sudden unsteadiness.

"Kaladria!"

I'm fine, I want to tell him. But I can't make out the words past the dizzying pain.

I'm vaguely aware of the General crouching down in front of me. "You know more about Earth's defenses than most, don't you, Captain Astrana?" he asks. "How do we defeat them?"

"You can't expect me to just tell you," I choke out.

I can barely make out the General's smile. "We've administered a very powerful truth serum," he says. "The more you fight it, the more it will hurt."

I clench my fists. I am the Captain of the *Resistance,* a respected Protector of Earth and the entire system. If he thinks he can force me to betray them with a little pain, he's going to be disappointed.

Still, I take several gasping breaths, trying to blink away the fuzziness in the room. He's right. It's getting worse. With every second that I hold my tongue, the more the pain presses against my skull, ripping through every thought.

The General leans forward. "Let's try again. Mr. Faraway has created quite the name for himself as Earth's defender. I suspect that is largely due to the influence of a certain lightning-wielding protector. But there must be something we can use to our advantage. Any thoughts?"

I spit.

"The sooner you talk, the sooner your pain can end."

I force out a huff of weak laughter. He's forgotten. He allowed Callaghan to rip my lightning from me, harvesting its power against my will. The pain of his truth serum is nothing to that. Even if it was, this pain could not break me. Not when I have already witnessed more pain than any drug, any poison can ever supply. Witnessing my mother's death, listening to Emma Blake scream for help before the infection overtook her, seeing Malcolm get hit by my lightning, being forced to kill that human woman so that she wouldn't become an Aklev'Zol. Those are the pains that break me.

The General doesn't understand that. He thinks my body is what makes me weak. But he doesn't know there are so many things so much worse than a broken body.

"You can torture me all you like," I growl, "Break my body, rip away my power, steal away everything that I once was. I will welcome death long before I surrender."

The General says nothing, silently waiting for me to give in to the pain he believes I will yield to. But I am the Lightning Demon. And a demon does not yield to pain. She only delivers it.

I grit my teeth as I lift my head once more. *You better be ready for the storm that's coming*, I think. *Because, if you're not, it will lead you to a destruction so great that not even your precious power will be able to save you from it.*

HAVING FADED away after hours of writhing on the floor, retching from the force of that horrible pain, I wake on the cot. Dad leans over me, his face pale, worry drawing his eyebrows together. "Kaladria?"

I put a hand over my eyes. Exhaling, I sort through the foggy memories I have, of writhing and retching, screaming even as I refused to give in to the truth serum's demands. "What happened?" I croak.

"You fainted."

I peek at him. "I didn't tell him anything, did I?"

"No." He shakes his head, studying my face. His eyes, while still haunted, are almost awe-struck. "You have remarkable self-control."

I smile weakly. "I'm a soldier, remember? I've been trained to withstand all kinds of torture." I turn my head, studying his worn expression. "Have they ever used that on you?"

"Many, many times."

I shake my head. The pain he's endured...In one swift moment, he had been stolen from his entire family and has spent every moment since then being physically and psychologically tortured, likely knowing that someday the General would come for Xalin and I.

I force myself into a sitting position. "We need to get out of here."

Dad raises his eyebrows, still seated on the cot. "There is no way out, Baby Girl."

My heart aches at the sight of the defeat in his face. After all this time, after everything he's witnessed, he has no fight left to give.

I rake my fingers through my hair. He might not have the willpower to fight back but we can't afford to just sit here. The General won't give up so easily. He'll be back, possibly to inflict other forms of torture. We have to get out of here before that happens.

"Everyone I love is out there fighting for their lives. I won't sit here and wait for the Aklev'Zol to kill them."

He sighs. "Alright. Let's think this through." The gears of his mind begin to turn, eyes brightening as he uses the tool he was always so skilled with. Where the lightning has been my greatest strength, my father was always the smartest out of all of us. He nods to the door. "The door is too thick to force open. The only other way out that I can think of would be by teleporting out of the room. But something about this place blocks the lightning. We can't..."

He trails off as I start to laugh. "What?" he asks.

I grin. "I think I can fix that."

Looking across the room, my eyes fall on one of the panels on the wall, just behind the cot. As Dad stands, I push the cot out of the way and kneel at the panel. Then, I take a breath. I never saw exactly what Malcolm did. I'll just have to rely on my own tinkering abilities and hope they're enough to match his.

"What are you doing?"

Fingers digging into the panel, I yank it off the wall. "The General is as foolish as he is arrogant," I say, inspecting the mess of wires. "This is not the first time he's tried to contain my lightning."

I finger the wires, tracing them through the open panel. Then, I yank one free. Instantly, I can feel it. Electricity dances across my skin, the bright blue light raging through my body. Dad staggers, that same lightning sparking across his skin.

Thanks, Malcolm.

Dad stares at his hand, flexing his fingers. "How did you do that?

"No time to explain. We need to go." I hold out my hand. "What do you say you and I steal a wormhole generator?"

6 5

KALADRIA ASTRANA

HAND IN HAND, my father and I dart in and out of the electricity in the air. We race through the building, teleporting through long winding hallways. I blast the Aklev'Zol soldiers that dare to get in our way. I refuse to let anyone stop us. No one is going to torture him ever again. And no one is going to keep me from returning to my friends and family.

I focus my attention on the thrumming of the wormhole generator, following its electricity through the building. But we stop as my father's lightning disappears, the sparks dissipating in the air around him.

Dad grimaces. "Sorry, Kala. I've been too long without the lightning."

"It's alright." I don't mention that my lightning could give out at any moment. That, since Callaghan's torture machine, using the lightning strains me, too. "Let's run instead."

He nods. We take off again, darting through the long corridor in the direction of the wormhole generator.

I stop as we enter the room, both of us panting hard. Across the room, the wormhole generator is hovering, still opened to our home on Saturn.

I pull my father forward. He stumbles next to me, utterly exhausted. "Almost done," I say softly, tugging him toward the portal.

Pausing, I glance back as the General strides into the room. His face is satisfyingly shocked as he stops, frozen by the sight of us.

I grin, stepping toward the wormhole. "You're too late."

Grabbing my father's hand, I pull him through the wormhole. Then, I turn around, smirking at the General as he lunges. I snatch the wormhole generator out of the air. Just before his talons breach it, the portal closes.

I exhale, straightening. Then, I swallow as I look around. *I'm home.*

I move through the room in a daze. I stare at the familiar walls, the cracked window on the other side of the room. Pausing, I stoop down to pick up a broken picture frame, depicting Xalin and I laughing together.

Tears brim in my eyes. *Oh, Uncle.*

"You okay, Baby Girl?"

I take a breath, blinking away my tears. "I didn't think I was ever going to see this place again."

Dad smiles sadly. "Me, neither."

"I…"

Trailing off, I turn to the window. Down the glass-encased pathway just outside the house stands a soldier. Two Aklev'Zol press closer and the young man swings a sword, gripping a long spear in his other hand.

I don't bother warning Dad of my plans before leaping forward. I teleport through the window and hit both the Aklev'Zol with a blast of electricity that sends them both crumpling to the road. Then, I glance back as Dad teleports through the window, grimacing. He runs across the pathway to catch up.

I turn to the soldier, who is staring at me like he's seeing a ghost. "C-captain Astrana," he stammers, "We thought…we thought you were dead."

I smile, holding out a hand. "Not yet." I pull him to his feet, glancing across the ruined city. "What's the situation? I'm a little out of the loop."

The soldier salutes. "Yes, Captain. The Aklev'Zol have invaded every planet. Due to our small numbers, we're spread pretty thin. Most of the Protectors were killed on the Satellite but those that survived lead the civilians in the war effort. Here on Saturn, your uncle leads the troops."

My knees wobble. *He's alive.*

I exhale. "Where can I find him?"

The soldier points across the street. "The city center's remains."

I nod, looking in the direction of the city. Then, setting back my shoulders, I look back down at the young man. "I need your spear, Soldier."

"It's yours, Captain."

I take the spear from the soldier, twirling it between my fingers. I glance at Dad, sighing at his troubled expression. But I don't remind him what I said about living for the fight. I'm sure he can see it in my eyes, the fire sparking inside of me.

"Come on," I say to him. "I think it's long past time for a family reunion."

He nods and I stride through the long pathway in the direction of the city with my father close to my side. We make our way through glass-encased streets, moving as quickly as we can while watching for Aklev'Zol.

"What exactly did you do to earn that kind of awe?" Dad asks.

My eyes slide over to his, cheeks flushing in embarrassment. "I developed a bit of a reputation for ignoring orders from my higher ups. My captain at the time wanted me off his ship but the Council could see that I was too skilled to kick me out of the Protectorate. They gave me the *Resistance* instead. Eighteen years old and a captain. It earned me a lot of renown."

He shakes his head.

"My success on the *Resistance* only made it worse. I became known for being ruthless against our enemies. People started to call me by a nickname behind my back. *The Lightning Demon.*" I sigh. "I used to hate it."

Dad scrutinizes my face. "You don't anymore?"

"We're in the middle of a war." I shrug. "It seems like a pretty good time to have a demon on our side."

I slow my pace, looking across the long road before us. Several paces ahead, in the middle of the glass-encased street, there are several Aklev'Zol fighting a single Saturnian soldier. He swings a blade above his head, lightning sparking around him.

"Uncle," I breathe.

Without waiting to see if my father will follow, I lunge forward. Lightning sparks around me as I stab one of the Aklev'Zol with my spear.

"Kaladria!"

I duck under an Aklev'Zol's swiping talons. Next to me, Xalin blasts one of the soldiers. He spins around to stab another with his blade. The Aklev'Zol press closer, refusing to back down. It works for me. I refuse to back down, too.

I close my eyes, releasing the lightning inside my body as I transform into my Lightning Form. Opening my eyes, I raise a hand. My fingers, now no more than sparking strands of lightning, are extended toward the glass ceiling. I blast the ceiling with every ounce of lightning inside of me. The glass shatters, raining down from the sky. I drop to the ground, slipping out of my Lightning Form.

Lightning sparks around us, the storm raging across the street without the glass encasing to protect it. The Aklev'Zol fall in smoking heaps, powerless against the storm.

I push myself to my feet, throwing my arms around Xalin. "Uncle."

He holds me tightly, his hand against the back of my head as he holds me to his chest. "Kala," he whispers huskily. "I thought I lost you."

Closing my eyes, I hold onto him tightly. "I missed you," I whisper.

Xalin leans back, searching for any life-threatening injuries. When he finds none, his expression softens. "What happened, Kala?"

"It doesn't matter." I shake my head. "Right now, there's someone you need to see."

I lead him back to where my father stands, leaning against a building in exhaustion. When Xalin sees him, he stops, staring at his brother in disbelief. Then, dropping his sword, Xalin rushes forward to embrace him.

Leaning back, I watch them with tears brimming in my eyes. It's been fourteen years since they saw each other, since they had even the faintest hope of speaking again.

Dad leans back, clasping Xalin's arms as he speaks. Xalin smiles.

I strap my spear to my back, glancing across the city. Then, I sigh, wishing we had more time for reunions. But I know the General will come quickly. He'll know what I'll do first now that I'm home. We have to hurry. I run over to join Dad and Xalin.

"You used the Lightning Form," Dad says, shooting me an accusatory look.

"It's not the first time. The Aklev'Zol are quite familiar with my second form."

Dad shakes his head.

"I wouldn't worry about it too much, Herren," Xalin says. "Kaladria has proven to be quite adept at controlling her Lightning Form."

As Dad sighs again, I face Xalin. "What happened to everyone else?" Panic swells within me and I struggle to push it back. "Did everyone make it off the Satellite?"

Xalin nods. "They're all alive, although their conditions vary from moment to moment. Everyone returned to their respective planets, trying to hold the Aklev'Zol back as much as possible."

"And Malcolm?"

Xalin smiles knowingly, making a blush spread across my cheeks. "Doing well," he assures me. "From what I've heard, he's giving them the hardest time. Humanity is putting up more of a fight than the Aklev'Zol expected."

Even if I knew Malcolm has been giving the Aklev'Zol a hard time, it's still nice to hear that he's okay from someone I trusted rather than one of the General's men. I exhale. "What about my ship?"

"Zeru has it on Jupiter." Xalin sighs. "From what I understand, Jupiter is ready to fall. The Aklev'Zol already control the city. There aren't many survivors left."

I nod. "Then, that's where we start."

66

MALCOLM FARAWAY

AFTER A YEAR of training and planning and battling, it seems like I should be able to sleep when there's finally a moment of quiet. But, even though I know sleep is necessary if I'm to keep fighting, I still find myself avoiding it until I nearly collapse from exhaustion.

Laying back on the bed, I stare at the ceiling. I feel restless. I can't stop trying to come up with a way to survive this fight. But the Aklev'Zol have already taken most of the system. The Protectorate worlds have all but fallen and Earth is close behind them. All that survives of humanity are the small safe zones pocketed across the world. Even as we do our best to stay in contact with one another, there's too much distance from each safe zone for us to do more than just survive the waves of enemies.

What would you do, Kaladria? I wonder. Then, I shake my head, sighing. Kaladria Astrana can no longer give me the answers I seek. It's up to me to figure this out.

I stand from the bed, grabbing my rifle and heading outside. As I head for the barricade, I sling my rifle's strap over my shoulder. I slip out the barricade and begin walking through the desolate city.

The city is unnervingly quiet. It almost feels as if something is coming, something more than the endless waves of enemies we've barely managed to fight off. Perhaps, it's my exhaustion, perhaps it's

271

just a feeling, but the silence puts me on edge. It feels like the calm before a storm.

As I turn onto a new street, rounding the corner of an abandoned building, I stop.

A group of Aklev'Zol stand in the street, surrounding a young woman. She falls on her back, face pale as she grips a bleeding arm. As one of the Aklev'Zol soldiers lunges for her, I drop to a knee, swinging my rifle around. I fire quickly, shooting the Aklev'Zol straight through the skull. The monster falls soundlessly.

For a moment, there's silence. Then, as the other Aklev'Zol soldiers turn, I fire again, shooting two more. The third lunges for me and I fire once more, shooting it straight through the chest as its talons reach for me.

I lower my weapon, approaching the young woman. She stares at me with wide eyes as I crouch next to her.

"You okay?"

She nods slowly. "I…I think so."

I set my rifle down. "Can I see your arm?"

As if remembering her injured arm, she looks down. Then, she nods again. As she holds out her arm to me, I check the gash for the Aklev'Zol's black taint. But there isn't any. They must have just scratched her.

I release her arm. "There's no infection but it's still a deep cut. You should still see a doctor."

She looks genuinely surprised. "Do you know a doctor? I didn't think there were any left."

I smile half-heartedly. "I know one. Come on. I'll take you to her."

The young woman falls into step next to me and I lead her through the streets in the direction of the barricade.

"What are you doing out here alone?" I ask. "It's dangerous to leave a safe zone."

The girl scrutinizes me. "*You* were alone."

I gesture to my rifle. "I'm not unarmed."

She sighs. "The Aklev'Zol took control of the safe zone I was at and I had to run. I was searching for another one to take refuge at."

I grimace. Another safe zone down. That doesn't bode well.

"What about you?" she asks. "What were you doing out there alone?"

I shrug. "Sometimes I just go out on my own. It helps me think."

She studies my face. "I've never seen anyone fight like that. You didn't look scared at all. Who are you?"

"My name is Malcolm."

She stops. "Wait. As in Malcolm *Faraway?*"

I sigh. *Here we go again.* I nod. "Yes."

She watches me with new eyes, her expression filled with that awe I will never be comfortable with. "I've heard so many stories about you."

"I'm sure they're exaggerations."

She shakes her head. "I don't think so. I just saw you take on four Aklev'Zol by yourself. The stories must be true. You're the only reason we've lasted this long. You're a hero."

No, I think. *Just someone following one.*

"There's something I've always wanted to know," she says slowly. "Something about the early days of this war, about the gang camps."

I grimace. *Gang camps.* In the beginning, when the Aklev'Zol first started invading, there were safe zones being completely run by groups of criminals. They wouldn't let refugees in their camps, instead stealing everything from those that drew too close to their safe zones. Those that were robbed lost their food, extra clothing, weapons, anything the gangsters thought would be useful. They'd leave the robbed refugees in the street to be found by the Aklev'Zol.

"I know most of humanity's leaders didn't care about the gang camps. They just wanted to worry about the Aklev'Zol." She shakes her head. "But I heard that you didn't let the gang camps continue. I heard you broke down their barriers, stole their weaponry, and left them to fend for themselves the same way they left the refugees they robbed."

I sigh but I don't deny it. Those early days had been filled with a lot of hard decisions. Choosing to leave those gangsters to the Aklev'Zol is a decision I will never forget. There was no mercy in such a choice. And yet I had known making that decision was the only way to keep the gang camps from rising up again.

The young woman studies my face. "Why did you do it?" she asks. "Wouldn't it have been easier to just worry about the Aklev'Zol? Aren't they the bigger threat?"

I pause. "Maybe. But I learned a long time ago that the easy thing isn't always the right thing. Sometimes doing the right thing means straying from the path everyone else expects of you."

Kaladria had taught me that. She'd always followed the path she thought was most right. Often times, that path went against the rules set by her society. But that had never stopped her. I can't let it stop me either.

We slip through the barricade and I stop, nodding to the house at the end of the street. "My mother is a doctor," I explain. "Go to her house, there at the end of the safe zone. She can make sure your arm gets properly taken care of."

The girl nods. "Thank you." She pauses. "And Malcolm? Thank you for being willing to do the right thing."

67

KALADRIA ASTRANA

XALIN WAS RIGHT. Jupiter is a mess.

The city was once the pinnacle of Protectorate technology. The ground was metal, laced with circuits, and had been built right on top of the atmosphere. The city was a sprawling phenomenon of castle-like houses and a thriving people. But now the ground is laced with cracks and the buildings are abandoned and crumbling. The city is empty, ghost-like.

With Xalin and my father flanking my sides, I walk through the abandoned city. The silence puts them on edge but it soothes me. After a year completely on my own, silence is easy.

I pause, eyes narrowing as something silver glints in the building to my left. Lightning sparks in my hands, my eyes fixed on the building as I reach behind my back for my spear.

"Kala?"

I don't turn, searching for the glint of silver I'd seen moments ago. "Watch my back," I say in a low voice. Then, I move closer to the building, eyes never straying from the broken window where I'd seen that flash of metal.

"Kala!"

I barely register Xalin's shouted warning before a Zol Beast slams into me. I fall on my back, head striking the ground. The beast snaps its jaws at me, teeth inches away from my face. When I push against it, the beast tries to bite down on my shoulder. *Oh, no you don't.* I slip through the lightning, teleporting several feet away. I reappear in front of Dad and Xalin, falling into a crouch.

The Zol Beast lowers its head with a mechanical growl. I clutch my spear, waiting. As the beast lunges again, leaping through the air, I tense. But then the beast is thrown back, suddenly sent skittering back by an invisible force. Definitely a Jovian's telekinesis. I don't turn to look. Lunging forward, I stab the Zol Beast through its plating, sending a bolt of electricity through my spear and into the beast. It staggers and then crashes to the ground.

I turn to see who aided me but then I freeze at the sight of the tall Jovian holding a long dagger in one hand. He stares at me, his expression as frozen as mine.

"Zeru," I whisper.

He blinks. "Kaladria?"

I launch at him, dropping my spear as I throw my arms around his neck. Zeru staggers back but then hugs me back, gripping me tightly as if he expects me to disappear.

"It's so good to see you," I whisper hoarsely, cursing the tears on my cheeks.

Zeru leans back, gripping my arms tightly. He looks down, his expression hardening. "Don't you ever force me to make a choice like that again," he says fiercely. "Leaving you behind was the hardest thing I've ever had to do."

"I know. I'm sorry."

He sighs, releasing me. "Where have you been?"

"Oh, you know," I say weakly, "Just on the homeworld of the Aklev'Zol."

"Of course you were." Zeru rolls his eyes but he's smiling. "Where else would you be?"

I resist the urge to stick out my tongue. "Where's my ship?"

"In stealth mode, near the city's perimeter." He nods behind him. Then, he studies my face. "Do you have a plan?"

"Get the team back together." I shrug. "That's as far as I've gotten."

"It's more than we had a few minutes ago." His expression turns solemn. "I say we go for our pilot next. Neptune is just as bad as Jupiter."

I nod. "Let's go."

As I sit in the captain's chair on the bridge of the *Resistance*, my throat burns with the tears I'm holding back. I smooth my fingers across the panel in front of me, smiling softly.

This ship was always my home. And that hasn't changed. Being here, my electricity almost sings, synchronizing with the ship's own power.

"Kala, we're approaching Neptune."

Exhaling, I nod. "Do we have any idea where Vale might be?"

"Most of the Neptunians have made camp at the edge of the northern city. Vale is likely there."

"Take us in, then."

As we draw near the planet's surface, the entire bridge falls silent. Very slowly, I stand and approach the window.

I stare at the surface of Neptune. The frozen tundra and the ice spires of the city have been tainted with a tar-like blackness. And it's spreading. The blackness seeps into the planet's surface, covering most of the city.

"What is that?"

Zeru grimaces. "It looks like the Aklev'Zol's dark matter."

I watch the blackness spreading across Neptune, thinking of the Aklev'Zol's homeworld. It looks much the same. Are they turning Neptune into one of their worlds?

I shake my head, looking past the dark matter, at the camp of Neptunians hunkered behind a wall of ice. If that blackness hits them…

I look at the expanse of ice between the Neptunian camp and the dark matter slowly slinking in their direction. A large group of Aklev'Zol soldiers stand there, assuredly waiting for the dark matter to overcome the Neptunians.

"Zeru, fire at the ice below the Aklev'Zol."

As he does, shooting the *Resistance*'s weaponry at the ice beneath the Aklev'Zol's feet. The ice cracks, fissuring. Then, the ground crumbles, sending the Aklev'Zol into the abyss below the surface of Neptune. The Neptunians cheer.

Exhaling, I slip back into my chair. Hopefully, we've at least bought the Neptunians some time. At the very least they should be able to flee to a safe distance without the Aklev'Zol there anymore.

"Go ahead and land," I tell Zeru.

Zeru lands the ship and I gaze out the window, watching the dark matter. As it reaches the huge crevice in the ground, it slows, the blackness slinking down into the hole.

I look up as the elevator doors open and Vale Taladauss rushes onto the bridge. "Zeru, what is going…"

Smiling wryly, Zeru nods to me. As Vale looks at me, he halts. "Kaladria?"

I push out of my chair. "Hello, Vale. It looks like we got here just in time."

He blinks. "How are you here?"

"She was on the Aklev'Zol's homeworld," Zeru explains. "She's been playing saboteur for us."

Vale surprises me by laughing. "You never change, do you? Same old Kaladria, single-handedly saving the galaxy."

I grin. "I did what I could."

As Vale shakes his head, I look back out at Neptune. The Neptunian soldiers have begun to pack up, likely to move themselves further away from the dark matter across the crack in the ice.

I look back at Vale. "I know your people are suffering," I say slowly, "But I'd like to ask for your help. If we are to defeat the Aklev'Zol, I think we need to work together again. Would you be willing to—"

Vale holds up a hand. "You don't need to convince me, Kaladria. If you hadn't asked me to come, I would have volunteered."

I smile. "Well, then, are you ready to get back in the sky?"

"It would be my pleasure."

"KALADRIA?"

Sitting in the airlock, I look up at Zeru. He steps further into the room, studying my face carefully. "You okay?"

I sigh. "I just needed a little quiet for a few minutes. I'm still not used to being around people again. I grew accustomed to the isolation."

"Because Xalin, your father, and Vale are all so loud, right?" He chuckles. "We haven't retrieved our loudest companions yet."

I smile.

Zeru sinks to the floor next to me. "What was it like?" he asks. "On their world?"

"Empty. The entire planet's surface is barren. If it weren't for the buildings, I would have had nowhere to hide. Even so, I never expected to survive it. I was certain I was going to die there. But I was determined to go down fighting."

"We shouldn't have left you behind."

I tilt my head back, studying his haunted eyes. "No, you made the right call. I know it was hard but I doubt we would have made it off the Satellite if you went back for me. And someone had to prepare the rest of the galaxy for war."

Zeru glances at me. "Malcolm blames himself for what happened, you know."

I sigh. *Of course he does.* Even if I wish he wouldn't, I'm not surprised. He'd blamed himself for Emma's death too, after all. "How is he?" I ask.

"He's alive. Doing as well as anyone in his position could be."

"You know, the Aklev'Zol find his success infuriating."

Zeru chuckles. "I can imagine. He was supposed to just be a human. He wasn't a soldier. They weren't expecting him to put up a fight."

And yet he had. Even as isolated as I was, I heard the way the Aklev'Zol soldiers spoke of him when they didn't know I was there. He's proven himself a worthy adversary.

"We should get up to the bridge," I sigh. "We must be getting close."

Zeru nods and we both stand. Together, we walk up to the bridge in silence. I can't decide if the silence is a comfortable one or if Zeru is trying to give me some space after what I admitted about struggling to be around other people. Hopefully, not the latter.

As we step onto the bridge, I cross the platform to stand next to Vale. I lean forward, looking out the window at Venus. Vale glances at me. "What's the plan?"

"Fly in low. Let's see if we can't give the Venutians a little backup."

The *Resistance* dives down. I watch as a battleground comes into view. On one side, hunched behind a wall, I can see the red-skinned Venutian soldiers. On the other side are the black forms of the Aklev'Zol, slinking across the red planet.

"Kala?"

"Fire."

Zeru fires on the Aklev'Zol. After several minutes, Vale lands the ship. I sit down, clasping my hands in my lap. After that display, there's no way our most reckless squadmate won't come running.

As predicted, Azar races onto the bridge. He skids to a stop when he sees me. He opens his mouth but he doesn't speak. He just stares.

I smirk. "Well, Azar, it would seem I've finally managed to stun you silent."

He blinks. "Kala?"

"Come on. Stop standing there like a slack-jawed idiot and sit down. We've got work to do."

6 8

KALADRIA ASTRANA

THEY'VE all been through a lot.

I knew they would have. With the Aklev'Zol invading, it hasn't been easy for anyone, least of all my squad. They had to take charge, step up to an enormous challenge, while grieving for the friend they thought they lost. I never envied their task. Still, even expecting it, seeing them this way is impossibly difficult.

Zeru watches the window, leaning against a wall. He still appears to be his carefree self but I can see the tense set of his shoulders, the tightness deeply wound into his spine. That haunted look remains in his eyes, as if he's constantly thinking of whatever he's witnessed in the last year. Both my uncle and my father lean against the wall, too. Dad looks exhausted, not surprising considering everything he's been through, and Xalin's face is drawn. Vale is quiet, as usual, but his expression looks particularly worn, almost aged. And Azar...

His body is taut with rage. His eyes are like a living flame, his face set in an endless sort of fury.

I can't imagine what horrors they've witnessed. It was bad living in isolation, always wondering what day would be my last, but at least I never saw any friends die. I never witnessed the destruction of all we'd once built. The only war I played a part in was my own.

"We'll be landing soon, Kala," Vale says.

I nod, grabbing my helmet. I glance at Azar. "Come with me. We'll need to search the underground cities for Hassuun."

Azar hesitates, then nods. Together, we head outside, walking straight into the tunnels that make up the Martian city. Or what was once the city. Some of the city's tunnels are closed off, their entrances caved in. Others have been completely abandoned.

"Why am I coming with you?" Azar asks in a low rumble. "Why not Zeru? Or Xalin?"

I know why he's asking. Azar and I are too much alike. Reckless, impulsive, brave to a fault. In the past, it was a bad pairing. Fire and lightning are too disastrous together. But, right now, with the whole system falling apart, we could use our destructive combination.

"Xalin looks dead on his feet and I need Zeru to serve as backup in case things go awry. Besides, neither of them have limitless supplies of pent-up anger."

He's silent, glaring out at a tunnel.

"Look, I get it, Azar. I really do." I glance down an empty tunnel. "The Council failed us. They were supposed to ensure this never happened. But they refused to believe us about the Aklev'Zol and look where it led us." I shake my head. "That makes me furious. I just wasted a year of my life on a hostile world because of their inaction. It feels like everything we did to stop them was a waste. But I don't let it get to me."

Azar's jaw is clenched.

"Anger makes you fight harder, Azar. But I don't need you to fight harder. I need you to fight smarter. All the anger in the universe won't mean a thing if you can't control it."

A sudden cry fills the air, followed by the sounds of gunshots. I whirl around. A Martian soldier collapses to the ground as two Aklev'Zol soldiers slink into view.

"We need to find Hassuun. Fast."

"You go." Azar pulls out his gun. "I'll buy you some time."

"Azar—"

He shakes his head. "You want me to fight smarter? This is me doing that. You and I both know I'm better at causing distractions. Let me handle this. I'll find you in a couple of minutes."

"You'd better." I grasp his arm. "Promise me."

I can't lose any of them. Not now.

He nods. "I promise. Now, go." He faces the Aklev'Zol. He charges down the tunnel toward them with a battle cry of absolute fury.

I zip in and out of electricity, moving in the opposite direction. Finally, I find a group of Martian soldiers. Several are continuously building up barricades around the city at a frantic pace, creating walls to block the onslaught of Aklev'Zol. Other soldiers fight to keep the Aklev'Zol from breaking through the slowly forming barricades.

Hassuun stands with them, firing a rifle at the attacking Aklev'Zol.

I teleport across the scene, yanking out my spear. Lunging, I stab one of the Aklev'Zol in the chest, just as Hassuun points his gun at its head. He lowers his weapon slowly.

I face the barricade, adding my electricity to the stone wall. The Aklev'Zol stagger away from the lightning barrier. The few foolish enough to attack my barrier are blasted back, their bodies smoking.

"We thought you were dead."

I face Hassuun, smiling faintly. "Didn't stick." I look him up and down, tilting my head back to meet his gaze. He looks exhausted. "I've got everyone else on the *Resistance*. Well, almost everyone. I haven't gone back to Earth yet."

"How..."

Hassuun trails off. I follow his gaze, looking past my lightning barrier. Most of the Aklev'Zol have withdrawn but the General stands there, watching me carefully.

I grimace. I suppose it was only a matter of time before he caught up to me. After all, he knows who I care about. He likely knew exactly what I'd do once I made it back to this system, if not the order of the planets I'd visit.

I teleport through the barricade. "General."

"Captain Astrana, I wondered if you'd be here."

"Oh?" Lightning sparks across my hands. "And now what?"

The General's eyes are narrowed but his tone remains light. "I was rather surprised to see you and your father escape."

I smirk. "That's always your problem, isn't it? You're completely incapable of keeping me and those I care about contained. From the very beginning, your soldiers have been incompetent against my squad."

"It is not my soldiers that keep getting captured."

"You aren't capturing anyone today. My father and I will never be your prisoners again."

"Oh, I have no intentions of taking either of you," the General says, glancing behind me at the lightning barrier. "I'm much more interested in some of your other companions."

My eyes are narrowed. "In case you hadn't noticed, you might have some difficulty reaching Hassuun at the moment."

His expression darkens. "Take down the barrier."

"Not a chance."

The General leaps forward and I swing up my spear to block him. Expression contorted with impatient anger, he grips the spear and jerks it out of my grip. He tosses it aside, lunging again. I stumble back a step as his talons swipe through my cheek.

I forgot how much stronger and faster he is than the other Aklev'-Zol, how much more powerful he is than the rest of his kind.

"Are you certain you don't want to reconsider?"

I lift my head. "I'm not afraid of you."

Inhumanly fast, the General lunges. He grabs my jaw, lifting me off my feet. *Take down the barrier.*

I spit. *Not on my life.*

The General throws me back into the wall. I gasp, coughing blood as my back strikes stone. I fall to the floor with a tight grimace, wiping blood from my mouth.

"I won't ask again," the General says. "Take down the barrier."

I push myself to my feet. "Not happening."

As the General steps toward me again, I clench my fists. I'm not ready to face him, not like this. I've been pushing myself at a nonstop pace, barely resting since Dad and I escaped the Aklev'Zol's world. I'm not going to be able to keep it up. And yet, I'm not sure I have a choice.

Just as the General draws close, a sudden blast of flames erupts between us. Grinning, I zip though electricity. I stay crouched down, spear in hand once more, as I reappear at Azar's side. "Perfect timing."

Azar glances at me. "You good?"

"Never better." I shrug back my shoulders as more Aklev'Zol join the General in the tunnel. "What do you say we show them why it is you and I are such a destructive combination?"

Azar almost smiles. "Ready when you are."

With fire on his fists and lightning on mine, we both charge. Fire and lightning explode across the air, sending tremors through the tunnel. With a roar, Azar launches himself at the nearest Aklev'Zol soldier, sending flames across the room.

I teleport through those flames, lunging for the General with my spear in hand. Reappearing above him, I launch myself at him, driving my spear at his head. The General shifts and I stagger past him.

I sidestep as the General tries to grab me. Then, glancing at my barrier, I drop it. The Martians fire at the Aklev'Zol and, within minutes, the only Aklev'Zol still standing is the General.

"You think you've won here, don't you?" the General snarls as I smirk. He collects himself quickly, a cruel tone replacing his anger. "You've forgotten. There's still one person in your team, your little *family*, that you haven't found yet. And I'm willing to bet I'll find him first."

Eyes widening in realization, I lunge forward. Azar grabs my arm. "Don't," he says, glaring at the slowly retreating General. "It's what he wants."

I grit my teeth. He's right. I wish he wasn't but I know he's right. The General knows me well enough to know how to best goad me. Letting him do so won't help Malcolm.

Turning, I face Hassuun as he rushes over. He looks first at me and then at Azar. "Does someone want to tell me what's going on?"

Spear in hand, I stalk toward the tunnel. "We're leaving."

69

KALADRIA ASTRANA

I WALK through Earthen streets at a furious pace. My fingers shake and my chest feels impossibly tight. I clench and unclench my fists, forcing my breath out in an attempt to calm my nerves. But I can't shake the anxiety out of my limbs. Even if I know my panic won't help Malcolm. Even if I know a calm head serves me so much better right now. I just can't push aside the fear that I'm going to be too late.

Xalin grabs my arm. "Kala, you need to calm down. Malcolm will be fine. He's completely capable of handling himself."

"This isn't just some Aklev'Zol grunt soldier, Uncle. The General is faster and stronger than the rest of them. He's clever and he's cruel."

"I know," Xalin concedes.

"We'll find him, Baby Girl," Dad promises. "Before the General. But you need to think this through. Your head is your best ally."

I exhale but I'm so tightly wound that it doesn't calm me down. Xalin notices. He grabs me by the shoulders. Then, he does something he hasn't done for many years. He leans down until we're at eye level. "Kaladria, you are bigger than your fear."

I nod, letting the words set in. Exhaling, I look between the two of them. My squad opted to spread out across this area, heading in different directions across the city. Dad and Xalin decided to come with me, likely knowing they'd be the only two capable of getting me to think straight. It seems they were right.

"Okay, okay." I take a deep breath, closing my eyes. I force myself to think like Malcolm would. "It's too quiet." I look across the empty street. "Malcolm would know that." I think for a moment, imagining what he would do with that information. This is the human that got humanity to fight together, the human that has kept the Aklev'Zol at bay for a whole year. "He'd want to figure out what the Aklev'Zol were planning before they could attack so he could prepare and plan a counter offensive."

"Out on reconnaissance," Xalin agrees.

Panic sets in again. "But that means he could be *anywhere*."

"Then, our best option is to start looking. Remember, the General doesn't know where he is any more than we do."

"Right." I take a deep breath. "Let's—"

A shrill cry pierces the air, chilling my bones. It's the scream of a small child, far too young to survive on these streets alone.

Everything clicks into place. Dad is right. The General doesn't know where Malcolm is, not exactly. But he does know how to lure him in. Malcolm has the biggest heart of anyone I know. If he's around here, if he hears a child in need of help...

The General intends to draw him in. This is how he'll catch him before I do. I'm suddenly certain of it.

"A trap," I breathe.

"What?"

I don't bother explaining. I take off running. "Come on!" I dart down the street toward the sound of that scream, yanking out my spear.

70

MALCOLM FARAWAY

THE MOMENT A SCREAM fills the air, the street is suddenly swarming with Aklev'Zol. I look at Noah. "Find that kid. I'll keep them off you."

Noah hesitates.

"Go!"

As he runs off, I yank out my rifle. I fire shot after shot at the Aklev'Zol slinking into the streets. When they're too close to make use of the rifle's scope, I pull out my dagger, stabbing one in the head.

Another charges. I reach behind my back, yanking out a long metal pole, the weapon I've yet to test. The staff buzzes with electricity. I swing it low, swiping several Aklev'Zol off their feet. Then, pulling my knife free of the dead Aklev'Zol, I throw it at a charging Zol Beast. The beast skitters across the street and I lunge forward. I drive the pole through its side, sending electricity through the Zol Beast's body.

Several more Aklev'Zol soldiers move in. At one point, I might have been doomed. But it's been a long time since I was helpless.

I slam the pole against the street. Electricity sparks across the road in a storm of lightning. The Aklev'Zol shriek, falling to the street.

"Well, I suppose she would be rather proud of the soldier you've become, wouldn't she?"

I swing the pole around, facing the Aklev'Zol approaching. He's flanked by two Zol Beasts and followed by many more Aklev'Zol soldiers. His body is heavily scarred, proof that he must be one of the oldest of his kind, having survived in this form long enough to have so many scars. He's slightly taller than the rest, more muscled even. There's something else different about him, too. Casual and confident, he carries himself with importance.

I narrow my eyes as he steps closer. "Do I know you?"

"We're all the same to you, aren't we?" He laughs. "All of us are just another enemy for you to kill."

Some days I do think I regret what I've had to become, even if I would gladly do it again to keep humanity alive. But I refuse to show any remorse to this monster. Not after everything they've stolen.

"You'll have to excuse my lack of compassion for the monsters that want to destroy my world."

The Aklev'Zol smirks. "Oh, you are without mercy, aren't you?" He shakes his head. "What happened to the boy afraid to kill?"

"He grew up," I say flatly. "It's not as if you'd extend that same mercy."

"Oh, but I do. My mercy just comes in a different form. The transformation can be rather enlightening. Is that not merciful?" When I say nothing, glaring at him, he shrugs. "I've shown many people mercy, Mr. Faraway. Emma Blake, for instance," he says slyly.

I grip my staff tightly, finally recognizing him for what he is. The first of these monsters I ever met, the one that killed Emma. The General.

His expression twists in its cruelty. "I even had mercy for Kaladria Astrana."

Hot anger twists in my gut. "I swear I'll kill you."

The General raises a taloned hand, signaling to his soldiers. As they move forward, I grip my weapons tightly.

He smirks. "Unfortunately, I do not intend to share my mercy with you, Mr. Faraway."

71

KALADRIA ASTRANA

A SMALL HUMAN girl sits in the middle of the street, screaming. Tears run down her cheeks and Aklev'Zol soldiers and Zol Beasts prowl around her.

I lunge forward, spear in one hand, a burst of electricity in the other. Somewhere nearby, Xalin lets out a roar. He rams into one of the Aklev'Zol with blast of power. Even my father rushes forward, forcing himself to teleport across the street. He scoops up the little girl, cradling her to his chest. As a Zol Beast lunges for him, he turns his back to the beast, allowing the Zol Beast to tear through his spine rather than let the beast hurt the girl.

He staggers, falling to one knee. Still, he holds the girl to his chest.

"Dad!"

I yank out a knife, launching at the beast. I slice through its side. Then, I shove it to the ground, blasting it with lightning. As I stand, I strike an Aklev'Zol soldier with my spear as he draws too close.

I stab a soldier but another grabs me, talons curling around my arms. The monster wrenches me forward. Others crowd closer. I growl, swinging my legs out, kicking the nearest of the soldiers in the head. I squirm but, before I manage to free myself, a gunshot rings through the air. The two closest Aklev'Zol fall dead.

I look past the fray. Noah Hilliard stands with a rifle in both hands. My heart is suddenly pounding. If Noah is here, does that mean Malcolm is close by? I look across the street but I don't see him.

Swinging my spear around, I stab the Aklev'Zol that launches itself at me.

Finally, all of the Aklev'Zol soldiers are dead, the Zol Beasts crumpled in the road. I turn to look at my father. The little girl clutches onto him for dear life, burying her face into his shoulder. I'm surprised she'd latch onto a stranger so quickly but I suppose she must have been through quite the ordeal to be out here alone, used as a trap like this.

"Are you okay?"

Dad grimaces, adjusting her in his arms. "I'll live."

I look at Noah. "Where's Malcolm?"

Thankfully, he doesn't waste any time asking what I'm doing here or how I'm alive. He nods down the street. "He was with me. He's still back that way."

I rake a hand through my hair. This was planned too perfectly. The General is definitely behind this. He's the only one who knows Malcolm and I well enough to play us so easily.

"Is Lori here somewhere?" I ask, glancing at my father and the blue blood staining his back.

Noah nods. "Back at her house."

I look at Xalin. "Make sure they get to Lori. She can help Dad. I'd assume her house is also the safest place to go."

"Kala—"

"I swear, Xalin, do not argue with me." I take a deep breath, pinching my eyes shut as fear takes hold. "Make sure everyone gets there. I'll be there shortly."

Sighing, Xalin waves to my father. Dad frowns, shooting me a worried look. I meet it with sharp eyes, face hardening. Little girl or not, someday he's going to have to accept that I'm not a child anymore and that I'm capable of defending myself. Dad relents with one last stern look. *Be careful.*

Noah glances at me. "We'll meet you at Lori's."

I nod.

As they walk off, I turn away. I take off running through the street, teleporting in and out of lightning. Fear coils in my gut and I push it aside. *You are bigger than your fear.*

Paces away from where I left Xalin and Dad, I stop, lungs aching. The lightning goes out, my body still too messed up from Callaghan's machine to handle it as long as I once could. I curse under my breath.

Gunfire explodes through the air. As I look up, my breath catches in my throat.

Malcolm stands in the middle of the street. Entirely focused on the Zol Beast slinking toward him, he swings a long, pole-like staff in one hand. He slams it down against the road and electricity sparks all around him in every direction.

I blink. *Lightning? Did he...?*

I shake my head and turn my attention to the Zol Beast. It stumbles before charging Malcolm.

Staggering to the side in exhaustion, I take off running. But Malcolm doesn't need my help. He yanks out a rifle, firing at the beast. As another Zol Beast charges, Malcolm spins around. He hits its jaw with the butt of his rifle. The beast staggers and he slides a knife down its side, jamming the electric pole into its body.

I freeze, gaping at him as the Zol Beast falls. *This is not the boy I left behind a year ago.*

Looking past him, I tense. The General stands behind Malcolm, just beyond the quickly forming pile of bodies surrounding Malcolm.

I take off running again, gritting my teeth as I teleport in and out of the street. *Just a block to go. You can do this—*

The General launches forward. He ducks under Malcolm's electric staff, swinging his talons across his chest and slicing through his entire front side.

"No! Stop!"

Malcolm freezes, staggering back. I don't know if it's the General's attack or my voice that stills him. Regardless, the General takes advantage of it. He lunges, driving his talons straight through his stomach. Malcolm collapses.

A lethal silence falls over the street. All I can see is bright red blood. Suddenly, it's the only thing that matters.

I launch forward. Teleporting across the street, I lunge for the

General. Just as he leans down to grab Malcolm again, I ram into him, throwing a blast of lightning in fury. *"Don't you dare touch him,"* I snarl.

"If it isn't the Lightning Demon herself," he sneers. "A little late, aren't you?"

With a roar, I swing my spear. The General pushes it aside easily, still smirking. But I'm not done.

I launch forward, lightning sparking across my body. Fury fuels every motion as I arc forward and throw a blast his way. The General stumbles back, swinging his talons. I jump back. Then, I throw my spear like a javelin. The General staggers as my spear is embedded in his shoulder.

He lets out a hiss, full of pain and fury. Then, he yanks out my spear, tossing it aside. But he pauses at the storm raging across my skin. *Try it. I* dare *you.* If he moves toward Malcolm again, I will kill him.

The General takes a step back. "I'll be back for you," he vows.

As he turns away, disappearing down the street, I drop to my knees. I press my hands over Malcolm's stomach. At my touch, he grimaces, eyes barely opening. "Kaladria…" Voice slurred, he starts to close his eyes again.

"No. Stay awake." I pat his cheek. "You stay with me. I didn't cross the universe for you to die on me now."

He blinks slowly.

I pull him to his feet, draping his arm over my shoulder as I pull his weight forward. *Stay with me, Malcolm. Please, just stay with me.*

72

KALADRIA ASTRANA

As we reach the barricade protecting the safe zone around Lori's house, Malcolm slumps against me, no longer able to hold his own weight. I stagger, looking desperately ahead at the barricade.

Noah appears at my side. He slides through the barricade, waving me forward. I follow him through the wall. Then, Noah puts Malcolm's arm over his shoulder. I put the other across my shoulders, gripping him tightly. Malcolm's head drops forward. *Almost there, almost there.*

As Noah and I carry Malcolm toward Lori's house, Noah throws orders to soldiers through the base, sending them across the street and to the barricade.

"What's happening?"

"Scouts have reported the Aklev'Zol are closing in on this base."

Likely because of my actions. The General said he'd be back for me. I hadn't anticipated it would happen so quickly.

We stop as we reach Lori's house. Noah glances at me briefly, moving away. "Take care of Malcolm. I'll take care of everything else."

I nod gratefully, doubting he'll ever know how much it means to not have to worry about this particular battle. I stagger into the house, one arm around Malcolm's waist, the other holding his arm over my shoulders.

Just inside the door, I lay Malcolm on the floor. His stomach is still bleeding but at least the wound isn't gushing. I press my hands over it, looking up. "Lori! Help!"

Lori Faraway rushes down the stairs, staring when she sees me kneeling on the floor. When she notices her son, she launches forward. Lori slides to her knees, touching his cheek and then his stomach. "What happened?" she asks, fingers brushing the inside of his wrist.

Bigger than your fear, bigger than your fear.

"A...a trap. Meant for both of us." I look down. "There's no infection though."

Lori takes a moment to check vitals. Then, she places her hand over mine, pushing it against his stomach. "Keep the pressure on. I'll be right back."

She rushes out of the room and I look back down at Malcolm, blinking back tears. "You have to live, Malcolm," I whisper. "I need you to pull through this."

I SIT ON THE FLOOR, staring up at the ceiling, more tired than I've been in a very long time. When was the last time I slept? Before I was captured by the General? Before I'd killed that human woman to save her from her infection?

Lori sinks down next to me. "It really wasn't as bad as it looked."

I look up. Across the room, Malcolm sleeps on the couch. His eyes are closed peacefully, his breathing even. I relax. "He's going to be okay?"

"His wounds weren't deep," Lori assures. "He's going to be fine."

I lean my head back against the wall. A year of running and hiding, followed by being captured, tortured, escaping, and running across the system to find my loved ones. I know it's far from over and yet...I truly have no idea how I'm supposed to keep this pace up.

Lori studies my face, likely seeing the fatigue there. "Are *you* alright?"

I bark a laugh. "Not quite sure yet."

Lori's eyes soften.

I sigh, hesitating. "I do have a bit of a confession. That day, on the Satellite, I may have sort of torn my stitches open."

She scowls.

I laugh. "I really tried, Lori. Promise." When she sighs, I continue, "An Aklev'Zol slashed me good. I didn't have much in the way of medical supplies where I was but I did my best to take care of it. Still, my arm aches pretty bad most of the time."

When I push my shirt aside, Lori fingers the scar. "You're lucky you didn't end up with an infection. I suspect the aching in your arm is due to some nerve damage. I did warn you there would be permanent repercussions if you opened up your stitches."

I smile faintly. "I know."

Lori sighs. "There's not much I can do for it right now. Regular medical care was one of the first things we lost. If this war ever ends, I might be able to repair the nerves. But until then, I'm afraid I can't ease any discomfort you're feeling."

I shrug, eyes sliding over to hers. "Let's call it penance for not following my doctor's orders."

Lori smiles faintly.

Looking down, I flex my fingers, focusing on my aching hand. Grimacing, I close my fists to hide the dried blood staining my fingers.

"Kaladria?"

I look up, surprised by the tears brimming in her eyes. "Lori? What is it?"

"Malcolm told me what you did on the Satellite," she says softly. "You fell off your ship because you let go of his hand. Because you didn't want to take him down with you."

I frown, eyebrows knitting together. "Of course I did. I couldn't—"

"The last time you were here, you promised me that you would protect him. You promised me you would make sure he came back, no matter the cost. I…"

Oh. Now, I understand. She blames herself. Because I promised her I'd protect Malcolm. Because I swore to keep him safe, no matter what it cost me. And when I fell back on the Satellite, it seemed as if it was that vow that killed me.

I reach out, grasping her hand in both of mine. "Lori," I say gently, "What happened is not your fault. Yes, I made you a promise. But I would have made the same choice even if I hadn't made that promise to you." I take a breath. "I care for your son very much. I let go because I didn't want him to get hurt."

She blinks back her tears.

I squeeze her hand. "I'm sorry for making you feel as though I died keeping a promise to you. Don't ever feel guilty for a choice I made. I chose my own path and I don't regret it."

As I release her hand, Lori wipes away her tears. "Thank you."

I smile slightly. Then, leaning my head back again, I sigh. I wonder if I can close my eyes, even for just a few minutes…

As footsteps come down the hall, I open my eyes again. Dad steps into the hallway, eyebrows knit together at the sight of Lori and I sitting on the floor. I glance at Malcolm's still sleeping form and then at Lori. She smiles understandingly, nodding to Malcolm. "I'll let you know when he wakes up," she promises.

Exhaling, I push myself to my feet. I walk across the hallway, joining Dad on the stairs. "You okay?" I frown. "What happened to that little girl?"

"She's here, sleeping right now. I've been trying to track down her parents but…" He shakes his head. "I've had no luck."

I sigh, too. It's extremely likely that her parents are Aklev'Zol now. "What will you do if you can't find them?"

"I don't know." Dad rubs the back of his neck. "I was considering taking her in. If you'd be okay with that."

I raise both eyebrows. "Really?"

"I've grown rather attached to her." He shakes his head. "Of course, this is all dependent on any of us surviving the Aklev'Zol."

I nod, then glance down the hall. Lori still sits on the floor but now there's a book in her lap. On the couch, Malcolm stirs in his sleep, sighing heavily.

"Is that him?" Dad asks, following my gaze.

I look down at my hands, stained red with Malcolm's blood. "The

General found him before I did."

He puts an arm around my shoulders.

"Lori says he's going to be fine but..." I clench my fists again. "I never should have allowed him to get involved in my messes. He's just a human. He's not—"

"Kaladria, if everything you've told me is true, he's not just a human. He's part of your team and a close friend. To discount that would be shameful. Give credit where it's due."

I sigh. He's right, of course.

"None of this is your fault, Baby Girl, and I think you know that." His eyes soften. "I think this feeling has very little to do with what happened today and more to do with you not being able to live with the possibility of him dying."

I close my eyes. Lightning flashes through my memory, followed by screaming, a still body and desperate tears. I push it away.

"You're right," I say softly. "That's exactly what my problem is." I let out my breath. "I lost him once and I would do just about anything to prevent that from happening again."

Dad watches me silently, trying to understand.

I swallow. "This was before the invasion. We were on Earth and we were captured by this human general." I look down. "He wanted my lightning and he wasn't all that particular about how he got it. Long story short, he used this machine that drew it out of my body by force."

He stiffens. *"What?"*

"I'm fine. That was a long time ago."

His face remains pale. "For them to do that..."

"Was rather unpleasant for me." I wave him off, pushing aside the memory of that pain. "The point is that, while this was happening, they threw Malcolm in the room with me." I clench my fists. "The blast stopped his heart. If I hadn't escaped, if I hadn't been able to restart it..."

"It haunts you."

Yes, I think. Even when I've witnessed so many more haunting things on the Aklev'Zol's world, nothing has ever broken me as much as seeing Malcolm on the floor, dead.

Dad studies my face. "Kala," he says slowly, "I know I don't know you as well as I would like, not after so long. But I'd like to believe that I will always know you well enough to understand how you're feeling." He hesitates. "Are you in love with him?"

I silently curse the heat rising to my cheeks. "I—"

A sound like thunder shakes the house's frame. Then, a single soldier races into the house. His face is pale and he looks across the room, clearly searching.

I stand. "Soldier?"

He hesitates, taking in my pale blue skin, blood-stained hands, and worn expression. "Where's Faraway?"

"Malcolm is unavailable at the moment." I clasp my hands behind my back tightly. "What can I do for you?"

"Look, lady, the Aklev'Zol have broken through the barricade. We need soldiers, not pretty little—"

Lightning sparks across my skin as I teleport across the room, reappearing inches from him. "In case no one has informed you, Soldier, I am not here by chance, nor am I some sort of helpless refugee of this war." I glare up at him. "Now, what can I do to help?"

Eyes suddenly wide, the soldier nods. "Right. We—"

He gasps as sudden talons rip through his chest. Crying out in surprise, I stumble back as the Aklev'Zol steps into the room, dropping the soldier. As the monster steps closer, I launch forward with a blast of lightning. The Aklev'Zol shrieks as it falls, smoke rising from its dead form.

I face my father. Dad stares at the dead Aklev'Zol, frozen. I stiffen, realizing what he's thinking. The little girl. She's still asleep, upstairs and alone.

I snatch up my spear. "Go. I'll handle this."

As he whirls around, darting upstairs, I race down the hallway. Something slams against the front door. I curse, running toward it. "Lori!" I call behind me. "Stay with Malcolm! I'll keep them back!"

Without waiting for her response, I launch forward. I run into the entryway of the house, just as two Aklev'Zol soldiers step inside the house.

I grip my spear tightly, wordlessly launching forward.

73

MALCOLM FARAWAY

I WAKE to the sound of someone shouting. Somewhere down the hall, there's a roar of unbridled fury. Even closer, a woman cries out with fear.

I open my eyes as the door swings open. I look down. My rifle rests on the floor. Grimacing, I roll off the couch. I land on the floor, gritting my teeth as I grab the gun. I find a hiding place just behind the end of the couch.

An Aklev'Zol soldier steps into the room, gripping my mother by her hair. She screams and my fingers tighten around the rifle. *Not yet,* I tell myself.

"Stop!" Mom cries. "Don't you dare touch him!"

I take a deep breath, exhaling slowly. My breath hitches with pain. I grind my teeth, ignoring it. I peer around the couch carefully, watching them draw near.

Mom's eyes are wide as she stares at the empty couch. "Malcolm..."

The Aklev'Zol grabs her jaw. "Where's your son, Mrs. Faraway?"

I lift the rifle, propping it on the edge of the couch. Wordlessly, I shoot the monster in the chest. As it falls, I stand slowly, staggering a step.

"Malcolm!"

300

I grimace, doing my best to ignore the sharp pain in my stomach. "I'm okay, Mom."

Tears brim in her eyes and Mom takes a step toward me. But we both freeze at the sound of a scream down the hall.

"*No!*"

I look toward the door at the sound of a furious yell, followed by crackling electricity. I stiffen, gripping the edge of the couch. *She really* was *there, then.* Not a dream, not a wish. She had been there in the street, pushing back the General with that unending rage I've always associated with her.

I step toward the door. I can't lose her again.

"Stay here, Mom."

"Malcolm—"

"Stay here!"

I rush out into the hall. At the other end of the hallway, there are several Aklev'Zol soldiers crowding around a woman. One of them grabs her arm, yanking her forward. She snarls, swinging a lightning-covered fist. But, before it strikes the Aklev'Zol, the lightning vanishes. The Aklev'Zol laughs. She lunges forward, slamming her head against him and driving a knife through his chest.

Two more Aklev'Zol grab her, slamming her back into the wall. She swings her legs out in an attempt to escape. A third Aklev'Zol puts a long talon under her chin, sneering. Sudden fear touches her face.

Gritting my teeth, I drop to a knee, peering at her through my rifle's scope. As she spits, the Aklev'Zol snarls, claws digging into her cheeks.

I steady my aim, shifting a few inches to her left, and squeeze the trigger.

74

KALADRIA ASTRANA

I STIFFEN as the Aklev'Zol gripping my jaw releases me and collapses to the floor. His companions freeze and I look down the hall. Malcolm kneels at the other end of it with a sniper rifle in his hands. He lowers his weapon, nodding to me. I swallow, chest tight. I suppose this is as much of a reunion as we can afford right now.

The remaining soldiers grip my arms tightly. They yank me toward the door, talons holding me firmly.

With a strained cry, I force my body into electricity, slipping into my Lightning Form. The Aklev'Zol scream, the electricity blasting them back. As they fall, I return to my normal body, dropping to a knee.

"Kaladria!"

I push myself to my feet with a heavy grunt, staggering closer. "You're awake."

"And you're alive."

"Come on, you didn't think the famed Lightning Demon would go down *that* easy, did you?"

I pick up my spear, pushing open the front door. I pause, assessing the situation. Aklev'Zol are everywhere, working together to pick off the human soldiers. Still, they're struggling more than I'm sure they expected to.

I glance at Malcolm. He drops to a knee, firing his rifle at the Aklev'Zol. I lunge forward, lightning blasting from my open hand. A Zol Beast launches at me and suddenly Zeru appears next to me, slicing the beast with a dagger. I swing my spear, exhaling at the sight of my other squadmates. Xalin and Vale bring down another Zol Beast and Azar and Hassuun charge a group of Aklev'Zol soldiers.

As I stab an Aklev'Zol, another grabs my spear, ripping it from my hands. I growl but, as per usual, my lightning chooses the worst possible moment to sputter out.

"Kaladria!"

I look up as Malcolm tosses me the metal pole I saw him fighting with before. As I catch it, electricity dances in my hands, my own lightning thrumming to life. Grinning, I swing the staff, sending a bolt of energy through the Aklev'Zol.

As two more Aklev'Zol launch at me, I swing the pole again. One is thrown back and the other pauses, staggering away from the lightning around me.

I swing again and again, using the pole in my hand to keep my lightning from dissipating again, drawing from its energy. As the Aklev'Zol's numbers thin out, a small smile curves up my lips. *They never should have let us back together.*

ONCE THE AKLEV'ZOL HAVE RETREATED, driven back by the combined efforts of the human soldiers and my own squad, I stand in the street with my arms crossed, watching the soldiers rebuild the barricade. The entire street is in disarray, littered with fallen bodies and the shattered pieces of buildings broken in the attack.

I glance back at the porch. Dad sits there, holding the little girl in his lap. Thankfully, she looks unharmed.

"Kaladria!"

I turn, smiling as Dean and Tyler hurry over. Both carry weapons, their faces worn. Still, it's good to see them alive.

"Hey, guys."

Dean wipes sweat from his brow. "We heard you died."

"Not quite. Almost though."

"Where's Malcolm?" Tyler asks, surprisingly serious.

I jerk my head back toward the house. "Inside. Resting, I hope. He took a pretty hard hit before the attack."

Dean nods solemnly. "Lori told us."

Tyler looks me up and down. "So," he says slowly, "Nice dress."

And that's the Tyler I remember. Rolling my eyes, I turn away from them with a casual salute. "And that would be my cue to leave. I'll see you guys around."

I head back into the house in search of Malcolm. But I stop as I find him, stunned.

Malcolm stands in the middle of the living room, wearing nothing but a pair of jeans, a bandage still wrapped around his torso. He paces the length of the room, hands laced behind his head. Automatically, my eyes fall on the sculpted muscles of his chest. Gone are the soft edges of the boy I met a year ago. They've been replaced by the chiseled body of a soldier who has seen too many fights.

I study the scars crisscrossing his skin, as marred by war as mine is. A long scar slides through his abdomen before disappearing below the bandage, an ugly raised line that must have cut deep. Another slides across his collarbone, moving down to his—

I blink. *Stop it,* I scold myself, shaking my head. There is far too much going on right now for me to be so distracted.

Clearing my throat, I step into the room. "How are you feeling?"

He starts, head jerking up as if he'd forgotten I was back. "Good," he says as he recovers. "I've certainly had worse."

"I know."

Malcolm pulls a shirt over his head, tugging it down. "What happened?" He looks away, drawing out a weary sigh. "On the Satellite, I mean."

I sigh, too. I slump back on the couch. "When I fell back on the Satellite, it was abundantly clear I wasn't going to survive if I stayed there. So, I jumped through the wormhole."

He sits next to me. "You were on their world?"

"Not the most habitable place in the universe." I lean my head back, staring at the ceiling. "When I jumped through the wormhole,

I'd sort of accepted that I was going to die there. Every day I survived, I couldn't decide if I should feel lucky to live another day or despair because it was another day alone." I sigh. "I figured I could do my part and buy you guys some time, maybe even cause a lot of destruction until they killed me."

"They were so disorganized when they arrived on Earth." It clicks. "That was because of you."

I smile softly. "I'm glad I could help, even a little."

"It helped a lot," he assures me. "It gave us the edge we needed."

I nod, still smiling. We're both quiet now and I steal a glance in his direction. He looks as exhausted as I feel. His eyes are bloodshot, lined with dark circles. Clearly, he hasn't been getting much more sleep than I have.

"You've done well," I tell him. "I'm sure most would have considered it impossible for all of the human nations to work together."

"I certainly thought it was." He shakes his head. "Getting them to believe us was the hardest part. They thought I was crazy."

"How did you convince them otherwise?"

Malcolm rubs the back of his neck. "I lured one of the Aklev'Zol to a meeting with some of humanity's leaders," he admits.

I blink at him in surprise. Then, I laugh. "I guess that would do it."

He smiles faintly. "After that, it wasn't too hard to convince the rest of the world what was coming. When the Aklev'Zol showed up on Earth, we were ready."

"I heard some interesting stories about you on their world," I say.

Malcolm sighs. "I'm starting to understand why you hated going to the Satellite so much. The way people look at me..."

"At least people don't call you a monster."

Malcolm's face turns serious. "You're not a monster, Kaladria."

I swallow, tilting my head back to look up at him. "Thank you," I say softly, wishing I knew the words to convey how much it warms my heart to know that.

Malcolm meets my gaze. There's some unreadable emotion in his eyes as he searches my face. Then, it disappears as he turns his head to look across the room instead. "I noticed you seem to be having issues with your lightning."

I flex my hand, watching the lightning beneath my skin. "It hasn't been the same since Callaghan used that machine on me," I admit. "Most of the time, it's fine. But, sometimes, it just goes out. Usually at the worst time possible."

Malcolm shakes his head, tensing at the reminder of that particular memory.

I look down, feeling suddenly uncertain, almost awkward. I worked so hard to survive, to make sure he survived. And now I don't know what I'm supposed to do, what I'm supposed to say. There are so many things I want to tell him but none of them would be fair.

"Malcolm?"

"Yes?" he asks softly.

I swallow my conflicted feelings. "I'm glad you're okay."

He doesn't speak. He merely reaches down, placing his hand on top of mine. I sigh. For now, this will have to be enough.

75

MALCOLM FARAWAY

I STARE up at the ceiling, head against the couch, fingers curling around Kaladria's. She exhales softly, surprising me by leaning her head against my shoulder. I stiffen but she doesn't move. As her breathing evens, I look over. *Did she fall asleep?*

Kaladria doesn't move, remaining slumped against my side. I hold her hand tightly, remaining still next to her even as my heart constricts.

She's really here. When she fell back on the Satellite, that had truly felt like the end of it. Even she couldn't fight off all the Aklev'Zol there. That was the whole point of running. And we'd left her there, left her to die in the most horrible way imaginable. But nothing would ever bring her back from that.

I shake my head. I should have known better. Kaladria has always had a knack for the impossible.

Holding onto her hand like it's an anchor, I close my eyes. Then, exhaling, I allow myself to drift off to sleep with thoughts of the lightning-wielding Protector at my side.

KALADRIA SITS in her captain's chair on the *Resistance,* drumming her fingers against an armrest as she gazes out the window.

I watch her carefully, still trying to wrap my head around the reality that she's here. She's discarded the torn Protector dress she was previously wearing, trading it for her normal black body armor. Her skin is covered in scars, the result of more battles than I can imagine. While there are still shadows in her face from whatever she's had to witness in the last year, her eyes are fierce and she sits tall, her head lifted proudly.

I can't help but marvel at how strong she is, despite everything she's gone through. She's still the same fierce creature that had showed up in my lab a year ago. Unbreakable and unyielding, a storm wearing skin.

She catches me staring. She raises an eyebrow, a small smile curving up her lips.

I'm saved from my own embarrassment as Zeru steps onto the bridge. He hesitates, glancing between the two of us. "Am I interrupting?"

"No," I say quickly.

Something flashes across Kaladria's face but it disappears too quickly for me to identify it. She clears her throat. "What is it, Zeru?"

"You've successfully rallied your allies." Zeru sits down. "What now?"

"Defending our worlds isn't going to be enough for much longer." Kaladria sighs, rubbing the exhaustion from her face. "We need to take the fight to the Aklev'Zol."

"I might have an idea for that." I lean forward. "Our scouts report the Aklev'Zol are amassing huge numbers here." I glance at Kaladria, knowing she'll understand. "Particularly at the college in town."

"Your lab?" she guesses.

I nod. For the thousandth time since learning they were gathering around it, I kick myself for not destroying my lab. The wormhole generator was my most advanced invention but it wasn't the only thing there. The last thing I want is for them to use my notes to create anything else to use against us.

Kaladria leans back in her seat, thoughtful. "The General is a master schemer. He knows us both. I wouldn't be surprised if he was trying to make use of your lab."

"It's impossible to reach it," I warn. "Every scout we send never returns. We can't get anyone close enough."

Kaladria winks. "Ah, but you didn't have Zeru and I before. We can get into almost anywhere."

Zeru watches her warily. "Why do I have the feeling you're about to suggest something I won't like very much?"

"Admit it, you missed this."

Zeru smiles, even as he shakes his head. "Alright, fine. Yeah, I did."

Kaladria's eyes glitter, oddly mischievous considering her obvious exhaustion. "You up for some reconnaissance?"

"That does seem to be our specialty."

Kaladria frowns, brow furrowing. "I thought our specialty was charging in head first, asking questions later."

Zeru rolls his eyes. "No, that's *your* specialty."

I chuckle. "From what I've seen, that's a fairly apt description."

Kaladria grins as she stands. "We'll be back shortly. Hopefully with some news about whatever it is they're planning."

I nod slowly. She turns to the elevator, Zeru following behind her, still shaking his head slightly. I lean back in my seat, watching them go. Even after they've gone, I still stare at the elevator's closed doors.

"Be careful," I whisper.

76

KALADRIA ASTRANA

I TELEPORT in and out of lightning, leading the way through the city. I reappear behind a building before teleporting to another street corner. Zeru keeps behind me, staying in his Ghost Form as he follows from the shadows.

I crouch behind a wall, one hand outstretched behind me to signal for him to stay back. Then, peering around, I study the street ahead of us. An enormous monolith stands in the middle of the street, almost completely blocking the door to Malcolm's lab. It's an enormous black monument, taking up most of the road. Soldiers stand guard around it and a couple of Zol Beasts prowl around its perimeter.

"Well?" Zeru asks.

"There's something in the street," I whisper. "Just outside Malcolm's lab. It's..." I sigh. "Honestly, I have no idea what it is. I've seen a lot of technology on their world but never anything like this."

"What is it?"

I nod ahead. "Take a look."

Slipping past me, Zeru peers onto the street. He frowns. "Does it give off any electricity?"

I look back at the monolith. "Sort of. I can sense...something. It's almost like electricity and almost like the energy the Aklev'Zol give

FORGED IN STORMS AND SHADOWS

off. But there's something off about it. Honestly, just trying to sense anything on that thing is making me dizzy."

I rub my temples, shaking my head. "I don't think we can just blow it up. The Aklev'Zol's technology is too advanced." I sigh. "I think we need more information."

"We should get Malcolm to see this. He's spent a lot of time looking for weaknesses in their tech. He might have a couple of ideas."

I nod. "Let's…"

Trailing off, I stiffen at the sight of a Zol Beast. It lowers its head with a low growl. Next to me, Zeru curses.

"Time to go," I whisper harshly, not taking my eyes off the beast. "Meet me back at the barricade. Now, go!"

As Zeru phases through the building, disappearing easily, I take off running. I race across the streets, teleporting across the college campus and through the city in an effort to lose the Zol Beast. All the while I'm kicking myself for not paying more attention. Clearly, the year I spent alone on their home world has taught me nothing about stealth.

Suddenly, the lightning fizzes out. *Not now.* Cursing under my breath, I reappear in the middle of the street. I glance around me. At least the Zol Beast is gone.

I start to trudge forward in the direction of the barricade. I clench my fists, muttering under my breath. If he wasn't already dead, I would kill Callaghan for making my life so difficult.

Pausing, I slow my pace at the sound of soft scuttling somewhere behind me. I turn my head. *That energy…*

Before I can finish the thought, a figure launches at me. As I'm knocked to the ground, my head strikes the pavement. Talons dig into my arms, shoving me against the street.

"Are you always this reckless?" the Aklev'Zol-Emma taunts. "Or do I just keep getting lucky?"

Even as my head spins with a sharp pain at the base of my skull from her attack, I glare. I try to shove her off but she just shoves my hands back down, pinning my wrists down with her knees. "How's Malcolm?"

I spit.

"Oh, you're not very nice, are you?" she pouts. "You're going to make me do something very nasty."

Her fingers curl around my shoulder. I stiffen, gritting my teeth against the sudden pain as she digs a single talon into my scarred shoulder. Her lipless mouth turns up in a hideous smile. At the cruelty in her face, I realize what she's doing.

No.

My eyes widen with horror. I writhe beneath her, screaming. "No!"

The Aklev'Zol-Emma rolls her eyes. "Stop squirming," she growls in annoyance. With her free hand, she pushes my head back to the street, her talons covering most of my face. The talon in my shoulder sinks deeper. I scream again, the sound muffled, as an icy cold creeps across my skin, spreading from her talon.

She leans closer. "It's time to see just how brave you are, *Lightning Demon.*" Sliding her talons free, the Aklev'Zol-Emma pushes me the ground as she stands. "I'm betting you turn before the day is out."

I don't move. Shivering, I lay in the street, fingers clutching my shoulder.

As she walks off, I push myself to my knees, nearly tumbling over as hysteria threatens to overtake me. I grit my teeth, fighting for some sort of control as I tug at my shirt with trembling fingers. I yank the fabric away from my shoulder. There's no blood, no sign that she touched me other than the small, tar-like blackness spreading from my shoulder. Dark tendrils creep down my skin toward my arm.

I drop into the street with an angry cry, slamming my hands against the pavement. Shaking, I dig my fingertips into the cracks in the street. I pinch my eyes closed, an awful sound escaping my throat.

My mind spins as I desperately search for some sort of escape. But I know better. There is no escape from this. I'm going to die, twisted into the monster I've fought for so long. Just like Corvar, just like Emma. The iciness spreading down my shoulder will never stop.

I slump to the street, shaking with my tears. It isn't death that fills me with grief. It's the could-have-been's. It's all the hopes and dreams that will never be fulfilled. It's my squad and my family. It's knowing there are things I should have said that can't be said now. It's knowing I won't make it long enough to see the system through this war.

No. I grit my teeth. *I have to find a way to see that they survive this.*

I take a deep, shuddering breath as I look up. I have to slow this down. I have to last a bit longer. Exhaling, I force myself to relax, convincing my body that nothing is wrong, that the piercing cold is just in my head. I sit up, closing my eyes, hands clasped in my lap. As if this is just another day, as if sitting in the middle of a monster-infested street is the safest place in the world. I convince myself that it is.

I yank my shirt back into place. There's only one thing left for me to do. If I'm going to die, I'm going to ensure no one else has to first.

Pushing myself to my feet, I take slow, measured breaths. I feel strangely calm. Perhaps I don't fear death after all. Maybe I can be braver than I thought.

I hurry down the street in search of Zeru.

He stands just outside the barricade. I exhale, rushing over to him. As fear fills up inside of me, I can feel that sharp cold prick my skin. I take a breath. "You good?"

Zeru nods slowly, glancing down at my hands, which are fairly scraped up. His brow furrows. "Are you alright, Kala?"

I nod, forcing calm into my face. He can't know. None of them can. They would waste precious time trying to cure something that can't be cured. I can't let them get distracted, not for me. They have to stay focused, now more than ever. And so no one can ever know what's happening to me.

"I fell," I say lamely.

Zeru raises an eyebrow, knowing just as well as I do that I don't trip. The iciness in my shoulder feels like a beacon but Zeru doesn't press the matter. He nods back to the *Resistance*. "Come on."

MALCOLM FARAWAY

As Zeru leads me into the city, I glance back at Kaladria, frowning. Opting to stay back this time, she stands near the barricade. Staring at her feet, she slumps back against the wall. She looks exhausted, far more so than she did before investigating my lab.

"Is Kaladria okay? I thought she'd want to come with us back to the lab." I hesitate, thinking of her silence as Zeru explained what they'd seen. "She seems a little distant."

"Hard to say." Zeru slows his pace. "She's always been private. If something is wrong, I doubt she'll tell anyone until either she's ready or she feels she doesn't have another choice."

I frown, trying to push aside my fears. Her mood changed so quickly. Before they left for their little reconnaissance mission, she was laughing, teasing Zeru. But the moment they returned, she was quiet, solemn even. The change is stark.

"She's been through a lot in the last year," Zeru reminds me. "There's no telling what she's witnessed. We'll just have to be patient with her."

I nod silently, even if I'm certain her sudden solemnity has little to do with her year on the Aklev'Zol's homeworld.

As we near my lab, Zeru stops. He waves me forward, nodding ahead. I crouch down at the wall, lifting my rifle to use its scope. An enormous black box has taken over the street, almost completely blocking off my view of the lab.

I lower my rifle to find Zeru watching me. "Well?"

I shake my head. "I've never seen anything like it." I look back at the monolith. "Did Kaladria sense any electricity?"

"Not exactly. Apparently, it gives off a similar energy as the Aklev'Zol do. But she wasn't sure if it's true electricity or just something akin to it."

I sigh. "Well, I have no idea what this thing is capable of."

Zeru rubs the back of his neck. "Then, I think it's time we act without captain's orders."

"What do you mean?"

He leans forward, studying the black box for a moment. "We need information, badly. And I don't think Kaladria is in the right mindset to help us with that."

"So, we do a little searching without her?" I assume.

He nods. "I say we handle this one on our own."

I study the black box, thoughtful. It's risky. The monolith is well guarded. And I've already lost so many scouts to this street. But I'm not all that inclined to get Kaladria's help when she's already so out of sorts. I lost her once. I can't risk losing her again.

I nod. "Let's go."

We sneak closer to the box, staying close to the walls and sticking to the shadows. Once we're mere feet away from it, Zeru stops. He watches the Aklev'Zol guarding the box. "If I cause enough of a distraction, do you think you can figure out what we're dealing with?"

"Depends on how good of a distraction you've got in mind."

"It'll be good. Go."

He turns transparent, running headfirst into the street. I slip forward, slowly approaching the black box. Zeru turns solid, just long enough to throw a knife at one of the Aklev'Zol. When it falls dead, the others give chase, along with the Zol beasts previously circling the black box. Smirking, Zeru transforms back into his Ghost Form, leading them on a wild chase through the streets.

I shake my head. *And he said Kaladria is the one who's always rushing in headfirst.*

I dart across the street, racing for the box. I run my hand across its surface until my fingers catch on a lip. I pause, pulling on it to reveal a mess of wires. I push them aside, searching for anything to clue me in as to what this thing does.

A small black chip comes free, similar to the memory we received from the Zol Beast we fought a year ago in that old abandoned house. Glancing back, I listen to the chaos down the street. Then, I take off running.

Within minutes, Zeru is back at my side. "Got anything?"

I hold up the chip. "Don't know. Hopefully."

Zeru nods. "Let's head back. It looks like you've got work to do."

***

I work in contented silence, plugging in the chip to examine what's stored on it. An immense amount of information shows up on the monitor. I exhale, beginning to sift through it.

It feels good to be more than a soldier again. Working on stuff like this, researching tech, using my head, that's home. Far more than any of the fighting I spend all my time doing these days. Creating weapons is close but finding answers is much more like the kind of work I used to enjoy.

"Find anything?" Zeru asks, leaning against the wall.

"Not yet. It might take some time…"

I trail off, eyes scanning the computer screen. *Blueprints.* I study the mapped-out designs, face paling as I realize what they're implying, what that black monolith's presence means.

"Malcolm?"

I rake my fingers through my hair. We're in so much trouble now. "We need to talk to Kaladria."

78

KALADRIA ASTRANA

"Have the two of you completely lost your minds?"

I cross my arms, eyes flitting between the two of them. Zeru, I can believe, would pull something like this. If only to keep me from doing something similar. I look at Malcolm, who crosses his arms too. I wouldn't have expected him to agree to something so risky. I don't remember him being reckless. But I suppose he's probably had to make more dangerous calls as of late.

"Kaladria," Zeru says impatiently, "You're my captain, not my mother. This was our choice. And it was a good call."

I sigh.

"Kaladria," Malcolm adds, more gently, "If we didn't get this information when we did, it might have been too late."

I hesitate. "What do you mean?"

"That thing is a machine capable of transforming all living beings into Aklev'Zol."

I set my jaw, very much aware of the iciness spreading down my arm. *Bigger than your fear, Kaladria.*

"We aren't talking about one at a time, either," Zeru adds.

Malcolm nods solemnly. "Once turned on, the machine will set off a reaction, infecting every being in the system in a single swoop."

"What?"

"Remember what we saw on Neptune?" Zeru asks. "That dark matter spreading across the surface of the planet. It's the same concept, even if it's happening at a much slower rate. Anything organic touched by the dark matter is infected. This machine will speed up the process. If they turn it on, anything living in this system will be transformed. If we don't figure out how to destroy that thing and fast, we're all dead."

I close my eyes, pinching the bridge of my nose. "How much time do we have?"

"Based on the information we retrieved, we know they haven't finished the machine. But it won't be long. Maybe a week. A month, at most."

I slump back in my seat. *So, that's it.* If we don't stop this now, if we can't work out some kind of miracle to destroy that machine, it will be over for much more than just me. It'll be over for everyone. My heart aches at the thought and I focus on that pain over the iciness creeping across my skin.

"Zeru," Malcolm says quietly, "Do you want to update everyone else on what we've learned?"

I open my eyes. Zeru nods slowly, watching me carefully for a moment. Then, he steps off the bridge and into the elevator. As the elevator doors close, Malcolm stands. He leans his rifle against the wall before approaching. He crouches in front of me, watching me carefully. "You okay?"

"Was it all pointless?" I ask softly. "Everything we did to keep them from invading. Everything we've done since then. Was this inevitable?"

Malcolm sighs. "I'm not sure I believe anything is inevitable. We had choices and we've done our best to make the right ones but the Aklev'Zol had choices, too. The best we can do is give everything we've got. And either we'll survive or we won't."

I smile faintly. "When did you get so smart?"

His cheeks redden slightly. "I'm not that smart. If I was, I'd already know how to stop them from turning that thing on."

I sigh. "I'm certainly not doing any better."

A machine that can wipe us out in minutes. How long have they been working on such a thing? Months? Years? Perhaps this was the plan all along.

Malcolm takes my hand in his. "We're going to figure it out, Kaladria."

I look down at our hands. I'm suddenly hyperaware of the iciness spreading through my shoulder. I swallow, twisting my hand free. "We need to figure out how to exploit that machine."

Malcolm stands, taking the chair next to mine. He fingers the memory chip. "I'll take a closer look at the data. Maybe I can find a weakness we can use."

I nod. "In the meantime, I'll take a team off world. Regardless of how we end up destroying that thing, I suspect we'll need help from the rest of the system. This is bigger than Earth."

Malcolm nods silently.

"I'll leave my father here," I decide. "He might be able to help." The two of them are the smartest people I know. Perhaps, with the two of them working together, the system might stand a chance.

"We'll find something," Malcolm promises.

I stand, walking toward the elevator without another word. There's work to be done and I don't have much time left to do it.

MALCOLM FARAWAY

KALADRIA'S FATHER IS A GENIUS.

As we go through the stolen data, it doesn't take me long to realize he's much more than a scientist. Herren understands the information much faster than I do, figuring out what we're up against almost immediately. As morbid a thought as it is, I can't help but wonder if that's why the General kept him alive for so long.

"It looks like they've been working on this for a long time," he says. "They've been trying to figure out how to instantly change a system since our ancestors fled the Zeta Arae system centuries ago."

"That long?"

Herren leans away from the monitor. "It would seem that they are quite determined to wipe us out."

"What would make them hate your ancestors so much that they'd put so much effort into destroying your people?"

Herren shakes his head. "I don't believe they were always this way. Once they were a thriving people but they became twisted and dark when they turned to a powerful entity for help in prolonging their race."

"The Queen of Tethra," I murmur.

Herren nods. "She was a great point of interest for me. But I still don't know if she ever existed. The General has never mentioned her."

I frown. There's no way that this queen could be the source of the Aklev'Zol's power without there being mention of her. If she exists, she must play a huge role in this war. Yet no word has ever been breathed about her involvement. Still, where could the stories have come from? If not this powerful being, who was the Queen of Tethra?

Herren, having returned to his reading, lets out his breath. "Herren Astrana," he mutters, "You are a fool."

"Did you find something?"

Herren points to the screen. "Read there. Carefully."

I scan over the words. "They don't have a power source," I realize. "That's the missing piece. That's why they haven't turned it on yet. They don't have the necessary energy to turn it on."

Herren nods.

I continue to read, searching for anything that might prove useful. Then, I scan over a sentence again. My breath stops. "Kaladria."

"What?"

I look at him. "Last year, a human made a deal with the Aklev'Zol, which resulted in an attempt to harvest Kaladria's lightning."

Herren grimaces. "She told me."

"What if the Aklev'Zol intended to use the harvested lightning to power this machine?" It makes so much sense now. Both Xalin and Kaladria had their lightning stolen in that facility. But it never seemed to affect Xalin the way it affected Kaladria. After all, Kaladria is the only one who struggles to use her power even a year after that experience. Which means they must have been stealing her lightning more aggressively.

Understanding lights on Herren's face. "They were trying to get the humans to create a power source for them."

"Exactly."

Herren frowns. "Then, why didn't they use me? I was held captive for over a decade. Why wait until her?"

I drum my fingers against the table. All three of the Astranas have been held captive. All three share the lightning of their homeworld.

That electricity lives within all of them. But I know there's at least one difference between Kaladria and her family.

"The Lightning Form. Kaladria uses it without serious repercussions."

Herren exhales heavily. "She has control over an immense amount of power. With that second form, she generates far more electricity than the rest of us. If they harnessed that, the Aklev'Zol could power just about anything they wanted to."

I rub the back of my neck. "So, why aren't they trying to use her like that now?"

The General had captured her. Why didn't he use that machine to steal her lightning again? If this is what he's been planning, why didn't he use her? As grateful as I am that she's been spared that pain, it doesn't make much sense.

We both glance at the computer. I scan over the document again, more slowly this time. Then, I look back at Herren. "Read here."

He leans forward, reading carefully. When he starts nodding, I know he's realized the same thing I have.

"The machine can be overloaded. That's why they don't want to use Kaladria as a power source anymore. Her Lightning Form is too volatile."

"So, we need to come up with something just as powerful to overload their systems," Herren says. "If we can do that, the whole thing will shut down. The machine will be dead."

"What's strong enough to overload something that large, other than your daughter?"

"I wonder if we could create something powerful enough to overload it," he muses. "Your wormhole generator puts off a lot of energy. Perhaps something similar would do the job."

I nod. This all started with the wormhole generator. Perhaps, it will end with something similar.

Herren stands. "I'll tell Kaladria."

As he leaves the room, I lean back in my seat. I glance at the computer screen with a weary sigh. It looks like the work has only just begun.

KALADRIA ASTRANA

"How long will it take?" I ask as my father finishes explaining that he and Malcolm are working on a device capable of frying the machine intended to be our doom.

His holographic form pauses on the comm, rubbing a hand across his face. "It shouldn't take long. Maybe a few days, provided we can find the proper supplies."

I exhale. "Good. The Jovians and the Martians have already agreed to send what remains of their forces to Earth for a last assault. Once we've gathered our armies, we can use our forces to get this device to the machine."

"I'll let Malcolm know." He studies my face. "Anything else?"

"No." I keep my expression calm, neutral. "Thanks, Dad. I've got to go."

As I end the call and the holographic version of my father disappears, I slump back in my chair. Keeping up appearances has proven to be exhausting. And pushing my fear away completely has proven to be impossible. Every time I think of that machine, I can feel the infection spread.

There's a knock on the door. I wipe my face, straightening. "Come in."

Vale pokes his head inside. "The Neptunians are in. Where next?"

"Venus." I hesitate. "Zeru should go with Azar. He's the only one who can handle Venus's temperature, thanks to his Ghost Form, and I'd prefer to send someone with Azar."

I don't want to imagine what Azar would do if there's even a hint of proof that the Venutians aren't interested in working with the rest of us. He's too angry as of late. Hopefully, Zeru can help him keep his cool so we don't completely alienate the Venutians before we know they'll come.

Vale nods, pausing in the doorway. "Are you alright?"

"Fine," I lie. "Just tired. I haven't been sleeping much."

"You should rest. I'll let you know if we need you."

I sigh, nodding. With one final troubled look in my direction, Vale leaves the room, shutting the door behind him.

Reluctantly, I stand and walk over to the bed. I fall onto it, curling around my pillow. I don't bother kicking off my shoes or removing my armor. I close my eyes with a weary sigh. It doesn't take long before I drift off into a world of dreams.

MALCOLM DROPS TO HIS KNEES, *his face full of such despair it nearly splits me in two.*

"Oh, don't feel bad." The Aklev'Zol laughs. "You really did try. But Kaladria Astrana is gone. I am all that remains of her."

No. Please, no.

Malcolm's expression is so broken. His eyes are hollow as he stares back at the Aklev'Zol. He doesn't even respond.

The Aklev'Zol leans forward and stabs Malcolm straight through the chest.

I GASP, sitting straight up. Sweat runs down my face, long strands of hair sticking to my skin. I push it away, chest heaving. I look down at my blackened arm. The cold creeps down to my elbow, slithering through every nerve.

I close my eyes, slowing my breathing. Still, it doesn't stop the tears spilling down my cheeks. *How am I supposed to keep this up?* My façade is crumbling with every breath, my resolve cracking every time I shut my eyes. I don't know how to stop that nightmare from becoming my reality. I don't know how to not become that dark, cruel thing. Or from hurting Malcolm—

No.

My fingers clench into fists. I won't let it happen. I'd rather die.

Of course, that might very well be the only thing that can stop it.

81

KALADRIA ASTRANA

IN THE END, all of the Council races prove they're willing to do what we always swore we would. We were protectors of the system before the invasion and every race is prepared to be so once more. Every planet vows to come to Earth, bringing every ship, every able-bodied soldier to help us make our last stand. It's not a lot but it's still more than we had before.

I go through the list in my head as we make for Earth, counting the armies now at our disposal. Saturn has the largest army remaining out of all the Council planets, giving our forces a large boost in both foot soldiers and ships to aid us on Earth. Venus and Mars have mostly foot soldiers, though not as many as Saturn. But they should provide good support with their abilities. Neptune has some soldiers but very few ships left to speak of. Jupiter has the least left to offer. Most of those alive are citizens. Still, even they vowed to fight with us. I suppose they have nothing left to lose. If they refuse to fight, it will assuredly mean the end of their race.

I shake my head as we land, standing and heading for the airlock. Even with so much help being offered, I doubt we'll succeed without clever tactics.

Stepping out of the airlock, I glance across the base. My gaze falls on my father, who hurries to my side. "How did it go?"

"Every race has agreed to join us in our efforts," I reply. "Everyone knows what's at stake now."

He nods. "Malcolm and I have made a lot of progress on our device. He's putting the final touches to it now. It'll be ready soon."

"Good. As soon as the other races show up, we need to destroy that thing."

There's too much emotion in my voice. It feels thick and my shoulder responds to my fear, making me stiffen in pain at the thought of the cost of failure if we can't pull this off.

Dad watches me. He touches my arm, the one still untainted by the infection. "Are you alright, Baby Girl?"

I force composure into my expression. "I'm fine. Just ready for this nightmare to end."

It's not a complete lie, I tell myself to push away my guilt.

"Agreed." He looks back at the ship, then across the street. "Where's Xalin?"

I nod behind me. "Still on the *Resistance.*"

Touching my arm gently, Dad brushes past me. He steps through the airlock, disappearing onto my ship. Taking a deep breath, I head for Lori's house. Noah leans against the barricade, rifle in hand. Nearby, Dean and Tyler stand in the street. Dean rolls his eyes as Tyler speaks animatedly. I move more quickly. I don't have the energy to deal with Tyler's antics today.

Lori sits in the kitchen, that small human girl Dad saved before on her lap. The girl cuddles close with her eyes closed. Lori smiles, sipping a mug as she rubs the girl's back. She glances at me as I slow my pace.

Malcolm? I mouth.

She nods toward the living room.

I stride into the next room. He sits on the couch, leaning over a small device. He scowls at it, eyebrows knit together in annoyance.

I slide into the seat next to his. "How is it going?"

"Slowly." He continues to scowl at the device in his hands. "I don't know what the deal is but I always seem to struggle to get things to turn on and *stay* on."

Despite everything, I find myself smiling at his exasperation. "May I?"

Sighing, Malcolm relinquishes the device. I turn the small box in my hands. It's no larger than the wormhole generator but it's much less elegant in design. It has a few switches on top and several ports on the side that must be meant to connect to the Aklev'Zol's machine and fry its inner workings.

I slid open the device, adjusting a couple of wires. Then, I hit it with a small burst of electricity. I hand it back to him. "Try it now."

He flips a switch on the box, eyebrows lifting in surprise as it thrums to life. "What did you do?"

"I've always liked to tinker," I admit.

"That's awfully convenient, considering your abilities."

"It certainly helps."

Malcolm sets the device on the table. "Well, provided whatever you just did holds up, we should be ready."

"Good. We should have a fairly sizable army within a day or so."

Malcolm exhales, drawing out a very slow sigh. "Then, it's almost over."

His voice is so confident that I have to turn my head away so he doesn't see my despair. He's right. Without their machine, the Aklev'-Zol's plans will be severely crippled. And, with every race standing together, everyone stands a chance against the Aklev'Zol. Everyone here has a strong chance of surviving this war. Everyone but me.

Instantly, that horrible nightmare flashes through my mind. I shake it away, swallowing hard. "I need to go," I tell Malcolm.

I walk toward the door without another word. Wanting desperately to crumble, I hold back the sudden emotion threatening to steal away any resolve I have left. I want to fall to the floor and scream in frustration.

I was so close. So very close.

I stop at the door. Cold seeps into my forearm. At the same time, it spreads upward, slinking into my collarbone. It creeps into my bones, sinking further and further into my arm. I stiffen, biting down a cry.

Malcolm notices how motionless I've become. "Kaladria?" He stands. "Is something wrong?"

I grit my teeth, refusing to look at him. "I'm fine."

8 2

KALADRIA ASTRANA

I DON'T KNOW how I manage to fall asleep. Even more surprising, I don't dream at all. I wake, bleary-eyed, but surprisingly well-rested. I stare at the ceiling for a moment before willing myself to look down. The damage has barely moved all night, the blackness still stopped halfway down my forearm, just as it was before I fell asleep. I suppose that's something to be grateful for.

Pausing, I look across the room at the window as sudden chaos fills the air. Screams shatter through the silence, followed by the sounds of gunshots. I sit upright, rolling out of bed and snatching up my spear. Adjusting my sleeve so it covers my arm, I dart outside. But I stop at the sight of the war zone I have just walked into. The whole base is under attack.

An Aklev'Zol lunges for a human. I reach out a hand, extending my fingers as I blast it with lightning. As the monster falls, I leap forward in search of my next enemy. As I move across the base, I run into Zeru. He moves just as quickly across the battlefield, flicking his fingers and knocking several Aklev'Zol soldiers to the ground with his telekinesis. I drop to a knee, pressing my fingers against the earth, sending electricity through the street and striking the Aklev'Zol Zeru has knocked down.

I stand. "What happened?"

"It would seem the Aklev'Zol are onto us," Zeru grunts, pulling his knife free of the head of an enemy.

"They must have noticed our forces gathering here."

I blast another couple of Aklev'Zol, desperately trying to ignore my rising panic. We need more time. We won't be able to reach the machine without an army. And our army is not all here yet.

Forcing my mind back into the task at hand, I swing my spear at a Zol Beast. Zeru fights alongside me, swinging his dagger expertly. As we bring down our enemies, we're quickly joined by our allies. It's not until the remainder of the Aklev'Zol's forces disappear out the broke barricade that I realize Malcolm is nowhere to be found.

I turn in a circle, heart pounding. "Where's Malcolm?"

Zeru frowns, looking across the base. "Lori's house?" he guesses.

I nod and we run to Lori's house. I clench my fists as we move through the house, finding nothing but silence. As I step into his room, I stiffen.

It's been completely ransacked. The bed has been shredded, long lines raking through the mattress, his things thrown across the room in disarray. Someone has clearly been searching for something. And then there are the bodies. Aklev'Zol bodies, their corpses strewn across the floor, limbs at awkward angles in death. I stare at the drops of bright red blood on the floorboards, suddenly ill. *Not black like Aklev'Zol blood,* I think. *That's human blood.*

I stoop down, picking up the small device meant to be our salvation. The thing has been completely torn in two, the pieces missing most of their interior parts. They found our plans. They figured out what we intended to do and destroyed the device we'd planned to use against them. Then, they took Malcolm, our only source of creating another.

Pain slices through my panic as fear urges the infection to progress. The iciness spreads down the rest of my arm, almost to my wrist now.

"The Aklev'Zol must have taken him." Zeru's voice sounds so far away, muffled by my pain and fear.

I blink, staring at the drops of blood. There's only one thing left

331

that matters. "I have to find him." My voice sounds mechanical, empty, even to my own ears.

"Kaladria, think about this." Zeru grabs my wrist. "That's exactly what they'll expect of you. I want to find him as much as you do but if we rush in blind—"

"I'm out of time!"

He drops his hand. I sink onto the bed, hand over my face as my last bit of willpower vanishes. I can't do this. I can't let *them* do this. The very thought of falling to the darkness while Malcolm is who-knows-where is too much to bear.

Zeru crouches in front of me, brow furrowed as he studies my face. "What do you mean, Kaladria?"

I don't look at him, staring down at my hands. Tears race down my cheeks but I ignore them, focusing on the spreading mark. It won't be easy to hide for much longer.

"Kaladria—"

I exhale. There's no point in trying to conceal it anymore. He won't let this drop until I explain myself. And I can't waste any more time trying to convince him that there's nothing to worry about. "I can't afford to wait, Zeru." I still can't meet his gaze as I yank down my sleeve. "I'm a walking time bomb."

He grabs my arms. "Kaladria..."

I take a deep breath, willing myself to be calm. *You are bigger than your fear,* I remind myself, using Xalin's mantra like an anchor. I have to slow the infection down. I need to buy myself a little more time.

I force myself to look up into his face, allowing myself to see the distress there. "I don't know how much time I have left," I whisper hoarsely. "If I don't go after him now, I may not have the will to go after him at all."

He releases my arms. "Kaladria—"

"I love him."

I expect him to be surprised. But he doesn't seem to be. He just smiles, if a little sadly. "I know." He stands, drawing out his breath very slowly, as if these next words are the hardest he's ever had to say. "Kaladria, you and I have been friends for a very long time. I know you better than almost anyone. I know what you'd do for the people you love. And I know there's nothing that would keep you here with Malcolm in trouble." He exhales. "I won't ask you to stay. I won't tell you to wait. All I wanted to say is try to get both of you back here in one piece. I'll take care of everything here."

I blink away my tears, wrapping my arms around him in a fierce hug. "If this spreads too far before I get back," I whisper, "I want you to know that you are the best lieutenant I could have asked for."

He hugs me back. "Serving under you was the greatest honor I've ever had, Kaladria." He steps back. "Now, go."

I STRIDE through the city at a furious pace, lightning sparking off tightly closed fists. Several Aklev'Zol soldiers, intending to stop me, lunge. But I don't stop. I flick my fingers in their direction, not waiting to watch them fall to my power.

As I reach the Aklev'Zol's monolithic machine, I pause. I don't know where they took him but I know the General will. And I know he's going to be closely watching this machine.

Leaning against a building, I peer around the corner, searching. Several Zol Beasts and half a dozen Aklev'Zol soldiers stand in the street. I turn back, spear clenched in both hands.

I take a moment to breathe. *You are the Lightning Demon,* I remind myself. *And a demon fears no one.*

Lightning sparking across every inch of untainted skin, I launch from my hiding place. I lunge at the nearest of the Aklev'Zol soldiers. I stab my spear into his forehead. As I rip it back out, the remaining forces charge.

I duck under a set of talons, using the back end of my spear to jab the soldier in the stomach. Swinging my staff back around, I swipe its sharp tip across another soldier's front. He staggers, talons over his stomach in an attempt to hold in the blood and gore now spilling from his body.

As two more lunge for me, I drop into a crouch. I press my hand to the ground. Electricity sparks across the street. The Aklev'Zol and

Zol Beasts around me stumble back. I lunge forward, slamming into one of the soldiers.

"Where is the General?" I demand.

"There are easier ways to get a hold of me, Captain Astrana."

Electricity sparking, I grip the soldier in front of me by the skull, electrocuting him. Tossing his body aside, I whirl around to face the General. *"Where. Is. He?"*

The General looks me up and down, undoubtedly searching for signs of the mark I'm hiding beneath my clothing. "I'm surprised you haven't turned yet."

"Don't change the subject," I snap. "Where's Malcolm?"

"What makes you so sure I know?"

Fury snaps my patience in two. I lunge forward, lightning ready. Two soldiers grab my arms, yanking me back. Even still, I snarl, squirming to break free.

I will kill him. If it's the last thing I do, I'll kill him.

"You really are something." The General laughs, shaking his head in disbelief. "That fire will make you an excellent soldier, I think."

I turn my head, clenching my jaw.

The General nods, signaling to the soldiers holding me in place. "Come. I suspect Mr. Faraway could use some company."

83

MALCOLM FARAWAY

I WAKE IN COMPLETE DARKNESS. Groaning, I push myself into a seated position. I touch my head with a wince. As I pull my hand back, there's blood on my fingers. I clench my fist, leaning back against the wall. My head is spinning.

They were really out for blood. I don't think so many Aklev'Zol have ever banded together to attack me before. Not like that. And when they broke the device, it all became clear. They wanted it destroyed and they wanted me removed from the picture.

A sleeper agent must have slipped through our defenses. It's the only way they would have known what we were planning.

My eyes flash up as the darkness around me eases away. Dim lights flicker above my head, revealing the once pitch-black space around me to be an almost empty room. Other than me, the only thing in here is a single Aklev'Zol soldier.

Her skeletal features twist into a smirk. "I was starting to wonder if you'd ever wake up."

The sound of her voice rips the breath from my lungs. I stiffen. I'd recognize that voice anywhere. I've been hearing it in my head since the day they turned her. "Emma."

She rolls her eyes. "When are you going to get it? *Emma* is dead."

I clench my hands tightly. "What do you want?"

"Other than you to stop getting in the way?" Her mouth twists up in a lipless smile. "Kaladria Astrana. The boss is convinced that, without the two of you, this will finally be over."

I grit my teeth. "You'll never catch her."

"Never say never." She turns on her heel. "Enjoy what little time you have left, Faraway. It won't be long."

As she leaves the room, I slump back against the wall. I wish she was wrong but I know better. Kaladria will come. Normally, she'd even stand a chance against them but something has changed in her. Something inside of her has snapped. She's unraveling.

The door swings open again. The General steps into the room, wearing a mocking smile. Even knowing she would come, my heart sinks at the sight of Kaladria. She's dragged in behind the General, staring into his back with such a raw hatred that it sends a chill down my spine. I stare at her, at the gore and grime covering her body like a second skin. Black blood—Aklev'Zol blood—coats her armor. Capturing her must have been a bloodbath.

Our eyes meet and the wrath in her face abates but only slightly.

"You didn't really expect her to just forget about you, did you?" The General chuckles at my fallen expression. "Particularly when she has so little time left."

Kaladria's face falls, pain contorting her expression. Her shoulders slump and she drops her gaze.

On seeing the obvious confusion on my face, the General looks at Kaladria incredulously. He barks out a surprised laugh. "Don't tell me you've been keeping it a secret."

Kaladria turns her head away, setting her jaw in a hard line.

The General raises his hand to signal to his soldiers to drop her. She falls to her knees, eyes still cast downward.

Before the General had spoken, I'd expected her to continue her wrathful bloodbath and kill them all. But now? Something about his words, about the secret she's keeping, has broken her.

The General steps away, grinning wickedly at Kaladria. "Well, by all means, let me give you the time to tell him the truth now."

I glare at his retreating form as he and his soldiers file out of the room, closing the door with absolute finality. Kaladria doesn't move, remaining frozen on the floor. I walk across the room, sinking to my knees in front of her. "Kaladria?"

She clenches her fists, glaring into the floor, but is otherwise completely still.

"Kaladria, what did he do?" I press. "What was he talking about?"

She looks up. Her eyes are bright with unshed tears, her features twisted with a kind of pain I've never seen before. "I..." She pinches her eyes shut. "I didn't want you to find out, not like this."

The pain in her voice genuinely frightens me. I stare back at her, searching her face. I wait for her to explain but she says nothing more. She just sits there with her eyes closed, fists clenched tightly in her lap.

"Kaladria, *please.*"

She exhales slowly. Then, she opens her eyes and forces herself her feet, creating some distance between us. Every motion is so careful, almost painful. When she yanks down the sleeve of her shirt, I understand why.

I can't breathe. *"No."*

Her shoulder is black, tar-like tendrils creeping up her collarbone and disappearing down her arm. I think of Emma, clawing at the blackness as it spread across her skin. Kaladria has been acting strange since scouting out the Aklev'Zol's monolithic machine with Zeru. This is what she's been hiding. This is why she's been so distant.

"The infection is spreading too quickly. I can't stop it."

Sudden anger bubbles inside of me, ugly betrayal swelling in my chest. *She lied.* To me, to everyone. I've asked her half a dozen times if she was okay and, every single time, she said she was fine.

"Why didn't you tell me this before?" I grab her arms, tugging her toward me. "Why didn't you let me help you?"

Kaladria twists out of my grip. "Because there's nothing you can do," she says sharply. "There is nothing you or anyone else can do to stop it."

I rip my fingers through my hair, looking away from the black matter covering her arm. Turning away, I slam my hands against the wall. Wishing she was wrong, knowing she's absolutely right.

No one can save her now.

84

KALADRIA ASTRANA

MALCOLM LEANS his head against the wall, hands clenched into tight fists as he strikes the wall in frustration.

Standing in the middle of the room, I swallow. Silently, I wish there was something I could say to make this right, even if I know there isn't.

Malcolm doesn't move but his entire body is taut with tension. Even though I know he's angry with me, even if I know I know he would have preferred honesty, I stand by my choices.

Despite all appearances, despite everything he's witnessed, I know a small part of him has never changed. He's still that boy who cared so deeply about so many. Creating the safe zones, ensuring there were places for the weak to go during this horrible war, even becoming a soldier. All those things were done to protect people. He's seen so many horrors, played a roll in so many deaths. But I know he doesn't like taking lives—even the lives of monsters—anymore than he did before. He's still that same kind soul, his compassion somehow untarnished by this cruel war.

He deserves so much more than I can give him. He deserves someone better than me, someone that can stand by his side when the dust settles. And, if I have to keep him at arm's length to make sure he gets that, so be it.

"I never wanted to hurt you." I take a step toward him against better judgment. "I was just trying to protect you."

He whirls around. "I didn't want your protection." His expression contorts with pain. "I never wanted it."

"Malcolm—"

He crosses the room in just a few aggressive strides. He grabs my arms again. I'm not breathing as he looks down at me. His eyes are so intense, burning into me. "Don't you get it, Kaladria?" he whispers fiercely. "I *love* you."

My heart is going to ram out of my chest.

Malcolm leans closer. "I thought..." He trails off, releasing me with a tight grimace as the door swings open again.

The General pauses, taking in my tear-streaked despair and Malcolm's tight frustration. He grins wickedly. "Was that so hard?"

Even with tears still leaking down my cheeks, I glare.

"I thought the two of you would be interested in some news," the General says. "We have finished the Machine, which the two of you are sitting in, by the way."

My heart sinks. I knew we were taken to the Machine. But I didn't realize they'd actually finished it. I thought it was just a good place to store a couple of prisoners. I'd hoped that was the case.

I swallow past the lump in my throat. We failed. Within minutes, it's going to be over. For everyone. All across the system, every being will be infected. Any chance of anyone surviving this war is about to vanish.

I look at Malcolm. He doesn't look at me, staring back at the General with a sullen expression.

My fists tighten, nails digging into the palms of my hands. I can't let him die. He's already lost so much. He's done so much to make it this far. After all of the suffering, all of the struggles, I won't let him share my fate. I don't have the power to give him what I know he wants but I do have the power to give him a chance to live.

As the General leaves again, slamming the door shut and leaving us in what I'm sure he assumes is our tomb, the floor lights up with strange circuitry. The center of the room glows with electricity.

I know what I have to do. I know how to stop this. Malcolm and my father invented a device capable of destroying this machine by overloading its systems. But my body holds more electricity than any machine could.

I drop to my knees.

Malcolm speaks up, voice hoarse with emotion. "Kaladria—"

I hush him, refusing to meet his gaze. Then, I press both hands to the floor. Slipping into my Lightning Form, I reach within myself and yank out every bit of power inside of me. Careful to keep the electricity away from Malcolm, I focus on the Machine. Lightning crackles around me and I push every ounce of it into the floor.

I extend the lightning throughout the floor, letting it seep into the machine. Long strands of electricity arc below my body. Even still, the effort pushes my power further than my body can reach, even in this form.

No. I won't give up.

Exerting my power with a roar, I push the lightning further, willing it to force the Machine past its limits. I will not yield. For Malcolm, for my squad and my family and everyone else desperately trying to survive this war, I will ensure this machine is destroyed.

Very suddenly, I gasp sharply. Everything splits apart in a torrent of electricity. Then, there's nothing.

MALCOLM FARAWAY

"KALADRIA!"

I watch in horror as her bright blue form splits across the room, losing any kind of shape as she spreads her power further and further. She screams, lightning flashing with white-blue light, before her form sizzles out into nothing. Her body dissipates into a thousand strands of electricity. And I am left standing here with nothing but silence.

A low whine fills the air as the whole room flickers into darkness.

She did it. She overloaded the machine. But the effort was too much. It split her body apart, tore her into a million pieces, just as she warned me it would if she wasn't careful with her Lightning Form.

She saved everyone. She destroyed their Machine, obliterated her own body in an explosion of lightning to save everyone from becoming an Aklev'Zol.

I drop to my hands and knees with a cry that splits my soul. I bow my head, pinching my eyes shut. I would have done anything to keep her from doing it. If I had realized what she was planning, I would have grabbed her. I'd rather be struck by her power a thousand times over before watching her sacrifice herself.

"Well, the General will not be pleased."

I look up. The Aklev'Zol-Emma slinks into the room, talons

curled around her hip. She looks across the room, taking in the sudden darkness of the Machine and the lack of Kaladria. As she puts two and two together, she shakes her head.

"Look at you," she purrs. "First Emma and now Kaladria, both dead in your company. You're earning quite the reputation, aren't you, Mr. Faraway?"

My hands curl into fists.

"It's a shame really. A *waste*." She sighs. "She really would have made an excellent soldier."

Sudden fury rips through me and I lunge for her.

86

KALADRIA ASTRANA

THE MOMENT MY LIGHTNING EXPLODES, I am certain I've been sent to some sort of purgatory state as punishment for pushing the limits of my Lightning Form past where it was meant to go.

Everything is numb. I can't feel my body. I'm not even certain I still *have* a body. I can't feel the lightning either. If there is electricity in this empty space, I can't sense it. I've become deaf and blind in a single instant, completely desensitized.

I don't understand how I can be conscious right now. I should be dead. I should cease to exist.

This must be what becomes of those who split apart in the Lightning Form. This is why it's forbidden. It's not just volatile. It's not just a death sentence. It's torment without an end. I am no longer alive, nor am I dead. I am stuck in limbo, trapped between two worlds. Destroying my Lightning Form has not killed me but my lightning is spread out too thin to be pulled back together and give me form again.

Will I remain this way forever? I wonder. *Will I fade away or am I doomed to remain trapped in this bodiless form, nothing but a conscious thought?*

Regret pierces my numbness, somehow making a heart that no longer exists break. There were things I still wanted to do.

I remember everything that led me here. I remember the Machine. I remember it was turning on and I remember my need to stop it. I remember the agony of my body splitting apart. I think I even remember Malcolm screaming my name before the numbness overtook me.

Malcolm.

Even with no form at all, everything inside of me aches for him. I wonder how it's possible to feel this kind of heartache without a heart. But, I suppose, some emotions are too strong to not be felt. I have loved him so fiercely without ever finding the words. And now I know he has loved me just as fiercely, even when I tried to keep him from feeling anything for me at all.

I can't let him go. It's unfair and it's wrong. I was so afraid of hurting him but, if I fade away in this nothingness, if I leave him to fight this war alone, I will have hurt him far worse than I would have if I'd told him the truth. This can't be the last thing he has of me.

I think of him gripping me tightly, staring me down with such intensity that I could barely breathe. *Don't you get it, Kaladria?* he'd asked. *I love you...*

I hold onto that memory, letting it be my anchor. I focus on the memory of him, those nebula-like eyes, soft brown curls, a gentle smile. Every warm touch I've ever felt since the day we met.

A scream rips its way out of the nothingness, tearing through me. I yank on the emptiness around me, somehow able to find the pieces of my lightning strewn across this blank space I've been banished to.

You are the Lightning Demon. You do not surrender. Not even to death.

I accept the name the Protectorate gave me. I accept that I am a demon, that I will always be known for destruction and death. I have caused much death but I will not succumb to it.

I scream through the silence again and again, refusing to back down. My roars echo across the empty expanse until suddenly I am dropping to my knees, gasping for breath. My fingers tremble and my body still feels hollow but the numbness has dissipated.

Returned to a body of flesh and blood, I've left behind that horrible nothingness.

I look up. Across the room, Malcolm is on the floor. The Aklev'-

Zol-Emma is on top of him. She straddles his body, perched on his chest as she reaches talons for his neck. He grits his teeth, barely holding her at bay with both hands.

My breath stops. *No.*

I barrel her off him, sending us both rolling across the floor. I catch myself with my hands but my arms are shaking with the effort. *I've used too much energy,* I think, huffing in exhaustion. *I can barely stand, let alone fight off an insanely strong monster.* But I know I have to. If I want my return to the real world to matter, I have to beat her.

I start to pull myself up but I fall back to the floor as talons rip through my spine. Kicking me onto my back, the Aklev'Zol-Emma pushes me to the ground. She pins me down, claws digging into my stomach. "You are annoying me."

I kick her hard, sending her sprawling. As she gets to her feet, I launch forward. Lightning sparks across my skin as I throw a punch, striking her jaw. She staggers against the force of my power. I don't let up. I slam forward, hitting her harder and harder. With each strike, she stumbles further and further back until she's backed against a wall.

She grabs my next punch, snarling. "You think you've won? You're still dying."

"Maybe. But not yet."

I grab her head in both hands. Fingertips pressed into her skull, I push lightning into my fingers. Lightning arcs between my hands. She screams, thrashing. Then, she collapses, those soulless eyes turning glassy.

I drop her body, swaying to the side as I trip over my own feet. Every ounce of energy left inside of me fades away without adrenaline to keep me going. My knees buckle and I collapse, too tired to catch myself.

Malcolm lunges forward. His arms encircling my waist, he pulls me against his chest. I tilt my head back to look at him wearily. Even still, I'm struck by those beautifully intense eyes. They're wide with fear now, like he expects me to evaporate.

"Kaladria?"

"Hi," I whisper weakly.

He exhales a heavy sigh of relief. Smoothing back my hair, he searches my face. "Kaladria, I—"

I stop him. "Not here." I blink back the dark spots in my vision. "The General will be back soon. We need to…" I blink again, working very hard to focus on his face. "We need to get out of…here."

Malcolm says no more. He scoops me up, cradling me close. As he carries me out of the Machine, he keeps my body tucked against his. I lean my head against his chest. For the moment, the only thing that matters is the steady beat of his heart.

KALADRIA ASTRANA

MALCOLM CARRIES me off the college campus and away from the Machine, walking down mercifully empty streets. He doesn't take me back to base, both of us simply too exhausted to make the trek. He slips into what appears to be some kind of old church. It looks abandoned but I suppose that's what makes it the perfect place for us to hide right now.

I look around the room as he sets me down. I've never seen anything like this. Huge stained-glass windows line the walls. The room is full of ornate carvings, tracing the walls between the windows. It's miraculous that something so beautiful could have survived the Aklev'Zol for so long.

Malcolm sinks to the ground next to me. He doesn't even look at me, focusing on the stained-glass windows.

"Malcolm?" I whisper, so softly I'm not certain he hears me.

He looks down, startling me with the emotion in his eyes. "Yes?" he asks huskily.

"I…" I take a deep breath. I don't think words could ever express how horrible I feel for what I could have done to him. "I'm sorry. I should have told you about my shoulder before. I…"

He pinches his eyes shut.

I will never forgive myself for hurting him like this.

I reach out a hand to touch him. But then I hesitate, drawing it back. I hold it to my heart, so very uncertain. My hands have only known war. They've killed and damaged so many people, destroyed so many things. My hands are weapons, extensions of the lightning meant to strike everything they touch. But, I suppose, it's time they learned how to be more than weapons.

I was wrong to hold back, to keep everything I've been feeling from him. And I was wrong to pretend that lying was better than admitting the truth. I was fooling myself, thinking that keeping secrets would protect him.

Exhaling slowly, I reach my hand back out. My fingers tremble as I brush them across the length of his jaw, sliding them up as I press my hand against his cheek.

Malcolm opens his eyes, staring at me.

For a moment, I say nothing. I just gaze into his face, searching those gorgeous nebula eyes. "I've been so stupid. I thought I was protecting you but…" I sigh. "I was wrong."

He opens his mouth, only to shut it again.

"I love you," I whisper. "I've loved you since the day Callaghan used my lightning against me and stopped your heart. I should have told you then but I was afraid. And then the whole system fell apart and I didn't think I was ever going to see you again." My words tumble out of me, wild and nonsensical. "By the time I found my way back to you, I'd convinced myself it would be better if I didn't love you, that you would be better off without me. But I wasn't thinking about how that might make you feel." I take a breath. "If you still—"

He cups my face between his hands, tugging me forward. His mouth crushes mine. He kisses me roughly at first, desperately even. As if this is the last moment we have, as if this is the only moment that matters. But then his lips soften on mine, becoming so gentle as he kisses me slowly, almost reverently.

I melt into him, all the sharp edges of the soldier I've always had to be yielding to his touch. I slide my fingers up and into his hair, pulling myself closer. I curve into him until there's no space left between us. Then, I slide my hand around his neck, marveling at how perfectly we fit together.

As he breaks the kiss, I'm suddenly breathless. His nose grazes mine as he leans back just enough to look into my eyes. "I promise you, Kaladria," he murmurs, "I'm going to find some way to keep you here." His thumb brushes my cheek gently. "I won't let them take you."

I hold onto him tightly. "Either way," I breathe, "I'm giving you everything I have. For as long as I have."

I pull him back down, kissing him again. This is all I have to give him. Even if the whole universe comes crashing down, even if he can't save me, I can still give him this. Something to hold onto, something to remember.

THE ONLY THING I'm truly aware of as we make our way back to base is that Malcolm is holding my hand. As we walk, I look up at him. He watches the streets ahead, of us, eyes scanning for trouble. His other hand is curled around the strap of his rifle, ready for anything.

Malcolm glances down at me, catching my stare, and a small smile curves up his lips.

"What?"

"It's nothing." He slows his pace, looking ahead once more. "Are you going to tell anyone?"

I stop, exhaling. "I should have done so before." I take a deep breath. "I need to be honest, with everyone." I swallow. "Especially my family."

I wince at the thought. The last thing I want is to hurt them but I now know that keeping secrets only hurts the people I love more.

Malcolm nods absentmindedly. We slow as we reach the barricade.

Zeru races to meet us. He pulls me into a hug and then claps Malcolm on the back. "Good to have you both back in one piece."

I share a look with Malcolm. "More or less. The Aklev'Zol's Machine is destroyed." When Zeru opens his mouth to ask, I shake my head. "I'll explain that later. First, I need to speak to my father and my uncle."

Zeru nods slowly. "They're on the *Resistance*. I didn't tell them everything but I did tell them where you went. I wanted to warn them in case you didn't…"

In case I didn't come back.

I take a deep breath. "I should go."

Malcolm leans in. "Do you want me to come with you?" he asks quietly. His tone asks a different question. *Do you need me there?*

I shake my head. "Go with Zeru. Gather everyone else. I'll come find you in a minute." I squeeze his hand. "I have to do this on my own."

Malcolm nods. He leans back, waving to Zeru. "Come on."

The two of them walk off and I take a deep breath. I stride over to the *Resistance* in search of my family. It's time to come clean.

Striding through the *Resistance*, I search every corner of the ship in search of my family. Finally, I stop, standing just outside my own quarters. The door is open and they're both in there. They're arguing.

"What were you thinking?" Dad is saying. "You let her become a soldier. You let her throw her life into mortal danger on a regular basis. What kind of life is that?"

I swallow, putting my hand over my mouth. Tears brim in my eyes.

"What did you expect me to do, Herren?" Xalin replies in frustration. "Do you know what it was like for us? You threw your life away, chasing legends and dreams, and we were left to pick up the pieces. I didn't know what else to do. She was *drowning*."

"You—"

I rush into the room, putting up my hands as I step between them. "Dad, Uncle, please," I beg. "Please don't fight."

They both sigh and I drop my hands. "If you would both take a seat," I say softly. "I have something very important to tell you."

Dad sits on the bed with a frown. Xalin sits next to him, watching me carefully. "Did you find Malcolm?" Xalin asks.

I nod. "He's safe." I take a deep breath. "And I destroyed their Machine. I overloaded it in my Lightning Form." I clear my throat. "But I sort of ended up splitting apart in the process."

"Kala!" Xalin admonishes.

"What were you thinking?" Dad asks at the same time.

I sigh, raising my hands defensively. "I know, I know."

Xalin shakes his head, a lecture on his tongue. "You could have died," he scolds.

"I'm not entirely sure I didn't," I say slowly. "I felt so...hollow." I shake my head, thinking of that nothingness. "That's not important right now. I didn't come here to tell you that. There's something else I need to tell you both, something I should have told you days ago."

They both fall silent.

They both deserve the truth, I remind myself. Then, steeling myself, I reveal the slowly spreading blackness moving across my skin. Instantly, they're both back on their feet.

"Oh, Kaladria," my father whispers, yanking me into a tight hug.

I pull back, reaching out to grab Xalin's hand. "I'm sorry," I whisper tearfully. "I am so sorry."

They both hold me, embracing me tightly. Xalin kisses my hair and Dad holds me more tightly.

I pinch my eyes shut as the tears start. More than anything, I wish there was some way I could spare them this pain.

88

MALCOLM FARAWAY

"I hate hurting them like that."

I glance over at her. Kaladria stares ahead but her expression is pulled down in her misery. She curls her arms around her sides. Her eyes are red-rimmed. Putting an arm around her, I pull her close. She leans her head against my shoulder.

"It would hurt them more if you didn't tell them," I say gently.

"Are you sure?"

"You weren't there so you don't understand. But I've seen it."

She looks up into my face, frowning.

I sigh. "The day the Satellite fell and we all thought you'd died, no one could pull themselves together." I shake my head. That day will always be one of the darkest in my memory. "We were all at a loss." I meet her gaze. "You mean a great deal to a lot of people, Kaladria."

She sighs softly, resting her chin on her knees. "Azar handled it about as well as I expected."

I raise an eyebrow. "You expected him to throw a fist through the wall?"

"He's always had a short fuse. He's been particularly angry since the Satellite fell. I'm surprised he didn't do more." She shakes her head. "I didn't expect Hassuun and Vale to be quite so upset."

"They care about you."

"I…" Kaladria stops, stiffening in pain. She grits her teeth, slapping a hand up over her collarbone.

I still.

"I'm sorry." She blinks away tears. "I'm alright." But she doesn't move her hand and her fingers are shaking.

"It's spreading, isn't it?"

Kaladria looks down. "I can slow it down but I can't seem to stop it."

"Can I see?" I ask softly.

She tugs the collar of her shirt down, revealing her blackened collarbone. The dark matter snakes up her neck, dark tendrils sliding across her skin. She shivers as my fingers brush past the mark. "Does it hurt?" I ask.

"Yes." She shivers again. "It's cold."

I pull her closer. "I wish I knew how to stop it," I say very softly, swallowing hard. The very possibility of losing her fills me with despair. The thought of witnessing her destruction again threatens to undo me. I push it aside, exhaling slowly. Fear will get us nowhere.

She adjusts her shirt. "Not that I'm terribly fond of the idea but could we cut out the infection?"

I shake my head. "If it were that easy, we'd lose a lot less people. It's almost like the infection is alive, determined to either change its victims or kill them." I shudder. "People have died doing exactly what you're suggesting."

She sighs. "Figures."

"I'll think of something," I promise.

"I know."

I put an arm around her, lightly tracing my fingers across her arm. "We need more information," I say thoughtfully. "We just don't know enough about how this works."

"Maybe we can use the intel you stole from the Machine. There might be something you and Dad missed. The Machine was made to infect people. Perhaps there's a way to reverse it." She sighs. "I don't know. Maybe that's wishful thinking. But the data might be able to at least explain what the dark matter that makes up the Aklev'Zol is."

I nod. "I'll go over it again."

She yawns. "I'll help you."

Absentmindedly, I trace my fingers up and down her arm. Silently, I marvel at the fierce creature at my side. There was a time when she terrified me. Her power was that of a vengeful god, wrathful, relentless. And, while that power remains, it's been a long time since I was frightened or even intimidated by it. She is the Lightning Demon, an unyielding force of nature, but I can no longer imagine what life would be without her at my side. I hope I never have to.

"Do you think..." I trail off, glancing down at her. Kaladria is slumped against my side, unconscious.

Her face is so peaceful, her sharp features softened in sleep. Her lips part slightly with a sigh. Either she's too tired to feel the infection or she has at last found enough of a respite from the horrible black matter that she can sleep easily.

I adjust her body so she leans against me more comfortably. "Later then," I say softly. "We've got a little time left."

89

KALADRIA ASTRANA

THE NEXT DAY, Malcolm and I sit on the bed in his room. The Aklev'Zol bodies have been removed and someone had the sense to remove the blood from the floor. The mattress has been replaced, though I can't imagine where a fresh bed was found in the middle of an apocalyptic war.

I glance up at the mess of papers strewn between us. Having printed all the files he retrieved from the Machine's memory chip, we've begun a mad search for anything that might help us.

Malcolm leans forward, reading the paper he's holding in both hands carefully.

"Find anything?"

He looks up. "Maybe. There's a lot of references to the Nadarani. That's what the Aklev'Zol were called before they became the Aklev'-Zol, right?"

I nod. "According to legend, the Nadarani were going extinct. That's what made them turn to the Queen of Tethra. They were desperate to survive."

Malcolm rubs the side of his face. "Okay, let's think about this. What do we know about the Aklev'Zol really?"

I lean back. "We know they go across the universe conquering worlds. We know they tried to conquer the worlds of my ancestors and my people fled when it became apparent they couldn't stop them." I look down at my blackened wrist. "We know they turn people into Aklev'Zol using fear."

"Do we know why?"

"What?"

"If they were after survival, why waste their soldiers chasing your people across the universe? Why risk their numbers in a war of this scale? If they were so concerned with survival, why not just stay where they were? It's not like your people would have ever gone back."

I think for a moment. He's right. It doesn't make sense. The Nadarani wanted their race to survive. But the Aklev'Zol are far more interested in dominance.

"The Queen of Tethra," I say. "She changed them."

"Something about the power she gave them changed the Nadarani, corrupted them."

"The Aklev'Zol, the Dark Ones," I murmur.

Malcolm nods thoughtfully, falling silent. He turns his attention back on his reading, scanning over a new document.

I sink back into my seat, looking out the window tiredly. Xalin and Dad are sitting outside, with the little human girl. Crouching in front of her, Xalin sparks electricity in his open hand, just enough to show the lightning to the girl. She squeals in delight, clapping her hands.

I smile.

"Kaladria."

I look away from the window, pausing at the stunned expression on Malcolm's face. "What? What is it?"

"Does anyone know why the Queen of Tethra gave the Aklev'Zol their powers? What she had to gain?"

"We don't know almost anything about the Queen of Tethra." I frown. "Why? Where is this coming from?"

He offers me a document. I take it from him, reading quickly.

My name is Kesan Dahmoth, ex-general of the Nadaranian Empire.

And this is my final record, a testament to what was done and what sins we have committed.

It began with a war against a rival world. There was a dispute between the Nadaranian king and the chieftain of the Druun. A single argument was all it took to throw us into war. It was a grave mistake on His Majesty's part. We did not have the military strength required to fight off the Druun. By the time war ended, our numbers had dwindled by the thousands. We were going to die out.

His Majesty did not wish for his legacy to be a war that drove us into extinction. So he sent his spies across the galaxy in search of a way to save us from our imminent destruction. The answer came to those spies on a lonely planet just across the system. There, they found an ancient being who claimed she could give them what they wanted. This being, calling herself the Queen of Tethra, only asked that she meet with the Nadaranian king.

Our king agreed and met with her in private. I do not know what he offered her in return for her generosity. But what came of that meeting has rocked the foundation of our society. The king returned to our world with promises of a peaceful survival, a second chance. He promised that, with this new alliance, we would become something new, something stronger.

Much debate came of his words. Some feared the Queen of Tethra's power, some argued that this would be our last chance to return ourselves to our former glory. Civil war erupted, bringing us even closer to extinction. In the end, the king's plan won out. It was decided that we would accept the Queen of Tethra's offer.

I will never forget the moment we first saw her. She was both terrible and beautiful, a monstrous mistress of obsidian.

She opened her arms to the people gathered in the palace. Black matter spread from her hands, moving through the air in the form of shadows. Everyone it touched was changed. They became like her, dark and tall, with long talons and soulless eyes. On seeing this change, many ran. Some escaped, some did not.

Very quickly, we learned that those changed by the Queen of Tethra's shadows were changed in more than appearance. They became slaves, completely dedicated to her wishes. They were husks of her will, unable to deny her command. And so those changed by the shadows were renamed. The Aklev'Zol, the Dark Ones.

The Queen of Tethra's new soldiers now scour the planet, looking for those of us untouched by her power. They stab their talons into the Nadarani they find, changing them into Aklev'Zol.

There are not many of us left. But those of us that remain have discovered what we can about the Queen of Tethra and her dark powers. There is little hope for us but perhaps this record will come into the hands of someone who can stop her madness.

As she changes us into her slaves and soldiers, the Queen of Tethra grows stronger. With each new husk added to the Aklev'Zol's ranks, her life is extended. As more are turned, she becomes closer and closer to immortal. But we have found her weakness. The Aklev'Zol are tied to her. And she is tied to them. To stop the Aklev'Zol force from growing, to stop her, the Queen of Tethra must be killed. The Aklev'Zol cannot survive without her. If she dies, so does her army.

This is the only way. The Queen of Tethra's hunger for power will end no other way. She will not willingly give up her immortality. She will spread across the universe until she is all that is left or until someone kills her.

Her death is the universe's last chance.

I look up, mind spinning. *How did this end up amongst the Machine's data? Is there some grand scheme I'm not seeing? Is someone trying to help us stop her? Or is she simply mocking us, goading us into action that could as easily finish us off as it could her?*

"It was always her," Malcolm says. "The Aklev'Zol, the Nadarani..." He shakes his head. "They didn't want this. *She's* the reason the Aklev'Zol chased your ancestors across the universe. Out of greed and a chance at immortality."

Anger flares inside of me. At the Nadarani and their foolishness. At the Queen of Tethra for causing so much pain, so much suffering. She's stolen so many lives, destroyed so many people, all for the sake of her precious immortality.

I look down at my blackened arm, glaring at the mark. *I will not serve such a monster,* I vow. *I'll die first.*

I take a deep breath. "Do you know what this means?" I ask.

"That the Aklev'Zol are zombies, fueling the lifespan of a crazy alien queen?"

"It means I know how to stop all of this. It means there's a chance of taking away my infection. And, more importantly, I know how to stop the invasion."

MALCOLM FARAWAY

WE'VE GATHERED anyone of importance we can find. With the armies of what remains of the Protectorate gathered on Earth, our current meeting includes officials from every planet, including Earth. Everyone sits in a conference room on the *Resistance* now, waiting for its captain to speak.

Kaladria stands at the head of the table. The leaders of the Protectorate worlds watch her with a sort of reverence. Even if the Protectorate is gone and the Council is dead, these men and women still know who she is and what she's capable of. The humans watch her warily, not sure what to make of the Saturnian soldier who possesses an authority they can't ignore. They've likely heard what she was once called. But I'm not sure any of them know what to think of meeting with someone called the Lightning Demon.

Still, even the humans have the sense to not say anything. For the moment, they simply watch her. She, in turn, watches them, her eyes daring them to voice their thoughts. But I can see the tight set of her shoulders, the stiffness in her stance. She hates being studied like this.

I cross my arms, waiting and watching. If they speak against her, I'll make sure they understand the foolishness of doing so. Not only does she have a plan that might save us all but she's already suffered more than her fair share on their behalf. I didn't unite them all for them to turn against us now.

Setting back her shoulders, Kaladria places her hands on the table, studying each person in the room. "We've discovered a way to finish this war once and for all," she finally announces. "One that will stop the Aklev'Zol and ensure they cannot change anyone else."

"How is this possible?" a Martian woman asks, leaning forward in her seat.

Kaladria glances at me. "Malcolm, would you care to explain?"

I nod. "We found what appears to be some sort of ancient record, left by the Nadarani before they were transformed into the Aklev'Zol. This record explains what the Queen of Tethra is and how she is connected to the Aklev'Zol. We've learned that, if we can kill her, all of the Aklev'Zol and their taint goes with her."

The room is silent with the implications.

"I propose one last push," Kaladria says, clasping her hands together behind her back. "We set our armies against the Aklev'Zol here in the city. Meanwhile, Malcolm and I will have our own covert mission. We will find and kill the Queen of Tethra. In doing so, this war will be over."

"Why you?" asks a human official. "Surely, there are more experienced soldiers."

Kaladria glowers. "I assure you, my size does not diminish my lethality."

"Captain Astrana is our most revered soldier," a Saturnian official interjects. "If anyone can succeed on such an important mission, it is her."

"Very well," the human yields, looking away from Kaladria's sharp gaze.

"How do you intend to find this Queen of Tethra?" asks a Neptunian.

"Kaladria and I are well acquainted with Aklev'Zol command," I say. "We intend to find the General of the Aklev'Zol and use him to get to the Queen of Tethra."

"Even if you do find her, how do you intend to get close enough to kill her?"

"Our best chance for success lies in getting close enough to strike while her guard is down. The Queen of Tethra is deeply connected to her soldiers. She must know what Malcolm and I have done to impede her progress. I doubt she'll be able to resist the allure of meeting us herself." Kaladria exhales. "Even if she doesn't care about Malcolm's actions over the last year, she will not be able to resist meeting me."

"Oh?"

Kaladria's eyes meet mine. I nod. *We stand together, no matter what they think.*

Taking a deep breath, she rolls up her sleeve. The dark matter has now crept halfway down her hand, covering all but her fingers. I clench my fist at the sight of the infection's progress. She doesn't have much time left.

The room is stunned silent.

Kaladria crosses her arms. "From what we understand, the Queen is responsible for some infections being slowed, in the case of her sleeper agents. However, that is not the reason my infection has not progressed more than this. The Queen will want to know how I've managed to stay myself for this long. We'll use her curiosity to our advantage."

"And how do we know you *aren't* a sleeper agent?" one of the humans asks.

I tense, prepared to call him out for his stupidity, but Zeru speaks before I can. Leaning back in his seat against the wall, the lieutenant of the *Resistance* twirls a knife casually. "Careful," he warns. His face is cool but his tone is dangerous. "She's done more to save the lot of you than you probably deserve."

"Excuse me—"

"I vow here and now that I will use my last breath if necessary to end the Queen of Tethra," Kaladria interrupts. "All I ask in return is that your armies provide the necessary distraction to get close. What do you say?"

The representatives and officials gathered share looks across the table. They murmur amongst themselves, nodding.

The Saturnian official clears his throat. "Very well, Captain Astrana. We agree to this plan of yours."

KALADRIA ASTRANA

ON THE NIGHT before our final battle, I find Malcolm in Lori's backyard. He stands there, his head tilted back as he watches the stars.

Crossing the yard, I join him there. He says nothing but his fingers find mine and he squeezes my hand.

I look up at the night sky, searching its glittering starlight for the assurances we need to pull through tomorrow. The path we're setting out on is one I put us on. I pray it leads to our survival.

"What happens if we somehow make it through tomorrow?" I ask softly.

"I think we'll just have to take it one day at a time," he says slowly. "Honestly, I don't care where we go, as long as we stick together."

"Agreed." I tilt my head back, studying his face. "You know, I never would have thought I'd end up falling for a human."

A smile twitches at his lips. "And I never thought I'd fall for an alien. I wasn't even sure aliens existed before I met you." He chuckles suddenly, as if remembering something. "You know, I was kind of afraid of you when we first met."

I smile sheepishly. I was so angry that day. Angry at my squad for not supporting my decision to go to Earth, at the Outsiders that had managed to get past our Borders, even at Malcolm for creating the wormhole generator.

He'd received the brunt of that anger. I wish it was the only time that happened, the only time I've pointed a weapon at him. Sadly, it's not.

"I was having a bad day," I admit.

"Yeah, you have a lot of those."

As I scowl at him, Malcolm laughs. "Honestly, you still scare me sometimes."

"Is that so?" I ask with an impish smile.

"You're sort of the most intimidating person I've ever met," he admits. Then, he tugs me closer, his own smile turning roguish. "I don't mind anymore. I've been told I can be a little intimidating, too."

"That I can believe." I shake my head. "I was so shocked the first time I saw you when I came back to Earth. I've never seen anyone fight like that."

He winks. "You pick up a couple things while fighting off an alien invasion."

I study his face. He's so relaxed, so confident, more so than I think I've ever seen him. "You're in an awfully good mood for someone about to face off against the most powerful entity in the known universe," I remark.

"I figure, if something happens to me, I want people to remember me happy."

My eyes soften.

His face sobers as he considers our possible failure. "Kaladria, if something goes wrong tomorrow, I want you to know that I don't regret anything." He stops, his eyes searching mine with an intense solemnity. "Meeting you was the best thing that ever happened to me."

I step closer, sliding my hands around his waist. My cheek pressed against his chest, I hug him tightly. He slides his arms around me, holding me tightly.

I never imagined I could feel anything like this. But standing under the stars, listening to his heartbeat, I know I've found a piece of eternity. The chill across my right side, where the infection has spread from shoulder to hand, collarbone to hip, is easily ignored.

With the stars watching over us, I know this is a moment not even the whole of the Aklev'Zol army can steal from us.

I tilt my head back to look at him. "I love you, Malcolm Faraway," I whisper. "And it doesn't matter if I die tomorrow, it doesn't matter if I become her slave, nothing will ever change the way I feel about you."

He dips his head down, kissing me softly. I pull myself closer, standing on my toes as I kiss him back. As we stand there, wrapped up in starlight, I hold onto him so tightly, knowing this may very well be the last time we can stand like this.

"I will never stop loving you," I whisper, lips brushing his skin. "Not even if the whole universe comes crashing down."

KALADRIA ASTRANA

MORNING COMES TOO QUICKLY, leaving us with too many difficult goodbyes.

We know there's a chance this is the last we'll see of anyone. But I don't know what to say. What am I supposed to tell them, knowing we could be parting for the last time? How am I supposed to convey how much I care for them all?

I didn't get to say goodbye on the Satellite. There wasn't enough time. In some ways, I wonder if that was easier. I didn't have to give all of them something to remember. I didn't have to find a way to tell them they shouldn't be saddened by my death, should we fail. But, this time, everything is different and I'm not sure there are enough words for everything I want to say.

So, I simply hug my uncle and kiss my father's cheek. "It'll be over soon," I tell them, wishing I knew if my promise held any merit.

Malcolm hugs his mother tightly, speaking softly to her. Lori returns his embrace with tears in her eyes. Then, she looks at me. "You be careful, sweetie," she says. "And take care of him."

I glance at Malcolm, who is currently speaking to Dean and Tyler. He rolls his eyes at something Tyler says. Dean shakes his head.

"I will, I promise," I tell Lori.

I look at Zeru, who smiles softly. "We've been through the wringer together, haven't we, Captain?"

I return his smile. "That we have." I put a hand on his arm. "Thank you, Zeru. I never would have made it this far without you."

My voice is thick with emotion. Zeru has been at my side longer than almost anyone else. He's stood with me in nearly every fight I've ever been in. I would have failed long ago without his support.

"You and Mal will have the hardest go," he tells me. "Be careful out there."

"I know. You, too."

I face my remaining squadmates. Vale smiles and I smile back, knowing that's the only exchange that needs to pass between us. Our silences have always spoken much louder than words.

I look up at Hassuun and Azar. I pull them both into a hug. "Don't do anything too reckless," I whisper. "I need to know you guys are going to be bothering me for a lot longer."

Hassuun chuckles.

"Don't worry, Kala. We'll all be back on the *Resistance* before you know it," Azar promises. "Soon enough, you'll be yelling at us for doing something stupid."

"Or shocking Azar for annoying you," Hassuun adds.

I smile. "I'm counting on it."

As I step back, Malcolm holds out his hand. I take it, lacing my fingers through his, and look back at Xalin. "Are we ready?"

He nods. "We'll have our armies head through the city the same time you do. The Protectorate and the human army will do everything we can to keep the Aklev'Zol off your back long enough for you to do what you need to do."

I nod, taking a deep breath. Even if I fear for all of them, I know this plan gives us the best chance for success. With our armies moving through the city, the Aklev'Zol will be too busy to worry about a single human and Saturnian sneaking through the college campus.

"We'll be ready."

With one last goodbye, Malcolm and I step away from all the people we love. We start down the street, ducking in an abandoned building, watching for our signal that it's time to wage war.

93

MALCOLM FARAWAY

I watch as Kaladria leans against the wall, peering out of the half-broken window. She studies the streets in silence, calmer than she's seemed in a long time. Perhaps, she's made her peace. Win or lose today, she knows this is likely her last chance to free herself of the Queen of Tethra.

I swallow, wishing I could be half as brave as she is. To be able to hold onto courage, even in the face of such a horrible fate.

"I need you to promise me something, Malcolm."

I hesitate, studying her suddenly solemn expression. "What is it?"

She doesn't look at me, brushing her fingers across her infected collarbone absentmindedly. "If defeat is imminent and it looks like I might turn..." She takes a deep breath. "I want you to kill me."

I stiffen. "Kaladria—"

She faces me, eyes brimming with tears. "Please," she whispers. "I don't want to be her puppet." She looks down. "Since I was infected, I keep having these nightmares of an Aklev'Zol version of myself doing such horrible things." She looks up again. "I would rather die than become a monster, Malcolm."

"I won't kill you."

"Malcolm—"

"It's not going to come to that," I say stubbornly, meeting her fierce stare. "This is going to work."

She sighs. "And if it doesn't?"

"If it doesn't, I doubt the Queen of Tethra is going to just let me walk away, regardless of what happens to you."

She sighs again, looking back out the window. Still, her fear is clearly on display in the infection slowly taking over her body. I can see the shadowy tendrils creeping up her neck. I swallow. Logically, I know she deserves to die in control of herself, rather than as the slave of a monstrous queen. But I don't think I could ever bring myself to do it. I can't let her go. Not for my sake and not for hers.

An explosion sounds through the air, followed by the crash of lightning in the distance. I look out the window. A storm ravages the sky, clearly the work of the Saturnians. Ships fly through the air and fire explodes across the city every couple of minutes.

Kaladria yanks out her spear. "Let's go."

Stepping into the street, we keep to the shadows as we move quickly through the city. Aklev'Zol soldiers run past us, rushing to meet our armies. When they draw too close, we step into alleys, pressed against the nearest wall as we wait for them to pass.

Kaladria stops as we near the center of campus. She leans back against the building, just behind the Aklev'Zol's now useless Machine. She leans against the wall, looking at me. I swing my rifle around, lifting its scope to look around the corner more discreetly.

"We've got two Zol Beasts and five Aklev'Zol soldiers." I lower my rifle. "I don't see the General yet."

"He'll be there soon enough. We're too dangerous a threat for him to ignore." Kaladria peers around the building. "I'll charge in. Cover me?"

I nod, lifting my weapon to watch the street. Kaladria teleports away, reappearing in front of the Machine. She blasts one of the Aklev'Zol soldiers, stabbing the Zol Beast that charges her. As she turns to face the soldier lunging for her, I fire. The Aklev'Zol collapses and I fire three more times. With the remaining soldiers dead, Kaladria stabs the other Zol Beast in the head.

Kaladria straightens and I lower my rifle. Glancing left and right, I run to her side with my hands still tight around my weapon. I nod to the Machine. "Do you think he's in there?" I ask in a low voice.

"Only one way to find out."

She pushes open the door, stepping inside the Machine. Then, cursing, she spins around the empty room.

"Where else could he…"

Kaladria stills, body rigid with pain. She staggers a step forward. Then, she falls to one knee, clutching her infected arm. I step toward her but stop as the General appears behind her. Kaladria stiffens, crying out as he grabs her, talons digging into her hair. He yanks her head back.

My fingers itch for the trigger but I don't move. *You can't do anything,* a voice in the back of my head reminds me. *You're helpless here.* I grit my teeth. Still, I know the voice is right. The General is too fast and too strong. If I make a move now, he'll kill her.

"I'm growing rather tired of the two of you," the General growls.

He slams her head against the wall. With a gasp, Kaladria goes limp, head lolling back. She slumps to the floor as the General releases her body in disgust.

"Kaladria!"

The General straightens. "I suggest you don't make this difficult, Mr. Faraway. The two of you have caused enough problems that Her Majesty is demanding to meet you." He leans down, aggressively snatching up Kaladria's jaw, drawing thin lines of blue blood across her cheeks. "For her sake," he spits as anger taints his mocking tone, "I suggest you cooperate."

I look at Kaladria's limp form. I know what she would want. She'd want me to find some way to finish what we started, she'd want me to make sure she never turned. But I can't. Not if she's the price I'd have to pay.

Shoulders slumping forward in defeat, I throw down my rifle. "You win."

KALADRIA ASTRANA

WHEN I WAKE, it's in the most nightmarish place in the universe. I open my eyes, breath hitching at the sight of that starless sky, the horizon lined with the stout black buildings of the forsaken world I'd hoped to leave behind forever.

Even though I know coming here could help us find the Queen of Tethra, fear still swells within me. I lived through so many desperate battles here, struggled through so many lonely nights. I don't appreciate the reminder.

Exhaling, I look over to find Malcolm watching me carefully with worried eyes. I push aside the dread coiling in my gut. *You're not alone this time,* I remind myself.

I look past Malcolm. Several Aklev'Zol soldiers stand nearby, watching us warily. *So we don't run,* I think.

I sit up slowly, shivering. The extreme cold has spread down my neck, inching its way toward my heart. I don't have much time left.

The memory of that nightmare, of an Aklev'Zol-Kaladria, flashes through my mind. I have to convince him to end it, before it's too late.

"Malcolm—"

Long talons curl around my arms, dragging me to my feet. Another soldier grabs Malcolm. The General steps forward, looking between the two of us with annoyance. Likely, he's thinking of the last time he saw either of us, when I destroyed his precious Machine.

I lift my head, meeting his gaze. *You should have killed me when you had the chance.*

"Come," the General says with none of his usual bravado. "Her Majesty is not patient."

Without giving me the chance to look at Malcolm, the soldier gripping me arm yanks me forward. The General leads the way into a huge black building. Unlike the rest of the simple structures across the planet, it's tall and brooding form is castle-like. Enormous slabs of obsidian line its walls and tall black turrets spiral toward the empty sky. A palace for a self-proclaimed queen.

I clench and unclench my fists, reminding myself that we're not done yet. Even if this isn't how I'd hoped today would go and I wish I had a little more control over the situation, we still have a chance. The General is taking us to her. All I have to do is escape long enough to kill her and this will all be over.

The General leads us into a huge chamber, a throne room of sorts. It's mostly empty, except for the long lines of soldiers standing against the walls on either side of us.

I grimace. They could prove challenging. If I make a move, they'll likely pounce.

As we stop, I look up at the dais across the room, at the huge black throne there. Then, my eyes fall on the figure sprawled across it.

The dark matter in my skin starts to tingle in her presence, as if it sings to her as a lightning storm sings to me. This must be her, then. *The Queen of Tethra.*

I study my enemy carefully, trying to account for every strength, every potential weakness. She's different from her soldiers. Her skin, while as black as an Aklev'Zol's, is hard like the obsidian of her palace, making her appear as though she's made of stone. Her face is beautiful, so unlike the skeletal faces of her soldiers. With her high cheekbones, full lips, and perfectly smooth skin, she possesses an otherworldly regality. The wrongness of it has me clenching my fists. Such a monster should be hideous and yet, despite her talons and the strangeness of her stone-like skin, she's beautiful.

Silvery eyes watching with an ageless sort of boredom, the Queen of Tethra observes us with cool indifference. She lounges across her seat with her legs over the side of the throne, long taloned fingers resting against her cheek.

The General stops before her, dropping to one knee. "My Queen."

Slowly, she stands. She towers above her soldiers, at least a head taller than any of them. I doubt I come any higher than her waist.

As she crosses the room, long black hair falls around her, brushing past her legs. It swirls around her body, almost haunted in the way it slithers around her. She pushes it back, sending it flowing behind her.

"General," she says as she stops before him, looking on him with cold, unreadable eyes, "I see you were successful."

The General bows his head. "Yes, my Queen."

She brushes past him, studying Malcolm and I with cold calculation. "Kaladria Astrana and Malcolm Faraway," she greets dryly. "You are the two most vexing creatures I have ever had the displeasure of meeting."

"We try."

The Queen's eyes betray sudden irritation. She steps closer, looking down at me haughtily. I clench my fists, tilting my head back to meet her gaze.

"You should be one of my soldiers by now," she says. I glare up at her as she strokes my infected jaw with a talon. "I'm impressed. It has been a long time since I met someone as brave as you."

As if to test me, she wraps her talons around my throat. I hold her gaze, unmoving, as she tightens her hold.

"Stop it," Malcolm growls.

The Queen turns on him. "And *you*. At first, I was grateful to you for allowing my soldiers onto your world. But then you had to go and make war with them." She grabs his jaw. "I will enjoy killing you. Perhaps, once I've finished with your lovely companion, you and I will get better acquainted." Sudden hatred flashes across her face. "I wonder how many ways I can make you *writhe*."

Not happening, I think.

I twist an arm free, throwing a heavy blast of lightning at the Queen. Any other being would be dead, their body smoking, with

FORGED IN STORMS AND SHADOWS

such an attack. But not the Queen of Tethra. The lightning fizzles out around her.

The Queen of Tethra brushes aside the sparks of electricity. "You didn't think you could really kill me with your silly lightning, did you?" She shakes her head, staring down at me haughtily. "I am ancient, endless. A god."

She steps away from Malcolm. Bending over, she slides a talon across the floor, cutting through it easily. As she draws her fingers across it, a loud shriek echoes across the room. The floor splits to reveal dark matter brewing beneath the surface of the crevice she's created.

I stare at the fractured floor. *I've seen this before,* I realize, remembering the first time I arrived in Malcolm's lab. There was a giant crack in the floor, like something had torn the floor in half. I remember the lifeless laughter I'd heard when I put my hand in it.

I look up at Malcolm, seeing my shock mirrored in his face. He knows, too. It was *her*. Somehow, for some reason, the Queen of Tethra had split the floor there, just as she has here.

"Oh, yes," the Queen says slyly, "You have seen this before, haven't you?" She laughs, the sound just as lifeless as it had been the day I first heard it through the crack in Malcolm's lab. "I must confess, I do enjoy toying with my slaves."

I glare. "We're not your slaves."

"Not yet." She turns, sauntering back across the room. She sits on the throne again, crossing her legs. The Queen watches me, smiling coldly. "You still don't understand, do you?" She laughs incredulously. "Even if you had the power to destroy my body, you could not kill me."

I narrow my eyes. *Watch me.*

The Queen of Tethra smirks, sliding a hand across her obsidian skin. "This isn't my true form." She points to the floor. Black matter lifts out of the crack, swirling through the air. She flicks her fingers and it twirls through the air, forming the shape of a woman made of obsidian.

I stiffen.

The Queen waves a hand dismissively. The figure splinters before vanishing back into the crevice. "You see now, don't you?" The Queen waves a hand and the crevice widens to reveal dark matter churning below the floor. "*That's* my true form."

My heart drops. I stare at the dark matter swirling in the crevice. It's the same tar-black color as the infection currently spreading across my skin. That matter is what connects the Aklev'Zol to the Queen of Tethra, what connects her to them.

Now, I understand. The Queen of Tethra is not this woman standing before us but the dark matter swirling below the ground. Dark matter she has placed into anyone ever turned into one of her Aklev'Zol. It's not her power she placed inside of them. It's *her*.

My skin crawls at the thought. *That means a part of the Queen is inside of* my *body. And if I'm changed...*

"You can't kill me," the Queen taunts. "Not unless you can destroy the entire planet. Your people may know you as the *Lightning Demon* but not even a demon can kill a god." She laughs. "You never stood a chance."

I look at Malcolm. His eyes mirror the same despair I'm certain he can see in my face. We failed. And now there will be nothing to stop me from becoming a part of the Queen of Tethra. Even if I thought Malcolm would grant me the death I'd asked him for before, I doubt the Queen would let him give it to me. She wants me as her slave too badly.

The sharp features of her face contort with cruelty. "I must admit that I find your audacity somewhat charming, Captain Astrana. It has been a very long time since anyone was brave enough to refuse my influence." Her eyes darken. "However, the time has come for this obstinance to end."

The Queen signals to her soldiers and they drag me forward. I stagger along with hands clenched into fists. Behind me, Malcolm shouts my name, struggling against the Aklev'Zol holding him in place.

The Queen stands from her throne, looking down at me with disdain. As she stares at me, ice shoots through my body. My breath hitches, the cold of the infection spreading much faster than it ever has before. It slices through my skin like frozen wildfire, covering my neck, most of my arm, wrapping around my chest.

I scream, her soldiers' tightening grips the only thing keeping me from thrashing.

"Kaladria!"

Everything sounds muffled, as if my head has been dunked underwater. I can barely hear Malcolm's voice as that piercing cold rushes through my body, despite all my attempts to stop it. I can't control the infection anymore. Pushing back my fear does nothing.

Because it's not fear that's making the infection spread, I realize. *The Queen is forcing it to spread faster than it otherwise would.*

I strain to look up at the Queen. Eyes unwavering, she continues to stare at me. I grit my teeth, fighting to regain control even if I know it's absolutely futile.

Hush now. Soon enough, you will be nothing but a memory and the pain will be gone with you.

I stiffen at the sound of her voice in my head. Despite the pain that makes me writhe, her voice is more important than my spreading infection. And she's right. It would be so easy, to just let it spread, to let this be done.

Yes, she soothes. *You have fought enough.*

I blink. I *have* fought for a long time. I've been fighting my whole life. But what was the point of all that struggling if I was always going to end up here? Releasing my fists, I sigh.

That's it, the Queen purrs. *Sleep now—*

"Kaladria, *fight!*"

As muted as it is, Malcolm's voice wrenches me from her spell. Horrified, I lift my head to meet the Queen's disappointed frown. My hands tremble as I realize just how close death had been. I was so close to giving up the fight, to allowing her to take control. Another moment and she would have had me.

Sighing, the Queen refocuses her attention. The pain snakes around my chest, drawing another scream from my lungs.

Come now, slave, she says in my mind. *Your time draws near.*

I clench my fists tightly to still their shaking. *I am no one's slave.*

You can't—

My scream gives way to a battle cry, a roar that pushes out the sound of her voice. Electricity explodes around me as I step into my Lightning Form. The Queen stops, unable to force the infection to spread while I'm in this form. Knowing I can't hurt her, even like this, I whirl around to face the General.

"KILL HER!" the Queen shrieks.

Unable to deny his puppeteer, the General lunges. I launch forward, ramming straight through him in the Lightning Form. He screams, collapsing to the floor. Smoke rises from his body and he doesn't get up.

I drop to the ground in my regular body, only barely aware that the Queen is still screaming inside and outside my head. I stagger to my feet as Malcolm twists an arm free of the soldier gripping his arm, slamming an elbow against the soldier's skull. As he darts forward, I grab his hand. With the rest of her soldiers giving chase, we run for the door.

I CLUTCH Malcolm's hand as we race out of the Queen's throne room and out of the castle that houses it. We run across the dark planet, only stopping when we are sure we're no longer being chased. We stand between two buildings, panting as we lean back against the wall.

Malcolm turns, cupping my cheek in his hand, his other moving down one of my arms to assess the damage done by the Queen.

"Are you alright?" I ask, searching his face.

"Not particularly. You?"

"I'm running out of time." I close my eyes, desperately trying to slow my heartbeat against the piercing cold wrapping around my entire body. "What are we going to do?"

For a long time, he's silent. He leans his head back against the wall, glaring up at the starless sky. Finally, he exhales tightly. "I don't know." Pain flits across his face as he realizes what that means for me.

He can't save me. Despite all his efforts to do so, all our plans to reverse my infection, there's simply no way to save me from the Queen and her dark matter.

"We can't kill her with conventional means," he says. "The only way to kill her is..." Malcolm trails off, expression freezing in place. He blinks once, in surprise.

"Malcolm?"

He meets my gaze, grinning proudly. "The only way to kill her is by destroying the planet."

I nod slowly. "Yes. The Queen said as much." I scrutinize his face. "I don't understand why you're so excited. It's not like we have a way of obliterating the entire planet."

Still grinning, Malcolm holds up a small, silver orb. "That's where I'm going to have to disagree with you."

I frown. "The wormhole generator?"

"We can change the polarity," Malcolm explains. "Reverse the wormhole generator to—"

"Create a black hole," I realize.

Kaladria Astrana!

I grimace, pushing aside the pain as the Queen of Tethra's voice screams in my head. Clearly, distance has not made her power any less potent.

"The only problem is I don't know if the wormhole generator is strong enough to make a black hole large enough to pull in the whole planet." Malcolm runs a hand across the side of his face. "Our chances would be better if we could create a black hole in the planet's core. That would rip the whole planet apart and it would collapse in on itself."

I nod, looking down at my hand. The obsidian infection has spread to cover all but my fingertips. I lift my hand, studying the dark matter.

The Queen of Tethra and I are connected. A part of her resides within me. I think of her slicing through the floor, revealing the dark matter below the ground. Could I do that? Could I use her power, simply because of the link we now share?

I consider the odds. If I'm wrong, our only other option will be hoping the wormhole generator can create a large enough black hole to suck in the whole planet. But, if I'm right, I can ensure the entire planet and all of her dark matter is swallowed up.

"I might have an idea about that." Inhaling slowly, I look up at him. "We could really do it. We can destroy the whole planet. The Queen of Tethra would be destroyed, her dark matter and the Aklev'Zol gone with her."

Malcolm nods solemnly, looking out across the desolate planet. "I mean, I don't think there's a way out of this for us but we can still save everyone else."

"And prevent the Aklev'Zol from ever returning."

Malcolm says nothing, holding up the orb, waiting.

Kaladria, the Queen croons in my head. Her thoughts snake through mine as she tries to put me back under her spell. *Kaladria, where are you hiding?*

I push against her, forcing out my breath. I will never let her get so close to making me surrender again.

"You should let me do it," I tell Malcolm. "You go through a wormhole back home first. I'll reverse the wormhole generator's polarity once you've gone. We don't both have to die."

"Not a chance. Even if I thought you could change the polarity without me, I'm not leaving you."

"Malcolm—"

He shakes his head fiercely. "No. I already know what it's like to live without you. I'm not doing that again." He exhales slowly, calming himself. "We're in this together, Kaladria. Until the end."

Tears well in my eyes. "Malcolm—"

"Kaladria." His eyes soften and he touches my cheek. "I couldn't live with myself if I got to live and you didn't." I open my mouth but he shakes his head. "And, again, you need my help to change the polarity of the wormhole generator. So it doesn't really matter, anyway."

I sigh. "Alright. Let's do it," I whisper, sentencing us both to death.

95

KALADRIA ASTRANA

My heart thunders in my chest as Malcolm and I kneel together, working to pull apart the wormhole generator. I gently move a wire aside as he switches some of the connections.

Malcolm looks up at me. "Do you mind?"

"Not at all."

I take both pieces of the orb, holding them gently. As I close my eyes, electricity sparks in my hands. Bright blue light shoots through the wires.

I stiffen at the sound of a low snarl. We both look up as a Zol Beast prowls toward us. Cursing, I press the orb into Malcolm's hands. "Keep going. I'll buy you as much time as you need."

Lunging forward, I blast the Zol Beast with lightning as I ram into it. As it falls, the street swarms with enemies.

I grimace. She must know what we're doing. Perhaps the dark matter connecting us is strong enough she can sense what I'm doing, what I intend to do. I only hope the connection is strong enough to do what I'll have to in order to reach the planet's core.

A soldier slashes talons for my face. I jump back, throwing a blast of lightning. As two Zol Beasts charge, I throw lightning with both hands, yelling wordlessly. Behind me, Malcolm works at a frantic pace to finish the alterations to the wormhole generator.

Almost done. But almost out of time, too.

At the reminder of what's coming, pain tears through my body. A scream claws its way free without permission. Holding my hand to my chest, I duck under the swiping talon of an Aklev'Zol soldier. When I look down, I grit my teeth. Long black talons have replaced my fingers.

"Kaladria!" Malcolm calls, likely having heard my scream.

I don't turn, staggering to my feet. "Keep going!"

As an Aklev'Zol's lipless mouth contorts with a sneer, seeing how close I am to joining them, I let out a roar. I swing my newfound weapon, driving talons across the Aklev'Zol's chest. I slice through his skin, sending him stumbling back.

The Queen of Tethra shrieks in my head, furious that I would dare use her dark matter against her.

I swing again. *If you didn't want me using them, you shouldn't have given them to me.*

I kick a Zol Beast in the snout. It skitters back before lunging once more. I throw a blast of lightning with my untainted hand.

"Kaladria, it's time!"

I throw up my hand. Lightning strikes through the air, sending the Aklev'Zol stumbling back. Then, I lift my hand, creating a barrier of electricity between me and the Aklev'Zol racing forward. They slam against it, falling to the lightning.

STOP!

I kneel down next to Malcolm, looking down at my tainted hand, staring at the sword-like talons. Mouth set in a grim line, I exhale. *You can do this, Kaladria.*

I relax, allowing myself to feel the infection as it continues to spread. The moment I stop pushing, the Queen's thoughts rush through my mind with a great burst of power. She doesn't try to lull me back under her spell. She just screams, in a rage over what I'm about to do.

Gritting my teeth, I blink back tears. I focus on the cold, allowing it to become a part of me. Then, I slide a shaking talon across the ground. The Queen screams as the ground splits apart at my touch.

Malcolm's eyes widen. "Kaladria—"

"The black matter connects her to me, just as I am connected to her," I choke out.

Malcolm touches my cheek. "Are you ready?"

"If we don't do it now, it will be too late."

Malcolm picks up the orb, twisting its alternating parts. Taking a deep breath, he drops it into the crack. The wormhole generator spins erratically as it falls into the fissure I've made, disappearing amongst the black matter swirling below the planet.

I bite my lip as I look at Malcolm, not sure what to say when we have so little time left. "Malcolm, I..."

He nods, understanding. Leaning forward, he cups my cheek in his hand. "It's okay," he whispers. "It's almost over."

I lean forward, pressing my forehead to his. The ground rumbles beneath us, the whole planet quaking, as it knows what has already begun. I gasp as the earth around us disintegrates, disappearing as it's sucked into the center of the planet.

I close my eyes. *We did it.*

The Queen screams. Both her fear and fury are palpable. *NO!*

I scream in agony as her thoughts cleave mine. As she shrieks in rage, my knees buckle and suddenly I'm slipping. Malcolm grabs me, shouting my name amongst the chaos around us. Then, everything tumbles around us and the world goes black.

96

KALADRIA ASTRANA

I GASP, eyes flying open in surprise. Chest heaving, I look up. Instead of the starless sky I'm expecting, I find myself staring up at a white ceiling. I sit up, staring at the room in disbelief. This is Malcolm's lab. I look across the room, frowning at the crack in the floor just a few feet away. *How did I get here?*

"Kaladria."

I turn my head, exhaling when I see Malcolm kneeling next to me. He looks mostly unscathed but his brow is furrowed with worry. He reaches down to touch my cheek, his expression distraught.

"Malcolm, what—"

He grimaces. "Your arm, Kaladria."

I look down, cursing at the sight of the black talons. "Does that mean it didn't work?" I look around the room. "How did we end up here?"

"I don't—"

My scream cuts off whatever he was going to say. Pain rips through my head and I press my hands to my face, pinching my eyes shut.

You fools, the Queen of Tethra laughs. *You don't think I've planned for this exact eventuality? You don't think I've prepared for the day someone clever enough tried to kill me?*

I grit my teeth. *You should be dead.*

Open your eyes, my little demon.

I force my eyes open. Malcolm is gripping my arms, his eyes wide with fear as he searches my face. As I look past him, my breath catches in my throat.

Spiraling like smoke, dark matter rises out of the crack in the floor. It snakes through the air, moving quickly across the room.

I dig my nails into the palms of my hands. *It's a piece of her.* This is why she made the tear in the floor when the wormhole generator turned on the first time. Malcolm once told me it had turned itself on. She must have done so. She made the crack in the floor and placed a piece of herself inside of it as a last resort. As long as that matter survives, so does the Queen of Tethra.

As the black matter hits me, I scream again, dropping to the floor. Her laughter echoes through my head and I pinch my eyes closed.

You destroyed everything, the Queen snarls, haughty mockery transformed to livid hatred in less than a second. *And now I'm going to return the favor.*

I bite my tongue to keep from crying out again. *Get out of my head.*

You'll never be rid of me, she vows. *Your body belongs to* me.

Never.

I have shown you mercy, the Queen says. *You almost killed me but I saved you and your pathetic human by bringing you here. Now, you will repay me with your own blood.*

The pain rolls through me, her icy touch raking across every nerve.

How? I manage between cries. *How did you bring us here?*

I can almost hear her smirk. *Again, you have underestimated my power, little demon. The crack, where the last piece of my dark matter resided in dormancy, created a connection to this world. With it and with the dark matter that has been working its way through your body, I was able to send you and Mr. Faraway here.*

I clench my fists. She sent us here, knowing she could use that final piece of her dark matter, the last surviving part of herself, to take over my body. And, with it, she could remake everything we destroyed. She could make Earth the new Tethra, housing her essence within its core, and with me serving as her first new slave.

"Kaladria?"

Malcolm's fingers brush across my spine. I force myself to sit up, trembling with the agony ravaging my body. "The Queen..." I rasp. "The Queen sent us back here. She wants revenge."

I can't let everyone I care about be lost to her greed, not after what we just did to make sure they survived. I have to stop her.

Perhaps I'll take Mr. Faraway as my next soldier, the Queen taunts. *That seems a fitting punishment for your insubordination.*

I clench my untainted hand into a fist, lightning sparking against my knuckles. *I won't let you.*

Pain shoots through my body and I release the electricity on my skin. A terrible sound rips its way out of my chest and I'm screaming again. Malcolm yanks me forward, cradling me to his chest.

I blink away tears. *I will never let you hurt him,* I vow. *Not Malcolm and not anyone else. You are never going to steal another life. You're going to die right here, right now, and that is going to be the end of it.*

The Queen's ice tears through me and I knot my fingers in Malcolm's shirt, gasping painfully. He holds me to his chest. "Kaladria," he whispers hoarsely, "What can I do?"

I exhale shakily. I know what I must do but I know he will never help me do it. Even if it would save everyone, even if it would prevent the Aklev'Zol from ever returning.

I pull his head down, kissing him hard on the mouth. He stills, surprised, but kisses me back nonetheless. Perhaps, he believes he can give me a moment of respite. I wish he could but I know that's impossible now. The Queen is too determined, too angry.

Ignoring the pain taking over every inch of me, I focus on him. The curve of his lips, the warmth of his hand on my cheek. Those are the things that matter, the things I want to hold onto.

He will probably never forgive me for what I'm about to do but at least he'll be alive.

As my lips brush his again, I slide a hand down to his side. My fingers close around the dagger sheathed there and I pull it free silently.

What—

I shove the Queen back, focusing on Malcolm. His fingers graze my cheek. His kisses are so tender that I wish I could find another way. But I know this is the only thing that will save him. *You are bigger than your fear,* I tell myself, knowing those words have never meant more than they do now.

"I love you, Malcolm Faraway," I whisper. "Never doubt that."

The Queen realizes my plan. *You won't do this,* she tells me, the first real trace of fear in her voice. *You are my last chance for survival. I will die without you.*

Exactly. She placed the last bit of her dark matter into my body. Her very existence depends on mine now. She put all her cards on me, believing there was no way I could stop her now.

You're wrong, I think. *To stop you, to save* him, *I would do anything.* My fingers tighten around the dagger. *And I think you have lived long enough.*

With the Queen of Tethra screaming in my head, I push Malcolm away from me. And drive the dagger through my stomach.

MALCOLM FARAWAY

I BARELY HAVE time to scream her name as she slams a knife through her body. Everything explodes, dark matter erupting into the air. I'm thrown back by the sudden blast. I roll across the floor, catching myself with my hands. Dragging myself onto my knees, I groan. But, as I look across the room at Kaladria, I stiffen.

She's crumpled in a heap on the floor. Her skin no longer shines with its usual bright blue lightning, leaving her body a dull, pale blue without the sparks to light it up. She lies in a pool of dark blue blood, the knife on the floor next to her.

Scrambling to my feet, I race across the room. I slide to my knees as I reach her side. The dark matter of the Queen's infection is gone. Her body is back to its pale-blue color and her fingers are no longer the black talons of an Aklev'Zol, but the delicate fingers of the lightning-wielding Protector.

As I lift her into my arms, her head falls back and her mouth falls slack. Heart silent, chest still, her body arcs back limply. Tears prick my eyes as I stroke her frozen cheek. "Oh, Kaladria." My voice cracks. *"Why?"*

I cradle her body, holding her head to my chest. She remains lifeless in my arms. My body curling around hers, I close my eyes, fingers knotting in her hair.

It wasn't supposed to happen like this. We were both going to live or we were both going to die. That's what I wanted. To live with her or die with her. But she had to sacrifice herself and take a path I can't follow. Just like she did when the Satellite fell, just like she did when she destroyed the Machine.

I love you, Malcolm Faraway. Never doubt that.

My heart hurts as her last goodbye echoes through my head. Now I understand what she was saying. She was apologizing for what she was about to do.

I break, body shaking with anguished tremors as I crush her to my chest. "Why do you always have to be the hero?" I cry. When there's no answer, I hold her even tighter. "I don't want to lose you." I bow my head, crying as I rock her body. "I can't lose you."

As if in answer to my desperate pleas, a sudden shuddering breath racks her lungs. She coughs, inhaling sharply.

I lean back, frantically pushing her hair out of her face. She takes another ragged breath. Her skin sparks erratically with lightning, as if even her body can't decide if it wants to live or not. Then, very slowly, she opens her eyes. My breath hitches at the sight of those sharp eyes.

She mouths my name weakly.

My hands are trembling as I smooth back her hair. "I'm here."

She blinks slowly. Then, her breathing slows and her eyes fall closed again. The lightning beneath her skin dims. She's fading again.

"No, Kaladria!"

I cup her face in my hands, stroking her cheeks, but she doesn't open her eyes again. I look down at her stomach, at the midnight blue staining her armor. She's losing too much blood. I lay her down, pulling my shirt over my head. I press the fabric to her stomach to staunch the bleeding.

"You are not dying on me," I whisper fiercely. "Do you hear me, Kaladria? If you and I can survive a wormhole, you and I can survive this."

98

KALADRIA ASTRANA

THERE'S a dull ache in my gut. I can feel it with every breath, sending a throbbing pain through my stomach. My breath hitches and I grimace. It's a reminder. Somehow, despite all the odds, I'm not dead yet.

Blinking, I stare up at the ceiling.

"Kaladria?"

I turn my head. Malcolm sits next to the bed, searching my face. He watches me cautiously. His eyes are horribly exhausted, red-rimmed and bloodshot. He exhales, leaning forward to smooth back my hair.

"What happened?"

"Before or after you decided to stab yourself?" he asks, his eyes heartbreakingly sad.

I swallow. *Right.*

"Are you angry with me?" I ask softly.

He's silent for a very long time. I can't tell if it's because he *is* angry or if he's just thinking before he speaks. His face is unreadable.

Finally, he releases his breath. "Honestly, I'm just happy you're alive. But please don't ever do something like that again."

"I promise."

Relaxing, Malcolm leans back in his seat. "Even though it was terrifying, your stunt did do the job. After our black hole sucked up their world, the Aklev'Zol were all destroyed. The only remaining dark matter existed in your body. And, when you stabbed yourself, all traces of the Queen of Tethra were destroyed. There's nothing left of her or her slaves."

"What about..."

My eyes fall on my hand, which bears no trace of the dark matter. I flex shaking fingers, watching blue lightning spark through my veins. There's no sign of the infection, not a single black talon.

"You're free, Kaladria," Malcolm says softly. "The infection is gone."

Tears fill my eyes. "I thought I would be dead."

"You were, for a moment," he says huskily. He takes a deep, shuddering breath. "That was the only way the Queen of Tethra could die." His eyes are full of so much pain as he places a hand on my cheek. "Seeing you like that..." He blows the air from his cheeks. "I thought I'd lost you."

I put my hand over his, holding it there.

"When you started breathing again, I brought you to my mother. She saved you."

I sigh, closing my eyes wearily. It's really over then. The Queen of Tethra is dead. She'll never enslave another soul.

"What about everyone else?" I open my eyes, chest constricting with sudden fear. "Did they...?"

Malcolm smiles softly. "All alive." He pauses, studying my face. "Do you want me to get Xalin and Herren?"

When I nod, Malcolm kisses my forehead and stands. As he disappears out of the room, I look up at the ceiling. It's almost too good to be true. I keep waiting for the piercing cold to return, for her voice to rake my thoughts. But it never does. The only pain that remains is the dull ache in my stomach where I stabbed the dagger. I can't sense the Queen of Tethra at all. Our connection has been severed. She's really gone.

"Baby Girl?"

I open my eyes, blinking back tears, as my father and uncle sit down on either side of the bed. Dad has a small gash in his cheek but looks otherwise unharmed. Xalin looks fine but his eyes are very weary. He grabs my hand and Dad touches my cheek.

"You scared us, Kala," Xalin says softly.

"That's sort of a specialty of mine, isn't it?"

Xalin doesn't laugh. He shakes his head, giving me a stern look. *Not funny,* his eyes tell me. When I give him an apologetic smile, he squeezes my hand.

"How long was I out?"

"A couple of days," Dad says. "You lost a lot of blood."

"I…"

Childlike laughter suddenly fills the room and a small form jumps right on top of me. I gasp, wincing in pain, as I catch the small human girl we'd saved before.

"Ava," my father admonishes.

The little girl climbs off me. "Sowee."

I chuckle, taking her in. She looks so much happier than before, so much less afraid. The last I saw her, she was too afraid to speak, or even look most people in the eye. Clearly, she's adjusted to her new life.

Dad smiles. "Ava, you remember Kaladria, right?"

"Kala." The little girl's head bobs. "Big sister."

At first, I stop, lifting my eyebrows in surprise. Then, I smile. "I guess you've decided to take her in, then?"

He nods hesitantly. "Are you okay with that? It doesn't make you feel like you've been replaced?"

"Of course not. I know I'll always be your Baby Girl." I touch his hand. "But there's nothing wrong with you having two daughters."

His eyes soften.

I ruffle Ava's hair, causing her to giggle. "Besides, I always wanted a little sister."

He chuckles. "I do recall that."

I grin, settling back on the bed. Growing bored of sitting still, Ava takes off running. Dad smiles apologetically before standing and chasing after the little girl. "Ava!"

"She's just as active as you were at her age," Xalin comments.

"She'll keep him busy, then."

Xalin chuckles. "I'd better go help him." He squeezes my hand before standing. Just as my father catches up with Ava, Xalin rushes over. He scoops her into his arms, running off with her. The little girl squeals in delight.

I close my eyes, smiling.

I can't remember the last time I felt this peaceful. Everything feels so *right*. My family and friends are safe, the Aklev'Zol are gone, and I get to live out my life however I choose. After such a nightmare, my body feels like it's going to explode with contentment.

"You know, you're a real hypocrite, Kala."

I open my eyes. Azar, Hassuun, and Vale walk into the room together, each with only a few minor scrapes and bruises. I smile. "Hey, guys."

"You told Hassuun and I not to do anything reckless." Azar jabs an accusatory finger at me. "And what do you do? You nearly get yourself killed."

"As usual," Hassuun says, smiling broadly.

I grin back at him. "I'm nothing if not consistent."

Vale shakes his head and Azar chuckles. "I guess you wouldn't be our captain if you weren't doing something stupid."

I smile.

"Stupid is her specialty."

I scowl at Zeru as he steps into the room. His arms are covered in light scrapes and his right hand has been bandaged but he seems just as at ease as the rest of them. He winks. "You know I'm right, Kala."

I open my mouth to argue. But then, sighing, I shrug. "I suppose I can't argue with that."

Zeru's smile softens, his face turning solemn. He sits on the edge of the bed, patting my arm. "Reckless or not, we're glad you're okay. We were all really worried about you. It's a relief to see you awake."

"It's a relief to *be* awake."

I look away, wiping my cheeks. There have been too many tears as of late.

"You know," Hassuun says, eyes twinkling. "Malcolm has been here pretty much the whole time you were unconscious. I don't think he's slept in days."

I frown, thinking of his weary expression and his bloodshot eyes. "He should rest. It's not as if I'm going anywhere."

Zeru shrugs. "You did sort of die in his arms."

I sigh. I suppose that's fair. After all, I wouldn't have left his side for anything if our roles had been reversed.

"So, you and Malcolm are sort of a thing now, I guess," Hassuun says.

Vale surprises me by rolling his eyes. "You're just realizing this *now?*"

I chuckle as Hassuun scowls at Vale. Zeru shakes his head, meeting my gaze. His thoughts are clear in his face. *Can you believe them?*

I grin. *Of course I can.*

"The Saturnian and the human," Azar muses, interrupting our silent exchange with a wicked grin. "I wonder what we can expect of the babies. Will they be human or Saturnian?"

For a moment, I just stare at him, completely mortified. When he wiggles his eyebrows in a taunt, I growl and flick my fingers at him. The lightning is weak, thanks to my injuries, but he still yelps in surprise.

He rubs his arm, scowling at me. I glare back at him but it's not long before I'm laughing. After a moment, so is everyone else.

MALCOLM KEEPS a tight hold on my hand as he leads me through surprisingly busy streets. It's only been days since we destroyed the Queen of Tethra but already the humans are beginning to rebuild.

I stumble along beside him, body straining with the effort it takes despite his slow pace. Clearly, a few days is not enough time for my injuries to fully heal. "Where are you taking me?"

Malcolm flashes a smile. "Well, as happy as I am that we're all back together again and everyone we care about survived the invasion, I'd like a little time to have you to myself."

I smile as he pulls me down a new street, guiding me into an old church. I stare up at the glass-stained windows. This is where he kissed me for the first time.

Malcolm tugs me close as we stand in the middle of the chapel. He pulls me forward gently, carefully placing his arms around me. I slide my arms up and around his neck, ignoring the annoying ache in my stomach that serves as a reminder that I haven't recovered yet.

I focus on his face, searching his eyes. There's something there I don't recognize. He looks weirdly nervous. He pushes it aside with a long sigh.

Malcolm leans in, kissing me softly. It's the sort of kiss that builds, softly, slowly. It's tender and gentle. I place my hands on his chest, standing on my toes to kiss him back. His hands slide down my arms, trailing down my hands until his fingers find mine. He leans back. "I have something for you."

I lift an eyebrow. "Really?"

His smile wobbles, suddenly uncertain, and there's that anxiety again. He takes a deep breath before pulling something out of his pocket. He holds out a small ring to me. I take it, fingering the smooth band gently. It's simple in design, just a gray band.

"It's made of silicone," he explains. "I figured anything too pretty would be destroyed every time you used lightning."

"Malcolm, it's..." I look up, frowning. He's on one knee. "Malcolm?"

"Hold on. I'm not finished." He takes a deep breath. "That's not just a ring. It's a promise." He smiles softly. "I don't know what's going to happen next. I don't know where we're going to go or what we're going to do. All I know is that I want to be with you for the rest of my life."

I clutch the ring as I realize what he's saying.

"Kaladria, will you marry me?"

For a moment, I just stare at him. Then, I kneel in front of him and throw my arms around his neck. "Yes," I breathe. "Whenever, wherever."

Eyes bright, Malcolm cups my face between his hands and kisses me. I hold onto my ring tightly, kissing him back. As we kneel together on the floor, he loops his arms around my waist. As his lips brush mine again, I sigh contentedly.

He leans back, taking the ring from me. I hesitate, uncertain of this particular human custom. *Which hand? And which finger?*

Malcolm smiles knowingly. He takes my left hand, sliding the ring onto my fourth finger. Then, he leans forward until our foreheads touch. "I don't care what happens next," he murmurs. "I don't care if I have to follow you halfway across the universe. I'm staying with you." His soft exhale warms my face. "I'll follow you anywhere."

I smile up at him tearfully. "Nothing would make me happier."

18 MONTHS LATER

99

KALADRIA ASTRANA

"Azar Losali, if you throw food at me again, I will zap you into tomorrow."

He raises his eyebrows. "If you could do that," Azar taunts as he throws another piece of bread at me, "You already would have done it."

Growling, I flick my fingers. As he yelps, Zeru plops down at the table. "Well, I can see that things are already back to normal. Azar's already irritating the captain and we've only been here a week."

Vale shakes his head. "I guess some things never change."

Looking past them, I scan the room. Since we beat the Queen of Tethra and the Aklev'Zol, we've rebuilt the Satellite and the Protectorate. But things are different this time. The cafeteria full of Protectors houses more than the five alien races that once swore to protect Earth. Humanity has joined us in our efforts to protect the system.

I glance at a table across the room, where a broad-shouldered human laughs at something a Martian girl says. Then, I look at another table, smiling at the sight of Dean and Tyler. Dean rolls his eyes, shaking his head at something Tyler says.

Tyler had practically jumped at the opportunity to join the Protectorate. And, while Dean hasn't joined the Protectorate as a soldier, he ended up coming to the Satellite as an engineer. Both of them have been doing well here, awfully comfortable with all of this after spending so much time with my own squad.

"How's your father?" Zeru asks, drawing my attention back to our table.

I don't look at him, still searching at the cafeteria. "Good," I say, distracted. *Where is he?* "Ava keeps him very busy though."

Zeru chuckles at my less than attentive response. "Looking for anyone in particular?" he teases.

"Nope," I lie, still looking across the cafeteria. He'd said he wanted to call his mother, to let her know how the week was going. But what's taking him so long?

"You sure?" Zeru asks. He smiles, nodding across the room.

I follow his gaze. Malcolm steps into the mess hall, walking casually in our direction. I look him up and down. He wears black Protectorate armor, just as we all do. The color contrasts against his fair skin, making the nebula-like color of his eyes appear even more striking than before. My eyes fall on the silicone ring on his left hand, the twin to mine. He smiles when he sees me, winking. As he sits down next to me, he kisses my cheek.

"Hey, none of that." Azar points an accusatory finger at us, wrinkling his nose in disgust. "This is a public sitting area."

I grin, leaning closer to Malcolm. "Do you want to help me gross out Azar?" I whisper conspiratorially.

Malcolm chuckles. "What did he do this time?" he whispers back.

"Azar is right," Hassuun interjects, shaking his head. "You guys are sickening."

I laugh. *Oh, I'll show you sickening.* I start to lean closer to Malcolm but stop at the small ding sounding from my comm link. I pull out the comm device. It's from Xalin. Likely regarding the new Council. I open it, reading the message carefully.

A lone ship was spotted near Neptune. The Council wants you to check it out.

I put away the comm link, looking at everyone at the table. "Fun's over, boys," I announce, pulling Malcolm up with me as I stand. "We've got work to do."

Azar and Hassuun lead the way to the *Resistance*, with Vale and

Zeru right behind them. Malcolm and I trail behind at a slower pace than our squadmates, walking hand in hand. As we make our way to the ship, I slide my finger back and forth across my ring, spinning the silicone band absentmindedly.

"What do you say, husband?" I ask. "You ready for your first mission as an official Protector?"

Malcolm smiles. "Let's show the universe why no one messes with our system."

"No one," I agree.

As we step onto the *Resistance*, I stop, smiling up at him. He smiles back down at me, his eyes softening. And, never in my whole life, have I felt so at home.

ACKNOWLEDGMENTS

First and foremost, I want to thank my family. Thank you, to my amazing husband for everything you did for me and this book. Not only did you serve as the inspiration for Malcolm, but you also helped me really make this story the book it is today. Thank you for helping me to remember that this is a good story on the bad days and being excited with me on the good days.

To my children, thank you for all the giggles and play breaks. I love my boys and wouldn't be who I am without them.

I'd also like to thank my parents for being so amazing and supportive, for always being my number one fans.

Thank you to my amazing mother-in-law for being the first person to read this book. Thank you to Camille and Jennifer for your wonderful insights.

Thank you to my siblings, who I can honestly say helped me envision the close bonds between the squad of the *Resistance*.

Finally, I thank God for the talents and gifts I've been blessed with, for the opportunities I've received. I pray every day for the chance to bless others and touch hearts.

ABOUT THE AUTHOR

Brittany Oldroyd lives in Idaho with her husband and their two boys. She loves kickboxing, anime, and all things art-related. She's also obsessed with fantasy and science fiction and spends most of her reading time devouring books in one of those categories. She loves to write young adult and new adult science fiction and fantasy, stories with heroic characters and unique plots.

Brittany is the author of *Trapped*, *Forbidden*, and *Forged in Storms and Shadows*. For information about signups and events, more about her work or to contact her, visit her website at brittanyoldroydbooks.weebly.com.

ALSO BY BRITTANY OLDROYD

Made in the USA
Middletown, DE
31 January 2022

60119996R00246